MW00628089

Calling
Clarissa

Beth Worsdell

Calling Clarissa Copyright © 2023 by Beth Worsdell.
All Rights Reserved.
All rights reserved. No part of this book may be reproduced in any form or by any electronic or mechanical means, including information storage and retrieval systems, without permission in writing from the author. The only exception is by a reviewer, who may quote short excerpts in a review.
Cover designed by GermanCreative
This book is a work of fiction. Names, characters, places, and incidents are products of the author's imagination or are used fictitiously. Any resemblance to actual persons, living or dead, events, or locales is entirely coincidental.
Visit my website at www.bethworsdellauthor.com
First Printing: May 2023
E-book ISBN number 978-1-959775-03-4
Paperback ISBN number 978-1-959775-04-1

Wordsell Publishing.

Dedicated

To all who value family and friendship, and those who love to laugh.

Thank you to my family, friends, and readers for your constant support.

Quote

Feed your soul with love and laughter.
Beth Worsdell

Chapter 1

Clarissa stood at her kitchen sink washing yet another pile of dirty dishes as late afternoon sunshine streamed through her kitchen window, indicating the tail end of spring. She wondered if there was more to life. "Same shit, different day," she said while cleaning another dirty plate. She had hoped to marry a good man like her father, but her ex-husband was a no-good asshole, a total narcissist, and an ego on legs. In fact, if anyone looked up the meaning of the word narcissist, they would see Nigel's picture next to the definition, and the word narcissist would be printed in bold.

Clarissa had also hoped that Nigel would step up and be a decent husband and father when they had their two boys, Luke and Matthew, but no. Alas, the fucker was still the same selfish prick he always was. Hence, why Clarissa finally had the sense to kick out said fucker and was a lot happier on her own. Penniless but happier. Clarissa wasn't the first, nor would she be the last, to realize that sometimes women are happier alone than miserable with their own personal asshole.

The problem was Nigel had no interest in helping to keep the roof over their heads or putting food on the table for the two sons he was supposed to love. He wasn't interested in making the most of the joint custody Clarissa had agreed to in their divorce either. So, she was struggling to make ends meet alone. The only things that kept her going were her boys, close family, and best friends, Becky and Hayley.

Clarissa finished washing the last dirty plate, slipped off her yellow rubber gloves, and turned to her kettle, needing a cup of tea. She tightened her hair clip at the back of her head, barely keeping her mass of dark-auburn hair contained, and sighed. Her mum always told her that tea made everything better. "What a crock of shit," she told herself. She filled her electric kettle, switched it on, and grabbed her favorite large mug. It was the same mug she had bought when she and the asshole had bought their first place together, a small studio flat above a betting shop.

Placing her hands on her grey Formica countertop, she hung her head, slowly shaking it in disbelief. 'What on earth did I see in him?' she asked herself while thinking about how Nigel was ten years before. She had to admit the younger Nigel had been a catch, or so she had felt at the time. An ex-rugby player, he was pure muscle with natural olive skin, piercing blue eyes, thick dark hair, and a jaw you just wanted to kiss or used to want to kiss. Now, she would love to punch his jaw and dislodge a few teeth. Clarissa no longer found him attractive; she only saw a slimy, cheating bastard who couldn't keep his cock in his trousers and who thought he was God's personal gift to women everywhere. 'Never mind,' Clarissa thought, reaching for her tea caddy and grabbing a tea bag for her mug, 'At least I've got girls' night to look forward to.' She smiled broadly, knowing it was just what she needed.

Clarissa hardly ever got to go out and enjoy herself. Her low-paying sales and customer service job that she hated and childcare costs meant she couldn't afford a babysitter to go out. However, Clarissa did take turns with her best friends, Becky and Hayley, babysitting for each other when possible. However, when they wanted to go out together, they were pretty much out of luck because neither Becky's nor Hayley's husbands wished to look after more than their own kids, which she understood.

Clarissa was looking forward to her girl's night. The cul-de-sac where she lived was away from the main road and was no longer a drive-through area, and she loved the peace and quiet. She also had a young neighbor, Steve, a twenty-something computer programmer and drummer, who didn't mind a bit of loud music or laughter when her girlfriends were over. The rest of her neighbors were mainly older curtain-twitchers who never missed anything.

Becky and Hayley were the most incredible women that Clarissa had ever known. They had been friends throughout high school, always getting up to no good, and they were very good at not getting caught. They never did anything significant and always stuck by each other no matter what.

Becky and Hayley had warned Clarissa that her ex-asshole was indeed an asshole when they started dating, but did Clarissa listen to her best friends in the world? No, she did not. *'If love had been any blinder, I would have been Stevie Wonder.'* However, if she hadn't married her ex-asshole, she wouldn't have had her two sons, Luke and Matthew. Clarissa loved her two boys with all her heart and wanted them to have the best life possible.

Clarissa added a little honey to her tea while her boy's watched television before bedtime. Her boys were only seven and ten years old, so they went to bed at eight pm, although she let them read for half an hour. She was surprised that they were still awake. It had been Luke's tenth birthday the day before, and Clarissa had hosted a birthday party for him at their house with the help of her best friends. They had decorated the downstairs with Luke's favorite Marvel characters, made all the kid's favorite nibbles, such as pizza, chicken nuggets, and fries, and managed to entertain twelve kids for four hours. Clarissa, Hayley, and Becky were exhausted by the time all the kids had left.

Did her ex-asshole show up for his son's birthday? Hell no! The bastard didn't even have the decency to drop in or send a birthday card. Luke had been devastated that his dad didn't give a shit, and seeing her little boy cry yet again because of her ex, tipped Clarissa over the edge. Clarissa had sent Nigel a blazing text message, telling him what a low life dad he was, including plenty of expletives. Did the scumbag respond? No, he did not!

"Thirty more minutes, boys," she told Luke and Matthew as she entered her lounge.

Clarissa smiled at the sight of her boys sitting on her sofa with their blankets. They were both the image of their dad, from their thick, dark, unruly hair, to their olive skin. The only traits they inherited from her were her brown eyes and personality traits, which she was very grateful for. Clarissa sat between them on the sofa for a cuddle while her tea cooled a little in the kitchen.

"Mummy," Luke said as both boys leaned into her. "Do you think my birthday card from Daddy will come tomorrow?" he asked, looking up at Clarissa with hope in his deep brown eyes.

Clarissa's heart broke in her chest. She knew there was no birthday card coming for Luke from his dad. Nigel was too busy acting like a childless man-whore even to bother. However, she knew she couldn't bear to watch Luke's hope be destroyed again. Clarissa raised her arms and slid them around her boys, bringing them in closer.

"I don't know, honey, but look at all the amazing cards you have already."

Luke glanced at their fireplace and the colorful array of birthday cards displayed on the light-stained wooden shelf above.

"I like the Hulk card the best," Matthew told Luke with a grin. "I like the way his googly eyes wobble."

Luke grinned back at his little brother. "Can you imagine if our eyes looked like googly eyes, and every time we bounced on a trampoline, our eyes jiggled?" He giggled.

Clarissa and Matthew laughed at the idea, and as her boy's laughter faded and their focus went back to their television show, Clarissa thought about how lucky she was to have them.

—x—

By eight-thirty, Luke and Matthew were in bed, Aretha Franklin was singing Freeway Of Love in the small lounge, and Clarissa was taking out a cheap bottle of white wine from the fridge while swaying her curvy hips to the music. She was just getting her groove on when a tap on her kitchen back door interrupted her dance, instantly making her smile. She turned to see Hayley's large boobs pressed against the frosted glass windowpane of her back door, making her giggle.

"Put them away, you hussy!" she told Hayley as she entered her small but modern-looking kitchen with Becky following behind.

The evening chill swept into the kitchen with her friends, making goosebumps appear on her sleeveless bare arms.

"I come bearing gifts," Hayley replied, placing a shopping bag on the countertop, opening her thick red wool coat again, and jiggling her enormous boobs with her hands. "And I don't just mean these puppies!"

Clarissa and Becky burst into a fit of giggles.

"You are seriously too much. How does your hubby put up with you?" Becky said, removing her puffer coat and placing it on the back of a dining chair while trying to fake a shocked look.

"Lots of practice." Hayley smirked, sliding her coat off and placing it next to Becky's. "And I mean lots."

Clarissa finished opening the wine, found some wine glasses, and hugged her two best friends, instantly feeling light-hearted.

"You do know that big boobs are overrated," Clarissa stated as she released Becky from her hug.

"You can talk, woman." Becky chuckled while reaching for a wine glass. "You both have big enough boobs to suffocate any man who wants to die happy!"

Wine sprayed across the kitchen countertop as Hayley's mouthful evacuated with force, making them crack up with laughter. She coughed and spluttered as wine dripped down her chin.

Clarissa refilled Hayley's glass as her wet friend cleaned herself with a tea towel, dabbing her face and soaking wet boobs.

Becky looked at her friends with a grin. "Let's face it, girls, if either of you went in for a breast reduction, you'd go in with a list of women wanting your leftovers."

Clarissa's stomach started to ache from laughing, but it felt good to laugh with her friends.

Grabbing the bottle of wine, glasses, and snacks of peanuts, twiglets, and crisps, they made their way to the lounge. Hayley plonked her tall, slim frame on Luke's bean bag, her long dark brown hair splaying around her shoulders. While Becky, their petite, red-headed friend, sat crossed-legged on the floor next to the coffee table and snacks. Clarissa took the sofa with her wine glass in hand, sinking into the old but comfortable tan-colored cushions.

"Don't be jealous of the boobies," Clarissa told Becky with a smirk. "Men only love big boobs because they swing well, clap, and give them a round of applause while doing the deed, and when they see a nice cleavage, they imagine their todger sliding in between.

The truth is, there's nothing worse than lying down and watching your boobs slide and disappear under your armpits. Plus, you can't do sports because you give yourself black eyes and chest pains. The last time I went jogging, I nearly caused multiple car accidents because men were swerving all over the road. They were too busy watching my boobs behaving like two puppies fighting in my t-shirt."

Within seconds, Becky and Hayley were laughing so hard that they could barely breathe.

"I swear you should be a comedy act!" Hayley tried to say breathlessly as tears of laughter streamed down her cheeks.

Becky nodded in agreement while gripping her stomach. "Seriously, I'd pay to watch you do stand-up."

Clarissa grinned at her best friends and then sipped her wine, which was going down very nicely.

"In all seriousness, if I thought I could do stand-up comedy for a living, I would," she told them honestly. "I still hate my job at Janka Industries, and my childminder is putting her rate up again. I don't blame her with living costs going up again, but I'm barely surviving right now."

Her heart felt heavy as she admitted her frustration and lack of money.

"Is Nigel still not giving you any money for your boys?" Hayley asked, raising her brows.

Clarissa shook her head sadly, hating the fact that she was going to have to admit, yet again, that her ex was an asshole.

"Not only is he still not paying, but he didn't even drop in a birthday card or call Luke to wish him a happy birthday. And I know he knew because his mum reminds him of that kind of thing. I thought going to court again might do the trick, but every time they track him down, he changes jobs before anything can be deducted from his wages."

Her best friends shook their heads in disgust.

"He never deserved you and certainly doesn't deserve your lovely boys," Becky said gently.

Clarissa could feel tears welling in her eyes as her heart felt heavy. Feeling vulnerable wasn't a feeling she enjoyed, and she hated feeling like her life was out of her control even more.

"Agreed," Hayley added while giving Clarissa an understanding look.

Hayley's ex-husband had turned out to be quite the asshole too. There were numerous times when Clarissa and Becky had to rescue Hayley from her home when her ex was beginning to kick off, and she needed to leave. He hadn't been a man-whore like Nigel, but he did have a nasty temper and enjoyed using his fists until one day when Hayley lost it and gave him a taste of his own medicine before grabbing her bag and leaving for good. Her new husband, Adam, worshiped the ground she and their kids walked on. Clarissa was happy for her and a little jealous. Hayley was like a new woman since leaving her ex-husband, and she no longer took shit from anyone. Becky and Clarissa were in awe of her.

"Instead of your sales job, you need to find something that pays really well and will work around your boy's schedules," Hayley stated, "and I think I might have the perfect solution." She grinned mischievously.

Clarissa and Becky's eyes widened as Hayley looked at them wickedly.

Clarissa wiped her damp eyes and took another sip of her wine. "Well, don't leave us hanging. What have you got for me?"

Hayley took a deep breath and raised her brows. "Well, one of our junior lawyers, Stephanie, has just left our firm to change careers. When she was saving for her wedding and deposit for a house with her fiancé, she started doing an evening job for extra income. Turns out, not only did she make loads of money, but she was really good at it, and she loved it more than being a lawyer. She also gets to work from home."

Hayley took a long sip of her wine and grabbed a handful of nuts from the old wooden coffee table.

"Oh my god, don't leave us in suspense. What's the job?" Clarissa demanded, even though it sounded too good to be true.

Hayley bit down on her bottom lip while trying to stop laughing.

"Spit it out!" Becky chided.

"Okay, okay," Hayley told her in defeat. "A phone sex chat line operator."

"What the hell?" Clarissa blurted, nearly spilling her wine in shock. "You're suggesting I talk dirty for a living?"

Becky burst into laughter. Laughing so hard that she fell backward on the floor while holding her stomach.

"Seriously, woman, you're going to mummy-pee if you laugh any harder," Hayley told her while grinning like a Cheshire cat.

She turned to a stunned Clarissa, who couldn't believe what her best friend was suggesting. "Look, Stephanie told me all about it after a few vodkas at her leaving party last week. It's just acting but over the phone."

Clarissa still wasn't sure if her best friend was pulling her leg or not. It wouldn't be the first time. Hayley was a minx for winding you up and spinning a yarn, as her mum would say.

"Are you being serious?" Clarissa raised an eyebrow.

Hayley tried to look offended, pretending to stab herself in the heart, then laughed.

"I swear on my kids' lives; it's totally true," she said, looking at them with sudden sincerity. "Stephanie happened to see an advert in a local paper when she was job hunting, and the hours fitted perfectly around her day job. So, she decided to give it a go. Obviously, her fiancé wasn't too keen at first, but once he heard her acting like someone else and saw the money roll in, he was all for it. She was earning so much money and having so much fun that she decided she wanted to do it full-time, especially as they want to start a family after their wedding. Stephanie's new job enables her to have a full-time income and stay at home with their future babies."

Becky leaned against the coffee table with her mouth agape. Clarissa couldn't believe her ears either.

"She's really earning full-time money working from home?" Clarissa asked, shocked. It still sounded too good to be true. "I'm not sure I could talk dirty for a living," she admitted as her cheeks flushed.

Hayley gave her a stern look. "Are you seriously kidding me? Who was it, who used to do phone sex chats with asshole before living with the douchebag? Who used to send him very descriptive sexual texts, trying to keep his attention when he was being a cheating bastard? Girl, if anyone could do it and do it well, it's you!"

Becky nodded profusely in agreement.

Clarissa didn't know what to say. Her best friend was right. She had talked dirty and sent dirty texts to her ex, which had had the desired effect at the time. Maybe she could do it. She was desperate to get out of her current job at Janka Industries. It was crap money, and her boss, John Mason, always made her skin crawl. He was obviously a boob man. She was constantly catching him ogling hers. He had even told her once that he would love to get lost in her cleavage. She didn't think he meant to say it aloud, and he seemed shocked that it had come out of his mouth, but since then, it had made him brave with regular innuendoes and obvious stares. The pervert had even started to call her spanner eyes. When did she ask him one day, why? He told her that his nuts tightened whenever he saw her. Clarissa had nearly vomited in her mouth.

"Okay, I'm interested," she admitted. "I have to do something before the boys, and I lose the house and end up living on the street.

Hayley and Becky both grinned like cats who had got the cream.

"You're not going to regret this, honey," Hayley told her. "I have such a good feeling about this!"

"Me too!" Becky chipped in.

Clarissa wasn't as confident as her friends, but Hayley's good feelings were usually right.

"So, what else did Stephanie tell you?" she asked.

"Well, the first thing you need to know is, like any actor, you are playing a role. So, we need to come up with your alter ego. We also have to invent a new name and body description. You could even do an accent if you want," Hayley explained excitedly.

Becky started to giggle. "I swear this will be the best girl's night ever! I'm going to text Martin to tell him I'm staying over. He went on a boy's weekend with the rugby lot recently, so he owes me."

"That's a good idea." Hayley laughed. "I'll text Adam too. If your man owes you, then mine does too. Especially as I ended up washing all their kits this month, this is something that can't be rushed."

Clarissa rolled her eyes at her best friends, but she knew they were going to have a blast.

Once Becky and Hayley's husbands were notified that their wives were not coming home, they were all ready to return to business. Clarissa suddenly had butterflies in her stomach at just the thought of being able to quit her much-hated job. And if she was willing to admit it, she was also a little excited at the thought of talking dirty again.

Since she had kicked Nigel out for his cheating ways and for treating her like his personal doormat, she hadn't had a chance to date anyone else. Her ex-asshole had completely destroyed her confidence, and after she had filed for divorce, he had turned nasty, telling her that no one else would want her.

Since then, Nigel had made no effort to hide the fact that he was trying to fuck anything that looked slightly female—had a pulse— and still had breath in their bodies. Clarissa hoped that he would catch some nasty STD and that his cock would fall off. The thought would often make her smile.

"I think the best way is to think of a woman you admire and base your alter ego on her," Becky said as she put her phone back in her handbag.

"That seems logical." Hayley agreed. "Who are your favorite women?"

Clarissa had to think for a moment. She had given up trying to compare herself to other women years ago. Not just because of how Nigel had made her feel, but because there were not many well-known women with naturally massive boobs. Apart from the fabulous Dolly Parton, of course.

Clarissa was tall for a woman at five foot eleven. Luckily, Nigel had been six-foot, although he hadn't liked Clarissa wearing heels. She had long auburn hair that passed her slim shoulders, deep brown eyes, and a pretty oval face, so her friends told her. '*Who would I like to be?*' she asked herself. If she was honest, she loved movies and books about badass women like Hayley, who took no shit from anyone.

Becky and Hayley waited patiently, sipping their wine and munching on nuts and crisps as they watched Clarissa pondering. Movies and books popped into her mind as she mentally searched for the women, she admired the most. Then, Tomb Raider popped into her head, and she knew.

"Angelina Jolie," she blurted out to her patiently waiting best friends.

"Ooooh, good choice." Becky agreed.

"Oh, I love Angelina Jolie," Hayley told her, "She's independent, beautiful, and she does a lot of good in the world."

Clarissa nodded. "Exactly. Maybe I could base my alter-ego on her."

"Okay. So, tall, slim build, great boobs, legs that go on forever, long dark hair, stunning blue eyes, and a great butt," Hayley stated, with Clarissa and Becky nodding in agreement. "Next, we must think of a name and decide what age you need to pretend to be."

"Clarissa's got quite a husky voice. No offense, babe. I'm actually quite jealous, but you don't sound like a girly girl. So, maybe you should stick with your real age. That way, it's easier to remember," Becky suggested.

Clarissa wasn't offended at all. She knew she had a husky voice. She quite liked it. Nigel had once loved it too.

"Fair point," she told Becky with a smile, "and you could never offend me, honey."

"Right, that's settled. So, what about a name? It needs to be something sexy but classy," Hayley told them.

The three of them sipped their wine and mulled it over while Clarissa's iPod changed songs, and Adele started singing, Set Fire to the Rain.

"That's it," Clarissa declared, "Adele."

"Oh my god, that song coming on is a sign," Becky said with a grin. "I have a good feeling this is going to work out."

Before long, Clarissa's alter ego was written down in her notebook, along with the chat line details from Hayley, and another bottle of white wine was opened. Then the conversation changed to other women they admired and confessions of dirty talk with ex-boyfriends.

"I tried talking dirty with my ex, but it didn't go very well," Becky confessed, slurring slightly. "He was stroking his todger with his eyes closed while I was describing what I was doing, and his mum walked in on him with a cup of tea in her hand."

Clarissa nearly choked on her mouthful of nuts, and Hayley giggled.

"No way! I would die if I walked in on one of my kids doing that. What did she say?" Hayley asked, her eyes wide in horror.

Becky bit her bottom lip, trying to stop herself from laughing. "She screamed, holy fuck, apparently. Then she jolted backward, spilling the hot tea, which splashed all over his privates. Poor Neil had to go to the emergency room for burns."

Clarissa and Hayley didn't know whether to cringe or laugh.

"When I was nineteen, I slept over at my ex's. In the morning, we were getting it on, and before I knew what the hell was happening, his dad was outside cleaning Graham's bedroom windows. Then his mum walked in with tea and crumpets for breakfast," Hayley told them.

"You are kidding?" Clarissa laughed, trying desperately to swallow her nuts.

"Nope. And to make matters worse, his mum sat on the bed next to us, wanting to chat about the bloody weather."

Becky tried to breathe while holding her stomach. "What did you do?"

"There was nothing we could do but try to slide apart while keeping the duvet over us. That was the last time I stayed over at a boyfriend's place when they still lived with their parents," Hayley stated matter of factly.

"I'm starting to feel like I've lived a dull life compared to you two." Clarissa chuckled.

Becky rolled her eyes. "Come on; you must have some embarrassing moments. Confess, woman!"

Clarissa smirked. "Well, I nearly lost my virginity before Nigel, and I started dating. Do you remember Edward from college?"

Hayley and Becky's mouths fell open in surprise.

"You never mentioned getting it on with tall, blonde, and hunky!" Becky chided.

Clarissa clamped her lips and shook her head. "You wouldn't have said anything either," she told them firmly. "He came over to my house, supposedly to study, and before I knew it, we were snogging on my bed. One thing led to another, and within minutes he was thrusting on top of me. After a few minutes, I asked him if he was going to put it in, and he said he had. I think he was shagging my bedding because I wasn't feeling anything."

"Oh my god! No wonder you didn't tell us!" Hayley howled with laughter. "Then what happened?"

"He quickly climbed off me, and that's when I saw his little winky. That man definitely wasn't in proportion. Probably too many steroids."

"What did you say to him?" Becky demanded while rubbing her aching cheeks.

"Trying to make him feel better, I told him not to worry and that

I liked them small."

Both girls laughed so hard that Becky crossed her legs to brace herself, trying not to mummy-pee.

"Holy hell, I'm dying here!" Hayley gasped. "That must have gone down like a lead balloon. Talk about adding salt to the wound."

Chapter 2

Becky and Hayley left early the following morning. All three of them had woken with thick heads from laughing and drinking far too much cheap white wine, but it had been a blast, just like Clarissa thought it would be.

Luke and Matthew played in Clarissa's neglected back garden with her neighbor's kids, shooting at each other with Luke's Nerf guns he received for his birthday. So, Clarissa knew she had time on her hands before her non-stop eating machines wanted feeding again.

After making herself a mug of tea, she sat in her favorite armchair with her trusted, ancient laptop and notebook, which included Hayley's phone sex chat line company details. She rubbed her hands and then opened her laptop. *'Search engine, here I come,'* she thought as she prepared herself for investigating the chat line as butterflies appeared in her stomach. "Why am I so bloody nervous," she asked herself. *'Because you've never done anything slightly risky in your life,'* she admitted.

After reviewing her notes, Clarissa looked for the search engine icon on her laptop. She opened it, with the butterflies fluttering vigorously in her stomach, typing the words Castle Communications into the search box. Instantly, results pages appeared with their company information at the top of the first page. *'Here goes,'* she thought as she clicked on the Castle Communications UK link. Clarissa was instantly impressed with the company's website. It was professional in appearance, looked friendly, and was stylish. However, she wasn't sure what she expected. She scrolled down the website past the sales icon, general information, business address, and social media icons, stopping when she saw a box with hiring information.

We are now hiring PSO's.

Are you over 18 years of age and open-minded?

Do you have a landline?

Would you like to work the hours that suit you and get paid weekly?

If the answer is Yes to all these questions, then you may be ideal for our team.

Apply here.

Clarissa clicked on the Apply Here icon button, instantly going to a new page that was a lot less classy than their home page. Talk to Earn was the header, and Become a Phone Sex Operator was underneath, all in bright-red text against a black background. '*Well, that's setting the mood,*' she thought while sipping her steaming hot tea.

As Clarissa read all the available information, it confirmed what Hayley had been told by her friend Stephanie.

How would you like to work from the comfort of your own home and work the hours to suit you? We always want to snap up talented women over 18 years of age who want to work 15 hours or more from home. If that is you, register today and get started. We pay weekly

Give free training

Offer flexible hours

Pay top rates

No hidden fees

Call 0161-888-999 Or Register HERE

Clarissa didn't know whether to call the number or click on the register icon. *'I'm a coward,'* she clicked on the icon, taking her to yet another page with a registration checklist and an online form to fill out. *'Wow, they really want to make sure I'm over eighteen,'* she surmised as she read over the checklist.

Registration Checklist

You need the following criteria.

Female voice.

Be over 18 yrs.

Legal resident of the UK.

Have an available landline registered to you.

Be available to work 15 hours a week or more.

Then came the form to fill out, and Clarissa paused, thinking about her current job at Janka Industries and her lack of money situation. "How badly do I want a decent life for my boys and me?" she asked herself aloud as she listened to her two boys laughing and squealing with their friends from her back garden. "Whatever it takes!" She declared as a new sense of determination washed over her. She began to fill out the form.

<u>**Name**</u>

Clarissa Darcey

Email address

ClarissaDarcy1991@gmail.com

Confirm Email Address

ClarissaDarcy1991@gmail.com

Password

Nigel_is_an_asshole

Confirm Password

Nigel_is_an_asshole

Register

'I really must change my email address,' Clarissa thought, *'any idiot could probably hack me,'* she told herself, but she loved her chosen password. "Very apt." She took another gulp of her tea while clicking the register icon.

Before long, Clarissa had filled in the online registration forms with all her relevant information. Relief swept through her when she realized Castle Communications didn't want current employment details or references. The thought of her boss, Mr. Mason, discovering what she was thinking of doing made her stomach churn. If he knew what she was applying for, it would only encourage him.

Clarissa was feeling quite shocked at herself for going ahead and registering. She was hoping with all her heart that it was the first small step to a better future with Luke and Matthew. Asking Nigel for money for their boys was something that she hated doing. And because he never paid up, she had stopped asking and demanding, seeing it as a waste of energy while adding pure stress. Going through the court system wasn't getting her anywhere either. Meanwhile, the asshole drove around in a top-of-the-range sports car, had a posh apartment in the best area of Winchester, and was constantly out with a steady stream of women, shagging everything with a pulse. She abruptly pictured Nigel in her mind, standing naked with horror on his face as his cock dropped off, landing on the ground with a thud. *'If only.'*

Feeling more hopeful than she had the previous day before her best friends came over, she put her laptop away and decided to start making lunch for the boys.

—x—

The rest of Clarissa's day was the same as every Sunday, filled with cooking, cleaning, and catching up on the never-ending laundry. She was starting to think that the bloody thing magically refilled itself as it was never empty. Her boys were muck monsters, and there was no chance of them staying clean on any given day. She spent the evening ironing the boy's school uniforms for the week while they played Xbox. Then she bathed them, read them a story, and put them to bed after lots of cuddles, with them pleading for her to read more.

When Luke and Matthew were finally asleep, Clarissa made a cup of tea and plopped herself in her favorite armchair with her library book in hand, relishing the peace and quiet. She was about to open her fabulous new read when a ping sounded from her laptop on her coffee table.

At first, she wondered who would be emailing her so late at night, then she remembered and wondered if it was Castle Communications getting back to her. With a strong feeling of anticipation, she reached for her laptop and opened it on her lap. Opening her email, she spotted an email from Castle Communications immediately. Clarissa's pulse began to race as she clicked on it.

Dear Clarissa Darcy, thank you for applying to Castle Communications, and congratulations on taking the first step to earning great money at your convenience. I would love to chat with you and tell you more about working for us.

Please call Michelle or Rachael on 0161-888-999. Extension 9, between 9 am-12 pm. Monday to Sunday.

With Regards
Michelle Ryan.
Service manager.
Castle Communications
167 Eccles Rd
Manchester
M44 ELS

Clarissa was surprised at the odd hours stated, but she was relieved that there were evening hours. There was no way she would be able to call while she was working at her day job. And even if she called during her lunch or tea break, she wouldn't want to return to work with an embarrassed and flushed face. Her work colleagues didn't miss a trick. *'I should call now while I'm still feeling brave.'*

Taking a large gulp of her cooling tea as if it was a large brandy, she pulled out her phone from her favorite pajama bottoms and began to dial the number with slightly shaking hands. "I should not be so nervous," she scolded herself, "I talk to strangers daily on the bloody phone."

Clarissa dialled the number, pressed call, and waited.

"Welcome to Castle Communications. If you know your extension number, please select it now."

Clarissa pressed nine and again waited.

"Good evening, Castle Communications. Michelle Ryan speaking, how can I help you?"

'She sounds friendly enough.' Clarissa thought, feeling slightly relieved. She took a deep breath.

"Hi, my name is Clarissa Darcy. I registered earlier today on your website, and you emailed me, asking for me to call," she said in a rush of words, her bravery gone.

"Hello, Clarissa, and thanks for calling. How are you doing?"

"I'm good, thanks, but I'm a bit nervous, to be honest. I've never done anything like this before."

Michelle laughed down the phone humorously. "Trust me, Clarissa, most women haven't done this before when they reach out, but nearly all of them never regret it. Tell me a bit about yourself and why you're interested."

Clarissa wasn't sure how honest she should be, but she was a genuine person and hated liars—even more so since Nigel. She steadied her nerves and decided to lay it all out to bear. She told Michelle everything about the job she hated, the boss who made her skin crawl, her ex-husband being an asshole and not paying towards his kids, and the fact that she was struggling financially. It felt good laying it all out.

"We have so many women working for us in similar circumstances," Michelle told her sympathetically. "I think this job would be perfect for you and your situation, Clarissa. Would you like to know more about the job?"

"Yes, please," Clarissa replied, her bravery and determination seeping back.

"Okay. We offer many phone sex services to callers, such as barely legal, yummy mummies, hot and wet, wet and wild, and domination, to name but a few. You will receive a full list of our services if you decide to give it a go. We ask our ladies to record an introduction for each service, and if a caller selects you, you chat with them for a maximum of thirty minutes, tailoring your chat to the service they phone in on. The callers get disconnected at the half-hour mark, so they can't run up large phone bills. If they want to carry on talking to you, they must call in again and select you. Have you got it so far?" Michelle asked.

It all sounded straightforward to Clarissa. Although, she was starting to think twice at the mere mention of domination.

"It sounds okay so far."

"Good! Now the way it works is that the calls come through directly to us at our head office; we then put the call through to you using our secure system. Your landline is never called directly, and none of your personal information is ever shared. To protect your identity, you'll have to choose a different persona and name when talking to callers."

"I understand."

"Awesome. Now, let's get to the nitty-gritty about how much you'll earn. If you work between the hours of eight am to twelve am, you will receive twenty-five pence a minute; if you work between twelve am to eight am, it will be thirty-five pence per minute. We pay you weekly directly into your bank account, and you will receive an online statement of your calls and hours worked, and how much you earned on each call. How does that sound?"

Clarissa's mind was reeling from all the information, and she quickly calculated how much she could earn an hour. Fifteen to twenty-one pounds an hour was a lot better than what she was currently earning, that was for sure. *'I've got nothing to lose but maybe a lot to gain,'* she thought, *'it's worth a go.'*

"It sounds like a good opportunity," she told Michelle honestly. "Would I be able to work just evenings to start with before I decide to leave my current day job?" she asked, hoping she would get the right answer.

"Yes, of course. I think that would be the wisest option to begin with. You can pick your hours. All we require is that you work a minimum of fifteen hours a week."

'I can manage fifteen hours a week while the kids are sleeping,' she assured herself.

"I can do that," she told Michelle, feeling her determination strengthen.

"That's great. I'll email you all the information you need, and I'll email you the wage forms to fill out. When would you like to start?" Michelle asked cheerfully.

"How about next Monday, if you've received everything back in time?" she asked, thinking she should start as soon as possible while still feeling brave.

"That sounds like a plan. I'll be in contact soon. Welcome to my team, Clarissa!"

Clarissa was feeling more hopeful than she had in a long time.

"Wonderful, and thank you, Michelle."

"Bye for now."

The line went dead, and Clarissa was shocked at herself for going ahead and taking the first steps. The call went a lot better than she expected. Michelle had come across as friendly and professional, just like any decent manager. Clarissa was relieved.

Clarissa couldn't wait to tell Becky and Hayley that she had pulled on her big girl pants and made the first move towards a better and brighter future. She glanced at her fossil watch, a gift from her parents, to see if it was too late to call her best friends. It was only nine-thirty PM, so she knew that her best friends in the world would still be up.

She decided to message them first to see if they would like to do a video chat so they could talk and see each other.

Are you girls up for a video chat? I have news!!!!

Hayley quickly replied first. *Hell, yeah!!*

I'm free.

Clarissa was excited to hear what her best friends thought. They weren't just her best friends; they were as good as sisters. She logged into her messenger, clicked on their group chat, and clicked call. Within seconds, both of her best friends joined the call.

Becky looked like she had already had a nap, her curly, red hair making her look like she had been dragged through a hedge backward, and Hayley looked like a younger version of herself with no makeup. Clarissa knew she probably looked a sight with wearing her adult Harry Potter pj's and her hair in a messy bun.

"What's the news?" Hayley demanded with a grin—not waiting for any hellos.

"Yes, spill, woman!" Becky added excitedly.

"I did it," Clarissa exclaimed, "I registered with Castle Communications, the phone sex company. Their manager emailed me, and we just had a chat on the phone about it. I should be starting next Monday."

"Bloody hell, lady," Hayley declared. "I'm so bloody proud of you. I wasn't sure if you would go for it."

Clarissa laughed at the shock in Hayley's voice.

"Hayley took the words right out of my mouth. That's awesome, honey," Becky agreed excitedly. "Does this mean you're going to hand in your notice at work? And what's your new boss like?"

"She's called Michelle, and she was friendly and professional. She explained how it works and how much I could earn. Apparently, I only have to work a minimum of fifteen hours, so I should be able to do evenings at first, until I know whether it's going to work out or not before quitting Janka."

"That's smart!" Becky agreed, just as Clarissa's laptop pinged.

"Ooh, is that the information email from them?" Hayley asked, hearing the ping from her end.

"I don't know, but I'll check."

Clarissa balanced her phone against her now lukewarm mug of tea, reaching for her laptop. She opened up her email, and there it was. Instantly her pulse started to race with anticipation.

"Yep, it's the information from Michelle," she told them.

"Well, don't keep us waiting. Open it and tell us what it says!" Hayley demanded, sounding even more excited.

Becky nodded, agreeing profusely.

Clarissa laughed. "Okay, okay, I'm doing it."

Clarissa opened the email, not knowing what to expect, and then she read it aloud for her friends to hear.

"Hi Clarissa, it was lovely to chat with you. I've attached the wage forms for you to print off, fill out and send back to us. I've also attached a pdf document of our list of services. Please go over the list and think of an introduction for each service. Once you know what your introduction will be, please call the free number to record your introductions. You will have the opportunity to re-record until you are happy with each one. I look forward to your first day and getting to know you." Clarissa took a deep breath.

"Wow, you're right; she does sound friendly and professional," Hayley said, "Now tell us the list; we're dying to hear what's on it."

Becky giggled, "Yes, we are."

"Bloody hell, girls. Impatient much?" Clarissa scolded with a smirk.

"Why yes, yes we are," Hayley admitted with no shame, with Becky nodding on Clarissa's phone screen next to her.

With a tap of her finger, Clarissa opened the pdf attachment, and her eyes grew wide. Her girlfriends, who were watching her like a hawk, instantly spotted her reaction.

"What's wrong?" Becky asked, concern in her voice.

"The bloody list is huge!"

Hayley laughed at Clarissa's reaction. "Don't be intimidated and bashful, woman. Read them out!"

Clarissa could feel her cheeks already burning with embarrassment, and she knew her friends would notice. She took a deep breath and started to read them aloud.

1: *Barely legal*
2: *Busty babes.*
3: *Party girls*
4: *Naughty professionals*
5: *Yummy mummies*
6: *Big booty babes*

7: *Roleplay*

8: *Mature*

9: *Milf's*

10: *Gilf's*

11: *Submissive girls*

12: *Experienced women*

13: *Girl on girl*

14: *Hot and Wet*

15: *Lesbian ladies*

16: *Wet and wild*

17: *All the curvy ladies*

18: *Kinky*

19: *Extra Kinky*

20: *Fetish*

21: *Domination*

As Clarissa read the list, she could feel her cheeks burning hotter and hotter. She was sure that her face was probably glowing.

"I'm not sure I can do this," she told her friends. "I've never done girl on girl, been submissive, or done any domination or kinky stuff. The kinkiest thing Nigel and I ever did was use furry hand-cuffs once. Even then, he was a total pussy, whining about them digging into his wrists."

By the time she spoke her last word, her best friends were cracking up with laughter. Hayley was struggling to catch her breath, and yet again, Becky had laughter-tears streaming down her face.

Clarissa tried to look stern as she waited for them to stop and compose themselves, but they had a fit of giggles that wasn't going to end anytime soon.

"Right, I'm getting another cuppa while you two buggers sort yourselves out," she told them; unfortunately, it only made them laugh harder.

Clarissa left her phone on the arm of her chair while taking her mug into the kitchen. As she made her tea, she smiled and listened to her best friends laughing and talking about her dreaded list. Hearing their light-hearted banter dissolved her embarrassment. Clarissa was grateful.

By the time she had finished making her tea and was back in her lounge, her best friends were composed, discussing the various services.

"I could pretend I've done girl on girl," Hayley told Becky as Clarissa grabbed her phone and sat down again, putting her laptop back on her lap.

"You could?" Clarissa asked, her embarrassment now gone.

"Hell yes. Let's face it, who knows what we like better than we do? If I were you, Clarissa, I would just describe what I would like done to me but pretend I was talking about doing it to another girl. Don't forget; it's all going to be acting."

Clarissa could always rely on her friends to put things in perspective.

"But what about the fetish and domination stuff? I haven't got a clue," she admitted.

"I don't think you need to worry about all of that kinky stuff," Hayley told her. "When I had my chat with Stephanie, she said she hardly ever got those kinds of calls. They aren't the most popular chat lines. Most of her callers were just horny guys wanting to listen to a hot girl while they have a wank."

"I bet she's busy on the weekends when the pubs and clubs kick out," Becky added with a giggle.

The girls were making Clarissa feel a lot better about the list, and yet again, she reminded herself that she had nothing to lose by trying it. "Okay, so are you two going to help me come up with my introductions so I can record them?"

"Yes!" Hayley and Becky both declared in unison.

Clarissa couldn't help but laugh at their enthusiasm. "Maybe you two should be doing this with me."

"We need to be able to tell our hubby's that you're earning tons of money before we have a chance at doing it," Becky said with a giggle. "I've been thinking about what work I want to do now my kids are all in school."

Clarissa's brows raised at her comment. "Have you two already talked about doing it?"

"We talked about it after our girl's night while sharing your pull-out bed," Hayley told her honestly. "We're both rooting for you. And if you earn loads of money and we can convince our hubbies, then we'll go for it too."

Within a couple of hours, the three friends had come up with introductions for all the chat line services on Clarissa's dreaded list. Her cheeks were aching, and she felt like she'd done a hundred sit-ups from laughing with the girls. All three felt quite proud of themselves for what they had achieved. Clarissa knew none of the introductions were perfect, but she was sure she could probably redo them later on once she had some experience.

Chapter 3

After saying goodnight to Hayley and Becky, Clarissa popped to the loo and then made herself a fresh drink. While her tea was brewing, she wondered if she should record her introductions the following night or get it done now, while she was feeling more confident, and it was still fresh in her mind.

"Sod it," she said under her breath, "Now or never."

Finishing her tea, she made her way to her small Ikea desk and laid out her notepad, now filled with saucy introductions and notes, her laptop, tea, and her phone. She sat at her desk and took a moment to listen out for the boys, who had a habit of coming down in the night for drinks. The last thing she wanted was for them to hear anything. They may not see their asshole of a dad, but they did see their grandparents regularly, and Nigel's parents definitely didn't need to know what she was doing. Luckily, she couldn't hear a peep from upstairs, so she knew she was safe to start.

Steadying her breath and pulse, Clarissa dialled the number on the email, and it connected.

"Welcome to the team. This cost-free line is for recording your introductions. Select the number of the introduction you would like to record."

Clarissa looked at the list. *'I might as well do them in order,'* she thought as she selected number one, barely legal.

"This is the Barely legal line. Press zero to record your introduction, press one to end your recording, press two to listen to your recording, and press three to save. Press nine to listen to these instructions again."

Clarissa quickly picked up her pen and pressed nine, realizing that she should have been ready to write the instructions down. She listened to the message again, this time jotting them in her notebook. Clarissa knew that if she had to listen to the instruction message more than a few times, it would wind her up. She hung up, wanting to have a moment to practice her first introduction.

Once Clarissa was ready, she read her intro aloud a few times, trying to use a younger voice that she could maintain for a conversation. She was unsure if she sounded barely legal, those days were long gone, but she was trying. Clarissa felt like a total idiot. She was relieved that Hayley and Becky couldn't hear her.

Clarissa called the number again, pressing number one for the barely legal line. Taking a breath, she pressed zero and heard a beep.

"Hi, I'm Clarissa, and I. Shit, the wrong bloody name!" She said as she pressed one to end the recording and two to listen to it.

She was shocked to hear that she didn't sound too bad. She didn't quite sound barely legal, but she sounded younger than she actually was. Pressing zero, she restarted.

"Hi, I'm Adele, and I want you to teach me how to please a real man like you."

Clarissa pressed one to end and two to listen to her recording.

She was stunned at how well she sounded, instantly grateful for her years of experience in customer service and sales. Pressing number three, she saved her first introduction and hung up.

She knew that in sales you had to find a client's need and then try to fulfill that need. She decided that this was just another sales job, only she was selling a service and not a product. Other than that, it was all about boosting men's egos and making them feel like God's gift.

Looking at her list again, she saw that Busty Babes was the next line to record. Now that was a service, she did feel confident about, especially as she was a busty thirty-six H on a curvy frame. Clarissa had always been busty, and that was putting it mildly. At sixteen years old, she was already a thirty-four DD, which was one of the reasons Nigel pursued her. By the time Clarissa was six months pregnant with Luke, they had grown to the size she was now. And by the time Clarissa was due with Luke, she looked and felt like Budda. At the time, Clarissa didn't know where her boobs ended, and her bump started.

'Well, at least these big boobies are coming in handy now,' she thought as she read and practiced her next introduction.

After three run-throughs, she felt ready and dialled the number, pressing number two for the Busty Babes line. She hit zero and began.

"Hi, I'm Clarissa. Fuck, shit and balls."

Clarissa wanted to kick herself for making the same mistake. It was challenging to switch to a different persona and mindset. Then she had an idea. Hanging up, she quickly searched for Angelina Jolie, and when she found the perfect picture, she promptly printed it out.

Sticking Angela's picture above her laptop, she knew it would remind her to use her alter ego's name instead of her own. Moments later, she was pressing zero again to record.

"Hi, I'm Adele, and I have thirty-six H boobs that need some serious attention. Do you want to play?"

Clarissa listened to her recording, and her confidence soared. *'Wow, I'm not too bad at this.'*

As Clarissa worked her way down the long list of sex chat line services, her confidence increased. She was actually having fun recording all the introductions. However, when it came to the last two on the list, her nervousness grew. Her only fetish was for manly men with close beards, sexy nerds, and nice bums, if that counted. As for domination—she was clueless—apart from knowing that there were dominant's and submissive's.

Hayley and Becky were a great help with the introductions. Surprisingly, they knew much more about the whole fetish and domination scene than she did. From what Clarissa could gather, reading the Fifty Shades of Grey trilogy and others like it had made them both feel quite knowledgeable. Apparently, the books had increased their sex lives too. Hence, why they both now had new additions to their families since the books came out. Mind you, Clarissa hadn't heard their husbands complaining about it.

'Get it over with, woman,' she scolded herself, *'you only have two left, and you should be in bed already.'* Clarissa glanced at the time on her phone. It was already two in the morning, but she wanted to get it done.

She practiced twice and called again, this time selecting number twenty for the fetish line and zero to record.

"Hi, I'm Adele, and I want to hear what really turns you on."

Clarissa listened and saved it, pleased that it was short and sweet. After talking with Becky and Hayley, they decided it was best to have an open-ended introduction because none of them knew what fetishes the men would have. She hung up and looked at her last introduction, relieved that she was nearly finished.

After reading it aloud a couple of times, Clarissa was ready to do the last introduction for the Domination line. She called the number for the last time, entered twenty-one, then zero to start recording while glancing at Angelina's picture.

"Hello, you may address me as Mistress Adele. What are you going to do to please me?" she said sultrily down the phone.

After listening to her last and final recording, she was thrilled with how it sounded. *'I did sound quite dominant,'* she thought with a grin on her face.

The relief she felt for getting all the recordings done was immense, and if it hadn't been so late, she would have been tempted to have a glass of wine to celebrate her small victory. Instead, she quickly printed off the forms she needed to fill out, slipped them into her bag, and took herself off to bed.

—x—

As soon as Clarissa woke in the morning, she jumped into action. After getting her shower and getting dressed, she woke Luke and Matthew, herding them into the bathroom to wash and brush their teeth. Neither of her boys were morning people on school days, and she knew how they felt.

"I'm going to start breakfast, my little rays of sunshine. Toast or cereal?" she asked, smiling at their sleepy faces.

Matthew spat out his toothpaste. "Toast, please, with marmite."

"Same, please," Luke mumbled, wiping his mouth.

Clarissa ruffled their hair affectionately and made her way downstairs.

Clarissa grabbed her handbag as she walked through the lounge and headed for the kitchen. She knew her boys would be a while getting dressed, so in between making tea and toast, she filled out the forms for Castle Communications. Once Luke and Matthew were fed and ready, Clarissa slipped the forms into her handbag and led her boys to their front door. Like most weekdays, she took a deep breath, dreading that she would have to do the job she hated.

After dropping Luke and Matthew off at her childminder, Susan's, Clarissa stopped at a mailbox and posted her application. When she arrived at Janka Industries, she was starting to feel a little better about her day. Clarissa exited her old red mini, locked it, and strode towards the grey, looming offices of Janka Industries.

Clarissa got to work as soon as she pulled up to her desk. Her floor was a hive of activity, with her colleagues' answering calls and working on their computers. A couple of older ladies she worked with chatted with hushed voices by the large printer at the end of her floor, gossiping about the latest office scandal. She could see her creeper of a boss, Mr. Mason, hoovering in his office doorway, ogling her. She made sure not to give him eye contact. Her skin crawled.

Clarissa turned on her computer and opened her messages, folding her arms under her boobs—out of habit— as her eyes scanned the never-ending stream of emails from clients. Like a stealthy cat, Mr. Mason was suddenly standing next to her, and her stomach lurched as his gaze zoned in on her ample bust.

"Are those heavy?" he asked loudly.

Clarissa nearly choked on her own spit, aware that everyone had heard his booming voice. The office floor went quiet. Hushed whispers assaulted her ears. She felt sick to her stomach, desperately wanting to crawl under her desk and hide. Clarissa unfolded her arms and reached for her work folders next to her keyboard, picking them up and holding them to her chest to obstruct his view.

"I hope you're referring to my work folders, Mr. Mason, because referring to anything on my body would be sexual harassment, again." Clarissa looked up—glaring at him—willing him to leave with every fibre of her body.

He smirked, and Clarissa silently hoped that at least one of her colleagues would step in and help her, but no. Like always, they behaved like sheep, hiding from the lion stalking his prey.

Clarissa's phone began to ring with perfect timing.

"If you'll excuse me, I have work to do."

As she held her folders with one hand against her chest, she answered the call with the other. Mr. Mason strode away arrogantly, and Clarissa prayed he would trip over his own feet and land flat on his face.

—x—

The rest of Clarissa's week passed in a blur. *'Thank God it's Friday,'* Clarissa thought as she got in her old but trusted Mini in the company car park. She pulled onto the main road, heading for home. For a change, she didn't have to collect her boys from her child-minder. As luck would have it, her ex-in-laws had asked to take Luke and Matthew to a theme park for the weekend, something Clarissa couldn't afford to do. They even offered to collect the boys from school. It was great timing because she had received an email from Michelle at Castle Communications asking her if she was free to do some training over the weekend.

Clarissa immediately sent messages to Hayley and Becky to let them know. She wasn't surprised when they both messaged back to say they were free and were coming over to support her. *'Who were they kidding?'* Clarissa knew they didn't just want to support her;

they wanted to hear her in action. She giggled as she stopped at a red light, knowing she would be exactly the same if Hayley or Becky were about to work on a phone sex chat line. *'Because that's what best friends do!'* Clarissa and the girls usually did their girl's night two nights a month, but for her best friends, this was a special occasion.

—x—

When Clarissa arrived home, her best friend's cars were already parked by her house, and they were waiting inside for her. They all had keys to each other's houses in case of emergencies. Clarissa had locked herself out numerous times, and so had Becky.

As Clarissa stepped out of her car on the driveway, she heard music playing inside, making her smile.

Hayley opened the front door as Clarissa approached it. "Hurry up, woman, the wine is open, and the Chinese food is on the table."

Clarissa giggled. You could trust her friends to make a meal of something, literally. Her stomach growled at the thought of Chinese food. It was her favorite takeaway, and she hadn't had a chance to eat lunch; she had been so busy at work.

Hurrying inside, she grabbed her phone from her bag and dropped her purse on the hallway side table. As she entered her kitchen, she could see Hayley and Becky sitting at the dining table with a small feast in front of them, an open wine bottle and glasses at the ready.

Clarissa grinned at her best friends. "You two are seriously the bestest ever!"

"Ah, shucks," Becky told her, "You deserve it for putting up with your creepy boss."

"Did you have any more issues with him after Monday?" Hayley asked, concerned.

Clarissa rolled her eyes as the memories of his crude behavior during the week came flooding back.

"Well, let's see. On Tuesday, I made the mistake of wearing red lipstick, and John walked past and said, Oh, sexy blow job lips. Then on Wednesday, he accidentally, on purpose, brushed his crotch against my backside while I was at the coffee machine. Yesterday the perv asked me if it was cold outside because he said my nipples were going to poke someone's eye out. Then today, he asked me if I was wearing knickers because he couldn't see my knicker line. Within earshot of pretty much everyone! I swear if I dressed down anymore, I would look like a man."

"That bloody perv!" Hayley declared while Becky started choking on her noodles. "Did you report him to your HR department again?"

Clarissa scoffed and rolled her eyes. "Of course, I did. I went in first thing Wednesday morning."

"And what did they say?" Becky asked after managing to swallow her chow mien noodles.

"As usual, they said it's a he-said-she-said situation because no one will come forward and back me up," Clarissa told them, her blood boiling in her veins.

"Why the hell not?" Hayley asked, thoroughly enraged.

"Because I'm the youngest one there now," Clarissa stated. "Everyone near my age has left for better jobs because of him, and it's only the nearly retired people and me. They don't want to cause trouble just before they retire, and I can understand that." She felt stuck between a rock and a hard place.

Becky's face flushed red, camouflaging her numerous freckles. "They aren't backing you up because he's not doing it to them."

"You're probably right," Clarissa agreed, "but that doesn't change anything. Anyway, enough about the creeper; let's enjoy our dinner and wine."

—x—

An hour later, Clarissa and her best friends were chilling in her lounge, listening to Tina Turner's greatest hits and hitting their second bottle of wine. Clarissa couldn't help but check her watch. Her training with Michelle was due to start at eight pm, and she was beginning to wish that she hadn't eaten so much food. She was also starting to feel nervous, yet again wondering if the new job was a good idea.

"Feeling nervous?" Becky asked after seeing Clarissa checking the time for the fourth time in ten minutes.

"Yes, I am. I can't help it," she admitted, "apparently Michelle loved all my introductions, but talking dirty to someone live, is a whole different thing."

"Well, I had another chat with Stephanie this week, and she told me a bit more about it," Hayley said with a wicked grin while wiggling her eyebrows, instantly making Clarissa smile.

"And?" Becky asked impatiently, making Clarissa's smile turn to Hayley's matching grin.

Hayley took a sip of her wine, making Becky and Clarissa feel even more impatient.

"Oh, she gave me all the juicy info," she told them, laughing at her friend's scowling faces, "she said that she has regulars who call her all the time, who are lonely and just want some company. Some of them just chat with her like an old friend, telling her about their work week and dates they've been on, and asking for advice about women. Other regulars are guys whose ladies aren't interested in them anymore and aren't giving them attention, if you know what I mean. Then she gets lots of drunk men on the weekends, as I mentioned before. If you can build up regulars like she has, you'll be golden. And you'll be able to tell your creepy boss to go fuck himself."

"After the week I've just had, I bloody hope so," Clarissa admitted. "If I have to stay in that job too much longer, I might do something to John that I won't regret."

Becky abruptly started to laugh, nearly spilling her wine. "Can you imagine if he called the chat line, and you recognized his voice?"

Hayley's mouth, which was full of wine, exploded from her nose and mouth, spraying her friends with a fine mist.

"Oh my god, Hayley. Your mouth is like an out-of-control fire hose," Clarissa squeaked as she burst into laughter, "If John called, that would be my worst nightmare."

"Unless he called on the domination line." Hayley tried to say as she blew her wine-covered nose and wiped her wet face. "Then you could go to town on him and severely punish the creepy pervert."

Clarissa laughed so hard that she nearly repeated Hayley's wine explosion.

"Could you imagine?" Becky giggled, "What would you do or say?"

"I honestly don't know. Knowing me, I'd be so stunned that I'd probably hang up," she told them honestly.

After listening to Becky and Hayley's torture suggestions for her creepy boss, Clarissa began to prepare herself for her first training session. Becky and Hayley watched as she placed her notepad, pen, and chat line service list on her desk and put up her picture of Angelina. In preparation, she had already moved her landline phone over to her desk the night before. Just the sight of the chat line list had her nervousness growing. She could understand why some performers threw up before going on stage.

"You're going to do great," Becky told her sincerely.

"Yes, you are, and you have nothing to worry about," Hayley agreed.

Clarissa loved her friends for being so supportive and encouraging. "Thank you, besties," she told them with a smile as she glanced at her watch again.

Clarissa sat down at her desk with two minutes to go, pulling the phone towards her.

"You'd better put it on loudspeaker so we can hear what's being said," Hayley told her with a cheeky grin.

"Yes, we want to hear everything," Becky admitted with her own cheesy grin.

"Seriously, ladies, you are too much," Clarissa chided jokingly as she picked up the phone, set it to the loudspeaker, and dialled the number on her notepad. As she waited for Michelle to answer, she noticed Becky and Hayley sitting with their fingers crossed, making her smile.

"Hello and welcome to Castle Communication, Michelle Ryan speaking."

Clarissa's pulse suddenly sped up. "Hi Michelle, it's Clarissa; ready for my training."

"Hi, Clarissa. How are you doing?"

"I'm good but very nervous," she confessed, the phone slightly shaking in her hand.

"You don't need to be nervous," Michelle assured her. "I've listened to all your introduction recordings, and I think you're a natural."

Movement made Clarissa turn to her friends, who had switched from crossed fingers to matching thumbs-up and Cheshire cat grins. She covered her mouth quickly to stifle a laugh.

"Thank you, Michelle. That makes me feel a little more confident," she said, turning her attention back to her new boss.

"Your introductions have all been uploaded to our system. So tonight, you will be trying some calls while I listen in. If you have any issues, I'll be able to hear and rescue you," she said humorously. "Do you have any questions or concerns before we start?"

"No, but I'm still nervous about the fetish and domination lines, to be honest," Clarissa admitted.

"You'll probably get one a shift, maybe, if that. So, I wouldn't worry," Michelle said light-heartedly. "The way the system works is that you call the number at the bottom of the chat line list, enter your personal code, which is 91737, and press one to log in. Calls will be forwarded to you through our secure system. When you're ready to log out, call the number again, enter your 91737 code, and press two. Does that sound straightforward?"

Clarissa felt her skin flush while her hands began to tremble a little more, but she understood everything Michelle had told her. "It does."

"Wonderful, see if you can do an hour. I'll call you afterwards, bar any issues."

"Sounds good; speak to you in a bit," Clarissa replied, then hung up.

"She sounds nice," Becky told her with a large smile on her face.

"I second that, and it sounds straightforward enough," Hayley added. "You've got this, honey."

Clarissa wasn't sure or as confident, but she mentally pulled up her big girl knickers and gave them her brightest smile. "Sod it! Here goes," she declared.

Glancing at Angelina Jolie's picture and then the phone number on her chat line list, she dialled and entered her code, pressed number one, and then hung up.

When Clarissa turned to look at her best friends, she couldn't stop the grin that appeared on her face. Both Becky and Hayley were poised on the edge of their seats in anticipation of her first call.

"I don't know who's more excited, you or you," she said, pointing at them in turn.

"Definitely me!" Hayley told her with no shame.

"I don't know about that," Becky interjected. "I feel like I'm living precariously through Clarissa at the moment."

"I saw you two...," Clarissa said as her landline phone started ringing. *Shit, this is it.*

Panic began to flood Clarissa from her head to her toes. She picked up the phone with a shaky hand and glanced at Angelina's picture.

"Line two."

A woman's voice told her when she clicked the dreaded green answer button. Clarissa then heard a small beep as the call connected. She quickly checked her list. *Busty babes, I can do that; I'm busty.*

"Hi, I'm Adele; who's this?" she asked her in her best sultry voice.

"Mark," a deep, drunk, and shaky voice told her, "Are your tits really that big?" He slurred.

Clarissa could see Becky and Hayley attempting to stifle their laughter. "They are, with big and hard tingling nipples to match. What would you like to do to them?" she asked.

Abruptly moans emanated from the loudspeaker as the caller seemed to reach his peak. Then the line went silent for a minute, and Clarissa wasn't sure what to do. She looked at her friends, holding her free hand out as if asking for help. Becky and Hayley shrugged while keeping their hands over their mouths.

"Thanks for that" Mark slurred.

The line went dead, and as Clarissa hung up, Hayley and Becky exploded with belly laughs.

"Oh, my God. Thank God my hubby lasts longer than that after he's had a few beers!" Hayley said while trying to breathe.

Becky repeatedly slapped her knee while trying to catch her breath too. "He definitely must have started before he called in."

Clarissa didn't have a chance to reply; her phone began to ring again. She quickly answered, glancing at her list.

"Line thirteen. Beep."

It was Girl on Girl. '*Shit,*'

"Hi, I'm Adele; who's this?"

"Hello, Adele. I'm Gerry. How old are you?"

Clarissa paused, '*real age,*' she thought. "I'm thirty-one. Do you like girls who like girls?" she asked sexily.

"Oh yes," he told her breathlessly, "What do you like doing to other girls?"

Panic momentarily set in as Clarissa tried to think of what to say.

Suddenly Hayley and Becky leapt in action, Becky holding her hands up as if she was holding someone while snogging their face-off, while Hayley started to rub her own large boobs and pretend to tweak her nipples.

Clarissa nearly laughed down the phone. She quickly slapped her hand to her mouth to keep herself silent. Her mind was racing.

Slowly she removed her hand while trying to compose herself.

"My girlfriend loves it when I kiss her slowly, sliding my soft wet tongue into her sweet mouth," Clarissa told him seductively.

"Then she likes it when I slowly run my wet tongue down her body, taking my time to lick and suck her hard, swollen nipples. Mmm. Do you like the sound of that? Can you imagine watching me slowly licking her?" Clarissa asked.

All Clarissa and her friends could hear was a loud slapping noise and Gerry moaning loudly. Suddenly the line went dead.

Clarissa burst into laughter as she put down the phone.

"I swear you were made for this job." Hayley guffawed.

Becky snorted; she was laughing so hard. "I second that! But, if you want to earn some decent money, you need to try and make them last longer."

As Clarissa tried to get a grip and ease her aching sides from laughing, her landline rang again.

"Bloody hell, you're popular!" Becky declared through her giggles.

Clarissa didn't have a chance to reply. She picked up the phone and glanced at her Angelina picture, then her list.

"Line twenty-one, Beep."

Her heart skipped a beat when she realized it was the domination line. Clarissa didn't know what the hell to say. She took a long and slow deep breath to prepare herself.

"Hello, my name is Mistress Adele. Who am I speaking to?" she asked, desperately trying to sound sultry and authoritative.

Hayley did a thumbs up while Becky stood, bent over, and slapped her own ass. Clarissa glared at her hilarious friend and then grinned as Becky pretended to hang her head in shame.

"My name is Archie, Mistress Adele."

The caller had a rich, deep voice, and Clarissa pictured a top lawyer or a prominent company CEO.

"Are you calling to be dominated and punished, Archie?" she asked sternly.

The line went dead. Clarissa looked at her friends in confusion. "What the hell did I say wrong?"

Becky shrugged. "God knows."

"I thought you were nailing it, but there's only so much you can learn from spicy books," Hayley told her.

"Maybe it was his first time calling, and he got cold feet," Becky suggested.

Clarissa topped up her wine glass, hoping Becky was right.

Chapter 4

A few minutes passed before the phone rang again, during which time Clarissa, Hayley, and Becky analysed what she could have done differently with her domination call. By the time she picked up her phone again for her next call, none of them were any the wiser.

"Line twenty-one. Beep."

'Oh god, not again,' Clarissa thought as she answered.

"This is Mistress Adele. What's your name?"

"Hello, Mistress. I'm Michael, and I've been a very bad boy this week." A quiet, masculine voice answered.

"Have you, Michael? Tell me, what naughtiness did you get up to?" Clarissa asked firmly. She could hear his breathing pick up the pace at her question.

"I stole my girlfriend's G-strings and wore them to work. Then when I got home, I used them to masturbate," he admitted, his voice quivering.

"I think I need to spank you for being so naughty. What do you think?" Clarissa asked.

Click. The line went dead.

"What the hell!" Clarissa shouted, dropping the phone in frustration.

She turned to her best friends, who looked just as confused as she was. "I seriously don't know what I'm doing wrong!"

Hayley walked over to Clarissa, giving her a big hug. "Don't panic, honey; it's only your first time."

"I don't think we could do any better," Becky assured gently. "We think you're doing fantastic."

The rest of Clarissa's first hour at her new job was full of calls, and much to her dismay, the majority of them were on the domination line. She was sick of picking up the phone and hearing, line twenty-one. Beep. Nothing she said kept the domination callers on the line for more than a couple of minutes. Her other calls were mainly drunk guys feeling horny after a night out on the town. Of course, being drunk and horny, none of them lasted very long. Apart from one guy who was too drunk to be able to finish. Clarissa felt terrible for the guy, who, after ten minutes of trying, whispered down the phone, "Sorry, it's why my wife left me." Clarissa felt sorry for the man.

After realizing her hour was up, Clarissa called the chat line's secure number again, entered her code, and pressed two to log herself off. Before she could talk to her waiting friends, her phone rang again. "Shit, I didn't log off properly," Clarissa declared, annoyed at herself. Not wanting to be unprofessional and ignore the call, she answered. However, no line number was said.

"Hello," Clarissa said hesitantly, putting the call on the loud-speaker.

"Hi Clarissa, it's Michelle. Well done, you were terrific!"

"Really? I thought I was terrible," she told Michelle, feeling shocked.

Clarissa looked at Becky and Hayley with wide eyes, only to see them giving her the thumbs up again. She grinned at her friend's constant encouragement.

"Honestly, you were brilliant. And I have to apologize, Clarissa. Most of our ladies only get the odd domination call. Sometimes they don't even get any during a shift, but when I watched the system, nearly all of the submissive's were trying to get to you."

"Really?" Clarissa squeaked in surprise.

"Yes. I think it's your voice, and I do mean that as a compliment. You have such a sultry, husky voice; the submissive's are drawn to you."

Clarissa felt herself deflate in her desk chair. It was the last thing Clarissa wanted to hear.

Clarissa's silence down the phone spoke volumes.

"Trust me; it's a really good thing," Michelle told her with a chuckle.

"It is?"

"Oh my god, yes! The submissive's stay on the longest out of all of our callers," Michelle explained. "If they find a mistress they like, they will talk with her for hours, repeatedly calling back. Our domination ladies earn a fortune, and they have the longest lists of regulars."

"Wow," Clarissa said as the information sunk in.

"If you can get to grips with being a Mistress, you will definitely be able to earn full-time money in no time."

Clarissa was unsure of what to say, especially when she saw Becky and Hayley silently applauding.

"All of your paperwork has been processed, so you can start working on Monday if you want." Michelle continued. "Just let me know if you have any concerns or issues, okay."

"Thank you, Michelle, for everything," she replied, still in a daze. "I'll speak to you soon."

The line went dead, and Clarissa hung up, feeling speechless while looking at her two best friends, who were trying to give her positive vibes.

"Well, bloody hell. That's a surprise on both counts," Clarissa said. "I didn't think I did well at all, and I can't believe I'm a submissive magnet."

"You do have a very husky and sexy voice. I've always been jealous of your voice." Becky grinned.

"It's probably why your customers at work always try to keep you talking," Hayley added.

Clarissa had to admit that her calls at work were, on average, longer than everyone else's. John the creeper always brought it up during their staff meetings, but he couldn't do anything about it. Her customer reviews were always the best, and she consistently had more reviews than anyone else at work. The last time he had a go at her for it, she politely told him that she was making the company look good, so he should focus on the company's poor performers instead. And because he knew it was true, he just gawked at her in surprise and huffed away.

"So, what do I do?" she asked her friends. "Either I quit before I've started because nearly all my calls are going to be domination, or I learn how to be dominant and earn enough to leave my day job."

"I think it's a no-brainer," Becky told her confidently. "Let's face it; you have a fantastic attribute that attracts the customers who use the service the most and stay on the longest, by the sound of it. Why wouldn't you want to take advantage of that?"

Hayley nodded profusely. "I agree. You'll be earning more than most, and I'm sure the longer you work on the chat line, the more you'll earn. You heard what Michelle said, her domination ladies have lots of regulars who stay on for ages."

Clarissa knew that everything her friends were saying was true.

"You need to ask yourself how badly you want to leave the job you hate and how much you want a better life for you and the boys," Becky said bluntly.

She couldn't dispute her best friend's words. As always, they were the voices of reason. Clarissa was miserable with her work and money situation, and she knew that Nigel would never change. There was no chance of him suddenly becoming a decent dad, providing for his kids. Everything was down to her, and she had accepted that.

"I know, I know. You're both right. Nothing is going to change unless I make it," she admitted.

Becky and Hayley were beginning to look like the nodding dogs you see on people's dashboards in cars. She laughed, picking up her wine glass and holding it up in her friend's direction.

"Here's to going for it and making a better life."

Her girlfriends were quick to clink her glass.

"To a fresh start and a better life," Hayley said cheerfully.

"Here's to you earning a shit load of money and punishing naughty, kinky bastards!" Becky cheered loudly.

Clarissa grinned.

—x—

By eleven-thirty, Clarissa was sitting on her sofa in her PJs with a steaming mug of tea and her laptop on her lap, preparing to do some serious research on domination. Becky and Hayley had helped her finish a bottle of wine while giving her more words of encouragement, asking if they could come back the following morning.

Clarissa couldn't imagine not having her best friends in her life. They had always been there for each other, for the good times and especially the bad. They were each other's cheerleaders, therapists, and huggers whenever needed. And they all knew how lucky they were to have each other. Family wasn't always about blood. Her best friends were her sisters.

Sipping her tea as if it was a strong whiskey, giving her some much-needed courage, Clarissa opened her laptop and clicked on the search engine. "This is going to be the strangest thing I've ever had to research," she said to herself as she typed, domination.

At the top of her search, the first item gave her the definition. Exercising control or influence over another person or being controlled by another. *So, it's a total power thing, interesting.* she thought. As Clarissa glanced down at the search results, there seemed to be a lot of information about world domination too. "I don't think I'm feeling that determined." She laughed.

Although there were many results about the definition of domination, there wasn't much else that could be useful. Clarissa knew she had to be more specific. She typed in the search bar again, this time for how to dominate another person.

This time the results were much more interesting. Clarissa scanned down the results, stopping at one that caught her eye. *'Promising,'* she thought, clicking to open it. It appeared to be a whole article about a dominant and submissive relationship. She grabbed her notebook and pen to take notes.

The first thing that was obvious while reading the article was that it was all about power—the dominant asserting their sexual power over the submissive—and the submissive taking the dominance within safe and pre-agreed limits. Trust was clearly a big deal, which made sense to Clarissa. If she were being tied up and made vulnerable, she would want to be able to trust the person doing it. That had never been her ex-asshole, Nigel.

Clarissa started making notes.

BDSM-Bondage and discipline, dominance and submission, sadism and masochism.

Trust-limits.

Safe words.

She continued to read, and the article went on to mention fetishes, another thing Clarissa didn't know much about. She had no idea that there were so many fetishes and kinks, from feet and shoe fetishes to wanting to be a doormat, where a mistress literally wipes her stiletto boots on them. Her mind was blown.

Then Clarissa wondered. She always had a thing for nerdy guys, especially if they had muscles hiding under tight shirts. The new Clark Kent sprang into her mind. Would that be classed as a mild fetish? By definition, a fetish was something you liked that turned you on. In which case, she guessed that everyone had a fetish for something. Many men seemed to have a fetish for boobs, butts, curvy hips, and nice legs. Becky had a fetish for bald men, her biggest crush being Vin Diesel, and Hayley had a thing for very masculine men with beards, hence why she ended up marrying a great guy who looked like he had just disembarked a Viking longship.

Clarissa carried on reading and the next thing the article mentioned was the tools that may be used while dominating, such as sex toys and various props. Riding crops, blindfolds, nipple clamps, and spanking paddles, the list of items was long. The only problem was Clarissa wouldn't be doing it in person. She would have to ask the submissive's if they had anything at home to use. If they did not, well, she would have to try and wing it using whatever they did have.

Another issue abruptly popped into her mind, and a call she had during her training. The caller had come through to the domination line, but when she had told the caller to spank his own ass, he told her that he just liked the idea of being dominated but didn't actually want to do it.

Clarissa added the two things to her list.

Toys and props.

Physical or fantasy.

While it was fresh in her mind, she tried to think of things that were common in a home that she could use to dominate someone—things that most people had. She began to write a new list as ideas popped into her head, such as toothpaste, hair bands, hairbrushes, clothes pegs, spatulas, shoelaces, and utensil tongs. She was quite impressed with her list. *'I could use all of those things,'* she thought as she pictured the items and the body parts she could use them on. "It's a good job my grandparents aren't seeing this," she told herself, "They'd be rolling in their graves."

She sipped her tea, slipped her pen behind her ear, and carried on reading the article. It went on to explain boundaries and rules. Apparently, it was essential to have rules in place, not just for safety but also to cement trust and what was acceptable. It seemed to Clarissa that having rules was another way for a mistress to assert her dominance. She quickly added rules to her growing list.

Needing a break from her research, Clarissa left her desk and decided to open the large bottle of Baileys her best friends had bought her for Christmas. It was her guilty pleasure, and after the week she'd had, she knew she deserved it. Also, with her boys away with Nigel's parents, she wouldn't have to get up early for a change.

The thought of a blissful lie-in, with no squealing, wrestling boys waking her up, made her smile.

Once she had her large Bailey's on ice and had a bathroom break, she went back into her research. Clarissa had to admit; it was the most fun she'd ever had researching something.

The next section of the article was about permissions and punishments. Clarissa had no idea that domination was actually quite complex. She quite liked the idea of being able to give or deny permission for a man to pleasure himself and to punish a man for not doing as he's told. She suddenly wished that she'd had that control over her ex-asshole. Images flashed in her mind of Nigel bent over a wooden chair, wearing only a black leather thong and a studded collar around his neck, with her whipping his bare ass, telling him what a bad bastard he had been. *'If only.'* She added another two items to her list.

Clarissa scrolled down on her laptop, looking forward to what she would learn next. She stopped at a new section of the article titled Dirty Talk. She was surprised by what she read. Talking dirty to a submissive appeared to be more intricate, laced with other elements such as rules and adding suspense to their experience. It was also about tone and using your voice for pleasure or punishment.

Scrolling further, Clarissa came to a section about role-play and outfits. It described the most popular role-play dynamics, especially for newbies, such as teacher and student, doctor and patient, boss and employee. Her creepy boss, John, popped into her mind, *'Nope, not going there,'* she thought as she involuntarily pictured him in a PVC jumpsuit and matching Doc Martens, with his beer belly hanging out, waiting for her to punish him. Clarissa retched at the thought. "Eww, gross!" she said aloud, grabbing her large Baileys and taking a much-needed swig. That was an image she neither wanted to see again nor see in real life.

The outfit section had Clarissa extremely intrigued. She had always loved the leather and PVC look, and in her closet were two knee-high black leather skirts that she adored but didn't get a chance to wear very often. Clarissa had also once owned a sexy pair of tight leather trousers before she had Luke and Matthew. Unfortunately, on a girl's night out at a club, her zipper had broken, and her drunken best friends had persuaded the club DJ to duct tape her waist to keep them up, so she could keep dancing. Their drunken efforts to remove the leather trousers when they got home was something neither she nor Becky and Hayley would ever forget.

Clarissa knew that outfits were something she would also have to research, as well as what the toys and domination tools looked like, especially if she was going to have to describe them to her domination callers. She added both to her list.

After gazing at her phone to check the time, Clarissa knew she would have to call it a night soon. She was usually in bed by ten pm, exhausted from long working days and looking after her boys. She wasn't used to staying up so late. It was already two am, and her eyes were feeling heavy and tired. Clarissa scrolled down on her laptop, relieved when there was only one section left on the article, Bondage.

Bondage was something else that Clarissa had limited knowledge of. Apart from the furry handcuffs she had used on the ex-asshole a couple of times—she didn't think that counted. Clarissa, like most people, knew about whips, using tape and zip ties, especially after her best friends gave her details from reading spicy books.

However, she was surprised to learn that there was more to it than that. Not only were things like ball gags, chains, leather straps, and spreader bars used, but experienced Dom's also used contraptions. There were unique swings, chairs, cages, and all sorts of dominating furniture that Clarissa knew she would have to research to enable her to describe accurately. *'Another thing to add,'* she thought as she scribbled on her notes.

Clarissa took another sip of her drink and closed her laptop. She was beginning to feel proud of herself. Not only had she had a successful training session, as far as Michelle was concerned, but she had also done some excellent research. She looked at the growing list she now had to work with for her new job.

BDSM-Bondage and discipline, dominance and submission, sadism and masochism.

Trust-limits.

Safe words.

Toys, tools, and props?

Physical or fantasy?

Rules.

Permission and punishment.

Research.

Tools and outfits.

Bondage contraptions.

Clarissa's confidence was growing with her knowledge. She was starting to think she might have a chance at doing her new job and doing it well. She let out a big yawn, reminding her how tired she was. Finishing her glass of Baileys, she took herself off to bed with a feeling of pride.

Chapter 5

When Clarissa woke at ten am after a lovely lie-in, she lay in her warm bed, relishing the blissful peace and quiet. Then she began to remember some of the strange dreams she'd had about whips, chains, and dominating her ex-asshole, Nigel. Her cheeks began to blush as images sprang to mind of her punishing Nigel for all the crap he had put her and their boys through.

With Hayley and Becky due to come over at eleven, Clarissa knew she had to get a move on. Their husbands were taking their kids to a local football match—a sport that neither of her friends was interested in—so her friends were free to help her prepare for her new job.

As Clarissa showered, she thought about her day job. She had been a customer service and sales rep for years, and even though she had never enjoyed it, she had learned many skills. One of the things Janka Industries gave her when she started was a collection of scripts. There seemed to be a script for everything, talking to a new customer, going over service issues, talking to an existing sales customer, and signing up a new client. Clarissa didn't like using the scripts, finding them fake, mainly because she didn't talk like the scripts. However, she had to admit that they had helped her remember the vital information.

There and then, that is what she decided to do. Write a script to help her remember the key elements she needed to say and ask during her domination calls.

—x—

Clarissa was sitting at her kitchen table with a fresh pot of coffee, her laptop, trusted notes, and her new list when Becky and Hayley entered through her back door.

"Morning ladies, look through those while I pour your coffee," she told them, sliding her notepad in their direction.

"Damn, you were busy last night after we left," Becky said, impressed.

"I was," Clarissa admitted. "I didn't get to bed until the early hours. But I did get a lot done. I found a fantastic article that gave me lots of information. So, I feel much more confident now. This morning while I had a shower, I had an idea about writing a short script to help me set rules and find out what the domination callers want."

"Well, that sounds like a great idea," Hayley said as she grabbed her fresh coffee. As always, smelling it first. "Mmm, nothing beats the smell of fresh coffee!"

"Weirdo!" Becky teased.

Hayley pointed to her eyes with two fingers and then to Becky as if to say, I'm watching you. "You can talk, book sniffer!" she laughed. "Every time you buy a new book, you spend ten minutes sniffing it."

Becky held up her hands in surrender. "Okay, you're right. I do, and I can't deny it." She giggled. "It's the best smell ever. Nothing beats a new book smell."

Clarissa laughed at her best friends, "You are both weirdos."

"You can talk, Mistress Adele," Becky told her with a smirk.

Rolling her eyes at her friends, Clarissa grabbed her coffee and sat down with her friends, pulling her laptop towards her.

"I think the first thing we should do is write my script and then research what the Mistress outfits and domination contraptions look like. I believe the more I know, the more authentic I'll come across to callers. What do you think?" she asked.

Becky and Hayley were back to behaving like nodding dogs.

"Agreed."

"Sounds like a plan," Hayley added.

"Okay, I'm going to approach this like the salesperson I am," Clarissa told her suddenly confused friends, neither of which had any sales experience.

Hayley had always been a criminal lawyer, working her way up Haver & Sterns' legal ladder, and Becky was a nurse until she had her kids.

"Sales is all about finding a client's need and fulfilling that need, and that's what I have to do with this job. The more information I can discover from the caller, the happier the caller will be because they will be getting what they want."

"That does sound logical," Hayley told her, looking very impressed. "No wonder you've always been good at your day job."

Clarissa smiled at her compliment. "Are you sure you want to be doing this? Wouldn't you rather be at the football game with your hubbies and kids?"

Hayley and Becky looked at each other, then laughed.

Becky shook her head and raised an eyebrow at Clarissa. "Neither of us enjoy watching grown-ass men running up and down a pitch, occasionally kicking a ball. We'd much rather hang out with you and do this. Anyway, we are always doing stuff with the kids. It will do them all the world of good to have a break from us."

"Okay. So, first things first, my greeting," Clarissa said as she wrote No.1 on her notepad.

"I think you should keep it formal, firm but sultry," Becky suggested.

Nodding in agreement, Clarissa wrote it down.

No.1 Hello, I'm Mistress Adele. What is your name?

"I think you should also confirm that they've called the domination line," Hayley told her. "You did get quite a few callers hanging up after saying hello, so maybe some of them went through to the domination line by mistake," Hayley suggested.

Clarissa liked Hayley's idea. It made sense to double-check that the callers knew it was a domination line. She added it to her script.

No.2 You do realize you have called the domination line?
No.3 Do you want to be my submissive?

"From what I read last night, some submissive's want physical domination while others just want to talk about it. I think that has to be my next question," Clarissa told her friends, scribbling it down.

No. 4 Are you looking for physical or fantasy domination?

Becky raised her hand as if she were in a classroom. "What about trust limits and safe words? You have them on your notes. Do you need to do those next?"

Clarissa thought for a moment. "I don't think they apply because we'll only be talking about domination. They'll be able to control what they do to themselves on the other end of the phone. I think we should create my rules next. Aiming to try and keep them on the phone for as long as possible."

Becky and Hayley looked at each other comically.

"Yeah, we didn't think of that," Hayley admitted. "See, this is why you're going to be so good at this job."

Giving her best friends a grin, Clarissa looked at her list again as if it would give her all the inspiration she needed. "Okay, rules, rules," she said while chewing on the end of her pen.

"They must call you Mistress Adele all the time," Hayley suggested. "If they forget, you get to punish them."

"Oh, that's a good one." Becky giggled.

Clarissa scribbled it down quickly, smiling as she wrote. "Okay, rule number one done," she said as her mind went over how she could keep them on the phone. "I've got it." Clarissa grinned mischievously.

"Got what?"

"What she said," Hayley added.

"A way to keep the domination callers on for longer," Clarissa told them with a wicked smile appearing on her face.

"Well?" Hayley demanded, instantly intrigued.

"I don't allow them to finish until I'm ready!"

"Oh my God, Clarissa, you are evil," Becky blurted out with a fit of giggles.

Hayley sat with her mouth agape for a moment as she processed Clarissa's words, "You are a bloody genius? Wicked, but a bloody genius."

Laughing at her friend's reactions, she wrote it down on her rules script.

Rule No.2, You will not come until I give you permission.

"I think you have to tell them to obey you, too," Becky said as her giggles subsided.

"Nice one, honey," Clarissa told her, raising her hand for a high five. "I'm starting to think you two should be starting with me."

Becky joined in Clarissa's high five, clearly pleased with herself. Clarissa felt very proud of her friends and herself for how well they were doing. Her script with the new rules was coming along nicely. It was short, to the point, and was just what she needed to do a good job. Clarissa added, obey her rules to the list.

"I think there's one last thing I need to add," she told her friends. "If the caller wants to be physically dominated, I need to know if he or she has things they want to use."

Hayley nodded in agreement, "Another good one to add. That goes back to what you said earlier about finding their need, I suppose."

"It does, and from reading that article last night, it seems that toys and sex tools are used a lot for dominating," Clarissa added the final question to her list while sipping her coffee. "I think it's done."

"Let's hear it then," Becky demanded with a grin, "We can be your test subjects."

"Really? You want me to do it now?"

"Hell, yes, we do," Hayley agreed.

Clarissa couldn't stop herself from laughing at their eager faces. "Okay, but you have to tell me if I'm crap."

After another sip of her coffee and a deep breath, she prepared herself for the expected embarrassment.

"Hello, I'm Mistress Adele. What is your name?" she said in her sultry voice as her cheeks instantly began to flush pink.

"Simon, Mistress," Becky answered in the deepest voice she could possibly manage.

Coffee sprayed across the dining table from Hayley's mouth, all over Clarissa's notes and laptop. All three of the friends burst into laughter.

"Bloody hell, Hayley, do you have to keep spraying your drinks everywhere?" Becky tried to say as she grabbed a kitchen towel to wipe everything down while bracing her lady bits and trying not to mummy-pee.

Hayley began choking and sneezing simultaneously while trying to catch her breath. Clarissa passed her some tissues as she helped Becky clean up the coffee mess.

"That was so bloody funny," Hayley stated before sneezing again.

Becky grinned wickedly. "I couldn't resist."

"I can't believe you managed to go that deep with your voice," Clarissa told her as she threw away the soaked tissues and kitchen towel.

"I've had lots of practice," she said proudly.

"How on earth have you had practice talking like a man?" Hayley asked in disbelief.

"Well, all our bills are in Martin's name, which is fine, but when there's an issue with anything, I'm always the one who has to call to sort it out. He's always working during office hours. They won't speak to me because the accounts are in his name, so I have to pretend to be Martin to get things resolved," Becky explained.

"How many times have you had to do that?" Clarissa asked curiously, especially as Becky had nailed it.

"After Martin got laid off last year, more times than I care to admit." She giggled. "But it worked a treat, and now I can do it on demand. Martin doesn't have the patience to deal with all the questions they have to ask."

Hayley giggled as a thought popped into her head. "We could have so much fun with your man voice once Clarissa quits her day job. Creepy John needs to be taught a lesson."

The menacing laugh that escaped her made Clarissa and Becky look at each other in surprise.

"You scare me a little sometimes, woman," Clarissa told her with a smirk, "but I love how you think."

Hayley grinned. "Okay, back to your script."

Clarissa composed herself, ready to restart.

"Do you realize you have called the domination line, Simon?" she asked sexily.

"Yes," Becky answered just as deeply.

This time Hayley and Clarissa were expecting it, giving Becky grins.

"Do you want to be my Submissive, Simon?"

"I do, Mistress."

"Are you looking for physical or fantasy domination?"

"I want the real deal," Becky told her, trying to sound manly and sexy but failing terribly.

Hayley wiped her eyes as laughter tears began to stream down her face.

"If you want to be dominated by me, you must follow my rules. Do you understand, Simon?" Clarissa said firmly.

"Yes, Mistress."

"Rule one. You must call me Mistress Adele at all times. If you forget, you will be punished. Rule two. You will not come until I give you permission. Do you understand, Simon?"

"Yes, Mistress Adele," Becky replied.

"Rule three. You will obey me at all times, or you will be punished. Is that clear, Simon?"

"Absolutely, Mistress Adele."

"Do you have anything you want me to use on you?"

Becky suddenly looked like a deer caught between headlights.

"Err, no, Mistress."

Clarissa laughed at her friend's expression. "You are so good at the man voice. More Coffee?"

"Yes, please, I need one after doing that voice; it's quite a strain on the old vocal cords," Becky said as she stroked her throat.

Clarissa took the coffee mugs, rinsed them, and put some fresh coffee in the machine, adding the water and clicking it on.

"So, what are you going to do if a caller wants to be dominated for real, but they don't have any toys or things to do it with?" Becky asked curiously.

"I was thinking about that last night, and I think I can use what most people have at home," Clarissa said with a smile.

Both of her friends looked confused.

"Like what?" Hayley asked in disbelief.

Clarissa bit down on her bottom lip, trying not to laugh. "Well, I can get them to spank themselves with things like a hairbrush, spatula, or wooden spoon. I can also tell them to tie a shoelace around their cocks or use a rubber band. And clothes pegs would be excellent for their nipples and balls."

Becky and Hayley stared at her with shock written all over their faces. Hayley's eyes looked like they were about to pop out of her head, and Becky's mouth was nearly on the floor.

"Who's scaring who now?" she laughed as she refilled their mugs.

Once Clarissa and her friends had their fresh coffee, and she was back in front of her laptop, she glanced at her list again. "Right, next on the agenda, outfits."

"Now, I've really been looking forward to that bit of research," Hayley admitted, "Adam's always trying to talk me into getting hot and sexy lingerie for the bedroom."

Becky raised her eyebrows. "Then why don't you?"

Hayley grabbed her enormous boobs, flopping them on the dining table, much to their surprise. "How many hot and sexy outfits have you seen that would fit these puppies?"

"Get your tits off my table!" Clarissa laughed, trying to fake indignation while pretending to shield her eyes from the sight before her.

Hayley sat back with a grin, letting them slide off the table.

"Have you actually tried to find kinky lingerie to fit those big boobies?"

Hayley sighed, "I have, but there's nothing. I would have to have lingerie made to measure. You know what it's like, Clarissa. The bigger boobs you have, the less sexy the lingerie becomes. My mum used to call my bras over-the-shoulder-boulder-holders, and when they were on the washing line, they looked like bloody hammocks."

Clarissa knew precisely where she was coming from, as she had the same issues. Her own bras didn't have dainty little hooks on the back and thin straps like pretty bras; they had triple rows of reinforced hooks and eyes with thick back straps. Her ex-asshole was able to fit his whole head inside one cup.

"Well, you never know; we might find something that will fit while we're looking," Becky said hopefully. "Let's get to it." She rubbed her hands together excitedly.

Opening the search engine on her laptop, Clarissa entered female domination outfits and clicked images. There were pages and pages of results. Clarissa was impressed. As soon as Becky and Hayley saw her eyes light up, they quickly slid their chairs around the table to get a better view.

The three best friends slowly glanced over the images. There were bras and knickers, Basques, bodysuits, tops, skin-tight trousers, and dresses of various kinky and sexy designs. Most of the domination wear was black and red PVC and leather; some were adorned with laces, others sheer lace and even spikes. Clarissa had to admit the women in the images looked damn hot. Unfortunately for Hayley, there didn't seem to be much for women with big boobs.

"See, I told you," Hayley told them with disappointment.

Clarissa felt for her. "When I'm earning tons of money, I will get some sexy stuff made for you," she told Hayley, wrapping her arm around her shoulders in a hug.

"You always look hot anyway," Becky told her, "It's a miracle you haven't already got enough kids to create your own football team."

Hayley held her hands up. "It's true; there's no denying it." She laughed.

"At least I know what to describe during my calls," Clarissa told them. "Now for the last search, domination and fetish contraptions."

Clarissa typed the words into the search bar, and all three of them were stunned at the results. Some of the images were rather more graphic than expected, especially as they weren't just showing the contraptions but also the people using them. There were altars, special tables, throne-like chairs, sex swings, and even wooden crosses.

"There are some things that you just don't want to see," Becky said, stunned.

Hayley nodded. "And there are some things that you can't unsee."

Clarissa nodded in agreement. "But at least I can describe a few of these things during calls."

"I must say, I almost feel sorry for your soon-to-be callers. They have no idea what they're in for," Hayley told her before she and Becky burst into a fit of giggles again.

—x—

Clarissa had a fantastic time researching with Becky and Hayley, and when Luke and Matthew were dropped home on Sunday by her ex-in-laws, she was still in an excellent mood.

Clarissa opened her front door and smiled instantly as Luke and Matthew ran up her garden path towards her. She waved at her ex-father-in-law, Steve, who gave her a smile and a friendly wave.

Her ex-mother-in-law, Sharon, walked quickly up her path, trying to keep up with her grandsons.

Clarissa hugged her happy boys. "You two look like you've had fun?"

"It was awesome," Luke told her with a grin.

Matthew nodded.

Clarissa smiled and gave them the look to remind them of their manners.

Luke and Matthew released her, turning to their grandma and hugging her waist.

"Thanks for having us, Grammy," Matthew told her warmly.

"Thank you, Grammy," Luke added.

Sharon stroked their heads affectionately.

Clarissa smiled at her boys as they released their grandmother. "Okay, my little angels. Go and put your things away, please."

Sharon watched as her grandsons chased each other up the stairs.

"Thank you for having them, Sharon," Clarissa told her warmly.

Clarissa had always got on well with her ex-in-laws, and even after everything that Nigel had put her through, they had main-tained a good relationship. After all, it wasn't Sharon and Steve's fault that their son was a narcissistic, ego on legs.

"You are very welcome, Clarissa. Did you have a good week-end?"

Clarissa beamed. "I did, thank you."

Sharon's smiled reached her eyes. "It's lovely to see you so cheerful, did you get some good news or something?"

Clarissa wasn't sure how to answer. She decided quickly to tell the truth.

"I'm actually starting a new job in the evenings, working from home."

"You're leaving Janka Industries?"

Clarissa shook her head. "No, I'll be working both jobs for now."

Guilt swept across Sharon's face, and an awkward silence stretched between them.

Clarissa decided to end the silence before Sharon could think of any questions about her new job. There were some things that Sharon and ex-husband didn't need to know.

"Anyway, thank you for having the boys, they love spending time with you both."

Sharon smiled warmly as Clarissa waved to Steve, who was waiting patiently in their car.

"It was lovely to have them. Can we have them again soon? They grow up so fast; it won't be long before they'll think they're too cool to spend time with us." Sharon chuckled.

Clarissa knew that Sharon and Steve had been doting parents to Nigel. Unfortunately, he had treated them just as badly as everyone else.

"Of course, you can. They adore you both," Clarissa told her warmly. "Anyway, I'd better get them fed and sort their school things out. See you soon."

Sharon smiled and turned, making her way back to Steve and their car. Clarissa felt sad that Nigel had treated them like shit for so many years. They were decent people, and they didn't deserve it. Clarissa silently prayed that her boys wouldn't do that to her.

As her ex-in-laws pulled away, she closed her front door.

Luke and Matthew were so tired from their weekend trip Clarissa didn't even get a cuddle before they fell fast asleep on the sofa. As she carried them upstairs, one by one, she wished, not for the first time, that she wasn't alone. They were getting so big and growing so fast that it was hard to keep up with them. Clarissa knew it wouldn't be long before they were the same height as her.

Once they were both in their beds, snuggly under their duvets, she took a moment to admire her gorgeous boys. Both were so different, and luckily, neither was like their dad. Clarissa often prayed that they would stay more like her, even though she wasn't religious. She also often wondered if their dad would one day wake up and realize what a terrible husband and father he had been, but she doubted it.

Chapter 6

Monday morning didn't start well for Clarissa. As she slipped her feet into her low black heels, her phone pinged with a text message. Her eyes widened when she saw the name Asshole appear on her locked phone screen. Clarissa couldn't remember the last time he'd been in touch at first; it was so long ago. Then it popped into her head. It had been four months ago after a rare night out with the girls. One of his friends had seen her all dressed up, so Nigel had messaged her in the early hours, drunk and feeling horny. It had seriously pissed her off. So much so that she messaged him back, telling him to drop dead.

Clarissa knew she should probably just delete the message without bothering to read it, but as he had missed Luke's recent birthday, she hoped it would be an apology. She picked up her phone and opened the message.

Hi, babe

That pissed her off instantly. "I'm not your babe, prick!" she said under her breath, so her boys didn't hear.

My mum said you looked happy and have got a new job. Did you get a new man too? I miss you, hot stuff!!!

Clarissa was nearly sick in her mouth. 'Who the hell does he think he is? Oh yeah, God's gift to women.'

Various reply ideas came to her, such as drop dead, I hope your cock falls off, or why are you asking? Have you been dumped again because your latest girlfriend realized what a dick you are? Then Clarissa reminded herself that she didn't have to tell him anything. She decided to treat him with the contempt he truly deserved, especially as there was no mention of Luke and his recent birthday.

None of your business, and I am not your babe, ASSHOLE!

Clarissa clicked send, feeling like a badass bitch. She forwarded Nigel's message to Hayley and Becky, picturing them in her mind, rolling their eyes.

When Clarissa arrived at work, her phone was still blowing up with new messages. She knew it was her girlfriend's messaging her. She doubted there would be any reply from Nigel.

—x—

Traffic had been horrendous on the way to work, and Clarissa knew she was running twenty minutes late. She mentally prayed that her boss, John the creeper, was in a meeting and wouldn't notice her slipping in late.

Unfortunately, John was waiting to pounce as soon as she walked onto her floor, standing by her desk with his hands in his pockets. She could see his right hand moving and she knew he wasn't jiggling his keys in his trousers. Clarissa wanted to retch.

"Miss. Clarissa Darcy, my office, now!" he demanded loudly in front of the whole floor. Her colleagues hushed their voices.

Clarissa wanted a hole to appear so she could crawl into it and hide. She took a deep breath and followed as he stomped towards his waiting office.

As Clarissa walked past her watching colleagues, some gave her looks of empathy, while others pretended to be busy, either on their computers or phones. *'Pussies,'* she thought.

The moment she entered her boss's office, he was behind her, closing the door. Coming from behind, John accidentally-on-purpose brushed against her ass. She froze in front of his desk. *'What the hell'* her skin crawled, and her stomach turned.

She was hoping that he would sit behind his desk so at least there would be some barrier between them, but no. John turned and perched himself on the front of his desk facing her. His beady eyes running up and down her body.

"You, young lady, are over twenty minutes late."

Clarissa tried to keep calm, but her pulse began to quicken as a cold dread washed over her. Her chest rose and fell as her heart hammered in panic.

"There was a bad accident on the main road, and the police stopped all the traffic. It wasn't my fault that I'm late this morning, Mr. Mason," she told him, trying to keep her voice calm and even.

"Even so, I might have to report your lateness. Unless you do something for me," he told her as his hand slid across his black trousers to his crotch.

Clarissa wanted to vomit and run at the same time. Her pulse began to race faster as her fight or flight instincts kicked in.

"Mr. Mason, if you're suggesting what I think you are, that is not happening."

She clenched her fists at her sides. Her nails digging into the palms of her hands.

Mr. Mason slid off his desk, pulling his shoulders back as if it would make him taller. Clarissa's heart felt like it was going to burst from her chest. He strode toward her; his eyebrows narrowed in determination. She didn't know what to do. She was frozen to the spot, unable to move. Her breath quickened, making her large breasts rise and fall faster, which seemed to grab Mr. Mason's unwanted attention.

Suddenly, he grabbed her—one hand grabbing her left breast—the other sliding forcefully between her thighs.

For Clarissa, it was the last straw. Buzzing sounded in her ears as adrenaline coursed through her veins. Fury swept through her like a wildfire as her instinct to fight kicked in. Grabbing both of his narrow shoulders—she pulled him towards her as her right knee rose with force—connecting squarely with his crotch.

His eyes widened with shock. He screamed loudly like a wounded animal. Clarissa knew everyone would hear, but by then, she didn't care. Instantly releasing her hold—he crumpled to the floor with a thud—both hands holding his injured crotch. Clarissa's rage was pulsing through her veins, her fear now gone. She stepped towards her boss feeling nothing but disgust, and she placed her foot and heel against his weeping, scrunched-up face.

"You are a disgusting excuse of a man, and you will never touch me again," she told him. Her voice shaking with rage. "I quit!"

Before her boss had time to recover, Clarissa turned on her heel and rushed out the office door. She stormed through the office floor while everyone stared in disbelief.

"You are all bloody cowards!" she yelled as she opened the exit door and left her much-hated job for good. 'There's no going back now,' she thought.

Clarissa raced out of Janka Industries as if a pack of wild animals were chasing her. She threw her arms onto her Mini's roof, trying to catch her breath, still shaking like a leaf. She had never attacked anyone in her life—and she was shocked that she had done it to her boss—no matter how much he deserved it.

Fumbling, Clarissa tried to extract her keys from her handbag, wanting to get away as quickly as possible. With shaking hands, she attempted to unlock her car and after a few failed attempts, her key finally slid home. She released a slow breath as she opened her car door and slid into the driver's seat. She shut her door, finally feeling safe.

Clarissa was almost expecting police sirens to sound in the distance. She wouldn't put it past creepy John to call the police on her and act like a victim.

Trying desperately to steady her nerves, she took long, slow, deep breaths, aiming to calm herself before attempting to drive home. Clarissa looked at her shaking hands, willing them to steady. She tried to listen for sirens in the distance but could only hear regular traffic and birds in the nearby trees.

When her shaking lessened, and no sirens could be heard in the distance, she pulled her phone from her handbag, messaging Becky and Hayley on their group message to tell them what had happened. After another slow breath, she started her car.

Pulling out of Janka Industries' car park for the last time felt liberating—and even though she was still shaken from what had just happened—she felt free for the first time in years. As she reached the main road, her phone started ringing, and she glanced to see who it was calling. It was Hayley. Clarissa was beyond relieved. Clicking her blue tooth, she answered.

"Hello," she said, her voice shaking.

"I can't believe it!" Hayley shrieked down the phone, "You actually kneed your boss in the balls and quit, seriously?"

Clarissa's eyes welled with threatening tears. "Yep."

"Oh my god, honey, I am so freaking proud of you! Are you on your way home?" Hayley asked, clearly concerned. She could tell by the one-word Clarissa had spoken that she was distraught.

"Yes," Carissa said softly with a sob.

"Becky and I will meet you there, okay? Martin's day off today, and I've told my office manager that I'm sick. We'll be with you soon, honey. Drive safe, alright."

"Thank you."

That was all Clarissa could manage.

—x—

Clarissa sobbed all the way home. By the time she pulled up to her house twenty minutes later, Becky and Hayley were both waiting for her at the front door.

No words were needed.

Both of her best friends raced to her car—wrapping their arms around her—hugging her while she cried.

After a few minutes of much-needed hugging, Clarissa raised her head, her tear-soaked face feeling hot. "I need a long, hot shower and a stiff drink. Shall we go in?" She asked with a weak smile.

Becky and Hayley nodded, leading Clarissa into the safety of her home.

"I'll pour the drinks; Becky can call the hubbies to tell them we'll be late," Hayley declared as they entered.

—x—

Clarissa stood naked in her shower, scrubbing her skin, washing away any trace of John's grubby hands. The thought of him grabbing her, made her blood re-boil. 'Never again, you bastard.'

Feeling clean again, Clarissa put on her favorite t-shirt and black lounge pants and made her way downstairs. Hayley had a large vodka and cranberry waiting for her on the coffee table in the lounge.

"Don't worry about Luke and Matthew; Martin's picking them up from your childminder, and they're staying at Becky's tonight for a sleepover. Martin agrees that the boys don't need to see you shaken up. It would only upset them and you. I've called Susan and told her," Hayley said with a sympathetic smile.

"I'll take them to school in the morning with mine," Becky added with a warm smile.

Clarissa's heart felt full of love for her best friends. "You two really are the bestest, best friends anyone could hope for," she told them sincerely.

Hayley handed Clarissa her large vodka cranberry as soon as she plonked herself on the sofa. "So, tell us exactly what happened."

Taking a deep breath, Clarissa told them everything in detail.

"That slimy, fucker!" Hayley shook her head, still feeling enraged.

"Wow, I still can't believe he went that far," Becky said softly. "I would have loved to have been there to see you in action though."

"That creepy pervert had it coming, honey," Hayley assured her. "I'd love to see him try to explain to your HR department why you attacked him, when this comes out."

Clarissa suddenly felt ashamed of her actions. She looked down at her glass, feeling guilty.

"Clarissa," Hayley said, grabbing her attention again, "don't feel bad about this; you were defending yourself, end of!"

"I agree," Becky told her, her face deadly serious. "He sexually assaulted you, and you had the right to take action."

Hayley sat up, a determined look in her eyes. "In fact, he has forced you out of your job with his behavior, and because you have complained about him to HR on numerous occasions, it's all on record. So, if you wanted, you could sue the company for constructive dismissal. As Becky said, he forced you to quit."

It was too much for Clarissa, especially now her adrenaline had worn off. She was still trying to process what had happened. And she knew that the phone sex chat line was going to be her only option for a while, and her only income.

"I don't think I could deal with suing Janka right now," she told them truthfully.

"Well, at least let me contact your HR department as your legal rep to lodge a complaint and inform them of the incident," Hayley urged. "And when you feel up to it, we'll also report it to the police."

Clarissa nodded and took a big gulp of her drink, feeling drained. "Okay."

The rest of the evening was spent watching movies. Becky and Hayley knew exactly which films would make her feel better, and the large vodka cranberries had Clarissa finally feeling relaxed.

—x—

When Clarissa woke on Tuesday morning, she slowly lifted her thick head and opened her eyes, looking around. She was still on her sofa with one leg hanging off, covered with Luke's fluffy Spiderman blanket. She smiled at her best friend's love and kindness. Becky and Hayley had even set the timer on the coffee machine. She could smell the alluring aroma wafting from the kitchen. Clarissa was just about to get up to wake her boys when she remembered that they had stayed at Becky's overnight. And after quitting her terrible job, she had the day to herself.

Thoughts of the day before came flooding back. John Mason trying to blackmail and assault her, and her attacking him in response. Goosebumps rose on her skin. Then she reminded herself of what Becky and Hayley had said. She defended herself. The justification made her feel a lot better about the whole situation. *'The bastard deserved it. He'll never touch me again.'* Clarissa knew that she would rather live in a tent in Hayley or Becky's back garden, than go back to working for John Mason and Janka Industries. Their HR department was a joke.

Clarissa unfurled herself from the blanket and made her way to the kitchen and the waiting pot of coffee. Becky or Hayley had also been kind enough to put her phone on charge; she grabbed it, poured her coffee, and sat at her dining table.

There were numerous messages on her phone, and not just from her best friends. The first message was from her creepy ex-boss, which shocked her. Her stomach lurched.

Clarissa had never given him her personal number. As far as she knew, only Janka's HR department had it on file. She had never given it out to any of her colleagues either. She read the message as her skin crawled.

I'm so sorry for my behavior, Clarissa. I thought we had a connection. My mistake. Please forgive me and come back. Your job is here waiting for you.

Feelings of anger began to simmer. "What freaking connection? The scum bag is delusional."

Clarissa knew that Hayley would be contacting Janka about the incident on her behalf, but clearly John Mason didn't think she was brave enough to report him. She knew there was no way she was ever going back, even if he got on his knees and begged. She couldn't bear the thought of being anywhere near him, ever again. Clarissa was glad that he at least admitted to his behavior. Hayley would be pleased too. She clicked on the following message, which was actually from Hayley.

Hi honey, I hope you got some decent sleep. I've filed a formal complaint with your HR department and given a report of what happened on your behalf. Let me know when you are ready to report it to the police, Okay? Love you xxxx.

Clarissa was shocked that Hayley had done so much already. She knew she shouldn't be too surprised; Hayley was like a dog with a new bone when she was passionate about something. She sipped her coffee, relishing the warmth and flavor, then messaged back.

Thank you, darling. You are the best. I slept like a log after all the hugs and vodka. I think I'll be ready for the police tomorrow. The perv texted me and said sorry. I will forward it to you. I'm not letting that slimy bastard get away with this! I appreciate your help. X

A very loud rumble came from Clarissa's stomach, and she realized that she hadn't eaten since the previous morning. 'No wonder I got so drunk so quickly last night,' she thought as she got herself some cereal. As she sat down to eat, she opened the following message, which was from Becky.

The kids all slept well. Martin spoiled them with popcorn and chocolate, sorry, lol. I dropped them at school, happy. Love you!!!

Clarissa smiled. She didn't get Luke and Matthew sweets or chocolate often, so she knew they would have been in their element. She was sure they would have had a lot of fun.

Thank you again for yesterday and having the boys. You and Hayley are seriously the best!! X

The last message on her phone was from her ex-asshole, which surprised her. Clarissa didn't know what was happening in his life—and she really didn't care anymore—but something was obviously going on.

You will always be my business, and you will always be my babe!

"What the hell!" Clarissa was so stunned she read the message three times in disbelief. She decided not to reply for the time being. Becky and Hayley's husbands both knew friends of Nigel's, and she hoped they would know something she did not.

After forwarding creepy John and Nigel's messages to her best friends, she decided to get a hot bubble bath—make herself feel human again—and maybe try her first shift at her new and now only job. The boys would be at school all day, and she wouldn't have to pick them up from her childminder until six pm. The childminder was another thing she knew she would have to deal with, especially since she didn't have a full-time job anymore.

After her bath, Clarissa sat at her desk feeling torn. Could she really talk dirty to horny men after what John Mason had just done to her. Her heart began to hammer in her chest as her blood ran cold. 'Not all men a like John Mason,' she reminded herself, 'it's just talking and acting. Taking a long slow breath, Clarissa began to feel calmer and more centered. Her heart slowing back to its normal rhythm. '*I can do this for me and my boys.*' With her feeling of determination seeping back and her laptop, notepad, pen, Angelina's picture, drink and phone set up, she was ready to give her first shift a go.

The last thing Clarissa wanted was another dead-end job paying minimum wage. What she did want was to be able to take her children on holiday, buy them decent quality clothes, and be able to enjoy time with her best friends. She knew that if she were successful working on the chat line, she would be able to achieve all those things.

Just as Clarissa was about to pick up her landline phone to start her shift, her mobile phone pinged. She picked it up and saw it was another message from Hayley.

I can't believe the two scumbags messaged you. I took a screen-shot of creeper John's message and emailed it to Janka's HR. I told them to warn him not to contact you again. What did you reply to the asshole.

Clarissa quickly replied.

Thank you, honey. I haven't replied to asshole yet. Something is going on with him.

Another ping and reply from Hayley.

You're welcome. I will see if my hubby has heard anything about the asshole. X

Putting her mobile phone on silent and away in her back pocket, Clarissa pulled her landline phone towards her, dialling the number on her chat line list to log on. Within seconds of logging on, the first call came through, and she answered.

"Line twenty-one. Beep"

'Surprise, surprise, it's a domination call.' Clarissa was suddenly

nervous again. It was the first time she would get to use her new script and try out her rules. She got ready to do her best firm but sultry voice.

"Hello, I'm Mistress Adele. What is your name?"

"Hi, Mistress, I'm Liam." A meek and quiet man replied.

"You do realize you've called the domination line?" she asked firmly.

"I do," he said with a hesitant voice.

"Do you want to be my Submissive, Liam?"

"Yes, Mistress."

"Good," she purred. "Are you looking for physical or fantasy domination?"

There was a long pause, and Clarissa didn't know whether he would hang up or speak.

"I want the physical, Mistress," he told her, speaking a little louder.

"If you want to be dominated by me, you must follow my rules. Do you understand, Liam?" She asked, her voice slightly firmer.

"Yes, yes, Mistress," his voice wavered.

Clarissa wasn't sure if he was getting more excited or nervous, but she was relieved he was still on the line.

"Rule one. You must call me Mistress Adele at all times. If you forget, you will be punished. Do you understand, Liam?"

"Yes, Mistress Adele."

"Rule two. You will not come until I give you permission. Do you understand?"

A loud moan came from the phone. 'Oh yes, it's excitement,' she thought.

"Yes, Mistress Adele."

"Rule three. You will obey me at all times, or you will be

punished. Is that clear, Liam?"

"It's clear, Mistress Adele."

"Do you have anything you want me to use on you?" she asked, curious as to what he would say.

"I have a beautiful inflatable penguin that I like to get slippy on, Mistress Adele. Shall I blow it up?" he asked, his voice wavering.

Clarissa couldn't believe what she was hearing. She also didn't quite know what he wanted to do with the inflatable penguin. She had never heard of getting slippy. A mental image of her kid's favorite penguin show popped into her head. 'Don't go there,' she thought. Clarissa's mind was reeling with so many questions and thoughts. What does getting slippy mean? What slippy stuff did he want to use? She decided to subtly find his need and pander to his unusual, kinky fetish.

"Yes, I want you to blow it up, Liam. However, first I want you to tell me what you are wearing and describe what your penguin looks like, so I can picture you both in my mind.," she told him seductively.

A loud moan came from the phone. Liam obviously liked that she was interested enough to ask for details.

"I'm wearing tight yellow and black swimming trunks, Mistress, and I have my body oil ready too. My penguin is as big as me when she's blown up," he said. "She's got a smooth black back, and her breast and belly are white. She's also got a beautiful yellow beak and yellow feet."

"She sounds amazing," Clarissa told him, trying to sound excited, "but you do realize you didn't address me by my full name, Liam?"

"I'm sorry, Mistress Adele, I deserve to be punished," he said with an excited whimper.

'Here goes my first stint at punishing,' she thought, 'what do I do? Then an idea came to her, and she knew she would have to be descriptive to get the best possible effect.

"Liam, I want you to slide your tight swimming trunks down to your knees. Then I want you to take your cock in one hand and spank it with the other, three times as I count. Do you understand?"

Clarissa didn't know if it would work, but from what she had read, domination was all about pleasure, pain, and reward.

"Oh god, Mistress Adele, I adore you," Liam whispered.

The sound from the phone changed, and Clarissa assumed he had put his loudspeaker on.

"I'm sliding my trunks down now." His breath getting heavy and loud. "I have my cock in my hand, Mistress Adele. I'm ready to be punished."

Clarissa took a deep breath, unsure if she was ready for what would happen.

"One," she said firmly. She heard the first slap, not knowing whether he was spanking his cock or something else.

A loud guttural moan emanated from the phone, and she could tell he was enjoying it.

"Two."

Another slap and a deep moan sounded.

"Can I please come, Mistress Adele?" He asked desperately.

Clarissa almost felt sorry for her new submissive, but she knew her job was to keep him on the phone for as long as possible.

"No, you may not come yet, Liam," she told him firmly, "I want to hear you get slippy with your beautiful penguin. And you haven't finished your punishment."

"Yes, Mistress Adele."

"Three."

Another slap, moan, and heavy breathing sounded.

"Well done, Liam. You are an impressive submissive. I think you may have become my favorite."

She could almost feel his excitement through the phone.

"Mmm, thank you, Mistress Adele," he whispered breathlessly.

"Now, I want you to blow up your beautiful penguin and tell me how she feels."

The moan Liam gave down the phone had Clarissa thinking she had sent him over the edge, but seconds later, the sound on his end of the phone changed. She could hear him taking deep breaths and blowing into the nozzle of his penguin.

"How does it feel blowing into her, Liam?" she asked.

He paused his blowing. "She feels so good, Mistress Adele. She's brushing against my cock as I blow."

Clarissa honestly didn't want the mental image that popped into her head as she listened to him, but there was no stopping it. Liam huffed and puffed, blowing up his beloved penguin. Then, unexpectedly the line went dead.

At first, Clarissa thought Liam had hung up. That was until she checked the time. Then she realized she'd managed to keep him talking for the full half-hour. Clarissa was so happy and proud of herself. She leaped from her chair, ran around her lounge, and then did a happy dance. For once, she felt in control of a man and not the one being controlled.

Chapter 7

Before Clarissa had a chance to relish the moment, her phone rang again. Quickly, Clarissa sat back at her desk, steadied her breath, and answered.

"Line seventeen. Beep."

Clarissa quickly gulped her drink while glancing at her chat line list. It was the curvy ladies' line.

"Hi, I'm Adele. Who's this?" she asked, trying to sound friendly and sexy.

"Hi, Adele, my name's Zack, but you can call me big boy."

If Clarissa still had her drink in her mouth, she would have done a Hayley and sprayed it all over her desk. Straight away, she involuntarily thought of Nigel and his colossal ego.

"Well, hello, big boy," she practically purred down the phone. "Are you wanting to play with me?"

"Mmm. Well, that depends on how curvy you are, Adele."

Zack was clearly used to flirting; she could hear his confidence in his tone.

"Well, big boy. I'm wondering if I'm too curvy for you to handle," she teased. "I've got a thirty-six H bust you could get lost in, curvy full hips for you to get to grips with, and a nice round ass that loves a little spanking. What do you think?"

When Clarissa started to hear a slapping noise, she knew she was on the right track. It sounded so comical, that she had to place her hand over her mouth to stop herself from giggling.

"I think I want to lay you on your back and slide my cock between those gorgeous big tits. Ah, ah, ah."

And just like that, the call ended, making Clarissa laugh even more. Being descriptive was obviously the trick, and Clarissa knew she was creating happy customers.

Clarissa answered four more calls, none of which were unusual, mainly horny and lonely guys calling on the most common chat line numbers for a quick wank on their day off. She had to admit that Hayley's friend, Stephanie, was right. Her new job was definitely acting, and she didn't feel turned on by any of the calls. There was no chemistry between her and the callers, and she wondered if that was because she was a woman or if it was because she couldn't see them.

The fifth call that Clarissa received did surprise her. It was another domination call, and she greeted the caller with her new script.

"Hello, I'm Mistress Adele. What is your name?" she asked in her firm but sultry tone.

"Hi, Mistress Adele. It's your favorite submissive again, Liam."

Clarissa was absolutely thrilled to hear Liam on the other end of the phone. Not only had she managed to keep in on the phone the first time for the entire half-hour, but for him to call back meant that her research and hard work had paid off. She sat at her desk, smiling like an idiot.

"Well, hello again, Liam. I'm so pleased you've been so obedient and have come back to please me," she told him, rewarding him with praise.

"Of course, Mistress,"

"Liam, you forgot to address me by my full name again. You know what happens now, don't you?" she asked more firmly.

"Oh yes, Mistress Adele." His voice trembled as his breath quickened.

Clarissa was starting to get the impression that he wanted her to punish him.

"Then you know what to do, my favorite. Slide down those black and yellow, tight trunks and hold that big, hard cock of yours," she ordered. "You will spank it three times. Are you ready?"

"Yes, Mistress Adele," he whispered in anticipation.

"One!"

Slap. A moan escaped him.

"Two!"

Slap. Another deep moan.

"This time, a little harder. Three!" she demanded.

"Ahh, ahh," Liam cried out, panting as if he had been running. "Thank you, Mistress Adele."

"How did it feel to be punished for being bad, Liam?" she asked, wanting to gauge how far to take things.

"It felt so good, Mistress Adele, thank you," he told her huskily.

"Tell me, Liam, how is your beautiful penguin looking?"

A deep moan from her new submissive made it clear he was very turned on by the sight of his inflatable penguin. Clarissa had to bite down on her bottom lip to stop herself from giggling at the mental images popping in her mind.

"She's looking really good, Mistress Adele. She's all smooth and shiny," he moaned loudly.

"She sounds amazing, Liam. I want you to run your hand all the way down her smooth, shiny back and tell me how she feels,"

Clarissa told him.

There was a slight pause, and Clarissa could hear his moaning deepen.

"She feels so good, Mistress Adele. Can I please get slippy with her now?" he asked, his longing evident in his voice.

Clarissa knew she would have to keep him engaged in conversation to keep him on the line. She also knew that he enjoyed telling her about his inflatable.

"You may, Liam, but I want you to describe exactly what you're doing, as that would please me. You do want to please me, don't you, Liam?"

"Yes, Mistress Adele, I do," he told her sincerely.

"Then you may begin. However, remember my rules, Liam. You are not allowed to come until I give you permission," she said more firmly.

"I understand. Thank you, Mistress Adele."

"Now, tell me what you're doing, Liam."

Clarissa could hear noises, but she didn't know what was happening at his end.

"Mmm, I'm squirting my body oil on my hands, and now I am smoothing it onto my body, Mistress Adele. I'm making my body all slippy for her."

Clarissa was starting to get an idea of what would happen next. "Do you think she's ready for you to get slippy on her, Liam?"

Heavy breathing came down the phone, and she could picture him looking at his penguin with passion in his eyes.

"She's ready for me, Mistress Adele."

"Then you may proceed and get slippy on her, but remember to ask permission before you finish, Liam."

For the next ten minutes, Clarissa listened to her first submissive, slipping and sliding all over his inflatable penguin, with him describing how it felt. She could hear his body squeaking against the vinyl of the inflatable. Clarissa repeatedly had to cover her mouth whenever she heard him slip to the floor with a thud, but it only added to his excitement. Every so often, Liam would beg for permission to finish, but Clarissa was checking her watch, and she didn't want him to hang up before his time ran out.

With just over five minutes to go, she decided to relent.

"Liam, you have been a fantastic submissive. You have pleased me greatly. You have my permission to come," she told him in her sultry tone.

"Oh, Mistress Adele, thank you!" he exclaimed, desperate for release.

Within moments Clarissa could hear him reach his climax, and it sounded like a big one. She wondered if that was because she had kept him hanging on.

"Mistress Adele, you are amazing and the best Mistress I have ever had. Can I call you again, please?" Liam asked while panting and trying to catch his breath.

Clarissa was thrilled by his response. "Of course, Liam. You're my new favorite submissive, and I definitely want to talk to you again," she emphasized.

"Oh, thank...," he started to say.

The line went dead as Liam was cut off.

—x—

Clarissa managed to work right up to two pm, and she was thrilled at herself. Not only had she managed to keep most of her domination callers on the line for the entire half-hour, but most of them called her back to get permission to finish.

Clarifying if they wanted physical or fantasy domination had helped her immensely. She still couldn't get over the fact that her domination callers wanted to be punished. Clarissa also had better success with her other callers too. Especially when she realized she could keep them talking after they finished. They seemed to like the fact that she asked them about themselves, and she was interested.

When Clarissa thought about how many hours she had worked, she got excited. She was dying to know much she had earned. Even if she could earn what she was making at her customer service and sales job, she would be better off, especially as she wouldn't have to pay for childcare anymore or petrol. The thought reminded Clarissa that she had to talk to her childminder, Susan, about no longer needing her service. It wasn't a conversation she was looking forward to, especially as Luke and Matthew were so attached to her. Clarissa didn't have much spare money, especially now, but she decided to get Susan a thank you present from her and the boys.

Before Clarissa started to get ready for her chat with Susan and collect her boys, she messaged Hayley and Becky to let them know her first shift had gone really well. She knew as soon as they got the message, they would be desperate to hear all about it. And she couldn't wait to tell them everything. She smiled to herself, finally feeling mentally stronger and more in control of her life.

Clarissa was about to leave her desk when her phone rang again. She had been working so many hours, that she half expected it to be another caller, even though she knew she had logged off.

"Hello?"

"Hi Clarissa, it's Michelle. How are you doing?"

Clarissa wasn't surprised; she got the impression Michelle liked to look after her team.

"I'm good, thank you. I've just finished my first shift, and I think I did alright," Clarissa said honestly.

"I can tell you; you did better than alright, Clarissa. You were brilliant. And I can't believe your domination call stats. What a difference!"

"Thank you so much." Clarissa felt even more proud of herself. "I spent a lot of time researching, and I think my sales experience has helped."

"Whatever you did, it worked. Congratulations, Clarissa. I knew you were going to be great. I think you'll be able to leave your day job in no time," Michelle told her enthusiastically.

"Well, that might be another reason why I did so well. I was feeling a lot more determined. My boss sexually assaulted me yesterday, so I quit my day job."

Michelle gasped down the phone. "I'm so sorry, Clarissa. Are you okay?" she asked, genuinely concerned.

"Yes, I'm ok, but I'll have to do a lot of hours on the chat line now, as it's going to be my only income. If that's okay with you?"

"Are you kidding!" Michelle laughed, "If today's anything to go by, you can work as much as you like, and you'll be earning a fortune."

Clarissa desperately hoped that Michelle was right. "Thank you, Michelle. I appreciate your encouragement."

"You're welcome. I'll check in with you again soon, but if you need me, you have my number. Bye for now."

"Bye."

—x—

Clarissa practically floated around the shop while looking for Susan's present; she was so happy. She couldn't remember the last time she felt like she was on cloud nine. And because she was no longer in a job she hated, she felt like a huge weight had been lifted off her shoulders. Clarissa didn't even mind the fallout with her old HR department or reporting creepy John to the police. Why? Because the slimy bastard would be less likely to do it to someone else. Also, if he got fired for his behavior, he would struggle to get another job and have more victims. Clarissa was smart enough to know that word gets around of bad behavior and scandal, especially a sexual scandal.

After seeing the cost of jewellery, Clarissa settled for a beautiful bouquet of flowers and a thank you card for Susan. It was the least she could do after Susan had looked after the boys for so many years. After writing the card out in her car, she drove to Susan's house—but the closer she got—the more uncomfortable she became. She hated letting people down, even if it wasn't her fault.

Susan was as friendly as ever when Clarissa arrived, inviting her in for a cup of tea and asking if Clarissa was alright. She was amazed to see Clarissa on a weekday, especially as Luke and Matthew were not sick or on a school break.

When Clarissa explained what her slimy boss had done and that she had been forced to quit her job, Susan's face was empathetic. She placed her hand on Clarissa's and told her how sorry she was. Clarissa was relieved Susan was as understanding as she hoped she would be.

"I've been in the same situation myself many years ago," Susan confessed. "My HR department was even worse than yours in those days. In fact, they told me to dress more manly to help prevent it from happening, as if it was my fault, the bastards. That's why I started childminding, and I haven't regretted it since. I wish I'd had the nerve to knee my old boss in the balls like you did." She laughed. "What are you going to do now?"

"I have got a new job, but it's commission only, and I don't know how much I'll be earning," Clarissa explained, "I'll also be working flexible hours from home, so I'm afraid I won't be able to afford or need any childcare. I'm sorry, Susan."

Clarissa felt like crying. Susan had become a good friend, and her boys loved her like a grandparent.

"You have nothing to be sorry for, love," Susan told her gently. "None of this is your fault. After all these years, you and the boys are like family. I hope you'll stay in touch and visit all the time. I can't imagine not seeing you all."

Susan began to well up with tears. Clarissa couldn't bear to see her upset.

"Don't worry, you'll still see us, I promise," she assured her. Clarissa wrapped an arm around her. "I got you a little present to say thank you for everything."

Reaching into her handbag, Clarissa pulled out the card and gave it to Susan.

"I got you something else, too," Clarissa told her as she rushed out to her car.

When Clarissa walked back in with the bouquet of flowers, tears welled in Susan's eyes and began to trickle down her cheeks.

"You didn't have to buy me anything." She sobbed.

Clarissa reached across and stroked her arm affectionately. "I know, but I wanted to show you how much we appreciate and love you, Susan."

—x—

By the time Clarissa arrived home with Luke and Matthew, she felt a lot better. Especially as Susan had been so understanding of her new situation, and it probably helped that Susan had been in the same tough spot in the past.

"Put your school bags down and sit at the table, please boys, I have something to tell you," Clarissa told Luke and Matthew as they walked through the front door.

"Why mummy?" Luke asked as he dropped his bag and looked at her with eyebrows raised "Are we in trouble?"

Clarissa smiled reassuringly. "No, honey. I just need to talk to you both."

"Race you to the kitchen," Matthew announced, unfazed.

As Luke and Matthew raced to the kitchen Clarissa repositioned their school bags out of the way of the stairs and followed them. She filled and clicked the kettle on as they played the hand-slapping game and poured them both a juice.

"Okay, I have some news for you," she said as she gave them their juice and sat down at the end of the kitchen table. "I have a new job that lets me work from home. So, we'll be able to spend more time together, especially during the school holidays. And I'll be able to take you to school and pick you up at home time from now on.

"But auntie Susan takes us and picks us up mummy," Matthew told her matter of factly.

"I know she normally does, honey, but now I work from home she doesn't need to, and because I won't have to pay auntie Susan to look after you anymore, we'll have extra money for your school trips and maybe a holiday.

"Does this mean we'll be able to ride our bikes to school and back like our friends, mum?" Luke asked, his eyes hopeful.

Clarissa nodded and grinned. "Yep, and we'll be able to go to the park after school if you're good."

"But what about auntie Susan? We like going to her house and playing with the other kids," Matthew told her, his bottom lip starting to quiver.

"We'll still visit auntie Susan, don't worry." Clarissa stroked

Matthew's head affectionately and ruffled Luke's hair, making him grin. "Okay, time for homework while I cook dinner."

Luke and Matthew took the news better than expected much to her relief. She suspected that was due to her promises of park playtime and allowing them to ride their bikes to and from school.

After dinner, Clarissa started a video call with Hayley and Becky while her boys finished their homework in the lounge. When Becky answered the call, Clarissa and Hayley nearly had heart attacks because Becky was wearing a dark-green face mask and looked like an ogre's wife.

"Holy hell, Becky, you could have bloody warned us!" Hayley declared while she and Clarissa patted their hammering chests.

Becky laughed, making her look even scarier. "I'm pampering myself, but I had a little accident during the process."

Clarissa and Hayley locked eyes. They both knew that Becky wasn't the greatest when trying to carry out self-maintenance. Clarissa remembered her eyebrow fiasco years earlier. Becky's eyebrows had been plucked so unevenly, that one eyebrow looked like it was constantly raised. It was most unnerving and made them feel like Becky didn't believe anything they said. It had taken Becky months to grow them back to normal.

"Oh God, what did you do this time?" Clarissa asked.

Becky began to look sheepish. "Well, I decided to try that new hair removal cream I've seen advertised on my hoo-hoo, but I was getting bored while waiting for it to work. So, I decided to tidy the kid's bedrooms as the stuff did its thing. Unfortunately, I think I moved around too much. I washed it off, and now my hoo-hoo looks patchier than a patchwork quilt."

Clarissa burst into laughter, and Hayley snorted loudly.

"Are you trying to tell us that you left your lady bits looking patchy?" Hayley asked incredulously while Clarissa tried to breathe.

"Mmm, yes," Becky admitted sheepishly.

Hayley and Clarissa couldn't believe their ears.

"I hope you aren't planning on having more kids because a patchy hoo-hoo isn't going to look very attractive to Martin." Clarissa giggled.

"I second that statement," Hayley added with a grin.

Clarissa was pretty sure that poor Becky's face was probably glowing red under her dark-green face mask.

"I think you need to do a baldy hoo-hoo after we've gone," Hayley suggested.

"And I second that," Clarissa chipped in, feeling relieved that her boys couldn't hear the conversation.

Becky held her hand up in surrender, "Okay, okay, a baldy hoo-hoo it is."

"Don't worry, honey. You aren't the only one to have gone the baldy way out of all of us. I remember when Nigel decided to do it one year on Valentine's Day."

"Was he trying to impress you?" Becky asked.

Clarissa laughed even before she got her words out. "I think he did it to try and make it look bigger. He even remeasured it, as if removing his pubes made it grow."

Hayley and Becky instantly exploded into belly laughs, and in seconds they were all trying to breathe.

"Oh my god, stop!" Becky declared, "You're making my face-mask crack."

That only made the girls laugh harder. And it took another few minutes for any of them to be able to speak properly.

"Anyway, let's get to the nitty-gritty. Clarissa, how did your first shift go on the chat line?" Becky asked, dabbing laughter tears from the corners of her eyes while trying to preserve her facemask.

Clarissa told Hayley and Becky all about her first shift and how well it went. They were thrilled for her when she told them that Michelle had called to tell her well done.

"That's fantastic!" Hayley exclaimed excitedly, "Did your new knowledge and script help with the domination calls?"

Clarissa couldn't stop the grin that spread across her face. "It sure did. I was able to keep most of the submissive's on the line for a full half-hour, and most of them called back for permission to finish," she told them proudly.

Hayley clapped enthusiastically. "That is bloody amazing!!"

"Well done, you kinky minx," Becky congratulated.

"I think the boys and me are going to be okay."

Hayley nodded. "Yes, you are! Now, tell us the kinkiest call you had today. We've been dying to know."

Clarissa giggled. "You aren't going to believe me, but it involves an inflatable penguin and some body oil."

"What the hell!"

"No way!"

After telling her best friends about Liam, her new submissive, and the rest of her shift, Hayley and Becky were hysterical. And Becky's dark-green face mask had cracked completely, making her look more like a zombie.

"So, you're telling us that a dude spent probably over one pound a minute to tell you how he was blowing up his favorite blow-up penguin?" Hayley asked in disbelief.

"Yep." Clarissa nodded.

"And then he called you back so you could listen to him slipping all over it and making a mess of it."

"Yep."

Hayley and Becky were in fits, barely able to contain themselves.

"Oh my god, I need to brace my lady bits," Becky stuttered, "This is too much."

"How on earth does someone get a fetish for pool inflatables?" Hayley wondered aloud.

Clarissa shook her head. "I have no idea, but how do any of us get fetishes? We all have a fetish for something, bald men, beards, and, as you know, I love hot nerdy looking guys. I know we're having a giggle about it, but fetishes are normal for everyone."

Her girlfriends nodded, not being able to deny the facts.

"There's only one downside," Clarissa told them.

Becky's face mask cracked a little more as her eyebrows lifted. "What's that?"

"I won't be able to look at another penguin the same way ever again without picturing Liam getting slippy." She grinned.

"I'm wondering if Liam had a partner or a wife, and if so, what they would think about his fetish?" Becky said with wide eyes.

"I don't know what I'd do if Adam told me he had an unusual fetish like that," Hayley told them honestly, "It's bad enough that he's got a thing for pregnant women."

Becky and Clarissa looked at each other in surprise.

"Why are you both looking at me like I've got two heads?"

Becky opened her mouth and closed it again, stunned.

"You've never told us that before," Clarissa told her.

"Really, I thought I had," Hayley said truthfully, "I didn't know myself until I got pregnant the first time. Most women get a rest when they're pregnant, but not me. Not that I'm complaining, mind you. I couldn't even get a shower without Adam following me in."

"Well, that explains why we didn't see much of you when you

were pregnant." Becky laughed.

"I think there are probably thousands of people who have unusual fetishes that they don't want to share with their partners," Clarissa said thoughtfully. "Many may be too afraid to share in case their partners leave them. That's probably why Liam called the chat line so that he could satisfy his fetish urges."

Becky nodded in agreement, "I've got to tell you, girls, this is becoming an eye-opener for me!"

As Hayley was about to speak, Luke walked into Clarissa's kitchen with a bloody nose dripping down his Spiderman PJs.

"I've got to go. Luke has a nose gusher. Love you," she told her best friends before quickly ending the call.

Luke looked like something out of a horror movie. Blood soaked his Marvel pajamas, mouth, and chin. Even with him pinching the bridge of his nose, blood was still seeping. Luckily, he was calm. This was a regular occurrence. Their family doctor still hadn't gotten to the bottom of why it was happening.

"Sit at the table, honey, and put your head back," Clarissa told him as she grabbed the kitchen towel roll off its holder, pulling off a handful.

Sitting at the dining table, Luke held his head up while trying to maintain pressure.

"Why does it keep happening, Mummy?" Luke asked, sounding like he had a cold.

Clarissa began to clean his face and neck as the blood spread down his exposed throat.

"I don't know, honey. Some kids are just prone to nose bleeds. Hopefully, you'll grow out of it. Doctor Simmons isn't worried, so we shouldn't be worried either."

After stopping Luke's gusher, cleaning him up, and putting his bloodied pajamas in soak, she put both boys to bed and read them a story.

With both her boys asleep, Clarissa made herself a cup of tea and checked her phone. She had decided to try and do shifts on the chat line while they were at school and in the evenings while they slept. That way, she hoped to earn full-time money.

'I can do this.' she told herself.

Chapter 8

When Clarissa looked at her phone, there were two messages, one from Hayley and another from her ex-asshole. Clarissa rolled her eyes, wondering what the idiot wanted now. Usually, it would be months between messages, so she couldn't understand why the sudden and more regular contact. She opened the message, feeling uneasy.

Hi babe, I was wondering if I could pop over tomorrow for a chat. Love and miss you!

'What in the hell?' Clarissa had to read the message twice just to check that she was reading it right. 'What on earth is going on with the idiot.'

What pissed off Clarissa the most was that there was no mention of his boys in any of Nigel's recent messages. No, sorry I missed Luke's birthday; how are my boys, or can I see my kids. Nothing.

"He's a bloody waste of space," Clarissa said, trying to keep her emotions and voice in check so she didn't wake the kids.

She sipped her tea and thought about the message before replying.

I repeat, I am not your babe! I don't love you or miss you. If you want to see your boys, you can have them over at your parent's place this coming weekend.

Instead of waiting for a reply, she opened the message from Hayley.

Didn't get a chance to tell you, but a policewoman is coming to see you tomorrow to take a statement. She'll be there at ten am.

Clarissa thanked her and also forwarded Nigel's message to her.

What the hell is he playing at? Hayley asked.

I don't know, but it's very odd behavior.

She forwarded her reply to Nigel with another text.
This is what I said to the bastard. Let's see how he responds.

Her phone pinged with another message from Hayley.
If he responds at all!

Yep

Clarissa put her phone on her desk, deciding to get ready for her shift. She had given her boy's plenty of time to fall into a deep sleep, and she wanted to get a lot of hours in. Only this shift, she was going to be more prepared. After her last shift, her throat had been sore from too much talking and not drinking enough in between calls.

In the kitchen, Clarissa prepared herself another cup of tea, a flask of tea, and a bowl of mixed nuts. She wasn't feeling nervous about the chat line anymore, and her mindset had switched to see it as another customer service job, only a lot more fun and interesting. Clarissa had a feeling she was never going to get bored, that was for sure. During her last shift there was barely enough time to take a sip of her tea between the calls.

As soon as Clarissa was ready at her desk with everything set up, she logged in on the chat line and began.

—x—

Three hours passed, and yet again, most of her calls were for domination. Clarissa was thrilled that her regular list of callers was building. She found that she was telling most of them that they were her favorite submissive, and they all seemed to like it.

During her calls, Clarissa could see her silent mobile phone flashing with new messages, and she wondered if Nigel had replied to her blunt message. She decided to take a bathroom break and then check.

Clarissa was surprised to see that all of her new messages were from Nigel, four messages to be precise.

Don't be like that, babe.
I miss you more than you know.
Please, can I come and see you?
I need to talk to you!

Nigel's messages had Clarissa reeling. She couldn't think of what he could want to talk about, and the fact that he still hadn't asked after his boys, let alone asked to see them, had her feeling seriously pissed off. She forwarded the new messages to the girls to see what they thought. Clarissa couldn't think of what could have caused his renewed interest in her. He had consistently shagged other women behind her back, and when they had the boys, he was more blatant about doing it, even coming home with love bites on his neck. Probably because he thought she wouldn't leave him due to the boys.

However, the asshole couldn't have been more wrong.

Nigel had been a sneaky bastard using two mobile phones—one for family and friends and the other for his women on the side. Then one night, he made a stupid mistake. Nigel forgot to take his extra phone with him on a supposed boy's night, leaving it in his sock drawer, and when Clarissa was putting the laundry away, she discovered it.

Clarissa remembered the sick feeling she felt when she opened the phone and saw all the messages and photographs between Nigel and his numerous girlfriends. All her worst fears became very real, and she knew she wasn't just paranoid like Nigel had tried to convince her.

That same night, Clarissa cut the crotch out of all his trousers and packed his belongings in trash bags. Her girlfriends and their husbands then helped her change the locks on her house and toss the trash bags outside his parent's house. She then called him and told him that he was done and not to come back. The only blessing for Clarissa was that the phone gave her enough evidence to get a quick divorce.

Clarissa couldn't comprehend what he was now thinking. She thought he would know by now that she would never, ever take him back.

Clarissa looked at her phone, wondering what she should say. She was curious about what he wanted to talk about and what must be happening in his life, but was she curious enough to want him in her house again? The answer was a resounding no.

She typed her reply.

No, not happening, scumbag! And your boys are doing great, by the way, you useless, poor excuse of a father!

Clarissa's phone shook in her hand. Venting her anger definitely felt therapeutic. She took a deep breath to reduce her temper, hating the fact that he could still rile her. Clarissa sipped her tea, made herself comfortable at her desk again, and got back to work.

—x—

The following morning, Clarissa walked her boys to school, trying to keep up with them as they rode their bikes down the over-grown path alongside their school. The morning sunlight shone through the mix of oak, sycamore and birch leaves, as Luke and Matthew pedd-led like crazy, trying to race each other.

As she no longer had set hours and no childminder, she was able to spend a lot more time with Luke and Matthew, and she was determined to make the most of it.

Clarissa's shifts at her new job were going brilliantly, and she found herself walking with a pep in her step. Her boys seemed a lot happier too. Clarissa not only forgot how much she enjoyed walking but also how lovely all the school mums and dads were.

After dropping her boys off and catching up with a few other parents, Clarissa power walked home, knowing that she had a policewoman coming to take her statement about creepy John, her old boss. Just the thought of his hands on her body gave her chills down her spine.

Clarissa made it home long enough to make a cuppa before her doorbell rang. When she opened the door, a slim, tall, policewoman stood on her porch with a folder in one hand.

"Hello, I'm Sergeant Jameson. Are you Clarissa Darcy?"

Clarissa nodded. "Yes, I am," she said, shaking her hand.

Sergeant Jameson shook Clarissa's hand surprisingly firmly and smiled.

"Please come in," Clarissa offered. "Can I get you a cup of tea?"

"Oh, yes, please. I think we have a lot of talking to do." She smiled again, this time sympathetically.

Leading the police officer to her kitchen, Clarissa offered her a seat and made them both some tea. She sat down opposite the officer, suddenly feeling like she was the guilty one. Clarissa knew the feeling was irrational, especially as she had never been in trouble with the police, but she still felt guilty kneeing her creepy boss.

"Thank you for the tea. And don't be nervous. From what I understand, you have done nothing wrong," Sergeant Jameson said, her eyes full of empathy.

'Easier said than done,' Clarissa thought as she watched the sergeant open her folder and retrieve a pen from her inside jacket pocket.

"Okay, Clarissa, in your own words, can you tell me precisely what happened, please."

Clarissa nervously tapped her fingers on the kitchen table. She told Sergeant Jameson everything that happened—from the moment she walked onto her floor at Janka Industries with Mr. John Mason waiting for her—to the final act of pressing her foot against his face and quitting. Sergeant Jameson quickly and efficiently wrote everything down as she talked. Clarissa didn't realize how quickly her nervous fingers were tapping until Sergeant Jameson placed her hand on top of hers to still them.

"I have to say, Clarissa, you showed amazing courage when your boss sexually assaulted you. And his behavior was indeed a sexual assault."

Becky and Hayley had pretty much said the same thing, but hearing it from a police officer, made Clarissa feel like a massive weight had suddenly been lifted off her shoulders.

"I was worried that he would report me for assaulting him," Clarissa confessed.

Sergeant Jameson smiled a knowing smile. "Sexual predators are usually cowards, especially when they get caught. However, they do get braver if they aren't held accountable," she said bluntly.

Clarissa sipped her tea, more out of comfort than thirst. Her skin crawled after describing what John Mason had done to her.

"I shouldn't be telling you this, Clarissa; but this is not the first time Mr. Mason has done this kind of assault. There are records of previous assaults. Unfortunately, it appears that after the reports were taken, he then contacted his victims, and they backed out. If you go ahead with yours, we can charge him and punish him this time. Hopefully, to prevent him from doing it to some other poor woman."

Clarissa couldn't blame John's previous victims. After her assault, all she wanted to do was to put it behind her and never think about him again. She knew that going to court meant other people would find out what he did. Then, Clarissa realized something, she had two best friends who would be at her side through everything, and maybe his other victims didn't have that support.

"I want to go ahead with this," Clarissa told the sergeant firmly, "I will not let that creepy bastard do it again to someone else, or maybe do something worse."

Sergeant Jameson smiled at Clarissa, impressed by her determination and emotional strength. "You've completed the first step, which is a great start. If you can read through your statement, then sign and date it, I will get the ball rolling."

After reading and signing her statement, Clarissa thanked Sergeant Jameson and showed her out. The sergeant gave Clarissa a card with her number, telling her to call if Mr. John Mason should get in touch again. Clarissa waved as the police car pulled away, grateful that Sergeant Jameson had been so sympathetic and understanding.

She had a feeling that Becky and Hayley wouldn't be surprised by John's sexually aggressive past record. "What a slimy, perverted bastard," Clarissa said as she closed her front door.

Clarissa looked at the time; it was already coming up to noon. Her stomach growled loudly in response. She knew that if she didn't eat something she wouldn't be able to concentrate—or worse—her stomach would growl while she was on a call and the caller would hear it. "Food, then work for a few hours," she told herself. It was the first time in years that Clarissa had looked forward to working, and it felt great. She made some lunch and set herself up at her desk with everything she needed, including a fresh flask of tea.

After taking so many domination and fetish calls, Clarissa found the more common calls super easy. All she had to do was be very descriptive, describing what she was supposedly wearing, how her body looked, and how she apparently felt during the call. Of course, Clarissa had to do sound effects too. She even had to run to her kitchen sink and trickle water on more than one occasion, pretending to pee. It truly was just acting, and nothing was fazing her anymore.

Two hours into her shift, Clarissa got a call on line nine, Milf's, which stood for Mum's I'd like to fuck. She wasn't worried. Her ability to switch persona to suit the various chat lines was getting easier with each call. 'Hot mum, hot mum,' she thought to herself while preparing to greet the new caller.

"Hi, this is Adele. Who's this?" She purred down the phone.

"Hello, Adele, I'm Chris, and I want to know if you're a loud moaner?" he asked with a deep and very masculine voice.

"That depends on how turned on you get me, Chris."

"Oh god, you have the sexiest voice, Adele. I'm desperate to hear you moan. Are you touching yourself?"

Clarissa was actually in the process of painting her nails a stunning shade of dark red after finding the nail polish in her desk drawer. She had completely forgotten that she had put it there.

"You have the sexy voice, Chris. You're making me wet, just listening to you," she told him, massaging his ego.

Clarissa knew precisely what he was doing on the other end of the line, wanking. After so many hours on the phone sex chat line, she could not only recognize the sounds easily, but she could usually tell how close they were by the speed and breathing pace. Although that was a skill, she had no intention of adding to her professional profile.

"Please tell me exactly what you're doing, Adele?" He asked, pleading.

Clarissa knew she had to slow Chris down, or he would come too quickly, and it would be a very short call.

"I want to tell you exactly what I'm doing, but I would love for us to come together. Hearing you come would turn me on even more. So, stroke that thick, hard cock slowly, and I will tell you."

"Oh god, Adele, I would love that," he said, panting down the phone.

Clarissa smiled to herself. She could tell by the sounds he was making that her plan had worked.

"I'm home alone, sitting on my armchair with my tight black

skirt pulled up to the top of my smooth thighs. Now I'm sliding my fingers into my panties. Oh god, you've got me so wet and slippery already, Chris," she told him as she painted another nail dark red, loving the color.

"I wish I was right there watching you, Adele. Rub your clit and imagine it's my tongue. I want to hear you moan."

Clarissa could tell that he had sped up again and was close, but she was determined to try and keep him going for as long as possible.

With her last nail painted, she described what Chris had asked for, and as she began to moan and pant, she blew her now beautiful red nails dry. Just as Chris reached his climax, and she was moaning loudly for him, a movement at her lounge window caught her eye. Clarissa couldn't believe it. Her ex-asshole was trying to peer through her net curtains.

Luckily for Clarissa, the line went dead.

"What in the hell!" Clarissa declared, slamming the phone down before remembering she had to log out.

When Nigel knocked on her front door, Clarissa was already fuming. She couldn't believe that he would just show up, especially as she had been positively rude to him, and made it clear he was unwelcome. Clarissa rushed from her lounge and opened her front door with force. Her flushed face clearly showed how pissed off she was.

"Hi, babe," he said, trying to sound smooth while attempting to look behind her for someone else. "Have you got company? I thought I heard a man's voice."

Clarissa glared at him for his audacity. "Firstly, I keep telling you; I'm not your babe. Secondly, it's none of your fricking business whether I have company or not," she told him, trying not to yell and alert the neighborhood's curtain twitchers of his presence. "I told you I didn't want you coming here. What do you want?"

Being mean to people wasn't in Clarissa's nature, and she had never been rude to anyone else, apart from her ex-boss John, recently, but her blood was boiling, and she was finding it hard to stop herself. If she was honest, all she wanted to do was to kick Nigel's ass back to his flashy red sports car.

Nigel's shoulders dropped as his eyebrows rose, and he looked at her pleadingly. He suddenly looked quite pitiful.

"I'm sorry, Clarissa, but I need to talk to you. It's serious!"

The look on Nigel's face began to dampen Clarissa's anger. He did look like someone had just died. *'Oh god, what if I've just been a total bitch to the narcissistic idiot, and someone has died,'* she thought, suddenly feeling a little guilty. She decided to try and keep her temper in check, and her mouth firmly shut until he told her what the hell was going on. Clarissa moved to the side of the doorway, allowing him entry. *'Yep, he's still got a sexy ass,'* she admitted to herself as he walked to the kitchen. She wanted to slap herself for even thinking about his ass.

Following Nigel to her kitchen, Clarissa indicated that he could take a seat at the table, and then she started to make some fresh tea. Although, what she really desired now was a stiff drink.

"What's going on, Nigel??" She asked.

"I just want you to know that this last month has been hard for me, Clarissa."

'You don't know the meaning of hard, you bastard. Hard is trying to feed and clothe your kids on a pittance.'

"Really, why?" She asked through pursed lips.

"I found a lump in one of my balls, and I've been having tests done," Nigel told her, sounding lost.

It was the last thing Clarissa was expecting to hear, and she could tell by his voice that he was scared.

"Did you find the lump, or did one of your many girlfriends find it?" She asked with a raised brow.

Nigel's awkward silence and the look on his face made her think that the lump wasn't his discovery.

"We're divorced, and I can't remember the last time you saw your boys. Why are you really here, Nigel?"

Clarissa had to admit, her ex-asshole looked pitiful, but his constant cheating and putting her down throughout their marriage had destroyed any empathy she would otherwise have for someone in his situation. To Clarissa, it felt like karma literally had him by the balls.

"I want us to get back together again as a family," he told her desperately.

"Are you freaking kidding me right now?" she demanded. "Have you completely forgotten how you treated me, cheated on me, and ignored our boys? I'm not even sure Luke and Matthew would recognize you anymore; it's been that long. What would make you think that I would ever have you back?" She yelled, no longer caring if her neighbor's heard or not.

"But I might have cancer!" he yelled.

Nigel's piercing eyes bore into hers. He rose from the kitchen table, walking towards her and reaching out his arms, inviting her to hold him.

Instantly, she stepped back, holding up her hands to stop him. Clarissa was floored by his undeniable narcissism. She tried to control her anger again, finding it more difficult with each minute. She felt like her boiling blood and the kettle were in sync, and her whole body began to tremble.

Nigel backed away from her in surprise. His body sagged and he retreated back to his chair, stunned by her rejection.

Clarissa turned away, placing her hands on the kitchen counter and hung her head, feeling emotionally drained.

"I'm sorry you might have cancer, but that's no reason for you to come here," she told him calmly, turning to face him once more.

Clarissa straightened herself to her full height while taking a slow, deep, measured breath.

"I'm not your wife anymore. You don't want a family; you just want me to look after you. And after how you've treated me and our boys, there's no way in hell that is going to happen!" Clarissa said, her voice low and serious. "Now, I want you to leave my house and never come here again."

Nigel's face looked as if she had just slapped him, hard. And in truth, she was still feeling like she wanted to slap some sense into him.

Nigel stood looking ashen, his shoulders slumping slightly in defeat. "You've changed, Clarissa."

Clarissa looked at him feeling gobsmacked. "Are you fucking surprised, you narcissistic bastard? Having you as a husband has that effect. Now get out."

Without saying another word, Nigel stormed out. Clarissa followed, slamming her front door behind him.

She refused to feel bad for having such a go at him, especially as he still didn't ask about his kids once during his unwanted visit. Clarissa didn't think he would be brave enough to try again, and she hoped her response to his bad news would stop him from messaging her anymore.

—x—

Clarissa wasn't in the mood to carry on working after Nigel's visit.

The last thing she wanted was to take it out on her callers, especially her domination callers. Instead, Clarissa poured herself a large glass of red wine and messaged her best friends to tell them about Nigel's visit.

Within seconds of her sending a text to their group chat, her phone exploded with replies. Becky and Hayley couldn't believe his audacity either. After texting back and forth, Clarissa's best friends decided to pop over in the evening. Their husbands were both going to be watching football, and their kids would be in bed.

Clarissa was grateful, knowing she would be able to vent to the two people who knew her and Nigel's history the best. However, she did warn them both that she had to do another shift on the chat line due to the days lost hours. That news got Becky and Hayley quite excited, with both saying they wanted to listen in. Clarissa couldn't stop herself giggling and rolling her eyes, while telling them they were both perverts before putting down her phone and finishing her wine.

Chapter 9

The moment Clarissa arrived home with Luke and Matthew, she put away their bikes, and settled them at the kitchen table before refilling her glass with more wine. She was still reeling from Nigel's visit, and when her boys came out of school, her heart broke yet again at the thought of their absent father, who didn't give a shit about them. Clarissa didn't want to tell her boys about their dad's visit, not seeing the point in upsetting them. She didn't want to have to lie to protect their precious little hearts.

—x—

When Becky and Hayley arrived, Luke and Matthew had done their homework, received lots of cuddles, and were watching a movie before bedtime. Clarissa was on her third glass of red wine for the day, feeling a lot more relaxed. They immediately made their way to the kitchen and out of earshot of Luke and Matthew.

"So, did Nigel honestly peer through the curtains while you were moaning your head off?" Hayley asked with a giggle.

"Yes, but he couldn't see anything. I think Nigel thought I had a man in the house." she grinned, "He tried to see if he could see anyone while he was at the front door."

"I still can't believe Nigel honestly thought you would take him back," Becky said with wide eyes, feeling flabbergasted.

Hayley shook her head, "I think he's getting his comeuppance for all the years he's been shagging around."

Clarissa nodded in agreement, "That's what I was thinking. It's like karma has come to make him pay. He didn't mention or ask about Luke and Matthew once," she told them with a heavy heart.

"You did the right thing, kicking the fucker out," Hayley assured her. "I will say it again; he never deserved you and your boys. Anyway, enough about that bastard. How did you get on today with the police?"

Clarissa told Becky and Hayley everything that was said while giving her statement, and neither of them was surprised when she told them John had a seedy past.

"It's such a shame no one before you went through with getting him prosecuted," Becky said sadly, "It might have prevented him from doing it to you, Clarissa."

"I know, but not everyone has best friends to support them as I do," she said with a smile, "I know it's not going to be easy, especially if they charge him and he pleads not guilty, but if I have to stand up in court and say what he did, I will."

"That's my girl!" Hayley declared with a huge grin. "You seem a lot more confident about the whole thing."

"I am. Any news on the HR front?" Clarissa asked.

"I think they're in panic mode now, especially as I've asked our top lawyer to assist me with this," Hayley said, grinning. "They've brought in their top lawyers too now, but they'll be even more panicked when I inform them that we know of John's past behavior, and that they did nothing about it."

Clarissa was also starting to feel panicked, "I haven't got the money to pay for you doing this, let alone two of you!"

Hayley held her hands up, "Don't worry, you don't have to pay anything. Creepy John and Janka Industries will be paying our bills when you win and compensating you too."

Relief swept through Clarissa's body like a wave. More money worries were the last thing she needed.

—x—

After Clarissa read Luke and Matthew a story, had another cuddle, and put them to bed, she and the girls relocated to the lounge.

"I need to get plenty of hours in tonight, as I lost so many today," she told them. "Please don't feel like you have to stay if you get bored."

"Oh, I don't think we'll be getting bored anytime soon," Becky told her, grinning like a Cheshire cat and reaching into her bag to pull out a notepad and pen. "I'll be taking notes tonight."

"Oh my god, Becky, you are too much." Clarissa laughed while Hayley rolled her eyes.

Clarissa logged on to the chat line, and before long she was in full swing with her calls, while Becky jotted down her notes while listening. Hayley chilled on Clarissa's sofa with a constant impressed expression. Clarissa's best friends would often cover their mouths to stop themselves from laughing, especially if a caller made weird noises or said something unexpected.

"Do you ever get turned on during a call?" Hayley asked while Clarissa was waiting for her phone to ring again.

"Er, nope," Clarissa said instantly, shocking her girlfriends

Their faces looked like they didn't believe her at all.

Clarissa laughed. "It's true. They could sound like Henry Cavill but actually look like a real fuggly, like creepy John."

Becky looked at Clarissa with a confused expression. "What the hell is a fugly?"

Hayley grinned. "I know that one. Freaking ugly."

Clarissa's phone rang again, and the girls instantly became quiet. She answered and put it on the loudspeaker.

"Line twenty-one. Beep."

"Hello, I'm Mistress Adele. What is your name?" Clarissa asked.

"Hello, my name is Alex," a masculine voice said quietly.

"Do you realize you have called the domination line?"

"I do, yes."

"Do you want to be my Submissive, Alex?"

Alex paused, leaving Clarissa wondering if he would speak or hang up. He hadn't said much, but she could hear the hesitation in his voice.

"I'm not sure, Mistress Adele," he answered again with hesitation.

Clarissa decided to go gently so as not to frighten him off.

"Are you looking for physical or fantasy domination or just to chat about what turns you on, Alex?" she asked gently in her sultry tone while shrugging at Becky and Hayley. Her best friends looked as unsure as she felt.

"I think I want fantasy, and I would like to tell you something, Mistress Adele," he told her, still sounding hesitant.

Clarissa didn't think it would be wise to go through all of her rules yet, especially as Alex didn't sound confident about what he wanted, but she did want to set some boundaries.

"I would love for you to tell me, but I have two rules, Alex," she told him a little more firmly. "You will address me by Mistress Adele at all times, and you will not come unless I give you permission. Do you understand, Alex?" She asked, half expecting him to hang up instantly.

"Yes, Mistress Adele, I do understand, and thank you," he said, sounding a little braver.

Becky and Hayley gave Clarissa a thumb's up, clearly just as surprised that he was still on the line.

"I'm so pleased to hear that, Alex, and I can't wait to hear what you have to tell me."

"Thank you, Mistress Adele. I've been doing some work on my house, and now I'm working on my living room."

"Are you doing it all yourself?"

"Yes, Mistress Adele, and I have all the tools too. I have a Senson workbench, a Senson hammer, and many other Senson tools," he said excitedly.

Both Hayley and Becky began mouthing, what the heck, at Clarissa, making her grin.

"It certainly sounds like you're well prepared and fully equipped, Alex. I'm very impressed," Clarissa purred.

"Thank you, Mistress Adele, but I have a confession," he said, excitement elevating his deep voice.

Clarissa raised her eyebrow at Becky and Hayley, making them grin.

"When I was tacking down my new carpet, I wondered how it would feel to have the tacks against my nipples, and I kept looking at my Senson workbench at the same time. The dark wooden top feels so good when I run my hands over it. I'm touching it right now, and the feel of it is making me hard."

It didn't take long for Clarissa to understand what Alex's fetish was. It was becoming evident that he sexually revered his Senson tools and fantasized about a bit of pain. Clarissa had an idea of how she could fulfill his need and fantasy. She turned to Becky and Hayley, who looked bewildered, giving them a wink and a grin.

"Alex, I want you to imagine that you're completely naked, standing against your Senson workbench, so you can feel the smooth, hard wood against your skin. Can you do that for me?" Clarissa asked.

Slightly heavier breathing and rustling sounds came from the loudspeaker. Clarissa had a feeling that Alex was busy getting naked.

"Yes, Mistress Adele."

She knew that using the Senson brand name was obviously important to her new submissive.

"Good, Alex. Now I want you to imagine that you're kneeling in front of your Senson workbench, placing your erect, hard nipples on the top of it, so they touch the smooth dark wood. Can you imagine that, Alex?"

"Oh yes, Mistress Adele, thank you," he said, clearly more turned on.

Not wanting him to get too excited too soon, Clarissa knew she had to try to control him so he could stay on the line longer.

"Just remember, Alex, you can't come unless I give you permission. And I don't want you stroking your big, hard cock unless I tell you. That will be your reward for being good. Do you understand?"

"Yes, Mistress Adele. I'm being good. I'm kneeling naked against my Senson workbench, and I'm resting my nipples against it. I can see the carpet tacks on top, and I'm wondering how it would feel to have them pressed against my nipples using my Senson hammer," he told her excitedly.

Movement caught Clarissa's eye, and when she turned, Becky and Hayley were positively cringing. Clarissa held in a giggle at her friend's reaction.

"I can hear how turned on you are, Alex. You're being so good, telling me your fantasies. I think I need to give you a little reward. You may slowly stroke your big, solid cock for five seconds, as I count. Are you ready, Alex?"

"Thank you, Mistress Adele. Yes, I'm ready."

"One...two...three...four...five...and stop."

Alex's panting grew stronger and louder.

"Good. Now I want you to close your eyes and imagine yourself picking up your Senson hammer in one hand and taking a carpet tack in the other, Alex."

"Mmm, yes, Mistress Adele."

Indistinct sounds of movement came through the phone, and Clarissa wondered what he was doing at his end.

"Imagine, Alex, that you're placing the carpet tack against your nipple, and you can feel its sharp end against your tender skin."

"Ahh, oh, Mistress Adele. Yes, it's so sharp. Mmm."

Clarissa looked to Becky and Hayley while quickly pressing mute. "Holy hell, do you think he's actually doing it or pretending?"

Both of her friends looked as shocked as she was.

"I don't know, but you did tell the dude to imagine, not do it for real," Hayley said with brows raised in astonishment.

Becky shook her head in disbelief, "Whatever he does in the comfort of his own home has nothing to do with you, honey."

Clarissa had to say something quickly, and she knew what he wanted to hear. "You're doing fantastic, Alex. I'm so pleased with you." She told him in a slow, sexy manner. "Now, I want you to imagine that you're resting your Senson Hammer against the carpet tack, so you can feel the tack's sharpness on your hard nipple, and the smooth wood of your Senson workbench underneath."

Louder moaning sounded, then panting, and suddenly loud bangs rang out, and he cried out loudly. Clarissa immediately clicked mute.

"Bloody hell, did he just do that for real?" She squeaked, looking at her best friends to confirm her worst fear.

"It sounded real, but who the hell knows? You are always doing sound effects," Hayley said. She was always the voice of reason, and Clarissa hoped she was right.

Becky removed her hands from her shocked face, her whole body still tense from cringing. "I can't imagine him doing that for real. Anyway, he was the one who told you he just wanted fantasy, and you haven't told him to hammer his nips," she reasoned while in disbelief.

Clarissa took a deep breath and clicked off mute. She knew she had to be professional and carry on.

"How did that feel, Alex?" She asked, trying not to sound panicked as a cold sweat formed on her forehead.

Alex was panting heavily. "Oh, it felt so good, Mistress Adele."

"I'm glad, Alex, and you've been so good. I'll allow you to stroke your throbbing cock for another five seconds, but slowly. Are you ready, Alex?"

"Yes, Mistress Adele."

He was breathing so heavily; Clarissa was starting to hope that he would come and hang up. The thought of him using the hammer and carpet tack for real was making her own nipples tingle, and not in a pleasant way. She could understand why Becky and Hayley were cringing.

Clarissa began to count. "One...two...three...four...five...and stop, Alex."

She could hear from his breathing that he was indeed getting close.

"Alex, I want you to imagine doing the same thing to your other nipple. Imagine picking up another sharp carpet tack and holding it against your hard, tingling nipple. Then imagine gripping your

Senson hammer tight in your strong hand, feeling the smooth wooden handle, and pressing its cold metal head again the tack."

"Argh!" Alex cried down the phone as loud banging rang out.

Suddenly the line went dead, and Clarissa released the breath she didn't realize she was holding. She quickly logged out to give herself a few minutes to recover.

"Holy hell, that was unnerving," she exclaimed to her shocked friends.

"I've got to be honest; the second time definitely sounded real," Hayley admitted.

Becky had both hands over her boobs, "I think my nipples are cringing."

Clarissa and Hayley both started to laugh. Becky's expression and her tensed body were precisely how they felt about Alex's call.

"Every time I see my hubby using his hammer or work bench, I'm going to think of that call," Hayley admitted, "I used to enjoy seeing my man at work; now that dude has ruined it for me."

It was a relief for Clarissa to laugh with the girls after such a tense call. She quickly glanced at her watch, realizing that Alex had been on for the entire half-hour.

"Damn, I didn't realize I kept him going for the full time," she said, feeling proud of herself. "I'm going to do another hour and then finish for the night, so we can have a nightcap before you have to go home," she told them.

Hayley nodded with a smile.

"Sounds good to me," Becky grinned, "I'm getting some great notes from your calls, apart from the last one." She giggled.

Clarissa took two more calls which were quick and easy, Busty Babes and Sporty Girls, which made her relax. When she answered the third call, she heard the familiar recording.

"Line twenty-one. Beep."

Immediately she switched to her domination persona.

"Hello, I am Mistress Adele. Who is this?"

"Hello, Mistress Adele, it's Alex again," the familiar voice said breathlessly.

Clarissa, Becky, and Hayley couldn't believe their ears. After what had previously happened, none of them expected him to call back in. Becky choked on her drink and was sputtering as quietly as she could, while Hayley covered her mouth to stop herself from swearing.

Taking a deep breath, Clarissa composed herself. "I'm so glad you called back, Alex. I think you're my new favorite. How are you feeling right now?" She asked.

"I'm so turned on, Mistress Adele. My cock is throbbing like crazy, and my nipples are stinging bad, but it feels so good."

"It makes me happy to hear that you're so turned on, Alex. It's been a little while since our chat earlier, so tell me what you're doing right now," she urged.

"I'm still nailed to my Senson workbench, Mistress," he said, breathing as heavy as if he had been running.

Clarissa nearly choked. She quickly clicked mute.

"Bloody hell, not only did he do it for real, he's still nailed the bloody thing."

She ran her hands over her face, quickly thinking of what to say next. She didn't dare look at Becky and Hayley for fear that they would make her laugh. Clarissa realized something; Alex hadn't called her by her full name. He seemed too switched on to make that mistake, which meant only one thing. He wanted to be punished.

She unclicked mute.

"Alex, you do realize you didn't address me by my full name. That means you've been bad, and I need to punish you. Are you really to be punished?"

"Mmmm, yes, Mistress Adele. I deserve it."

"Yes, you do deserve it," she told him sternly, "You will spank your hard, throbbing cock five times as I count, Alex. Are you ready?"

"Yes, Mistress Adele," he whispered in anticipation.

With each count, Clarissa and her friends could hear him carry out the spanking, his breathing becoming more rapid and his moans deepening.

"Now you are behaving yourself; I give you permission to come when ready," she told him.

"Oh, thank you, Mistress Adele."

Clarissa could hear the gratitude in his voice. She teased him, asking him to imagine her flicking his nailed nipples while knowing he was doing it to himself. She punished him every time he accidentally forgot to use her full name, and he enjoyed every minute. For over twenty minutes, Clarissa teased him with pleasure and pain until, finally; he found his release. Clarissa could hear his heavy panting, and she waited for the phone call to end.

"Thank you, Mistress Adele," he said, between laboured breaths, "Can I call you again soon?"

Clarissa was shocked that he asked but proud of herself for gaining another new submissive.

"Of course, Alex. I would love to do this again, especially as you're now my favorite," she told him, boosting his ego. "I want you to clean and wound dress your nipples, okay?"

"I will. Thank you."

Click, the line went dead.

Clarissa quickly logged out of the chat line system and turned to her friends.

"Thank god he didn't want to nail anything else to his Senson workbench!" she declared.

All three friends burst into laughter, more out of relief than humor.

"I wonder how he found his fetish?" Becky pondered aloud with a puzzled look.

Clarissa shook her head. "Who knows, but he's obviously into it big time."

"Guys are so weird," Hayley told them, "I once walked into my bathroom—only to find Adam in the shower—using the skin of his ball sack to catch water. He wanted to see how much his ball sack would carry, apparently."

That was it. All three of them exploded into laughter again.

—x—

Clarissa's first week at her new job sped by in a blur, and her second week was going well. It was already Wednesday, and she was sitting at her kitchen table with a cup of tea and her laptop. Clarissa had a nice routine going, long and soothing hot showers first thing, chatting with her boys over breakfast, then walking them to school. She was even hoping to get the puppy they longed for; now she was working from home and would have time to train and walk it.

As soon as Clarissa returned from the school run, she would spend an hour cleaning, doing laundry, and having tea in peace and quiet before doing a shift on the chat line. It was also her chance to catch up on her messages and emails.

Clarissa sipped her tea and checked her phone for any new messages. Some were from Becky and Hayley, and two were from ex-boss, John. As soon as she saw John's messages, her heart started to pound in her chest. Clarissa knew John had been told not to contact her again. She opened the first message hesitantly.

I told you I was sorry, bitch. You just got me fucking fired!

Clarissa was already shocked that he messaged her. She was even more shocked that he would message her after being fired. She hesitated to open his other message but decided she had to.

I'll get you back when you least expect it, you fucking bitch!

As Clarissa read the message, her blood ran cold. She thought Sergeant Jameson was right when she said most men like John were cowards. However, after reading his messages, she now wondered if he was dangerous or if it was an empty threat. Clarissa quickly shared the messages with Hayley. She knew that Hayley would pass them on to Sergeant Jameson if needed. As Clarissa held her mobile phone in her hand, it began to shake. Clarissa had no clue if her ex-boss was capable of being violent and irrational. She didn't want to find out.

Clarissa checked her messages from her best friends hoping to cheer herself up. The first was a message from Becky.

Martin heard through the pub grapevine that your ex-asshole got badly done over by his recent girlfriend. She took all his money, and he's fallen out with his parents. NO, CANCER scare. He lied to you. What a tosser!

To say that Clarissa was reeling was an understatement. She went from freaking out to furious in seconds. "That son of a bitch!"

Clarissa shouted, slamming her cup of tea on her kitchen table. Tea splashed everywhere, but she was too angry to care. Never in a million years did she think Nigel would be capable of such low-life deceit. To think that her ex-asshole would use a fake cancer scare to try and get her back was the final straw. She vowed there and then that she would cut him from their lives, her and her boys.

Clarissa replied to Becky with still shaking hands.

Unbelievable!! I'm done. Cutting him off permanently! What a total low life!

Chapter 10

Clarissa didn't know whether to open Hayley's message or not, in case it was even more bad news. She didn't think she could take anymore. Instead, she decided to clean up the mess she had made with her tea, make herself a fresh one, and steady her frayed nerves before daring to look.

By the time Clarissa sat down with her fresh cup of tea she was feeling better—still pissed off—but better. She opened the waiting message from Hayley and noticed a new one.

Your old company is trying to do damage control, and they have sacked creepy John. I think they will offer you a settlement to keep you quiet because they won't want any bad press. If they contact you, don't speak to them. Just refer them to me, okay. XX

Clarissa opened the new message from Hayley.

I'm going to hang that creepy bastard by his financial balls! Don't reply—but don't block his number—it's all fuel for your case. I'll request a restraining order so he can't come near you. Keep smiling, honey. Xxx

Hayley was always so controlled and calm that Clarissa envied her. Clarissa felt like her life was spinning out of control, and it wasn't even her fault. *'Fricking men.'* She sipped her fresh tea, determined not to let John and Nigel ruin everything she was trying to accomplish.

Ping. Another message from Becky came through. Clarissa clicked to open it.

Are you ok? Do you want me to come over during my lunch break?

Clarissa's heart felt so full of love and gratitude towards her best friends; they always had her back.

Sorry, Becky. I've had a couple of bad messages from John, and I was still reeling from them when I read your message about asshole. I'll forward them to you. I'm ok, just feeling shaken. Hayley's got it covered. No need to ruin your lunch. Xxx

After clicking send, Clarissa forwarded John's messages to Becky and then began to prepare for another shift on the chat line. She knew that within a couple of minutes of working, she would be cool, calm, and collected again like Hayley, and the distraction would do her good.

—x—

Clarissa had a brilliant shift that afternoon, and after taking Luke and Matthew for ice cream and a play at the local park after school, she began to feel happier again. Luke and Matthew could barely keep their eyes open when they got home.

As Clarissa was coming downstairs from putting her boys to bed, she heard a light tap on her front door. Instantly her pulse began to race as John's messages flashed in her mind. Usually, she wouldn't hesitate to open her front door, especially as she lived in a reasonably safe area. Another tap, then a familiar voice came through her letterbox.

"Clarissa, it's me, Becky. Let me in; I'm freezing my nips off!"

Hearing Becky's voice and sense of humor immediately made Clarissa smile. Relief swept through her. Rushing down the rest of the stairs, she quickly opened her front door to let in her best friend. The moment the door opened, Becky rushed towards her, giving her a huge and prolonged hug. Clarissa didn't realize how much she needed a hug until Becky's arms were wrapped tightly around her curvy frame.

"You didn't need to come over, Becky. I'm okay, honestly."

Becky released her hold and took a step back, looking at Clarissa with compassion written all over her face.

"I'm damn sure that if I'd received those text messages today, I'd be in desperate need of a hug and a friendly face. So, here I am," Becky declared, "Now, let's have a Bailey's and bitch about the bastards."

Clarissa led Becky to her kitchen with a grin on her face. A friendly chat and a Bailey's were definitely going to chill her out.

"I'm sorry about being the bearer of bad news today, honey," Becky said as they sat down at Clarissa's kitchen table. "But I thought you should know straight away."

"I appreciate it; I really do," Clarissa told her honestly, "I was beginning to feel guilty for throwing him out after he told me."

Becky's face was full of empathy and understanding. "I know, which is why I was determined to find out for you, so we could be sure."

"Did Martin say anything else?"

"Only that Nigel was pretty serious about this latest girl. He even added her to his bank account and mortgage. Apparently, she shagged a few of his friends behind his back, emptied their joint account, and kicked him out when he found out about her cheating on him." Becky laughed.

Clarissa decided that if she ever met Karma in person, she would snog her face off in gratitude. "That's seriously the best news ever. It's about time that git got a taste of his own medicine!"

"That's not all." Becky grinned "Apparently, Nigel went home crying to his parents, and they went nuts on him. They told him it was what he deserved for treating you and his sons so badly. When he asked to move back in, they told him that he'd made multiple beds, so go lie in one of them."

The news was too good to be true for Clarissa. She laughed so hard, she had to hold her sides as a stitch was forming.

"So, where is he now?" She managed to ask.

Becky smirked. "Well, he didn't treat any of his other girlfriends well either, so not one of them wanted to know when they heard his sob story. So, he's couch surfing at the moment because he's still penniless right now. Most of his friends don't want to know either because he's tried to shag most of their ladies."

"I wonder how long the last of his friends will let him do that. I doubt they'll trust him near their wives and girlfriends, knowing his history."

"Who knows." Becky shrugged. "Are you worried about the messages from creepy John?"

Clarissa wasn't sure how to answer. She didn't want Becky worrying about the bastard too.

"I don't know what to think or feel at this point," she said candidly. "Sergeant Jameson told me guys like him are usually cowards, but his messages seem threatening. I don't know him well enough to know what he's capable of or what his mental state is like."

"Hayley told me she would get a restraining order on the

bastard. Let's hope it scares him into reality," Becky told her. "Anyway, let's talk about something positive. Have you had your first pay statement yet?"

Clarissa could have kicked herself. She had forgotten entirely about getting her first pay statement from the phone sex chat line, especially as she was used to being paid monthly.

"Becky, I've been so knocked sideways by Nigel and John, I forgot all about it," she confessed.

"Well, what are you waiting for? Have a look now," Becky urged.

Needing some good news, Clarissa opened her laptop and emails. Sure enough, there was an email from Castle Communications, she opened it immediately. Clarissa's eyes scanned down the email until she reached two PDF files at the bottom. The first was a statement of her calls, and the other was her first-ever payslip for the chat line. Clarissa slid her laptop to a better angle so Becky could see too.

Nervously, Clarissa opened the statement. She couldn't believe the number of calls she had taken, but then again, she had worked, on average, over nine hours a day. The statement not only told Clarissa how many calls she had taken but also her average call durations per line, and her average compared to the other employees. Clarissa was thrilled to see that she was in the top ten for her calls.

"Bloody hell, woman, your stats are fantastic. No wonder your new boss, Michelle, is so happy," Becky told her with a huge grin.

Clarissa was positively beaming as she closed the pdf file and opened her payslip. The moment Clarissa and Becky saw how much she had earned for her first week's work, they both jumped up and began happy dancing around the kitchen. Clarissa was so happy she began twerking while shouting, whoop, whoop.

"That payslip is far better than my old ones," Clarissa said as they finally sat back down, still grinning.

Becky nodded. "It's more than Martin's on a week, that's for sure! You're definitely going to be much better off, especially as you're not paying your childminder or having to drive to and from work anymore. I'm so happy for you, Clarissa. Everything is going to work out for you."

After Becky left, Clarissa logged herself onto the chat line, feeling even more motivated now she knew what she could earn. Everything was feeling like second nature now, and most of the time, she didn't even have to look at her list of chat line services. Her regulars were beginning to build, and some of them would even call for a quick chat just to catch up and tell her how they were doing. Clarissa even had a few submissive's who would call her to let her know that they were behaving and completing the tasks she had set them, such as wearing women's lingerie to work or wearing nipple clamps and a cock ring while at home, so they would think of her when they got hard.

Clarissa soon discovered that for most submissive's, it was a way of life for them. Most didn't want to be dominated for just half an hour to an hour. They wanted to be dominated all the time, and by Clarissa giving them tasks and punishments in between calls, she was able to offer what they needed. It was working out really well. Not only were they calling to update her on how they had done with their tasks and punishments, but then they would have a domination session with her, and then she would give them new tasks and punishments. Clarissa felt like she and her submissive's were in a win-win-win situation.

After a few hours of working, Clarissa received an unusual call on the fetish line. She answered in her domination mode.

"Hello, I'm Mistress Adele. Who's this?" she asked sultrily.

"Hi Mistress Adele, I'm Tasha," a very deep, masculine voice said quietly.

"Hello, Tasha," she said in a gentler voice, "are you looking to please me tonight?"

"Yes, I am a mistress. I want to sing and dance for you."

Clarissa was gobsmacked and wasn't sure what to say to her new caller. She hadn't had a caller who wanted to entertain her before.

"I would love for you to sing and dance for me, Tasha," she said genuinely, "but first, I would love to know what you look like and what you're wearing, so I can picture you in my mind as you perform."

An excited squeal came through Clarissa's phone. "I'm six foot one, Mistress Adele, and I have a smooth and toned body. My legs are long and slender, and I've been told that I have a cute bum. My eyes are deep brown, I have high cheekbones and full kissable lips, Mistress," Tasha told her.

Clarissa thought Tasha sounded stunning, and she loved how Tasha described herself, full of confidence.

"You sound absolutely stunning, Tasha. What are you wearing for your performance?"

"I'm wearing a shimmering pink leotard and matching tights, Mistress, with a light purple tutu and silver high heels," Tasha said proudly as she tapped her heels on her floor.

The mental image of Tasha's outfit made Clarissa smile, *'who doesn't want to dress up like a ballerina?'* She thought.

"Wow, your outfit sounds amazing, Tasha. And what song are you going to perform?" Clarissa asked, genuinely eager to find out.

"I'm going to sing the Spice Girls song, Wannabe, for you, Mistress Adele," Tasha said, her excitement clearly elevated, as was her deep voice.

"I honestly can't wait to hear you perform, Tasha. You may begin when you're ready."

Clarissa heard Tasha's phone switch to the loudspeaker, and then she heard her heeled footsteps. Suddenly the nineties song started booming through the phone, and Clarissa could hear Tasha's high-heels clip-clopping on a hard floor as she began to dance.

Tasha started to belt the song out in her deep masculine voice, "I tell you what I want, what I really, really want."

Clarissa was seriously impressed. She had never heard the song sung in a deep voice before, and Tasha was nailing it. She listened intently as her new caller sang and danced to a song that brought back memories for Clarissa. Both Becky and Hayley loved the song, and so did she.

When the song ended, Tasha picked up the phone again and took it off the loudspeaker. "Did you like it, Mistress Adele?" She asked nervously.

"I think you are fantastic, Tasha, and I loved your performance. You have a real talent," Clarissa told her honestly.

"Really, Mistress?" Tasha squealed excitedly. "Can I call you again soon with another performance?"

Tasha's joy had Clarissa smiling, and she knew she had given Tasha a real confidence boost.

"I would absolutely love to hear you perform again, Tasha!"

"Oh, thank you, Mistress Adele. Speak to you soon."

The line went dead, and Clarissa was still smiling. She was actually looking forward to Tasha's next call, and she wondered what song it would be next time. Clarissa knew that no other call that night was going to make her smile as Tasha's would.

—x—

Clarissa closed her front door. She couldn't believe her luck. It was a beautiful Saturday morning, and her ex-in-laws had just picked up Luke and Matthew. Her ex-mother-in-law, Sharon, had called the day before, asking if they could take them to the zoo and have them overnight. Clarissa's boys were super excited when she asked them if they wanted to go.

Clarissa wasn't sure if Sharon would mention her son and his recent behavior. Clarissa was certainly not going to bring it up when Sharon arrived, and she hoped her ex-mother-in-law wouldn't either. Clarissa didn't want to talk about the asshole, especially to his mum. Luckily, Sharon didn't mention her son, and as Clarissa locked her front door, she breathed a sigh of relief.

With a rare free weekend, Clarissa messaged Hayley and Becky to ask them if they fancied a night out. As luck would have it, their husbands, Martin and Adam, had been out the night before playing in a darts contest at their local pub, The Red Lion, so Clarissa's best friends jumped at the chance of a girl's night.

After many messages back and forth, they decided that they would go dancing, something that all three of them loved to do. Martin and Adam were not keen dancers, so if Hayley and Becky could go dancing without them, they would. Clarissa's ex-asshole had been a fantastic dancer, which was probably why he had no problem attracting women on his supposed boy's nights out. *'Bast-ard!'*

Clarissa's plan was to get some housework done, shoot to her favorite lingerie shop, and work some hours on the chat line before getting ready to go out.

—x—

Within a couple of hours, Clarissa's housework was done, and she was on her way to Luscious Lingerie, which was just on the outskirts of Winchester town center. It was a bit of a trek, but it was the only place Clarissa knew of where they made and sold fairly pretty bras for girls with huge boobs. Her mum had been taking her there for years, and Clarissa knew the owner, Ann, very well. Her mum, Mary, and Ann were old friends.

Ann looked like a classy older lady, but the stories about her youth often had Clarissa blushing. Clarissa didn't know whether Ann would get her blushing this time after so many hours on the sex chat line. She was starting to think that she had heard it all now and nothing could shock her.

When Clarissa entered Luscious Lingerie, it was a lot busier than usual. Clarissa wasn't surprised. Every now and again, Ann would hold a large sale to clear her old stock, and for an older lady, she did well promoting on social media. Clarissa always loved her posts, especially when she modelled her products. Ann was fabulous and confident. Clarissa wanted to be like Ann when she was older.

Ann waved to Clarissa as soon as she entered the store, then she pointed Clarissa to the special big boobs section, as she called it. Clarissa never bothered looking at anything else in the shop; there was no point. Everything else in the shop would barely cover her nipples.

Buying new bras was a treat for Clarissa. What little spare money she had, was usually spent on Luke and Matthew, especially since Nigel wasn't helping to provide for them. Clarissa hadn't been able to treat herself to new lingerie since she had kicked the asshole out.

After finding a lovely couple of over-the-shoulder-boulder-holder bras in her size that looked quite pretty, Clarissa searched for some cute thongs to go with them. Clarissa always felt like a bit of a weirdo buying lingerie, dresses, or tops because her top half was a size eighteen due to the size of her boobs, but her lower half was a curvy size fourteen. Clarissa managed to find a few thongs to match her bras, so she headed to the sales counter feeling pleased with herself.

A few people were waiting to be served, so Clarissa waited in line. After a few minutes in the queue, she felt like she was being watched. With a quickening pulse, she looked around the shop. Clarissa couldn't see anyone staring at her, but she was almost expecting creepy John to pop out from one of the clothes rails shouting, "I'll get you bitch!"

Before long, it was Clarissa's turn to be served, and Ann was all smiles and banter as usual, even though her small shop was busy. Ann always had time for her loyal customers, and Clarissa appreciated it.

"I haven't seen you in ages. How are you, dear?" Ann said with a beautiful smile.

Clarissa gave Ann her brightest smile. "I'm great, thanks, Ann. I finally quit my office job, and now I'm working from home, I'm on more money, and I'm getting to spend more time with Luke and Matthew."

Ann positively beamed at Clarissa, and she knew Ann was thrilled for her. Clarissa's mum had always kept in touch with Ann, so Clarissa was well aware that Ann knew everything about her life. That is apart from her new job. Clarissa hadn't told her parents yet, but she knew that the news would reach them within days.

"That's wonderful news, Clarissa. What's your new job?"

Clarissa was abruptly unsure of what to say. She couldn't exactly blurt out that she was working on a phone sex chat line in a busy shop with many ears listening. "I'm now doing telephone sales," she answered, feeling like a liar, even though it was close to the truth. Sort of.

"Well, I am so happy for...." Ann started to say but was rudely interrupted by a male voice.

"Do you have anyone else that can serve?" A very masculine voice asked sharply.

'So fricking rude!' Clarissa thought while turning to see who had spoken.

The man Clarissa found herself glaring at was a tall and extremely handsome man of around six foot six. He was dressed in an expensive shirt and elegant trousers. And with his chiselled looks, wired-framed glasses—and muscles threatening to burst from his tight shirt—he was precisely the kind of sexy, hot nerd Clarissa was attracted to. However, his rudeness, interrupting Ann while she was talking, pissed Clarissa off. She was no longer in the mood to tolerate bad behavior from men, especially after the last couple of weeks.

Clarissa's eyes connected with his, and she stared him down.

"You will wait your turn, do you understand?" she commanded firmly, daring him to disobey her with her glare.

She waited for him to answer, and so was everyone else nearby, but she stood her ground and stared back.

He blinked at her. Then, unexpectedly the hot stranger lowered his eyes, and as he did so, Clarissa thought she heard him say quietly, "Yes, Mistress."

Stunned, Clarissa wondered if she had heard what she thought she heard. *'Maybe too many domination calls have got me hearing things,'* she thought.

Beginning to feel embarrassed with thoughts of the chat line and domination, she quickly spun around and turned her attention back to Ann and her lingerie purchase.

"I'll tell you more about my new job next time I see you, Ann. Thank you ever so much. It was great to see you," Clarissa said with a smile.

Ann smiled, rang up the lingerie through her till, and handed Clarissa her purchase.

"I hope to see you soon. Give my love to your gorgeous little boys for me."

"Thank you, Ann. I will. Bye."

Clarissa took her shopping bag and left.

When Clarissa got home with her new lingerie, she was still thinking about the sexy, hot, nerdy guy and what he said under his breath. She still wasn't sure if she heard him right, and she was also feeling terrible for biting his head off. The last thing Clarissa wanted to do was to take the anger she felt for her ex-boss and ex-asshole and dish it out on a total stranger who didn't deserve it. *'I'm never going to see him again, and he was rude,'* she told herself, trying to alleviate the guilt she was feeling.

Chapter 11

It was early evening, and Clarissa was feeling great. After a brilliant shift on the chat line and a lovely goodnight phone call with her boys, who'd had a wonderful time at the zoo, she was ready to go dancing with her best friends.

Clarissa looked at herself in her bedroom mirror. She had chosen to wear her favorite deep-red bodice top with her knee-high black leather skirt and six-inch black heels. For the first time in a very long time, Clarissa felt sexy. She imagined that being able to make guys orgasm with just her voice would have a knock-on effect. And she definitely felt sexually powerful for a change. Clarissa slipped on her black jacket and headed downstairs, knowing that Becky and Hayley would be arriving soon.

After two glasses of white wine, Clarissa was feeling ready to party. Hayley and Becky arrived at seven pm on the dot, and they looked amazing.

"Wow, look at you, looking all sexy and hot, you kinky minx," Hayley said as she walked into Clarissa's kitchen. "I might snog you myself later after a few drinks."

Becky smirked. "Woman, you try and snog everyone when you have had a few drinks. Clarissa and I always end up being your supervisors."

"And that's why you're both my best friends." Hayley declared with a cheesy grin.

Clarissa giggled as she poured them a glass of wine before their taxi arrived to take them into town. She couldn't remember the last time she was so excited to go out with her best friends.

"How was your child-free day?" Becky asked.

Clarissa grinned. "It's been great. I got the housework done, bought myself some new lingerie, told off an extremely hot nerd guy in the shop, and had a brilliant shift on the chat line."

"Woah, back up a second, lady," Hayley declared. "What hot nerd guy?"

"Yes, what hot nerd?" Becky added, placing her hands on her hips.

Clarissa laughed as her best friends glared at her in anticipation. Putting them out of their misery, she explained exactly what happened in Luscious Lingerie and what she thought she heard the sexy stranger say. Clarissa also confessed that she might have domination on the brain and could have possibly imagined it.

"I've got to be honest; you are oozing confidence since you started on the chat line," Becky told her happily, "I think your new job is doing you a world of good."

Hayley nodded profusely. "I agree. You've gone from a domestic goddess to a real kinky minx."

Clarissa laughed, shaking her head. "I don't know about that."

"You underestimate yourself," Becky told her. "You've found your inner goddess, and she's a hot, sexy little minx!"

A ping on Clarissa's phone let them know that their taxi had arrived. She looked at her phone to check.

"Our carriage has arrived, ladies; let's paint the town red, as they say."

All three girls danced their way out of Clarissa's house to the waiting taxi.

—x—

Once the best friends arrived in Winchester town center, they asked the driver to drop them at the Incognito cocktail bar. All three of them wanted to check out the bar's new look since it had been refurbished and try a couple of the new cocktails.

The cocktail bar was just starting to get busy when they arrived, and the venue looked amazing. The long walls were now a stylish bare brick, adorned with classy decor, and dark wooden tables were placed around the large room with matching chairs. Clarissa spotted a large and gorgeous ox blood-red Chesterfield sofa at the room's far end.

"I'll get the cocktails; you grab the sofa at the back before this place gets packed," she suggested.

Clarissa made her way to the bar to order the drinks as Becky and Hayley made their way to the other end of the room. By the time she had their drinks and headed towards them on the sofa, the bar was already filling up. Clarissa navigated her way to the couch, trying not to spill the drinks she'd only just paid for when someone touched her arm.

"Let me help you?" A familiar masculine voice asked.

Clarissa's eyes shot up to find stunning green eyes behind wire-framed glasses looking down at her. *'Oh my god, it's him.'* The cocktails nearly dropped from her hands. She opened her mouth to speak, but no sound came out.

"Here," he said, taking two of the glasses she was desperately trying to hold between her hands. "Lead the way."

In a state of shock and with legs like jelly, Clarissa walked towards her best friends, who were too busy to notice her coming their way with a hot and sexy stranger.

When Clarissa reached her friends, she put down the cocktail and turned to the hot, muscular man.

"Thank you for your help," she said politely, finally finding her voice. "And I'm sorry for snapping at you in the shop today. I've had a lot going on, and I shouldn't have taken it out on you," she told him sincerely while feeling guilty again.

The smile he gave her had her feeling like she was melting into the floor.

"No apology needed. I was having a shitty day myself and was rude. I shouldn't have interrupted you. I owe you an apology, and I am sorry," he told her.

Clarissa couldn't stop staring at his soft and sensual lips as he spoke. She imagined herself kissing them as his hands ran over her body. Her cheeks began to blush at the thought.

"I'll let you get back to your friends," he said as he placed the other two drinks on the table next to the sofa. He turned back to face her, giving Clarissa another sexy smile. "I'm Tobias Ellis, by the way." He held out his hand.

Clarissa took his hand and swallowed. "I'm Clarissa Darcy; it's nice to meet you," she said, almost stuttering.

Tobias smiled again and headed to the bar and his waiting friends. She watched him walk away while admiring his sexy ass.

"Holy shit. Who the hell was that?" Hayley asked with eyes nearly popping out of her head as Clarissa sat down beside her, still blushing profusely.

"That was the hot nerdy guy from Luscious Lingerie that I told you about."

Becky was practically panting, "He's the sexy dude you told us about?"

"Yep."

"The hot nerd you told off?"

"Yep."

Clarissa reached for her drink, still feeling like she was way too hot after her second unexpected encounter with the hottest guy she had met in a long time.

"I don't want to give you another hot flash, but he's still checking you out," Hayley told her as she took another gulp of her cocktail.

Sure enough, when Clarissa peered over her glass, he was watching her intently, with what looked like desire written all over his face.

"Damn, look at the way he's watching you. It's like you're the ice cream, and he wants a lick."

Clarissa nearly sprayed her cocktail all over the place.

"Seriously, woman, you can't say something like that while I'm drinking!"

In seconds, the girls were in fits, not caring who was watching or listening.

"This is our girl's night. No men are allowed tonight. We've got dancing to do," Clarissa declared while holding up her glass, "Cheers, besties."

Hayley and Becky clinked glasses, toasting each other and their friendship.

After a couple more cocktails, the girls decided to make their way to the Vodka Nightclub with the hopes of getting in. It was still pretty early, so they knew their chances were good.

Sure enough, on arrival at the nightclub, there was only a minimal queue to get in. Within half an hour, they were already dancing the night away. Clarissa did indeed feel like a hot minx on the dance floor. Her confidence was high, and her worries were temporarily forgotten. She even managed to keep her high heels on all night, which was quite a miracle.

—x—

It was two in the morning when the pre-booked taxi dropped Hayley, Becky, and Clarissa back at her modest home. All three were drunk on cocktails and dancing. They held each other up while Clarissa tried to find the keyhole on her front door. When they finally got in, they were already in a fit of giggles.

"I'll get us some glasses of water. I don't want a hangover in the morning," Clarissa declared as she removed her heels from her aching feet, flinging them on the floor.

"I'm not sure I can keep my eyes open long enough to drink one," Becky said through a giant yawn. "This is the latest I've been up in a while, and I'm shattered."

By the time Clarissa returned from the kitchen with the glasses of water, Hayley had already stripped down to her bra and knickers and was already snoring on the sofa, covered with Matthew's blanket. Becky had fallen asleep sideways across Clarissa's armchair, with her head back and her mouth open, making her look like she was catching flies.

Clarissa gently moved Becky to a better position, covering her with Luke's blanket, and after putting their glasses of water where they could find them, she went up to bed, hoping to dream of the hot and sexy Tobias.

—x—

When Clarissa got up the next morning, she found Becky and Hayley already awake, drinking coffee at her kitchen table, looking a little worse for wear. She was grateful to have drunk water the night before.

"Good morning, my little rays of sunshine," she greeted as she walked into her kitchen and poured herself a coffee. "Do either of you want some toast or cereal?"

Hayley and Becky began to turn green at the mere mention of food, and silence followed.

"I'll take that as a no, then." Clarissa laughed as she took a seat. "What a fantastic night. I think that was our best girl's night out so far."

Hayley nodded, "It was brilliant, but I think my feet might need a while to recover before doing it again."

"Why on earth do we women insist on wearing heels to go dancing instead of comfy shoes that don't leave us with aching feet and blisters?" Becky wondered aloud.

"Because we all think that guys find us more attractive when we're dancing on the balls of our feet," Hayley laughed. "And heels make us feel hot and sexy."

Becky slid Clarissa's phone to her across the kitchen table. "Your phone has been blowing up this morning, honey."

Clarissa couldn't understand why. She picked up her phone to check it. A message from her mum asking her about her new job made it clear that she'd been in touch with Ann at Luscious Lingerie. It was one of the downsides of having a trendy mum who used apps to keep in touch with friends.

"Looks like I'll be telling my mum about my new job today," she told the girls with a smirk.

"Your mum's so bloody cool. She'd probably work alongside you for the callers who need an agony aunt if she were here." Hayley laughed.

Clarissa grinned, knowing it was a true statement. She glanced back at her phone messages. Her blood ran cold. There was another message from John.

And so it begins, bitch!

Clarissa couldn't believe he had messaged her again. Her face reflected her horror.

"Are you okay, honey?" Becky asked, clearly worried.

"It's another message from John."

Hayley grabbed Clarissa's phone, instantly pissed off. She read the message aloud.

"What a bloody creep," Becky declared, just as pissed off as Hayley, "and what the hell does that mean, so it begins?"

Clarissa shook her head, "I've no idea, but it sounds ominous. Do you think he's got the balls to do something nasty?" She asked Hayley.

Hayley shook her head, "I honestly don't know, but maybe that's why his other victims were keen to drop their charges. I'm going to call Sergeant Jameson later and let her know. Send me the message too, so I can add it to your file."

Clarissa forwarded John's message to Hayley and took a gulp of her coffee. Her mouth suddenly felt drier than a surfer's sandy butt.

Just as Clarissa was about to put her phone down, a notification from her social media popped up on her screen. She didn't have many friends on her account as she liked to keep her private life private, especially as Nigel would get his friends to check out what she was doing.

"That's odd. I've got a notification on my social media account," she told the girls.

"I wonder if that's what John was referring to. Maybe he's hacked your account," Becky offered.

Clarissa opened her phone again and clicked on the notifycation, but it wasn't a hacker warning; it was a friend request from T.

Ellis. It took her a minute to recognize the name.

"I think it's a friend request from Tobias, the sexy nerdy guy from last night," she squeaked.

Hayley peered over to look. "Well, don't just sit there, woman; get out your laptop so we can all have a look."

Within a couple of minutes, Clarissa had her laptop open and the notification on her screen; she clicked to open it. Sure enough, there was Tobias's profile picture, and he was just as hot as he was in person.

As Clarissa looked at his headshot, it was as if his piercing green eyes were looking into her soul.

"I don't need a man in my life right now," she said, exasperated.

Hayley and Becky wanted to slap Clarissa for being silly.

"Are you kidding me right now, woman?" Hayley demanded. "Sexy, hot guys who seem decent don't come along very often, and you're talking about ignoring him!"

"Hayley's right. At least let us help you check Tobias out before you dismiss him. He might be the Mr. Right, you deserve," Becky added.

Clarissa knew her friends were right. She hadn't met many men she was attracted to whose personalities were as nice as their looks. She knew looks weren't everything, but Clarissa still felt you had to have a good physical attraction in a relationship. After all, everyone wanted to feel wanted and needed. It was human nature to want to be desired.

"Okay, okay." She relented. "Let's check out Tobias's profile."

With a couple of clicks, the girls looked at all of Tobias's posts and information. They were shocked to discover that not only was he hot as hell, but he was clever too. From what they saw on Tobias's information, he was a successful app developer and freelance software program developer with his own successful company called Destination Unknown Technologies.

"He looks very familiar, you know," Hayley told them.

"Of course, he does. You saw him last night." Becky laughed.

Hayley scowled and picked up her phone. "No, I mean, I think I've met him before. I'm going to look him up on the search engine," Hayley said as Becky clicked on his photos.

It became apparent to Clarissa that not only was Tobias physically active outdoors, but he was also very social. He also loved spending time with his family and the family golden retriever called Chester. The other thing that struck Clarissa like a bolt of lightning was that no matter what Tobias was wearing, he made everything look good, from smart trousers and shirts to grey sweatpants and t-shirts. Clarissa was suddenly feeling quite flushed.

"Well, bloody hell. Not only is the guy legit, but he also does a lot of charity work for sick kids," Hayley told them, "It says on this website that he lost his little sister to childhood cancer when she was only ten years old."

"Wow, not only is he hot as hell, but he's a bloody saint," Becky declared, "I think you should marry him and have his babies."

Clarissa laughed at her friend's sudden enthusiasm. "I think I should just accept his friend request and see what happens first," she said as she rolled her eyes.

Clarissa accepted his online friend request with one click, and a message came through in seconds. Clarissa looked at her best friends in surprise.

"Don't leave us hanging; open the bloody message," Hayley urged excitedly.

Becky nodded profusely while pointing to Clarissa's screen.

Grinning at her friends, Clarissa opened her first message from

Tobias.

Hi Clarissa, I hope you don't mind me reaching out. I can't stop thinking about you, especially after seeing you at the cocktail bar last night. Twice in one day felt like fate, and you blew my mind in the lingerie shop. I hope you had a great night with your girlfriends.
Tobias. X

A huge smile spread across Clarissa's face.

"Wow, he really has got the hots for you," Hayley told her.

"Agreed." Becky grinned. "I love the fact that he cares whether you had a good night or not. Your ex-asshole wouldn't have given two shits if you had a good time."

Clarissa knew that Becky was right. Nigel had only cared whether he had a good time. Sipping her coffee, Clarissa took a moment to decide what to message back. Then, she began typing.

Hi, Tobias. I don't mind at all. It's great to hear from you. Thank you for helping me with the drinks last night; it was appreciated. You're quite the gentleman. We had a great night, although our feet are aching from all the dancing, lol.

Clarissa didn't know what to say about her blowing his mind. She quickly re-read her message.

"What do you think?" She asked Hayley and Becky.

"It's good," Hayley said.

"Send it," Becky urged, "it's friendly and fun."

With another click, Clarissa sent her reply. She nervously bit down on her bottom lip, wondering if he was waiting for her message.

Becky and Hayley stared at her laptop screen as if they could use their sheer will to make Tobias reply.

Ping. Another message came through. Clarissa's heart began to flutter in her chest. She opened it immediately.

I'm glad you had fun last night. Maybe I could give you a long slow foot rub and then take you out for lunch?

Becky and Hayley squealed with excitement, like two teenage girls meeting their pop idol in person. Clarissa re-read Tobias's message three times, letting his words sink in.

"Bloody hell. I think you've found the perfect man," Hayley declared, "Adam has never offered to rub my feet. I have to bribe him with a blow job or a back massage. Guess which one he picks?" She laughed.

Becky shook her head while laughing. "You should suggest a sixty-nine, then he could massage your feet while you're repaying the favor."

Clarissa and Hayley nearly choked on their coffee.

"At least you can get your hubby to do it. If I ask Martin for a foot rub, he starts retching, and my feet don't even smell bad," Becky told them.

"I've only just met him. I think it's too soon to go on a date, don't you?" Clarissa asked her best friends.

"I think you should strike while the iron's hot," Becky said with a cheesy grin.

Hayley reached over and took Clarissa's hand. "Honey, guys like Tobias don't stay single for very long—and let's face it—you could do with a seriously long sex marathon. It's been way too long," she said with a deadly serious face.

Clarissa burst into laughter. "A sex marathon? Aren't you getting ahead of yourself? He's only suggesting a foot rub and lunch."

"I say accept and see where the foot rub goes. With a bit of luck, you might not make it to lunch. Hopefully, he'll end up snacking on you instead," Becky said while wiggling her eyebrows.

The three girls were in fits of laughter, and Clarissa was struggling to breathe.

"I swear, you two are too much."

"Quickly message him back," Becky told her.

Clarissa looked at Tobias's message again. A foot rub seemed too intimate for strangers unless you were in a massage parlour, but she could do lunch.

I would love to have lunch. Just tell me when and where.
Clarissa typed.

Ping. Another reply.
I can pick you up. That way, you can have a glass of wine or two.
Tobias offered.

"Bloody hell, chivalry isn't dead after all," Hayley gushed. "Tell him okay and give him your address, woman."

Biting the bullet, Clarissa thanked Tobias and gave him her address.

Ping.
I can't wait to see you! I'll pick you up at noon if that's okay.

Clarissa suddenly felt nervous. She hadn't been on a date in a long time. In fact, she couldn't remember the last time.

Sounds great. I look forward to it.

Clarissa messaged back.

"There you go, the deed is done," she told her friends with a smile.

Hayley and Becky started clapping and grinning at her, clearly thrilled.

"You'd better let us know how it goes when you get back!" Hayley demanded while Becky nodded in agreement. "In the meantime, I'm going to try and figure out how I know his face."

Clarissa held up her hands, "I will, I promise."

Becky stood up, placing her hands on her hips, "Well, we had better go, so you can start getting ready."

"Yes, go pamper yourself," Hayley ordered with a Cheshire cat grin.

Chapter 12

Clarissa started running a bath as her best friends were leaving.

"Bye honey, have a good time," Hayley called out from the hallway.

"Love you both. I'll message you later."

She heard the front door close and began to strip for her hot bubble bath.

A strange noise from downstairs stopped her in her tracks. Clarissa wasn't sure, but it sounded like metal hinges scraping.

"Clarissa, you need to come and see this!" Hayley shouted through the letterbox.

The urgent tone of Hayley's voice had Clarissa quickly turning off her bath taps and putting her pj's back on. She rushed downstairs and opened her front door to find Hayley and Becky standing next to her old Mini, which now had the words, Coming for you BITCH, etched deeply along its side.

Clarissa's whole body began to tremble, and her blood ran cold.

"He knows where I live," Clarissa whispered, tears springing in her eyes. Her body began to shake.

Hayley was already on the phone with the police demanding that they come straight away to Clarissa's address. The moment Becky saw her tears, she threw her arms around Clarissa, hugging her tightly.

"Let's get you a strong cup of tea and let badass Hayley deal with the police. She's already taken pictures," Becky told her.

"I don't think my insurance will cover what he's done," Clarissa sobbed, "I'll have to drive around with that on my car."

Becky stroked her back to comfort her, "Don't worry about that right now, honey. We'll sort it out, I'm sure."

Clarissa let Becky lead her to the kitchen, and she sat at her kitchen table with her head in her shaking hands. She couldn't believe the shit that was happening to her, just from defending herself and quitting the job she hated. Clarissa wondered what else John was capable of, and how far he went to get his previous victims to drop their charges. Her ex-boss was clearly not the coward Sergeant Jameson hoped he was.

Becky placed a strong cup of tea in front of her, and she took it in her hands, hoping the hot drink would somehow warm her up. Tears welled in her eyes, trickling down her cheeks. Walking back into the lounge, Becky returned with Luke's blanket, placing it over Clarissa's shoulders.

Clarissa sipped her tea in silence, not knowing what to say or do about what was happening, while Becky repeatedly tried to tell her that everything would be okay.

Moments later, Hayley stormed into the kitchen with a face like thunder. "If I ever get my hands on that sick bastard, I will rip his cock and balls off with my bare hands!" she raged. "The police are on the way, and Sergeant Jameson is on duty, so she's coming too."

Hayley took one look at Clarissa's tear-soaked face, and her own softened. "Please don't let that sick bastard scare you, honey. He's going to be locked up soon, and hopefully, they'll throw away the key."

"This is turning into a bloody nightmare," Clarissa told them, "And what about my boys? That slimy bastard knows where I live."

Hayley took Clarissa's hand. "I've told the police that, and Adam is on his way over. My mum will watch our kids while Adam and I install those door cameras on the front and back of your house. That way, Luke and Matthew won't know what's happening and get scared."

Clarissa was beyond grateful that her best friends were with her.

"I honestly can't imagine my life without you both," she told them with a sob.

Becky hugged her, and Hayley joined in, making it a group hug.

"Clarissa, you have always been there for us. This is what best friends are for," Becky told her warmly while gently squeezing her.

"I second that," Hayley said. She released her hold and stroked Clarissa's back affectionately. "I'm going to wait for the police and Sergeant Jameson to arrive, okay."

Clarissa nodded.

"I'll have a cuppa if you're making one, Becky," Hayley called out as she walked back outside.

Clarissa and Becky waited in the kitchen, with Becky trying to make small talk to calm Clarissa's nerves while she made Hayley's tea. Neither of them was checking the time, and both had completely forgotten about Clarissa's lunch date with Tobias.

That was until he walked into Clarissa's kitchen in all his sexy glory. Clarissa's mind went blank. She stared up at him with wet, red eyes.

"Are you okay, Clarissa?" Tobias asked with worry written across his handsome features. "Hayley's just told me what's going on."

All Clarissa could do was shake her head. She knew if she spoke, the tears would flow again, and Clarissa didn't want to cry in front of a man she hardly knew.

Before she knew what was happening—Tobias rushed forward—wrapping her in his strong muscular arms. That was it, Clarissa's floodgates opened, and she sobbed in his arms.

Becky didn't know whether to swoon or cry at the sight of Tobias caring for Clarissa like her ex-asshole Nigel never had. Instead, she decided to wait with Hayley outside and give Clarissa and Tobias some privacy.

Clarissa cried all her shock, frustration, and anger away on Tobias's shoulder. His thick arms made her feel safe and comforted. She could feel him stroking her neck softly underneath her messy bun.

As soon as Clarissa felt more under control, she raised her head, her gaze meeting his emerald eyes. Releasing Clarissa, Tobias raised his hands, brushing away her tears softly as she held his gaze. She couldn't remember Nigel ever touching her with such affection and care.

"I promise, I won't let that bastard hurt you or your boys," Tobias told her.

He said it so fervently that Clarissa instantly believed him, but she couldn't understand why he would be so protective.

"How do you know about my boys?"

Tobias smiled. "Your social media is full of pictures of you with them. I'm also best friends with Adam's older brother, so I've heard a lot about you over the years."

"Why would you want to protect me? You don't even know me."

"Clarissa, I feel like I've been waiting for you forever. When you turned, glared, and told me off in the lingerie shop, it was as if I was hit with a thunderbolt. By the time you finished admonishing me, I knew I was in love with you," he confessed. "I never believed in love at first sight until then."

Clarissa was speechless, and even if she could speak, she didn't know what to say. Her mouth opened and closed.

His stunning green eyes held her shocked gaze.

"You don't have to say anything. I know it's probably a shock to your system, especially as the timing is bad, but please let me be your friend. Let me take care of you and help to protect you."

"Okay," Clarissa said quietly.

She couldn't explain it, but it felt right that Tobias was there.

Tobias 's resounding smile warmed her a lot better than Becky's tea.

"Hayley told me you were trying to run a bath when they saw your car. So, why don't you go and have your bath while we're waiting for the police to arrive," he suggested.

Clarissa nodded, giving him a weak smile, even though she felt emotionally drained, and headed upstairs.

While Clarissa had her bath, Tobias was busy talking to his brother on the phone. He was determined to help Clarissa, and he didn't want her boys to see what had been done to her car.

His brother, Nicholas, owned a car dealership with a great selection of hybrid cars, so Tobias asked him to get his best one dropped off for Clarissa. Nicholas knew his brother would pay him by the end of the day, so he was happy to help. It wasn't the first time they had helped each other out.

With the car arranged, Tobias approached Hayley and Becky outside.

"How do I know you?" Hayley asked bluntly as he stood next to her. "I know, I know you, but I don't know how."

Tobias smiled. "I'm best friends with your husband's brother, Mitchell. We've played football for the same team for years and worked together when we left uni."

Hayley slapped her forehead comically.

"Of course, now it makes sense."

"Can you tell me more about the bastard who did this to Clarissa's car?" he asked.

Hayley and Becky told him everything they knew from how John Mason had been treating Clarissa at work—his recent sexual assault on her—to the discovery of his previous victims.

"Clarissa will be the first to make sure the charges stick. Although, as the sick perv has done this outside her house, it might change her mind," Becky told him.

"I'll make sure nothing happens to her and her boys!" Tobias told them.

Both girls turned to stare at him in surprise.

"I'm in love with Clarissa," he said, unashamed of his emotions.

Hayley and Becky stood looking at him, nodding their heads. The truth of his words was evident in his piercing green eyes.

"No shit, Sherlock," Hayley said with a chuckle.

Becky gave Tobias a stern look. "If you hurt her, you will end up buried under my patio!"

Hayley involuntarily snorted. She had never heard her best friend speak so threateningly, but Tobias held Becky's glare.

"I promise I won't do anything to hurt her or her boys."

By the time Clarissa had her bath, got dressed, and walked outside, her quiet road looked like a crime scene, and it horrified her. She could see her neighbors blatantly staring out of their windows, trying to see what was happening. Hayley was talking to Sergeant Jameson, who was making notes in her file. Becky was helping Adam to fit the first camera onto Clarissa's front door, and Tobias was talking to two men who were standing next to two cars. Tobias waved for Clarissa to join them.

As Clarissa walked over to the men, Sergeant Jameson gave her a sympathetic nod of her head before continuing to write.

"Clarissa, this is my brother, Nicholas, and his right-hand man, Brett," Tobias said, introducing the strangers who gave her warm and understanding smiles.

Clarissa shook their hands while wondering what the hell was going on.

"It's a pleasure to meet you," she told them politely.

Tobias could tell that she still wasn't feeling comfortable or safe.

"I hope you don't mind, but I asked my brother to bring you a car to use while yours gets fixed. I didn't think you'd want your boys to see it like that or have to look at it."

Nicholas pointed to the car, a brand-new Mercedes in silver, and it was stunning. Clarissa was blown away by Tobias's thoughtfulness, and she didn't know whether to thank him or snog him. She barely knew Tobias, but he seemed to be everything Nigel lacked.

"Are you sure you want me to use this car? I do have two young boys, you know," she said, glancing between the brothers. Nicholas smiled as Tobias wrapped his arm around her small shoulders, pulling her to his solid and muscular body.

"It's yours to use as you wish," he told her, giving Clarissa his sexy smile.

Clarissa instantly felt her pulse speed up as her cheeks flushed pink.

"You blow me away," she told Tobias, returning his smile, "Thank you so much for this. I really appreciate it."

"Clarissa, can you come over?" Hayley called over the chatter.

"You go and do what you need to do," Tobias told her, "I'll sort this out. I just need your car keys when the police are finished."

Clarissa nodded. "It was nice to meet you," she told Nicholas and Brett with a smile.

Sergeant Jameson was still writing notes down in her file when Clarissa approached. A police officer was taking photographs, while another was dusting for prints. Clarissa began to hope and pray that John was stupid enough to leave some prints.

"How are you doing, honey?" Hayley asked as Clarissa stood next to her.

Clarissa shook her head. "I'm holding it together now. I can't believe this is happening. I worked for that bastard for years and never knew he was capable of doing shit like this."

"Well, your old company is to blame for that. It looks like they've been covering for creepy John for years," Hayley told her. "It also explains why young women have never lasted very long at Janka."

Sergeant Jameson placed her folder under her arm and held out her free hand for Clarissa to shake. "Hi Clarissa, I am very sorry this has happened. I was wrong to think Mr. Mason was a coward like most sexual harassing predators I deal with."

"You weren't to know," Clarissa assured her, "None of us had a clue."

"We've recently discovered that Mr. Mason is closely related to your Janka Industries CEO, and that's clearly why he was never fired before. However, this time I think they know he attacked the wrong person. A woman whose best friend has the legal means and the balls to harm the company."

"That would be me." Hayley chuckled, making Sergeant Jameson smile.

"I think Mr. Mason being fired has sent him into a rage. Apparently, he trashed his office and drove his car through their entrance and into their foyer, costing the company thousands of damage," Sergeant Jameson explained. "He was caught on camera, but he'd gone on the run when we went to arrest him. I'm afraid we don't know where he is yet, Clarissa, but we will find him."

Clarissa could feel her legs trembling. She was glad her wide-legged trousers were hiding them.

"I hope you find him soon," Clarissa told her, "I don't want him coming back and doing something when my boys are home."

"I hope so too. Our local patrol car will be doing drive-by's on a regular basis until we catch him," Sergeant Jameson assured.

The other two officers finished processing her car, and one waved to the sergeant indicating they were done.

Sergeant Jameson nodded. "It appears we have everything we need for now. Again, I'm sorry this has happened," she told Clarissa.

Clarissa smiled warmly. "I know."

As the police drove away, Clarissa grabbed her car keys, giving them to Tobias. "Can I get any of you a drink or anything?" she asked politely.

Nicholas and Brett declined.

"I think we're all okay," Tobias said with a smile, "I'll sort your car out if you want to see how Becky and Adam are doing."

Clarissa had momentarily forgotten about the cameras.

"Thank you again. You guys are awesome," she said as she walked back to her house. She could feel Tobias's eyes watching her, and she smiled.

Becky and Adam were securing the second camera to the back of Clarissa's house when she found them. Becky loved doing things with her hands and was a huge do-it-yourselfer and crafter. She drove her husband, Martin, crazy with her projects. But he was always super impressed when she finished. He often joked that if he stood still too long, she would probably craft him into something else too.

"It's nearly done," Adam said when he saw her.

Clarissa watched as they finished and checked their work.

"Adam wants you to download an app if you want to grab your phone."

"I've got it here," Clarissa told her, pulling it out of her trouser pocket.

Adam brushed himself off, then got his own phone out. After making a few swipes on his phone, Adam showed her the app she needed to download. He grabbed the box that the cameras came in and passed it to her.

"You'll need the serial numbers to register the cameras on the app, Clarissa," he told her warmly, "Once it's all set up, you'll be notified if there's any movement front or back of your house. Also, the cameras will automatically record."

"Thank you so much for this, Adam. How much do I owe you for the cameras and your time?"

Adam shook his head, "After everything you've done for Hayley over the years, this is the least I can do, Clarissa," he told her while stroking his Viking beard. "Anyway, since you started your new job, she won't leave me alone, so I owe you for that, too." he laughed.

Becky sniggered, "Your new job is the gift that keeps on giving."

Adam and Becky's banter was starting to help calm Clarissa's nerves, and with so many people helping her and having her back, she was beginning to feel more in control and a little safer.

"Thank you for helping with the cameras, Becky," she said as she hugged her best friend.

"You're welcome, honey. Now go put the kettle on." Becky

grinned.

Clarissa grinned back at her friend, then walked out the front to see if anyone else wanted a drink. With the police gone, her road no longer looked like a crime scene, much to her relief, but her neighbor's net curtains were still twitching. She immediately noticed that her car was gone, and the new silver Mercedes was in its place, with no sign of Nicholas and Brett. Clarissa was expecting it to be still outside but covered over. She could hear Hayley asking about the Mercedes and its travel range.

"Where's my car?" Clarissa asked, confused.

Tobias gave her a guilty look. "My brother's taken it to get it fixed. He's got his own body shop," he told her with wide eyes, hoping not to piss her off.

Clarissa wasn't pissed off; she was panicked.

"I don't think my insurance will cover vandalism, and I don't have the money to pay for that," she squeaked.

"You don't need to worry about that," Tobias told her, holding his hands up. "My brother's going to get his apprentice to do the work, so he'll claim the cost back on his business expenses under staff training."

Relief swept through Clarissa. She was beginning to feel like she was on an emotional roller coaster.

"You've done so much for me already," she said, feeling over-whelmed again.

Tobias gave her such a beautiful smile; her heart skipped a beat in her chest.

"I'm making tea if you both fancy a cup," she told them as she blushed.

"Great idea. I'm gasping for another brew," Hayley said as she swept past them.

As Clarissa put the kettle on, Tobias grabbed mugs from her mug tree and put some tea bags in the teapot. Clarissa couldn't help but compare him to her ex-asshole. Nigel had been her only serious long-term relationship, and he would have just sat on his ass expecting to be waited on like his mother used to do. She smiled and felt her heart flutter. *'Am I falling for him?'* she wondered. She certainly couldn't deny the sexual attraction she felt toward Tobias.

Clarissa enjoyed her house being full of people, and it seemed that Hayley, Adam, Becky, and Tobias were in no rush to leave. They were chatting about anything and everything. Clarissa was starting to think they were doing it on purpose to take her mind off what had happened. The light banter was making her feel better, and what really impressed her was how well her best friends were getting on with Tobias.

A musical chime sounded on Clarissa's phone, and it was a sound that wasn't familiar.

"Well, at least we know your cameras are working," Adam said with a smile. "Open the notification, and the camera will show you who's out the front."

Opening the app, Clarissa could see that her ex-mother-in-law, Sharon, was dropping Luke and Matthew home, and Sharon was checking out the new Mercedes.

"The boys are home," she told her friends.

Clarissa put down her phone and made her way to the front door.

Luke and Matthew were full of chatter when Clarissa opened the front door, desperate to let her know all about the animals at the zoo.

"I can't wait to hear all about them," Clarissa told her boys with a big grin. Seeing her boys so happy and excited almost made everything better.

"Let me say thank you to your grandma. Why don't you go and tell Becky and Hayley about your zoo trip? They're in the kitchen."

Clarissa watched them run into the kitchen, and when she turned around, Sharon was peering around her to see inside, being nosy. Tobias was in full view, in all his sexy glory, chatting with Adam.

"Thank you for having the boys and taking them to the zoo," she told Sharon politely. "Sounds like they loved it."

Sharon smiled back, but Clarissa could tell she had seen Tobias. Sharon knew Hayley and Adam after so many years of barbeques and birthday parties; however, seeing Tobias in Clarissa's kitchen had piqued her interest.

"The boys had a fantastic time," Sharon said with another forced smile, "Is that your new car?" she asked, dipping her head towards the silver Mercedes.

"It's a loaner. Mine's being fixed," Clarissa explained.

Disbelief was written all over Sharon's face. "Ahh, I didn't know they loaned out brand new cars, especially top-of-the-range cars in place of Mini's."

Clarissa knew that Sharon had no real knowledge about cars and that her ex-father-in-law, who was still sitting in their car, must have told her.

"The loaner car was organized by a friend," Clarissa said, hoping that would be the end of the conversation.

"Mmm, must be a good friend," Sharon murmured a little sarcastically.

Clarissa was starting to get pissed off by the vibes Sharon was giving off.

Clarissa smiled sweetly, trying to keep her calm.

"Yes, he's the best. Anyway, I must go as I've got company," she told Sharon with another smile, waving to her ex-father-in-law, who gave her a nod. "Thanks again, Sharon."

Luckily Sharon realized that she wasn't getting any further information, so she turned and headed for her car, casting another side glance at Clarissa's loaner car. Clarissa shut the front door behind her.

Clarissa was gobsmacked when she walked back into the kitchen. Tobias was no longer standing and chatting with Adam. He was sitting on one of the dining chairs with Luke sitting on one knee and Matthew on the other, both trying to tell him about the zoo at the same time. Tobias was desperately trying to listen to both boys talking at once, asking them questions with genuine interest. He looked like a spectator at a tennis match, turning his head from side to side. Clarissa watched Tobias in awe, and she could feel herself falling for the sexy nerdy guy who her sons had instantly connected with.

"I think we need to get going, Adam," Hayley said with a grin. "My mum's probably been run ragged by the kids by now."

Clarissa snapped out of her reverie. Becky and Hayley were both grinning at her, and Hayley gave her an exaggerated wink.

"Yes, I'd better get home too," Becky told Clarissa, giving her another hug. "You know we're only a phone call away, and we'll come running," Becky whispered in her ear.

Clarissa nodded and hugged her friend back.

—x—

After Clarissa's best friends had gone, she made dinner while Luke and Matthew insisted on teaching Tobias how to play their favorite video game. Clarissa could tell that Tobias was in his element and enjoying himself. She couldn't stop smiling.

By the time Clarissa had dinner on the table, Luke and Matthew were wilting, barely able to keep their eyes open. It always tickled her that kids could be at warp speed one minute, then crashing and burning the next. She had cooked their favorite, spaghetti Bolognese, but her boys were too tired to eat much. Tobias, however, was tucking in and repeatedly grinning at her, making Clarissa's heart repeatedly flip.

When it came to clearing up after dinner, Tobias was right there helping, clearing the table while Clarissa filled the dishwasher, during which they would ask each other random questions. Clarissa loved finding out things about him, and their banter was light-hearted and fun. By the time they were finished, Luke and Matthew were fast asleep on the couch next to each other, sharing a blanket.

"Would you like me to help you take them up to bed?" Tobias asked.

Clarissa smiled. "Yes, please, if you could take Luke, as he's the heaviest."

With little effort, Tobias carried Luke upstairs, with Clarissa following behind carrying Matthew. However, Clarissa was a lot slower. She only got to the middle of the stairs before Tobias came back down to take Matthew from her arms.

"I'm guessing which beds to put them in." He grinned.

Clarissa giggled and followed him back up the stairs. As soon as the boys were on their beds, she turned to Tobias.

"I'm going to be a few minutes if you want to chill out downstairs," she told him as she started to pull off Luke's shoes.

"I'll make us a drink," Tobias said quietly once he realized what she was doing.

"Okay, and thank you for helping me carry them up," she whispered, giving him a smile.

Chapter 13

By the time Clarissa got back downstairs to her lounge, Tobias had a bottle of red wine open with two glasses ready on her coffee table.

"I thought you might be in the mood for some wine after the day you've had," he said humorously.

Clarissa grinned. "It's like you read my mind," she said as she plopped herself on her couch.

Tobias poured the drinks, giving Clarissa a glass which she sipped immediately, relishing the strong, fruity taste on her tongue. He took his glass and sat next to her, smiling.

"I didn't know whether to pour you a vodka or a wine after what happened today,"

Clarissa nodded. "Either would have been welcome. I was going to work tonight, but to be honest, I'd much rather be drinking wine with you. My nerves are shot." She looked into his striking green eyes. "You've been amazing today. Thank you."

The sexy smile Tobias gave her had her heart fluttering in her chest again.

"I'm not the sort of man who doesn't protect the woman he's in love with," he said with conviction, "I'll protect you even if we're only meant to be friends."

By the look on Tobias's face, it was clear he wanted to be more than friends. Clarissa smiled sultrily.

"I think it was fate that I told you off in the lingerie shop."

Tobias put down his wine, looking at her with eyes burning full of desire. "When you told me off, I wanted to kneel at your feet and kiss them."

Clarissa nearly choked on her wine. "You did?"

He smiled again, and Clarissa thought she was going to melt into her couch.

"Yes. Not only was I in awe of your beauty, but I don't think I've ever been so turned on. You made me feel like I needed to be punished, and I loved it."

Clarissa knew where this was going, but unlike her chat line domination calls, there was a sexy and hot guy right in front of her. She could either dampen his ardour or take what she wanted and needed. And right now, she needed to feel powerful and in control.

Clarissa put down her wine and met his gaze, staring into his piercing green eyes.

"Then you will address me as Mistress Clarissa," she told him in her husky, sexy voice.

His eyes widened, and he bit down on his full bottom lip.

"You have been a very bad man. Get to my room!" She demanded with a sexy smirk, pointing to her stairs.

Tobias looked at her like she was a goddess.

"Yes, Mistress Clarissa," he said, bowing his head.

Before Clarissa knew it, Tobias leaped off the couch, bolted through the lounge door, and was quietly making his way upstairs in seconds.

Clarissa was shocked at herself. She had a choice. She could either follow her heart and sexual desire to have her wicked way with Tobias— and dominate him— or continue plodding along with her life on her own. She realized life was too short not to follow her heart. And she had needs.

Clarissa made her way upstairs feeling excited and very turned on. She didn't know what to expect. After quickly making sure her boys were fast asleep, she shut their bedroom door and walked to her own.

Opening her bedroom door, she was greeted by a near-naked Tobias with his head tilted down, wearing nothing but a pair of women's black silky knickers with his hard cock bursting to get out. *'Well, that explains why he was in the lingerie shop,'* Clarissa thought to herself.

The situation was unknown to Clarissa, having never dominated in real life before. Although after so many domination calls, she no longer felt like a novice. Clarissa decided there and then to do what she knew.

"Do you really want to be my submissive, Tobias?" Clarissa asked sexily as she walked into her room.

Tobias's green eyes lifted to see Clarissa standing with her hands firmly placed on her hips, giving him a sultry and seductive look. When her eyes glanced at his barely contained hard cock, it switched as his heart pounded in his chest.

"Yes, Mistress," he whispered, barely able to contain his sexual excitement.

"Are you wanting physical or fantasy domination?" she asked, raising her brow.

"Physical, Mistress." His lips formed a pouty smile.

Clarissa moved towards him, close enough for him to admire her cleavage, and his eyes widened.

"If you want to be dominated by me, you must follow my rules, do you understand, Tobias?" she said firmly as she reached out her hand, cupping him in a dominant gesture.

She could feel him tremble in her grasp, and she had never felt so sexually powerful.

"Yes, Mistress," he said, reaching out his hand to touch her waist.

Instantly she slapped his hand away.

"Rule one. You must call me Mistress Clarissa at all times when we are in this room. If you forget, you will be punished. Understood?"

Clarissa could feel him twitching against her hand. She applied some gentle pressure.

"Yes, Mistress Clarissa."

"Rule two. You will not touch me unless I give you permission. Touching me in any way is a reward you must earn. Are we clear, Tobias?"

"Yes, Mistress Clarissa."

"Good. Rule three. You will not come until I give you permission. Do you understand?"

"Yes, Mistress Clarissa, I understand."

"Rule four. You will obey me at all times, or you will be punished."

"Yes, Mistress Clarissa."

"Excellent. Lastly, your safe words are orange for enough, and stop is red. Is that clear, Tobias?" she told him. Giving him another squeeze with her hand, making him moan loudly.

"Yes, it's clear, Mistress," he said, his voice breaking with anticipation.

'No, Mistress Clarissa?' Clarissa knew he had done it on purpose. She squeezed him harder. He raised his face, gasping at the pleasurable discomfort.

Clarissa stepped forward again, her body brushing against him.

"Oh, Tobias, you didn't address me by my full name," she told him, tutting her disapproval. "Now I'm going to have to punish you, so you don't forget."

He lowered his head slowly, locking his smouldering eyes with hers, his desire palpable.

"Release your cock!" she demanded.

Immediately Tobias did as commanded, and it sprang proudly from his silky knickers.

"Hold it at the base," she instructed—her voice laced with her own arousal.

Tobias took hold of himself, feeling his hardness while it throbbed in his firm grip.

Clarissa held his gaze. "I'm going to spank you five times as I count," she told him.

He closed his eyes, waiting for his glorious punishment to come. Never had he felt so aroused.

Clarissa steadied her breathing, abruptly nervous. She raised her hand.

"One…"

she slapped him firmly on his throbbing cock, making him cry out in pleasure.

"Two…" Slap.

Tobias moaned, his breathing picking up pace.

"Three…"

Clarissa slapped him again, this time a little harder, wanting to discover how hard he liked it. His loud moans made it clear that he was more than turned by what she was doing.

"Four…"

Clarissa spanked harder again, and this time his knees gave a little, his trembling body more pronounced.

"This is the last one, Tobias. Are you ready?" she asked.

The look he gave her was one of undeniable desire. His green eyes somehow looked brighter beneath his hooded brows, while his full lips seemed fuller and more kissable.

"Yes, Mistress Clarissa, I am," he replied slowly.

His voice was so deep and husky that she could feel her whole-body flush with desire. No man had ever made her so wet and wanton.

"Five..."

Clarissa spanked him harder again, taking his breath away.

Another loud moan escaped Tobias. Clarissa stepped back. He moaned again, releasing his grip. Leaning forward, he placed his hands on his firm, muscular thighs.

"Thank you, Mistress Clarissa," he half-whispered.

Tobias took a couple of deep breaths before standing straight in all his glory. Clarissa wanted him to take her there and then. She tried to control her racing pulse. Her whole body ached with desire. His eyes scanned her up and down like a starving man seeing his first meal in days.

Clarissa knew she had to reward Tobias as well as punish him, but as this was her first time dominating in real life, she wasn't too sure what to do. 'Wing it.' She decided.

"You did very well, Tobias, and I think you deserve a reward," she told him seductively, "What do you think your reward should be?"

"I want to kiss you all over and fuck you until you tell me to stop, Mistress Clarissa," he told her, his voice laced with so much desire that Clarissa wasn't sure how long she would last.

Clarissa smouldered under his gaze. Her inner sex goddess couldn't wait to get naked with him.

"Do it!" She demanded.

Tobias stalked forward, his black silky knickers sliding from his thick muscular thighs onto the floor. His hands trembled in anticipation as he started to unbutton her blouse. He leaned down, kissing the top of her cleavage and licking between her breasts. She couldn't stop imagining his tongue licking lower to where she was aching for him.

Once all her buttons were undone, Tobias gently slipped her blouse down her arms, brushing his fingers along her sensitive skin before letting it drop to the floor. His hands slid under her arms, and Tobias pulled her towards his firm body. His mouth met hers, kissing her for the first time. Clarissa melted in his arms, his hot body and solid cock pressing against her. Tobias deepened the kiss, his tongue teasing her, and she desperately wanted it to tease something else.

Clarissa didn't even notice that Tobias was unhooking her bra until she felt it loosen, and by her next breath, Tobias was trailing kisses along her neck as he slid her bra from her body.

Suddenly Clarissa was nervous, incredibly turned on, but nervous. No man other than her ex-asshole had seen her naked, and since becoming a mum, she had acquired stretch marks, cellulite, and extra curvy bits. Clarissa's heart began to pound as Tobias's kisses got lower, never faltering.

She realized that he either didn't see her imperfections or he didn't care.

Tobias dropped her bra to the floor, and he dropped to his knees, his hands gently cupping her large breasts. His mouth found her hard and tingling nipples, scraping them with his teeth, then sucking on them in turn.

For Clarissa, it was a pleasurable torture. She wanted him, and she didn't think she could wait much longer. Tobias sucked harder, and she moaned, placing her hands on either side of his head.

Before long, Clarissa's wide-legged trousers were undone by his nimble fingers, instantly falling to the floor. Tobias kissed and licked a trail down her flushed body to her knickers. He teased her through the lace material with his tongue, and she gripped his thick dark hair between her fingers. Tobias moaned at the apex of her thighs.

He was hungry for more.

For him, Clarissa was the best thing he had ever tasted, and after what she had done to him, becoming his first mistress, Clarissa felt like his forbidden fruit.

No longer able to deny his desire, Tobias rose to his bare feet, scooping Clarissa up in his arms. Her shoes tumbled to the floor, allowing her trousers to slip off completely.

Clarissa's pulse began to race faster, no longer worried about her imperfections. He carried her over to her bed, and he laid her down as if she were his prized treasure. As he kneeled on the bed next to her near-naked body, his eyes roamed, feasting on her form. Leaning over, he slid her lace knickers down her curvy thighs, removing them completely. Tobias kissed her again, and she ran her hands down his broad, muscular back, causing him to moan into her mouth. Clarissa could feel his hard cock pushing against her bare thigh, and she wanted him more than she had wanted anyone else. Tobias slid his body over her thigh while teasing Clarissa's tongue with his own, and the next thing she knew, his hardness was pressing between her thighs. She knew he could feel how wet and ready she was.

Tobias lifted himself up on his thick forearms.

"Are you sure about this?" Tobias asked, his voice deep with need.

Clarissa looked into his beautiful green eyes, feeling not only his need but also his love for her.

"I want and need you," she told him breathlessly.

Kissing Clarissa deeply, Tobias pushed against her, moaning on entry. She gasped, her fingers gripping his back as he started to thrust. Their bodies fit together as if they were made for each other.

Tobias and Clarissa moved together, their bodies fuelling each other's climb to ecstasy. She arched her back, her breasts moving with each motion. Tobias thrusted faster, her beautiful body spurring him on. Clarissa's gripping fingers and panting breaths indicating close she was.

"I need your permission, Mistress Clarissa," he panted, barely holding it together.

Clarissa's lust was overtaking her thought process, taking her a moment to register his request.

"You have it," she told him breathlessly.

Clarissa's thighs tightened around him, and he picked up his pace, thrusting deeply inside her. She cried out in ecstasy as she began to peak. It was Tobias's undoing.

The moment he felt Clarissa pulsing around him, he reached his climax, his whole-body tensing, then trembling as he released inside her.

It took a few minutes for Clarissa to truly comprehend what had just happened as they lay together, wrapped in each other's arms. Her body had never reacted to anyone as it had with Tobias.

Tobias raised his head, kissing the soft skin of her neck.

"You just keep blowing my mind, Clarissa," he whispered.

"I think it's you who's just blown my mind," she told him with a smile while running her fingers through his thick dark hair.

Tobias raised his arm, resting his head on his hand to look at the woman who had stolen his heart.

"How did you get into domination?" he asked, his curiosity getting the better of him.

Clarissa knew the conversation could go one of two ways. If she told him about her new job, he would either be okay with it or run for the hills, and she would never see him again. She decided to tell him and hope for the best.

"That was the first time I've ever dominated in real life," she confessed.

Tobias looked at her in surprise. "Really? I would never have guessed."

She smiled, taking it as a compliment.

"So, how did you know what to say and do?"

Clarissa took a deep breath. "I hated my previous job so much that Hayley suggested that I work on a phone sex chat line, like her colleague," she explained, "After what happened with my old boss, I quit, and I had no choice but to go for it."

"So, you do domination on the chat line?" Tobias asked, grinning at her.

Clarissa took his grin as a good sign.

"I didn't have much choice. It seems my husky voice is a submissive magnet." She giggled.

Tobias smirked.

"I'm not surprised. You know the effect you had on me at the lingerie shop."

Tugging Tobias's hair playfully, she kissed him.

"Anyway, because I was getting so many domination calls, I thought I'd better research what it was all about, so I educated myself and created my rules. It turns out I'm pretty good at domination on the phone and apparently not bad in real life either." She laughed.

"You certainly are," Tobias agreed, "but I think you should practice on me regularly and hone your craft," he told her, giving her an exaggerated wink.

Clarissa laughed even harder. "Oh, do you now?"

"Yes, and I think you should call me Tobi unless I've been very naughty; then you should call me Tobias," he told her with one brow raised.

"Just how often are you naughty, Tobias?"

Tobias grinned like a Cheshire cat. "Mmm, quite a lot. And I don't mind getting punished in various ways, as long as I get rewarded a lot, too," he said, lowering his head to tease and suck on her closest nipple.

Clarissa smirked and narrowed her eyes at him.

"Tobias, did I give you permission to do that?" She asked.

"Why no, no you did not, Mistress Clarissa?" He replied, his body already starting to respond to her look and the change of tone in her voice.

"You are a very, very bad man, Tobias. I think I'm going to have to restrain you, as you can't control yourself," she told him sternly.

Tobias's green eyes lit up, and she could feel him getting hard again. Clarissa slid herself from her bed, making her way to her accessory's drawer. She pulled out four of her silky scarves of various designs and colors. Tobias's eyes widened, and she could already see how turned-on he was getting.

—x—

For most of the night, Clarissa and Tobias got to know each other sexually and personally. Also testing Tobias's limits, what he did and didn't like, and what Clarissa was willing to do to him. By the early hours of the morning, they were exhausted, content but exhausted.

Clarissa was barely able to open her eyes and move her body when she woke the next morning. She had never been so sexually active in one night, even with her ex-asshole. Her ex had been okay-ish in the bedroom, but he was always so full of himself and his sex-god status, he never cared about her pleasure and fulfillment. Not that Clarissa ever thought of Nigel as a sex god.

Hearing her boys stirring from their bedroom, she turned over and checked her bedside clock. It was nearly six-thirty, and she knew she had to get up. Sitting up in bed, Clarissa glanced beside her and smiled as she admired the sexy, hot man lying next to her, still fast asleep. She was starting to wonder how she got so lucky. *'Maybe good Karma is finally looking out for me.'* She thought with a smile.

By the time Tobi walked into Clarissa's kitchen, Matthew and Luke were fed, dressed, and ready for school. As soon as they saw Tobi, they grinned at their new friend, clearly thrilled to see him. *'They never smiled at their dad like that,'* Clarissa thought as her heart melted.

"Would you like some breakfast, Tobi?" Clarissa asked as she picked up her boiled kettle.

Matthew giggled at the kitchen table, "It's not Tobi, silly mummy; it's Tobias," he told Clarissa.

"It's only Tobias when I'm naughty," he told the boys with a wink.

Clarissa nearly spilled the hot water she was pouring into mugs.

"Yes, please, gorgeous. I'd love some breakfast."

Matthew and Luke giggled.

—x—

After Tobi had left, promising to see Clarissa later, she dropped the boys off at school and did some grocery shopping, all while replying to messages from Becky and Hayley, wanting to know how her evening went.

When Clarissa arrived home, she was aching again. She wasn't used to so much physical exertion, and she had used muscles during the night that she forgot she had. However, she was determined not to start her shift until she had got her usual jobs done.

Within an hour, Clarissa was ready to start work, excited to start a fresh week. It wasn't long before she was in full swing taking calls. Some were regulars, and as always, she got lots of new callers. She was just refilling her mug with more tea from her flask when another call came through. She answered it, greeted with the very familiar recording.

"Line twenty. Beep."

It was another fetish call, and Clarissa seemed to get just as many fetish calls as she did domination. Luckily, they were usually closely linked, enabling her to keep the callers on for a decent amount of time.

"Hi, this is Adele. Who's this?" She asked in a sultry tone.

"Hello, Adele, my name is Harold," a quiet and well-spoken voice said.

"You have a beautiful accent and a very sexy voice, Harold," she purred down the phone, "Are you looking for some kinky fun with me today?"

"Yes, I am Adele. I am being incredibly naughty today," he told her, sounding excited by his naughtiness.

"Are you now, Harold? I love naughty, bad men. Tell me, what naughtiness you are up to; I'd love to hear," Clarissa coaxed.

Harold giggled like a naughty schoolboy making Clarissa smile.

"I was supposed to be in court today for a big case. Fortunately, due to unforeseen circumstances, it didn't go ahead. I knew my wife would be out today, so I have come home to have some fun," Harold explained, his voice becoming louder.

Clarissa was intrigued, especially now she knew he was either a top lawyer, barrister, or judge.

"Ahh, I see. So, while your wife's away, you want to play. Tell me, Harold, what exactly are you doing while you're home alone?" She asked.

Harold's breathing began to deepen into a low pant.

"I have taken some of my wife's lingerie, and I am laying on the floor in my office wearing her bright-red lacy bra and panties, with my knees up to my waist. I also took one of her vibrators, and I want to be naughty with it, Adele."

This was a new one for Clarissa. She'd had plenty of calls of guys wearing female lingerie, which was probably why she wasn't that fazed when she saw Tobi wearing silky black knickers. However, taking and wanting to use their partner's toys was something she hadn't come across. She knew he was excited about having taken the sex toy and using it.

"Harold, you really are a naughty man. Tell me what the vibrator looks like?" She asked, knowing her request would please him.

A buzzing sound let her know that Harold had turned on the vibrator.

"It is a bright-pink six-inch vibrator, Adele, and it has a bulbous end and rotating balls inside. Mmm, I am rubbing it against my hard penis and testicles through the panties, and it feels wonderful."

Clarissa could tell that he was getting extremely turned on.

"Harold, I want you to slide the vibrator into your mouth to make it slippery and wet, then I want you to slide it into your tight red lacy panties, so you can feel it against your hard cock," she urged, her tone firm but flirty.

Lots of moans and other sounds made it clear that Harold was doing what she had asked. His breathing and moaning becoming more rapid and loud.

"Tell me what you really want to do with that big, hard vibrator?" Clarissa asked, feeling like she already knew the answer.

"I, I want to fuck myself with it, Adele," he confessed.

Clarissa smiled. Harold's answer was exactly what she was expecting.

"I want to hear you do it, Harold, you naughty man. I want you to slide those red panties down. Then I want you to suck the vibrator to make it slippery and wet again, and then I want you to slide it in."

The saying, go fuck yourself, was now having a new meaning for Clarissa, and she never thought in a million years that she would ever tell someone to do it, literally.

As Clarissa heard Harold moaning and panting down the phone, she became aware of her phone flashing with messages, but after the recent messages from her ex-asshole and her ex-boss, she decided to ignore it. Her shift was going so well; she didn't want to read another awful message and ruin her good mood.

Loud moans from Harold brought her back to the present, and he was clearly enjoying himself.

"Does that feel good, Harold?" She asked.

"Oh, Adele, it feels amazing. I am so naughty. Mmmm."

Trying to keep Harold on the line for as long as possible, she coaxed Harold into slowing down, then speeding up for a very short time, and then slowing down again. Harold was on a pleasure roller coaster, and Clarissa had the controls.

"I don't want you to come, unless I give you permission, Harold," Clarissa told him with her sexy, firm voice.

"Oh, Adele, you are torturing me, and I love it!" He declared between pants.

Clarissa managed to keep him going for a few more torturous minutes, but it soon became apparent that he was too close to the edge.

"Harold, I give you permission to come, but I want to hear you moan like the naughty man you are. Moan for me," she ordered.

Seriously loud moans and vigorous movement sounded through the phone as Harold began to pleasure himself with his wife's vibrator.

Then, Clarissa heard loud banging on wood, and a female voice started to shout loudly at his end.

"Harold, what are you doing, Harold?" She shouted, banging on the office door. "Why is your office locked? Harold, what are you doing?"

Clarissa could almost feel Harold's panic.

"Shit!" Harold said as he desperately tried to get up off his office floor.

Clarissa heard the phone drop.

"Harold, I know you are in there. Open the door! What are you doing?" Harold's wife demanded.

Banging and things crashing to the floor were all Clarissa could hear. She could only imagine how Harold was feeling.

"I'm sorry, Adele, I have to go," Harold whispered before the line went dead.

Putting the phone down, Clarissa couldn't believe what had just happened. She was mortified for Harold, wondering how on earth he was going to try and explain what he had been doing. His wife certainly sounded pissed off, that was for sure. Clarissa needed to take a break, her pulse was racing, and she needed to get a grip.

Chapter 14

Logging herself off the chat line, Clarissa made a fresh tea and decided to check her phone, needing to know whether it was another bad text or a good one. The moment she saw the message, she knew it was from Tobi.

I hope you're having a great day, gorgeous. Don't worry about cooking dinner. I'm cooking for you and the boys tonight. PS: I've been a very bad man today!!! Love you, xxx.

There was no mistaking Tobi's message for anyone else's. Just reading Tobi's message had her grinning from ear to ear.

Thank you, you sexy, hot nerd. I hope you are ready to confess and accept your punishment, you bad man!

Clarissa was still grinning as she clicked send and saved his number. She wasn't sure how he had got her number. With everything that had happened the day before, she had completely forgotten to exchange numbers with him. Then Clarissa remembered Tobi talking with her friends, and she knew one of them must have given her number to him. She was glad that her friends had been thinking clearly.

Grabbing her fresh cup of tea, she got back to work, feeling even happier than before.

—x—

As Clarissa was driving home after picking up Luke and Matthew in the new Mercedes Tobi's brother had lent her, she was beginning to feel like a new woman. A new job, a new man, and true happiness, which was something she wasn't used to feeling. Luke and Matthew were very excited when she told them Tobi was coming over and cooking them dinner, and as she listened to their banter in the back of the car, she smiled.

After getting vegetable snacks for the kids, Clarissa sat down at her kitchen table to help Luke and Matthew with their homework when her camera app sounded. When she checked the app, she was stunned to see her ex-asshole, Nigel walking up her garden path. *'What the hell does he want now?'* Clarissa didn't know whether to tell her boys that their dad had turned up or not. The last thing she wanted was for him to ignore them on the doorstep. She decided not to tell them unless Nigel asked to see them.

"I'll be right back, boys, okay? I just want to pop the rubbish outside before I forget," she told them. "I'll only be a few minutes."

Luke nodded.

"Okay, mummy," Matthew told her, not looking up from his school project about insects.

Clarissa quickly went to her kitchen bin, pulling out the rubbish bag and knotting it as she promptly headed to the front door, closing her lounge door to minimize any noise. She took a quick big breath to prepare herself for whatever it was Nigel wanted and quickly opened the front door before he could press the doorbell.

Nigel had just raised his hand to ring the doorbell when Clarissa was suddenly facing him on her doorstep with her rubbish bag in hand. She glared at him.

"What are you doing here, Nigel," she demanded, trying to keep her cool.

Nigel looked at her with a sheepish expression. "I was going to text first, but I didn't think you'd reply."

She could already feel herself getting pissed off just at the sight of him.

"You're damn right I would have ignored you, you asshole, especially as I heard that your whole cancer scare was fake. What sort of sick bastard lies about possibly having cancer?"

Nigel lowered his head, but knowing her ex-asshole as well as she did, Clarissa knew he wasn't doing it in shame.

"I'll tell you what sort of bastard does something like that, a sick, narcissistic bastard," Clarissa raged. "I'll ask you again, why are you here?"

"I came to say I'm sorry for everything. I don't know if you heard, but I've had a rough time recently," he said, trying to look woeful.

'The idiot just wants sympathy. Probably because he's not getting it from his parents.' She thought.

Clarissa raised an eyebrow in disbelief at his audacity.

"I did hear all about it, but what has that got to do with you turning up here? After everything you did to me, you aren't getting my sympathy, Nigel. What goes around comes around."

Nigel was looking more uncomfortable.

"I was wondering if I could stay with you and the boys for a while. Just a couple of months until I can get myself straight?" he asked.

Clarissa was so stunned by Nigel's request that she forgot how to speak for a moment. She stared at him in complete astonishment.

Holding up his hands as if pleading, Nigel changed tactics.

"I'm sure if your mum knew I was in trouble, she'd suggest I stay with you."

"My mum wouldn't waste a cup of water on you if you were on fire, you tosser. She knows everything you did during our sham of a marriage and what a low-life dad you are," Clarissa told him bluntly. "I can't believe you have the nerve to ask me for help. When was the last time you bought shoes for your sons or even asked after them?"

Clarissa glared at him, waiting for the answer she knew she wouldn't get. Nigel opened his mouth to speak, then closed it again.

A loud car horn sounded, and when Clarissa looked down the end of her road, she saw Tobi's Mercedes speeding towards them. Straight away, she knew that Tobi thought Nigel was her creepy ex-boss from a distance, and he was racing to get to her. Clarissa waved at him, trying to show she wasn't in trouble. She turned her attention back to Nigel.

"We don't need you, and we don't want you here. Leave, and don't bother coming back!" Clarissa told him, instantly feeling calmer now Tobi was pulling up.

Nigel's face looked like she had physically slapped him, and when he heard the roar of Tobi's engine, he turned to see who it was. Tobi locked eyes with Nigel as he parked and turned the engine off. Instantly, Nigel puffed out his chest, trying to make himself look bigger than he was. *That isn't going to help you,* Clarissa thought.

When Tobi looked at her concerned, Clarissa smiled, hoping he would relax. She watched as he emerged from his car in all his manly glory and then opened his boot to retrieve the shopping he had bought—his muscles straining against his tight-fitting pinstripe shirt in all the right places.

Nigel turned and glared at Clarissa.

"Who the fuck is that?" He demanded.

Clarissa raised her eyebrows at his annoyance. "He's none of your business. Now, if you'll excuse us, my new man is cooking dinner for my boys and me. Goodbye, Nigel, and don't come back."

Tobi strode up the garden path, laden with heavy shopping but making it look effortless.

"Are you okay, gorgeous?" He asked.

Clarissa smiled. Just the sight of Tobi made her world right again.

"Yes, babe, I'm just taking out the trash," she told him, locking eyes with Nigel. "Go on in; Luke and Matthew are waiting to show you what they did at school today. My ex-husband is just leaving."

Tobi's eyes widened in understanding. When he reached them at the front door, towering over Nigel, he looked down at him and smiled.

"Excuse me; I have hungry boys to feed," Tobi said as he app-roached Clarissa, kissing her before walking into the house.

Clarissa stepped out onto her doorstep, still gripping the rubbish bag she had brought out, closing the front door behind her.

"I mean it, Nigel, leave, please."

Nigel blinked at her, obviously in shock that Clarissa hadn't only found someone else but that he was so different from him. His face began to flush, and Clarissa didn't know if he was getting angry or embarrassed.

Without saying another word, Nigel turned on his heel and stormed off back to a car she didn't recognize. Clarissa didn't give him a second glance as she walked to her rubbish bin at the side of her house, throwing in the half-empty bag. As she turned and walked back to her front door, she heard his wheels spinning as he got to the main road.

"Tosser," she said, shaking her head.

When Clarissa opened her front door, a delicious scent of garlic and seafood greeted her, and her mouth watered. She was expecting to find Tobi cooking up a storm, but she actually found Luke and Matthew helping Tobi cook. She grinned as she took the glass of wine Tobi had put on the kitchen table for her.

"Now that's what I love to see, handsome men cooking," she told them.

Luke and Matthew were thoroughly enjoying themselves. Clarissa knew her boys were destroying her clean kitchen and using every bowl and pan she had, but she honestly didn't care. Seeing her boys having such a great time making dinner with Tobi was worth the clean-up.

—x—

That evening, Clarissa enjoyed garlic prawns with noodles and vegetables with a glass of white wine. Tobi even persuaded Luke and Matthew to help him clean up the kitchen. It was the first time in years that she didn't have to cook or clean up. It was heaven.

Once the boys were in bed and reading, Clarissa curled up on her couch with Tobi, her body resting against his hard chest. He wrapped an arm around her and passed Clarissa her wine.

"Do you want to talk about your ex?" Tobi asked softly, not wanting to pressure her.

Clarissa smiled. "That could take all night, and I should get some hours in on the chat line."

Tobi put down his wine, wrapping both arms around her. "I've got to go to London to see a new client tomorrow, so how about you have tonight off? I can take Luke and Matthew to school in the morning, and that way, you can get an early start tomorrow," he suggested.

Resting her head against Tobi's chest, Clarissa thought for a moment. Did she really want to unload all of her ex-asshole baggage on Tobi? He obviously wanted to know, and Clarissa had no clue about his previous relationships.

"Okay, sounds like a plan," she said, deciding that she wanted to make the most of Tobi before he had to leave and hopefully get to know him better.

Clarissa told Tobi everything, why Nigel had shown up on her doorstep, his fake cancer scare, and their shared history. Tobi repeatedly shook his head in disbelief while letting Clarissa explain and vent.

"He doesn't realize how lucky he was, does he?" Tobi said in astonishment.

It was Clarissa's turn to shake her head.

"Nope. I know I'm biased, but Luke and Matthew are amazing kids, and he has no love or interest in them at all. I struggle to understand him," she said truthfully. "Anyway, enough about my ex-asshole and his narcissistic ways. Tell me about your recent and past romances."

Tobi grinned. "Mine haven't been as interesting and dramatic as yours. I've only had two long-term relationships. The first lasted three years. She was my high school crush, but she broke my heart when she went to a different college. The second and my most recent relationship lasted for four years and ended about a year ago after I walked in on her with another woman in our bed."

Clarissa took a sip of her drink and began to choke on her wine in shock.

"Seriously?" She spluttered.

Tobi nodded, raising his brows.

"Yep, I wasn't feeling too good, so I decided to work from home for the day. When I got home, I heard noises, and when I opened the bedroom door, there she was getting it on with a woman she worked with in our bed."

"You do know that's most men's dream, so see their lady with another woman?" she asked, laughing in surprise.

"I have to be honest, when I walked in on them, I didn't know whether to grab a seat and watch or ask if I could join in," he said jokingly. "But in all seriousness, how can someone compete when their partner cheats on them with the same sex? And cheating is still cheating."

Clarissa nodded. "If anyone knows how you feel, it's me. I think if I had caught Nigel in bed with someone else, I would have said they could have him. He made me feel like a paranoid idiot for years. Did you ever suspect your ex was cheating?"

Tobi shook his head.

"No, I didn't. Sara was a nurse, so I was used to her working extra shifts and odd hours. She recently married the woman she was cheating on me with."

Clarissa put down her wine and turned to face him.

"We are their loss, and you are my gain, Tobias," she told him with a sexy smirk on her face.

"Oh, oh, have I been naughty, Mistress Clarissa?" He asked, raising his brows.

"You most certainly have, Tobias," Clarissa gave him a stern look. "You made me choke on my wine and spill it all over my boobs. You need to be punished, and afterward, I might allow you to lick it all off," she said, already aware that she was getting him hard.

Clarissa leaned over and looked at the shoes he was wearing.

"I want you to pull out your shoelaces, take them and wait for me upstairs because you have been a naughty bad man. Now get to my room." She pointed upstairs.

Tobias didn't wait for Clarissa to move. Wrapping his arms around her, he slid off the couch, at the same time turning Clarissa over, so she was suddenly lying on the couch on her back. As Tobias rushed upstairs to Clarissa's bedroom, she laughed at his eagerness. She walked into her kitchen to collect a few clothes pegs from her cupboard, knowing exactly what she was going to do with them.

—x—

When Clarissa opened her bedroom door, Tobias was standing naked, apart from a pair of lilac lace knickers that she quickly recognized, with the shoelaces in his hand. She bit her bottom lip. *'Damn, he looks hotter in those knickers than I do,'* she thought as she approached him. Clarissa cupped him in her hand, squeezing firmly, and when he lifted his head to look at her, his eyes locked with hers. Her pulse began to race. She held up the clothes pegs in her other hand for him to see.

"Do you know what I'm going to do with your shoelaces and these pegs?" She asked with a sexy smile.

Tobias looked at the pegs with wide eyes. "No, Mistress Clarissa, but I'm looking forward to finding out." He smirked.

—x—

Tobi was true to his word the following morning, taking Luke and Matthew to school. She had never seen her boys get dressed and ready for school so quickly.

As she had some breakfast, she messaged Hayley and Becky on their group chat, who had been weirdly quiet on the message front.

Fancy a girl's night at mine tonight?

Becky, as always, was quick to reply.

Hell, yes. It's a school night, but who cares, lol.

I'm in, and I'll bring the stuff for Margaritas!
Hayley told her.

Clarissa couldn't wait to catch up with her best friends; it would be the first time in ages she would have something genuinely positive to chat about that wasn't kids or work-related.

Awesome, come over whenever you're ready. Love you!
She messaged back.

Before long, Clarissa was already working and getting some hours in when she received a phone call on her mobile phone from a number she didn't recognize. When she saw a voicemail notification, she quickly logged off the chat line to hear it.

"Hello Clarissa, this is Sergeant Jameson. I'm sorry to say we believe Mr. Mason is now armed and dangerous. Can you please call me back?"

Clarissa's heart began to pound in her chest. She couldn't believe John had managed to get a weapon from somewhere. With shaking hands, Clarissa called Sergeant Jameson back. She listened to the phone ringing, praying that Sergeant Jameson would answer.

"Good morning, Sergeant Jameson speaking."

"Hi Sergeant Jameson, this is Clarissa Darcy; I just heard your voicemail about Mr. Mason," Clarissa told her with a shaky voice.

"Hi, Clarissa; I'm sorry to have to give you bad news. I only just heard about the incident this morning as I was off duty yesterday."

"That's ok. I appreciate you letting me know as soon as you found out," Clarissa told her warmly. "What happened exactly?"

"It seems that Mr. Mason is on a vendetta against Janka Industries and you. On Saturday evening, Mr. Mason laid in wait in the company car park, and he threatened the CEO, Mr. Hardy, with a pistol, demanding that he receive a large payoff. Mr. Hardy agreed out of fear, and Mr. Mason got away. We're still actively trying to find him."

Clarissa's mouth went dry. Her heart was racing in her chest.

"Why do you think he's still coming after me? Since my car incident, I haven't had any more messages, and I haven't seen him near my house."

Sergeant Jameson paused, not wanting to give Clarissa more bad news, but knowing she had no choice.

"He told Mr. Hardy that he was going to...fuck you up. I'm sorry, Clarissa. I know you want this all over."

Tears sprang in Clarissa's eyes. She couldn't believe what she was hearing.

"Why is he doing this? All I did was protect myself."

"Mr. Mason is a sick man, Clarissa. This is strictly between you and me, okay?"

"Okay."

"I received some medical history on Mr. Mason, and apparently, he's always had a history of violent episodes. Unfortunately, getting fired has sent him on a downward spiral. Because he's now armed and has made another threat against you, we will be giving you and your son's protection until we can get you in a safe place," Sergeant Jameson explained. "I'm sending over a protection detail this morning, and they should be arriving at your house within the hour. Once you've collected your children and have packed some essentials, my officers will take you to a safe location."

Clarissa didn't know what to say. She was stunned it had escalated so far and so quickly. Sergeant Jameson sounded genuinely worried, and that scared Clarissa even more.

"Thank you for letting me know. I appreciate everything you're doing to protect my boys and me," Clarissa told her, desperately trying not to cry over the phone.

"I'll keep in touch and let you know of any developments, Clarissa," Sergeant Jameson assured her. "Call me anytime if you need me."

"Thank you," Clarissa said, putting down her phone.

Clarissa's first instinct was to call Tobi and tell him, but she knew he would turn around and head back immediately. She also knew that it was important for him to meet his new clients, and the last thing she wanted was to affect his business negatively. Tobi had worked extremely hard to build his company, and Clarissa knew that a business's reputation could make or break it. She decided to message Hayley and Becky to tell them not to come over. Clarissa didn't want her best friends to be put in danger too.

Within seconds of Clarissa messaging Hayley and Becky, her phone blew up with messages asking why. She knew she would have to tell them what was going on, so she suggested a group video chat to explain.

Moments later, Hayley initiated the video chat with a confused look.

"What's going on, honey," she asked Clarissa, "I was looking forward to us having margaritas tonight."

"I know, I was as well, but I've just spoken to Sergeant Jameson, and she's told me John Mason is armed and dangerous, and apparently out to fuck me up. She's sending a protection detail for the boys and me. She's putting us somewhere safe until they get him."

"Holy hell," Becky said, horror written all over her face, "are you serious?"

Clarissa nodded. More tears formed in her eyes as she told them everything Sergeant Jameson had told her.

"That sick bastard needs to be caught. God knows where he got the gun." Hayley growled.

"Agreed. At least they'll protect you until they catch him," Becky added, just as furious. "Have you told Tobias the news?"

Tears rolled down Clarissa's cheeks.

"No, I haven't. He's on his way to London to meet clients. I don't want this affecting his work, and I don't want all this drama to frighten him off."

"Don't tarnish Tobias with the same brush as Nigel," Hayley told her gently. "He seems like a genuinely lovely guy, and my brother-in-law, Michell, told me he's the salt of the earth. When I told him what was going on after your car incident, all he wanted to do was protect you and your boys. I honestly think he would put you and your boys before anyone and anything, honey. You need to tell him. He might get upset and hurt if you don't."

Becky nodded profusely. "I agree one hundred percent. And if he doesn't put you first, get rid! You don't want another Nigel."

Clarissa nodded as she wiped away more tears streaming down her face. She desperately wanted to escape the dramatic and emotional roller coaster she was on and just be happy with Tobi and her sons.

"Okay, I'll call him. Hopefully, I'll see you both soon," she told them quietly, ending the call.

Clarissa knew she had to call Tobi sooner rather than later. It had already been hours since he'd left, and it would have only taken him between one to two hours, depending on traffic, to arrive in London. Clarissa called his number, hoping not to interrupt anything important. Tobi answered immediately.

"Hi gorgeous, missing me already?" he asked cheekily.

She could tell by his voice that he was smiling, and she hated to ruin his good mood.

"I am missing you already," she told him truthfully.

Immediately Tobi knew that something was wrong.

"What's the matter? Are you ok?" He asked, instantly worried.

Trying to hold her tears at bay, Clarissa explained what was happening and what Sergeant Jameson had told her.

"The protection detail should be here already," Clarissa told him, "So don't rush back; there's no need."

"Please go and check that the protection detail is outside the house, gorgeous?"

"Okay, I'll look now," she told him, walking to her lounge window.

She could hear concerned voices asking Tobi if everything was okay.

"My family is in danger," he told them, "I've got to go. I'll reschedule with you asap."

Clarissa could tell that Tobi quickly left wherever he was, with a door slamming shut behind him. His breath quickened, and she wouldn't have been surprised if he was running. She pulled back her curtain to look outside. It took a moment to spot the police patrol car. She found it discreetly tucked between her neighbor's work truck and a black ford estate.

"I see the police car; it's right outside."

Tobi was panting and running at full speed to his car.

"Good, I'll be back as soon as I can. If that bastard shows up, please call me, okay?" He asked between heavy breaths.

"I will, I promise. Please don't speed back; I don't want to be worrying about you too."

Clarissa didn't want him to have an accident, speeding down the motorway.

"I'll be sensible." He promised. "See you soon, gorgeous."

As the line went dead, Clarissa held the phone in her hand, reeling from Tobi's words. "He called us his family. It's too soon. It's all happening too fast, but it feels right. I think he's the one."

Chapter 15

Putting down the phone, Clarissa decided to wash her face and get herself a fresh cup of tea before doing a couple more hours on the chat line. Clarissa didn't want to panic Luke and Matthew by pulling them out of school early, so she decided to pick them up at the regular time. She was also determined not to let John Mason take over her life, and with Tobi coming straight back from London and having to go to a safe place, she knew she wouldn't get any night-time hours worked.

With another two and a half hours worked and no sign of Tobi, Clarissa logged off, packed some essentials in a large holdall bag, and got herself ready to get Luke and Matthew from school. She hoped that if John did come down her road, he would assume that she was out because her vandalized car wasn't outside. Clarissa sent Tobi a text, letting him know she was leaving to get her boys and that she would meet him at her house before going with the police. Seconds later, she received a reply.

Sorry, gorgeous. I've hit traffic. I should be home by the time you get back. Be careful, please.

Clarissa smiled. The fact that he called her, Luke, and Matthew his family, called her house home and that he was also racing home to protect them spoke volumes about how he felt.

Grabbing her coat, the large holdall bag, and handbag, Clarissa left her house, ensuring it was locked up before getting in her loaner car. The police car edged out of its parking space straight away, waiting for her to drive off. It was reassuring for Clarissa to know that they would be following her.

—x—

The drive to the primary school was uneventful, and when Clarissa arrived and began walking to the school entrance, one of the police officers, dressed in plain clothes, got out to walk behind her. Clarissa reached her usual spot where her boys would exit and waited for the school bell to ring. A couple of minutes later, two other mums with big smiles sidled up next to her. Clarissa had known the friendly mums for a few years.

"Hi, Clarissa. Who was the hunk who dropped your boys off this morning, you lucky bugger?" The mum called Ashley asked, curiosity written all over her face.

Clarissa grinned at their nosiness.

"That was Tobi, my boyfriend," she told them.

Both women looked at Clarissa in surprise.

"Damn, I thought you were a lucky bitch having Nigel, but your new man looked like he could be Superman's replacement." She laughed.

"Trust me, Tobi is everything Nigel wasn't," she told them, "Nigel is an asshole in disguise."

Ashely nodded. "I did hear some rumours, but I didn't know if they were true," she admitted. "Anyway, I think you've landed on your feet with Tobi. He was great with your boys this morning. He walked right up to the doors, and they hugged him before going in. Tobi didn't leave until the bell went."

Clarissa smiled.

The school bell rang, and hordes of children of various ages streamed out of the school doors. It wasn't long before Luke and Matthew exited and made their way to their waiting mum. Clarissa was acutely aware of the policeman who was still avidly watching her, but no one else noticed. She said goodbye to the other mums and ushered her boys out of the school gates.

Luke and Matthew told her about their day as they walked to her car, and she was grateful that they had a better day than her. Soon, they were driving down the main road heading for home.

"I'm going to miss Tobi tonight," Matthew said sadly, "I wanted to show him the picture I made for him today at school."

"Don't worry, Matty, I think he's coming back tomorrow," Luke told him. "Isn't he mum?"

Clarissa smiled. "Tobi might be home when we get back. He left London early."

Luke and Matthew began to cheer in the back of her car, making her giggle. She still couldn't get over her boys connecting with Tobi so quickly and so well. It made her heart happy.

The traffic was minimal, and Clarissa was two minutes from home. The boys were already wilting from their long day at school, although they were trying to sing along to the songs on the radio.

A loud bang sounded from outside the car.

Suddenly Clarissa's car window smashed, showering her and the boys in shards and chunks of glass. Clarissa swerved as glass fragments hit her face and body, cutting into her soft skin. Instinctively she closed her eyes, turning her face away from the razor-sharp debris.

All she could hear were the screams of Luke and Matthew.

Clarissa couldn't see anything. Blood streamed down her face and into her eyes. Her first instinct was to slam on her brakes—but it was too late. The Mercedes' swerved, smashing into something solid. Clarissa, Luke, and Matthew's heads were immediately thrown forward—straight into exploding airbags—before the impact flung them back into their seats and headrests. Clarissa's tensed arms, shoulders, and back, taking the brunt of the impact.

She screamed in pain before passing out.

Sirens began blaring as the police protection unit jumped into action, pulling alongside Clarissa's car and the stationary parked van she had ploughed into. The driver, Officer Meadows, immediately called for backup and an ambulance on his radio as his partner, Officer Griffin, jumped out of their car, using the car door as a shield.

Having been partners for over five years, neither officer felt the need to communicate. They knew what they had to do.

Griffin's eyes scanned the road and surrounding buildings, trying to spot the shooter, Mr. Mason. There was no sign of the madman, and Griffin didn't know whether Mr. Mason was on foot or in a vehicle.

Cars in both directions stopped on the main road, now covered in debris, but the Darcy family was Griffin's priority. He rushed in a hunched position to Clarissa's destroyed car. Griffin could hear Luke and Matthew crying for their mum in total panic, but he couldn't hear any sounds from Clarissa. He began to think the worst.

Meadows knew their backup was already on the way. He quickly exited his car, eyes darting in all directions, unaware of where Mr. Mason could be. Traffic wasn't only at a standstill; it was also building up quickly. He silently prayed that their backup and ambulances would be able to get through the throng of vehicles.

When Meadows reached Griffin, he was already leaning in Clarissa's car, checking her vitals and injuries while Luke and

Matthew cried inconsolably.

"It's okay, boys, Officer Griffin is looking after your mum, and help is on the way. Are either of you hurt?" Meadows asked as he looked for obvious signs of injury.

Matthew was crying so hard that he couldn't form any words, and even though Luke was just as traumatized, he wrapped his arm around his baby brother.

"My, my head and neck hurt," Luke sobbed, "I don't know if Matt is hurt. Is my mum going to be alright?"

Meadows didn't think it was right to lie to the boys, especially as he didn't know if Clarissa had been shot.

"I hope so, little man," Meadows said honestly. "Griffin, what's the status?"

Griffin looked past Clarissa's blood-covered head. "I think he missed. I can feel her pulse, and it's fairly good. I'm seeing deep lacerations to her head and upper body, and after this impact, there could be possible spinal injuries. I don't want to move her. Better to wait for the paramedics."

Meadows nodded. He wanted to get Luke and Matthew out of the wrecked car, but with Mr. Mason still at large, it was too risky without their backup. Luckily, he could hear faint sirens in the distance, knowing they wouldn't be long.

Clarissa could feel searing pain as she started to regain consciousness. Her head felt like it was about to explode, and most of her upper body was searing with shooting pains. Even her skin felt like it was on fire. Clarissa was confused as she tried to open her eyes, she could hear muffled noises, but her brain couldn't filter them.

Officer Griffin could see that Clarissa was starting to come around. He saw her eye movement and her breaths quicken.

"Clarissa, can you hear me?" he asked. "Can you hear me, Clarissa?"

"Is my mummy waking up?" Matthew asked between sobs.

Meadows glanced at Griffin, who shook his head. "Not yet, little man, but hopefully she should wake up soon."

Griffin didn't want Clarissa trying to move in case she injured herself further, but he was getting frustrated. He could hear the ambulances and their backup, but they didn't sound any closer. Griffin knew other officers were probably trying to clear the road to let the emergency services through. Clarissa's phone began ringing from inside her handbag on the passenger seat, but he ignored it.

Clarissa's brain was trying to re-engage. Various strong smells and loud noises assaulted her senses as she tried to understand what was happening. Her eyes felt stiff and heavy, but she tried to open them anyway.

"Clarissa, can you hear me?" Griffin asked. "Squeeze my hand if you can hear me."

'Clarissa? That's me. I'm Clarissa.'

Clarissa squeezed his hand, and shooting pains shot up and down her arm. She moaned with the pain. She tried to open her eyes, but they were badly swollen, and she could barely see anything through the haze of red.

"My boys, where are my boys." Clarissa's panic began to rise.

"Mummy!" Luke called from the back seat, instantly trying to remove his seat belt.

Meadows pressed a gentle hand on Luke's chest.

"Stay there for a bit longer, little man."

Griffin gently squeezed Clarissa's hand.

"Your boys are here, and they're okay. Try and stay still, you're hurt, and the paramedics are just arriving," he assured her as the ambulances and backup finally pushed through the heavy throng of cars.

The pain in her head and body was too much—Clarissa passed out.

—x—

When Clarissa opened her eyes again, she found herself attached to a heart monitor and a drip in a hospital room. Clarissa had no idea why she was in the hospital. She sifted through her memories to remember what she was doing last. She remembered collecting Luke and Matthew from school and heading home—but that was it.

Her whole upper body ached as if she was bruised from head to waist, and her head throbbed uncomfortably. As she turned her head, she almost passed out again.

Taking it more slowly, Clarissa turned her head away from the brightness of the hospital room window. She tried to smile when she saw Luke and Matthew fast asleep on a large chair next to her bed, but her face felt tight and swollen. Clarissa slowly looked around the room she found herself in, spotting Tobi through the window in her room's door. He was on his phone, but the moment he spotted Clarissa was awake, he ended the call and rushed into her room.

Tobi's eyes were full of concern.

"Oh my god, Clarissa, I've been so worried. How are you feeling?"

Just as Clarissa was about to answer, Luke and Matthew woke at the sound of his voice.

"Mummy, you're awake!" Matthew squealed, his face lighting up with delight.

"We were so scared, Mum," Luke told her as fresh tears streamed down his young face.

Clarissa's heart broke at her children's mixed emotions. She couldn't imagine what they had been through, and she was relieved that they looked reasonably unhurt. She could see scratches on their faces through her blurry vision, but that was all.

"I'm okay, boys, I promise," she tried to reassure them.

Her throat felt dry and sore.

Tobi instinctively wrapped his arm around Luke, who buried his face into his side.

"Are they okay? Are they hurt?" she asked Tobi, needing reassurance herself.

"They have whiplash, cuts, and bruising, but nothing serious, gorgeous. I've had them thoroughly checked out. They're going to be sore for a while."

"What happened?" she asked, still feeling confused. "I was driving home after collecting them from school, and that's all I remember."

"Your ex-boss shot at your car," Tobi told her, his face instantly full of rage. "He was lying in wait on the main road because he knew you would be collecting the kids. He must have been watching you."

Clarissa couldn't believe what she was hearing. She wanted to ask a tirade of questions, but she didn't want to upset Matthew and Luke even more.

"How long have I been out of it?"

Tobi took a breath, trying to calm himself down.

"You've been asleep for days, gorgeous. They had to repair some damage to your spine, but you're going to be okay. You'll have to take things easy for a good few weeks at least, and you won't be able to drive for a while either."

A nurse tapped at Clarissa's door, and Tobi gave her a nod to come in.

"Hi Clarissa, my name is Nurse Kelly. I'm happy to see you

awake. How are you feeling?" She asked in a perky manner, as she approached the bed.

Clarissa tried to smile back at the friendly older lady, but her face hurt too much.

"I'm alright. I feel very bruised from the waist up, and my face doesn't feel right," she said honestly.

"You sustained many deep cuts to your face, neck, and arms when your car window smashed. I'm afraid you have a lot of stitches, but you won't notice the scars when they've healed. The doctor did a fantastic job," Kelly assured her as she placed her fingers on Clarissa's wrist, checking her pulse.

Tobi smiled at Clarissa as if trying to confirm Kelly's assurance, but Clarissa dreaded to think how she looked, probably like she had been beaten by a mob.

The hospital room's door burst open, and suddenly Hayley, Adam, Becky, and Martin rushed into the small hospital room, which abruptly felt smaller still. Clarissa's best friends started talking at once, and Clarissa couldn't keep up with either of them. They were clearly upset. She tried to smile to assure them she was okay.

After a couple of minutes, Clarissa held up a hand to halt their loud chatter.

"Whoah, ladies. My head is killing me. I can only listen to you one at a time," she told them gently.

Hayley and Becky instantly stopped talking, looking at her with apologetic faces.

"I'm sorry," Hayley said more quietly, "we've been so worried about you."

"I know you have," Clarissa told her, knowing she would be the same if they had been hurt.

Kelly stepped forward, checking Clarissa's monitors. "They've all been here every day," she told Clarissa quietly so only she would hear.

Clarissa wasn't surprised.

"Would you like some more pain relief, Clarissa?"

She tried to shake her head, but it hurt too much. "Not yet, thank you. I want a clear head for a while."

Clarissa had so many questions she wanted to know the answers to, but having a fuzzy head wasn't going to help her get them.

Kelly nodded. "I'll come back later on. In the meantime, would you like a cup of tea?"

Clarissa was dying for a cup of tea, and Kelly's words were like music to her ears. Her mouth felt like she had licked a hundred envelopes non-stop.

"Yes, please."

Giving her a warm smile, Kelly left the room.

Tobi leaned over to give her a gentle kiss. "I'll go and take the boys to get drinks and snacks," Tobi told her. "Let you girls catch up. We'll be back in a few minutes."

Luke let go of Tobi's waist to give Clarissa a gentle hug, and even though it hurt like hell, she didn't let on. Clarissa stroked Luke's back, and Matthew made his way around the other side of the bed. Clarissa put her other arm around him, kissing him on the top of his head as he lowered it to her chest.

"Thank you for being such good boys for Tobi. I'll see you in a bit when you've had something to eat and drink, okay?" Clarissa told them lovingly.

Clarissa smiled as Tobi winked and led them out of the room, heading for the vending machines.

"We'll go with the boys," Adam said, giving Martin a nod.

As soon as Luke and Matthew were out of earshot, Becky plonked herself on the chair next to Clarissa, while Hayley walked around the other side, gently sitting on the edge of her hospital bed.

"If that sicko weren't dead already, I would kill him for doing this to you!" Hayley declared angrily.

Clarissa's eyebrows tried to rise in surprise, and instantly her forehead hurt. She raised her hand to her forehead, and when she felt her stitches, she regretted it immediately. She felt like crying; her head and face hurt so badly.

"He's dead?"

Hayley nodded. "He sure is. The news stations and newspapers have been all over your story after what happened, and they were showing his picture. The police did a full-on search. The sicko didn't have anywhere to go, so he went to his sisters, but the police were watching her house. So, they nabbed him as soon as he pulled up outside."

"The bloody idiot started firing at the police, and they shot him dead," Becky added. "Good riddance! Now he can't hurt anyone else."

Clarissa's mind was reeling. So much had happened so quickly she was struggling to take it all in.

"So, does that mean it's finally all over?"

Becky nodded and smiled. "It sure is; life can go back to normal, thank god. Although the news reporters have been trying to get in here to see you and hound us all for information, but don't worry, badass bitch over there has been sorting them out," she said, pointing at Hayley.

"The bastard may be dead, but I'm still going to sue the ass off Janka Industries. That's if you want me to continue. Those bastards need to pay for everything you've been put through—and if they had dealt with that fucker years ago—none of this would have happened," Hayley raged.

Clarissa knew her best friend was right. "Yeah, you're right. I want you to keep going, please."

Nurse Kelly entered the room with a fresh cup of tea and a straw. "I thought you might need this," she said, showing Clarissa the straw. "It's going to hurt moving your head and face for a while."

She put the tea on the narrow unit next to Clarissa's bed and began to help Clarissa sit up to drink it. Becky and Hayley cringed as they watched Clarissa trying to move.

Holding up the tea and straw with one hand and supporting Clarissa's head with the other, Kelly helped her drink. She was so thirsty; half the cup was gone in seconds.

"I'll be back again soon," Kelly told her as she put the teacup down and left the room.

Laying her head back onto her pillow, Clarissa closed her eyes for a moment. "Do you know what they had to do to my spine? I haven't had a chance to find out," she said, reopening her eyes which were beginning to throb.

"We only know what Tobias told us," Becky told her, "Apparently, two of your discs moved, trapping nerves. So, they had to deal with it quickly before any permanent damage was done."

Clarissa was relieved, especially as it could have been a lot worse, and she was beyond grateful that it had been her that was badly hurt and not her boys.

"I have a question for you. Did your airbags," Hayley said with a grin, grabbing her large boobs, "help protect you as much as the car airbags?"

Becky burst into giggles as Clarissa tried not to laugh.

"Trust you to think of something like that, woman!" Clarissa exclaimed.

"We're going to keep taking the boys home with us until you come home," Becky said, still smiling at Hayley's question. "By the way, we've done some digging on Tobi, and he hasn't got an asshole bone in his body."

"What do you mean digging?"

Hayley grinned. "She means we've grilled my brother-in-law, Mitchell, and he told us that Tobias is a really decent guy. And I did a thorough background check on him. So you can stop doubting yourself and your new relationship," she said, just as Tobi and all the boys came back laden with snacks.

"How many snacks did you let them get?" Clarissa asked, trying not to laugh again.

Tobi looked at her guiltily. "They couldn't decide which snacks they wanted," he smiled.

His guilty look made Clarissa giggle, but it hurt so badly that she gripped her bedding. "Oh my god, please don't keep making me laugh you lot; it hurts too bad."

Immediately Tobi rushed forward, taking her hand in his. "I'm sorry, gorgeous. Are you okay?"

Clarissa took long slow breaths for a moment until the pain eased. "I'm ok; it just really hurts. It'll ease off in a second," she assured him.

"You need to get more rest," Becky told Clarissa as she approached Luke and Matthew. "Are you boys ready to come home with us?"

Luke and Matthew looked conflicted. They loved staying over at Becky's house, but they didn't want to leave their Mum, especially now she was awake. Clarissa could tell that her boys were torn.

"Why don't you go with Auntie Becky? I'm going to have to sleep for a while, my angels," Clarissa said, smiling.

Luke's face dropped. "Can we come back tonight after dinner?"

Tobi ruffled his hair. "Just ask auntie Becky to call me. I'll come to get you and bring you back to visit your Mum, okay."

Both Luke and Matthew brightened up, which made Clarissa feel relieved.

After saying goodbye with gentle hugs from Luke and Matthew, they all left, apart from Tobi. Clarissa hated to see her children go, but she knew they needed a little normality. Tobi pulled the big armchair closer to her bed.

"Are you doing okay?" He asked, taking her hand and stroking it with his thumb.

Clarissa tried to give him a reassuring smile. "I'm alright," she lied. "I never thought I would say anything like this, but I'm relieved and glad the bastard is dead. He could have killed my boys, Tobi."

Tears streamed down her bruised and swollen face as the reality of what had happened hit her. Within a split second, Tobi was out of the chair. He gently wrapped his arms around her fragile form as she sobbed.

Tobi knew how she felt because he had felt the same way. When he arrived at Clarissa's house, and she wasn't there, he started to worry. And when Clarissa didn't answer her phone, he went into panic mode. Tobi called the school just to confirm that the boys had been collected, and when he was told they had, he felt genuine fear for the second time in his life. The first time was the terminal cancer diagnosis of his sister.

Tobi had never loved anyone like he loved Clarissa, and his heart broke while she sobbed in his arms. "It's all going to be okay now, gorgeous. I promise," he told her comfortingly. "He's gone, and now we can get back to living our lives."

Clarissa realized that she couldn't imagine life without Tobi now, even though they had only recently met. She felt like they had known each other forever. Everything felt so easy with him, and she had never felt so safe and loved in someone's arms.

Tobi let Clarissa sob and shed all her traumatic emotions, and when her crying eased, he held her until she was ready to talk. Clarissa raised her tear-soaked face and saw nothing but love in Tobi's green eyes.

"Thank you."

He smiled, stroking her dark auburn hair away from her face. Tobi softly kissed her tears before smiling at the woman he would happily die for.

"You are welcome, beautiful lady. How about I get the doctor, so we can find out when you can come home?" Tobi asked.

Clarissa slowly nodded. All she wanted to do was go home; especially now it was safe.

Chapter 16

The doctor who came in to see Clarissa, armed with X-rays and scan photos, was just as friendly as Nurse Kelly, and Tobi already had a good rapport with him. Dr. Snow was the kind of doctor who gave you the impression he had seen everything regarding spinal injuries, which Clarissa found reassuring. When Clarissa saw him, he reminded her of Anthony Hopkins, not a large man but confident and friendly.

"Hello, Clarissa. I'm Doctor Snow. How are you feeling?" He asked, smiling and showing the whitest teeth she had ever seen.

Clarissa knew she had to be honest, but she didn't want Tobi worrying.

"I'm doing okay. I feel very bruised, sore, and like I've done a full twelve rounds with a heavyweight boxer."

"Well, I'm not surprised," he told her. "You've had a nasty head-on crash with a parked van, and unfortunately, because of the angle of the impact, you received a lot of impact force through your torso."

"Oh god, Tobi, your brother's car," Clarissa said, immediately feeling guilty.

"My brother and I don't care about the car, gorgeous. The car was insured, and it can be replaced. You, Luke, and Matthew are irreplaceable," he told her with a wink.

Clarissa was starting to feel grateful that she couldn't remember hitting the van. Seeing the damage to the Mercedes would probably make her feel even more guilty.

"These are your X-rays and scans we took before your surgery," Doctor Snow said, holding up each one to a lightbox on her room's wall. "As you can see here," he pointed, "these two vertebrae moved, putting pressure on your nerves. I had to realign your vertebrae and free the nerves."

Clarissa nodded, grateful for the doctor's layman's terms and not blinding her with medical jargon she wouldn't understand.

"I would like you to stay for another night. Now you're awake, you can tell me if you feel any pain down your legs and if you can control your bladder and bowels," he told her. "Your neck and shoulders took much of the impact force, so you will feel very bruised for a few weeks, maybe a few months, depending on how quickly you heal," Doctor Snow explained.

"Can I go home tomorrow if I do okay over night?" Clarissa asked hopefully.

Doctor Snow smiled. "Yes, you can. However, I want you to do at least six weeks of physiotherapy. And you will be signed off work for those weeks too."

"Shit," Clarissa exclaimed, "My new boss will think that I quit as I haven't been logging on."

Clarissa's heart sank. She didn't need to lose another job because of John Mason on top of everything else.

Doctor Snow looked at her sympathetically. "If your employer is a decent company, I'm sure they will understand."

"I hope so and thank you for looking after me," Clarissa agreed, giving him a smile of her own.

"Thank you, Doctor Snow," Tobi said. "We appreciate you."

Doctor Snow left Clarissa's room with a nod of his head and

another smile. Clarissa laid her head back onto her pillow, happy that she could be going home the following day and hoping she still had a job.

"I'm sure your new boss will hold your job open. You're probably one of their best," Tobi said as he sat back in the chair next to Clarissa's bed. "I'm going to work from home until you're all better. And when I get you home, not only will you not be lifting a finger, but I will kiss you better from your head to your toes," he told her with a very naughty-looking grin.

—x—

When Clarissa and Tobi pulled up outside her house late the following day, Clarissa had never been so grateful to be home. Not surprisingly, Hayley and Becky's cars were outside her modest home, as was another car she didn't recognize. She knew it couldn't be anyone from the press as Tobi had already told her that Hayley had frightened them off.

Clarissa had left the hospital with a supply of strong painkillers, a spinal brace for support, and a pair of crutches that hurt her already sore and bruised shoulders and arms. Not that Clarissa minded; it was a small price to pay for being home and back with her kids.

As soon as Tobi exited the car, he raced around to Clarissa's side, opening the door like a gentleman. He took the crutches from her and held them up.

"I know they hurt you. Do you want me to carry you over the threshold?" He asked. "It will give me some practice."

Clarissa's eyes widened. 'Is he hinting at marriage?' she wondered. 'Bloody hell, it must be love.'

She smiled at him, still feeling the stitches in her bruised face pull and sting. "And practice for the bedroom."

Tobi winked at her while placing the crutches across the back seat.

"Well, that too, you hot, sexy minx. I have a lot of bruises to kiss better, but you may have to show me the places without bruises that I need to kiss better too," he told her as he gently scooped her up in his arms, pushing the car door closed with his foot.

"You keep talking like that, and you'll be taking me straight up to the bedroom." She winked. "Becky and Hayley would totally understand."

Tobi laughed. "I'm sure they would. All three of you are saucy little minx's," he said as he carried her to the front door with ease.

"Don't tell them that," she grinned, "they already have crushes on you."

Tobi grinned. "Really?" he said cheekily, knocking on the front door with his foot.

Clarissa playfully tugged his hair.

The front door opened to cheers from inside the house, and as Tobi entered with Clarissa in his arms, she could see a large home-made welcome home banner across her lounge wall. Hayley, Becky, Luke, and Matthew were cheering her return home, and so were Clarissa's parents. Clarissa did a double-take—not quite believing what she saw—until her Mum burst into tears. Her mum and dad rushed over, hugging Clarissa while Tobi still held her. Clarissa couldn't stop fresh tears from flowing.

Once Clarissa's parents got a grip of their emotions and released her, Tobi placed her gently on the couch supported with cushions.

"When did you get back?" Clarissa asked while wiping away her tears.

Clarissa's dad, Daniel, wrapped an arm around his tearful wife.

"We flew out on the next plane after Hayley called and told us what happened," her mum, Mary, said tearfully.

Her dad shook his head as tears ran down his face. "I'm glad the police got him. I would have ripped his head off for going after you and my grandsons!"

Clarissa's mum hugged him. She was shocked to see her dad cry. It was something she had never seen him do. Angry, yes; tearful, no.

Luke and Matthew were thrilled to have their mum home and approached her with beautiful get-well-soon cards, welcome home pictures, and small bouquets of white roses, Peruvian lilies, and baby's breath sprigs. Their happy little faces were enough to lighten everyone's mood, including their grandparents.

"We made these for you, mummy," Matthew told her proudly, grinning from ear to ear.

Clarissa's heart was melting as she accepted the pictures and flowers.

"You made these all by yourselves?" she asked, smiling at her little boys.

Matthew eagerly nodded, feeling very proud of himself.

Luke nodded enthusiastically. "We made the pictures, and Tobi let us choose all the flowers we wanted in the shop, so we picked your favorites."

"I can see that, my angels. They are beautiful," she told them. "Maybe we can ask Tobi to put your pictures up in here, on the wall, and put the flowers on the coffee table so everyone can see them." She smiled, making her boys even more proud.

Tobi and Martin appeared out of nowhere, holding a bottle of champagne and a handful of glasses.

"Did someone mention my name," he grinned, "I thought we could celebrate you being home."

—x—

As Clarissa lay in bed propped up with soft pillows with Tobi lying beside her asleep, she thought about what a long day it had been. The day had been another roller coaster of emotions, especially the surprise visit from her parents, who had decided to stay for a month. Tobi's offer for them to stay at his house for the month had gone down very well with her parents, and every now and again throughout the evening, her mum had mouthed, he's a keeper.

Luke and Matthew lasted until ten pm, and Clarissa was grateful that they had no school the next day. There was nothing worse than tired and grumpy kids. They were so tired that they asked Tobi to take them up to bed, much to her surprise.

Tobi had not just bought one bottle of champagne; he had bought a whole case, which led to Hayley, Becky, and Clarissa's mum, Mary, getting rather tipsy. It made the rest of the evening hilarious, especially when Mary started asking about Clarissa's new job.

When Clarissa tried to explain what her new job entailed, her dad, Daniel, actually blushed, even though Clarissa made it clear that it was just acting. Unfortunately, Hayley and Becky couldn't stop themselves from describing some of the calls they had listened to, including the Senson tool man, making Daniel blush even more.

"I'm never going to look at my tools the same way ever again." Daniel had told them as his cheeks reddened.

Mary was surprisingly relaxed about Clarissa's new job. She was in fits of laughter as Hayley and Becky described more of the calls.

"Nothing would surprise me when it comes to men," Mary said with a knowing look on her face. "I once caught my ex-boyfriend with my knickers on his head and wearing my bra. It was quite a shock; I can tell you."

"You never told me about that," Daniel told her with raised eyebrows, enhancing his worry lines.

"I don't tell you everything," Mary stated. "We've been married for nearly forty years. There's nothing wrong with keeping a little mystery alive."

Daniel narrowed his eyes. "What else don't I know, wife of mine."

"Wouldn't you like to know," Mary grinned at her affronted husband.

"Why yes, I would."

Clarissa's dad pouted at her mum, making her giggle. She loved their banter, it never got old, and she had missed it.

Clarissa had given up asking all of them to stop making her laugh during the course of the evening. It hurt, but laughing made her feel so much better, and it seemed to be good therapy for all of them. When Clarissa told them about her recent caller, Harold, and him getting caught by his wife, they were laughing so hard, none of them could breathe. Becky nearly mummy-peed. Clarissa reminded them that everyone had a fetish for something, even her parents, which suddenly made Mary and Daniel go quiet. *"Interesting."* Clarissa thought.

—x—

"Can't sleep?" Tobi asked, reaching out a hand to brush his knuckles gently against Clarissa's cheek as they lay in bed.

Clarissa leaned into his hand. "No, and I should be exhausted after what you just did to me, you bad man." She chuckled.

Tobi grinned. "I warned you that I'd kiss all your bruises and places that hurt. I just didn't realize how many places there would be, or that there would be so many places that aren't usually connected to car accidents."

"Well, you did ask if I had twinges anywhere else, and by the time you kissed my top half, my lower half was having all sorts of twinges." Clarissa grinned.

"I do like to be thorough," he told her with a smirk.

"Yes, you do. Repeatedly, apparently."

Tobi kissed her. "Do you have things on your mind?"

Clarissa nodded. She looked at Tobi with worry in her eyes. "I never want to work for a man ever again. No offense."

"None taken. I don't blame you for feeling that way," Tobi told her, "I've had to work with some male assholes myself over the years. That's why I decided to start my own business and be my own boss."

Tobi could tell Clarissa's mind was working overtime.

"Would you like a cup of tea, gorgeous?"

Clarissa nodded, knowing she wasn't ready for sleep. Her brain had no intention of switching off.

When Tobi returned to the bedroom, he was armed with a tray of fresh tea and Clarissa's favorite chocolate-covered biscuits.

"I thought you might like a little snack too."

Not for the first time, Clarissa wondered how she had gotten so lucky to meet Tobi.

Tobi placed the tray between them on the bed.

"I've got an idea. Why don't you start your own company?"

Clarissa's eyes widened. Starting her own business was something she had never even considered.

"I don't have anything to sell, products, or service," she said, loving the idea of being a business owner but disheartened over having nothing to offer.

"Clarissa, you are so good at your new job; you do have a

service you can offer. I know enough about communications to know that you can rent phone lines and offer your own service. It's no different than any other company getting customer service lines; only you pick your own cost per minute. I could help you with a business website and even create an app for it," he said eagerly.

"You think so?" Clarissa said as her mind began going over the possibilities.

Clarissa sipped her tea and took one of the biscuits, literally needing some food for thought. She began to imagine having ladies working for her, and she knew she would be able to train them to do the job. She had been training new staff at her old job for a long time.

Tobi interrupted her thoughts.

"I have a bit of a confession," he said sheepishly. "When I started to get interested in being dominated, I did some online research and discovered there are whole communities of dominant's and submissive's. I'm sure there's a big market out there you can tap into, not just chat lines, but also the clothes, accessories, and toys."

"You don't need to feel embarrassed," Clarissa said, smiling. "I did a lot of research myself for my new job. It was quite an eye-opener. I suppose I could look into it while working on the chat line."

Tobi gave her another kiss. "Why not sleep on it? By the way, I was hoping to stay here while your parents are at my place, if that's okay?"

"Of course, you can stay for as long as you want."

He grinned like a Cheshire Cat. "Good. Then we can discuss your career more tomorrow if you want to go for it."

The night seemed to go on forever for Clarissa, with ideas and thoughts racing through her mind. And the more she thought about

Tobi's suggestion, the more she liked it. She even had a business name idea by the morning, Darcy's Domination Desires, the three D's.

—x—

As soon as Tobi woke up, he sprang into action. Before Luke and Matthew had a chance to wake up, he helped Clarissa get showered, which he thoroughly enjoyed, dressed, and helped her downstairs, placing her on the couch with a cup of tea and a bowl of cereal. When Luke and Matthew did wake up, Tobi made sure they showered, got dressed, and were ready for breakfast in record time.

"I'm so impressed," Clarissa told him when he gave her a fresh mug of tea.

Tobi looked just as proud as her boys had the day before with their pictures.

"I'm assuming your mum and dad will be around today to make the most of you, Luke and Matthew, so I thought I'd be prepared." He grinned. "Have you been thinking about my suggestion?"

"I have," she admitted. "I even thought of a name for my company too, but I'll tell you later when we don't have little ears around."

Leaning over her, Tobi kissed Clarissa, then brushed his nose against hers. "You are incredible, do you know that?"

Clarissa looked into his beautiful green eyes. "Yep, that's why you love me."

Tobi kissed her again and leaned further towards her ear. "Your confidence is so bloody hot. I've got a good mind to take you back upstairs and kiss all your bruises again," he whispered.

She giggled, knowing how serious he was.

No sooner had Luke and Matthew finished their breakfast, than

Clarissa's parents arrived with gifts for them. When Tobi went to answer the door, he grinned at Clarissa.

"Told you."

Clarissa shook her head, chuckling at him for being a smart-ass.

"You keep being cheeky, and I'll have to punish you later," she said, raising an eyebrow and giving him a stern look.

"Oh, promises, promises, Clarissa Darcy," Tobi said, winking at her.

Mary and Daniel had bought their grandsons an array of sports gifts, much to Luke and Matthew's delight, from footballs and pop-up nets to rugby balls and cricket bats. Luke and Matthew didn't quite know what to play with first, nor did Tobi. It became evident that not only was Tobi active with outdoor activities, but he was quite the sportsman too, which impressed Clarissa's dad greatly.

Clarissa was surprised that her parents had taken such a shine to Tobi, especially as they knew the hell her ex-asshole had put her through. Then Clarissa realized something. Nigel would have heard what had happened to her and the boys, but she hadn't received so much as a text from him to ask if Luke and Matthew were okay. *'What an absolute tosser.'* She could feel her blood starting to boil, hating the fact that the bastard couldn't be bothered to check on his kids after they were shot at and were in a car accident.

When Clarissa's parents and Tobi took Luke and Matthew to the park to try out their new sports gifts, Clarissa decided to call her boss, Michelle, to let her know what was going on, while she had a chance.

Within a few rings, Michele answered in her usual chirpy manner.

"Good morning, Castle Communications. Michelle speaking. How can I help you?"

Clarissa's pulse began to race. "Hi, Michelle, it's Clarissa Darcy."

"Oh my god, Clarissa, are you alright? I saw on the news what happened. That bastard could have killed you all," Michelle exclaimed in a rush of words, obviously concerned.

Clarissa breathed a sigh of relief. "I'm okay. I got out of the hospital yesterday, so I'm home again now. I'm sorry I couldn't work. I had to have surgery and was knocked out for a few days."

"You don't need to apologize, Clarissa. You take all the time you need. You'll always have a job with us; you're my best lady," Michelle told her warmly.

Her words were a massive relief for Clarissa. She didn't want to be in a position where she would have to borrow money from her parents. It was why she had stayed in the job she hated for so long. Although her parents were the sort who would never have wanted her to pay them back, however, that wasn't the point as far as she was concerned.

"Thanks, Michelle. I appreciate your understanding and kindness. I'd like to get back to work as soon as possible. I've still got bills to pay and little mouths to feed."

Michelle chuckled. "And that's why you are my best and favorite worker. You start back to work whenever you like, and if you have any problems, just call me, okay?"

"Will do," Clarissa said gratefully. "Thanks again."

The call had gone much better than Clarissa had expected, but after having a total bastard for a boss for years, Clarissa had wrongly assumed the worst. She smiled to herself, happy that her job was safe.

While she still had time to herself, Clarissa decided to research her possible new and first business venture. Unfortunately, her laptop was still on her desk, and there was no way she wanted to risk moving on her own with no one around. *'Thank God for smartphones and apps,'* she thought as she opened her notes app and the search engine.

The first thing Clarissa searched for was her company name idea, Darcy's Domination Desires. She was thrilled that no other company popped up on the results. With that good news, Clarissa typed her business name on her note's app, which gave her butterflies in her stomach. Doubts filled her mind, and she wondered if she could be a business owner. *'Sod it,'* she thought, *'I would never have thought I could work and raise two kids on my own, but I've done it. And I've done a decent job.'*

With a new sense of determination, Clarissa decided to look for quality wholesalers for domination and fetish tools, toys, and clothing, which wasn't as easy as finding other products wholesale. Quite a few companies sold wholesale domination and fetish products, but Clarissa couldn't see any reviews for the companies anywhere. She decided that she would have to try and delve deeper or trial some of the company's products when she had the money. The good thing was that the companies did seem to have a lot of products. Clarissa copied and pasted the company's details and links onto her notes.

There was still no sign of her parents, Tobi, and the boys, so Clarissa did a new search for domination and fetish, clothing, and lingerie wholesalers. And as Clarissa started to look at the various companies and their products, she noticed something extremely evident. Yet again, there were very few clothing items for busty and curvy women like her and Hayley. Then Clarissa had an idea. Ann, the owner of Luscious Lingerie was fantastic at making custom bras, corsets, and basques for brides and special occasion orders. From what Clarissa had heard, there was nothing that Ann couldn't create, and she wondered if Ann might be interested in a business proposition. Clarissa decided to contact Ann as soon as possible to talk to her about it.

She was starting to feel good about her possible new business venture, and she couldn't wait to tell Hayley and Becky to find out what they thought.

Using her notes app, Clarissa saved the links of all the clothing designs she liked, picking only the items that looked classy and hot as hell. If she was going to have her own company, she wanted everything to be top-notch and highly desirable.

By the time Clarissa's parents and kids returned, she had quite a list to go from, and she couldn't wait to show Tobi. Clarissa giggled when she saw the state of Matthew and Luke as they walked into the kitchen. Both were covered in mud from head to toe and were wearing huge smiles. Tobi was no better; neither was her dad. Mary made them strip in the kitchen, much to her dad's chagrin. As Luke and Matthew watched their grandad strip down to his boxer shorts, they giggled, and laughed even more when he began to roll his stomach. Even Tobi was impressed by Daniel's party piece.

Chapter 17

When Clarissa's parents left that evening, Luke and Matthew were exhausted, and when Tobi put them to bed, Clarissa went straight back to researching for her new business. Clarissa knew she should try and work some hours on the chat line, but she didn't think she had it in her to try and act like a nymphomaniac or domination diva just yet. *'Monday is soon enough,'* she told herself as she opened her search engine again on her phone.

"You look thoughtful," Tobi said as he walked back into the lounge.

Clarissa grinned. "I'm researching for my new business, Darcy's Domination Desires. I'm having such good vibes about this, Tobi. I think you're really onto something."

Tobi's responding grin was just as big as he adsorbed her excitement. "I love the name you've come up with. What do you need me to do, so I can help you?" he asked enthusiastically.

Putting her index finger to her lips, Clarissa thought for a moment. "A fresh cup of tea, my laptop, and your brains."

Tobi laughed. "That I can do. I'm on it."

Within an hour, not only had Tobi made Clarissa a fresh cuppa, but he had also moved her around on the couch, so her feet were up on a footstool. He placed a side table next to her for her tea and a tray to balance her laptop.

Tobi sat next to her holding his cup of tea.

"Okay, you are armed, ready, and dangerous. What's first?"

Clarissa smiled. She was thrilled that Tobi was so excited and enthusiastic.

"I have already searched for Darcy's Domination Desires, and there's nothing close to it online, so I think we're good there. I think we should look at phone rates and website designs first. I haven't got the money to buy any products yet, so that will have to wait. And don't even think of offering me money," she said, giving him a stern look as he was about to open his mouth to speak.

Tobi nodded and held a hand up in surrender. "I have it if you need it; that's all I'm going to say. Anyway, I think you're right to look at phone lines and a website first."

To say that Clarissa was impressed by Tobi's knowledge was an understatement. After doing a lot of research, they found two reputable companies that offered phone line services with various pricing costs. Clarissa knew that domination and fetish services were more specialized. Most chat line ladies were uncomfortable talking about domination and fetishes, so she decided to opt for the more expensive lines, especially as most of her callers were professionals.

While looking at website designs, Tobi became excited, telling and showing Clarissa which website designs worked better and were more accessible for site visitors. Even Clarissa started to get excited when he showed her how she could have her own online shop when she was ready.

"Do you remember Ann from Luscious Lingerie, where we met?" Clarissa asked.

"How could I forget?" Tobi grinned. "I think that if you hadn't told me off, Ann might have herself. Although it wouldn't have had the same effect."

Clarissa laughed as he wiggled his eyebrows at her.

"I'm thinking of asking if she'd be interested in creating some custom domination and fetish wear for my business. If I offer custom clothing and lingerie, I won't have to bulk order. I'll be able to offer clothing for busty and curvy women, and I can start offering the service sooner. What do you think?"

"I think it's a brilliant idea. Ann would be able to make extra money without doing all the legwork to get the sales. She'd also be able to keep that side of her business separate from her lingerie shop," he told her.

"Good point." Clarissa hadn't thought of that aspect. "I'm going to invite Ann and the girls over tomorrow night to see what they all think."

Glancing at the time and seeing it was still quite early in the evening, Clarissa decided to message her best friends and Ann, hoping that they would all be free the following evening.

Girl's night at mine tomorrow evening from eight. I have a business idea I want to run by you all. Are you free? Clarissa xxx

With the message sent, Clarissa waited for their replies while Tobi helped her to the bathroom. It was literally a pain having to ask for help to go for a pee, in more ways than one, but Tobi took it all in his stride.

Clarissa wished, not for the first time since she got home from hospital, that she had a bigger downstairs bathroom. Tucked into the left side of her front door, it only contained a toilet and sink, which were so close, if you had a bad stomach, you could evacuate at both ends of your body as the same time, if needed. She knew this from experience when her boys brought home a rather nasty stomach bug a year earlier. There was no room to manoeuvre, and Clarissa was grateful that Tobi was so strong. If she weren't hurting so badly with every movement as he lowered her to the toilet, she would probably be admiring his thick muscles in action.

"I can't wait to be back to normal," she told him, flinching with the pain.

Tobi smiled at her. "Don't worry, gorgeous; you'll be back to normal soon."

As Tobi helped her back to the lounge, Clarissa could hear her phone pinging with messages, and she hoped it was good news.

Once Clarissa got settled back on the couch, she checked her texts. There were yeses from Hayley and Becky and a heck yes from Ann. Clarissa was thrilled Ann was coming, and her 'heck yes' answer gave her the impression Ann was looking forward to it.

"Tomorrow night with the girls is on," Clarissa told Tobi as he put some soft music on, and Anita Baker began singing on the stereo. "If Ann agrees to my proposal, then it's just the toys and domination tools to sort out."

Tobi gave her a grin as he sat down next to her. "I was thinking about that. I think we need to do some market research," he said, trying to look serious.

Clarissa smirked. "You mean you want to try before I buy?"

"Exactly," Tobi wiggled his eyebrows at her again. "I think it's important to do thorough research so your customers are guaranteed to receive excellent products. Then you can add a badge to the items saying, Tobias approved."

"You are seriously too much, Tobi." Clarissa laughed. "If I wasn't hurting so bad, I would spank you!"

"I can get you a wooden spoon so you can reach," he told her cheekily, making Clarissa giggle.

She playfully smacked his thigh.

"I think we should have a look at the toys and domination tools together and pick some to try out. They're more for me than you, so I'll buy them," he said with a wink.

Clarissa rolled her eyes.

"I don't know who's more excited about this business venture, you or me."

Tobi shrugged, completely unashamed "I think it might be me. Now, let's see what we like the look of."

Tobi was like a child in a sweet shop, perusing the domination and fetish websites that Clarissa had found, and his shopping list grew to quite a size. Altogether, Tobi ordered a leather restraint kit, leather collar, padded blindfold, nipple clamps, an over-the-door bondage cross, and a male body harness.

"You're going to be like a kid at Christmas waiting for all of this to arrive, aren't you?" Clarissa asked him.

"Yes," he said, with the biggest and cheesiest grin she had ever seen.

—x—

Clarissa woke on Monday morning feeling better than the day before after having a better night's sleep. What had helped was Tobi insisting that he kiss all her bruises again, and by the time he had finished, she fell asleep with a smile on her face.

As Luke and Matthew had a day off due to teacher training, Daniel and Mary spent the day at Clarissa's house, making the most of their grandsons before the boys had to go back to school. And every time Tobi made fresh cups of tea, prepared lunch or snacks, and helped Clarissa go to the bathroom, Mary kept telling Clarissa what a Saint he was. Daniel was just as bad, although it was lovely to see the two men in her life bonding and joking around like old friends.

When Tobi happened to mention that Hayley, Becky, and Ann were coming over that evening, Mary's eyes lit up. Clarissa knew she had to invite her mum for the girl's night, especially considering she and Ann were old friends and both were good fun. Clarissa's dad was never one to miss an opportunity, inviting Tobi to the local pub down the road for a few beers. Clarissa wasn't sure who was going to lead who astray, her dad or Tobi.

Before Tobi left with Clarissa's dad, he had Luke and Matthew settled upstairs reading, wine opened for the girls, and snacks on the table, with the help of Clarissa's mum. Clarissa was still shocked and grateful at how different he was from Nigel. She was starting to think that sometimes people had to experience bad relationships to appreciate a good one when it came along.

—x—

As always, Hayley and Becky were slightly early, armed with more snacks that would probably go straight to Clarissa's waistline, especially as she wasn't really mobile yet.

"We've come prepared," Hayley said as she walked into the lounge. "Wow, you're looking perkier."

Clarissa thought Hayley was just trying to cheer her up. Every time she looked in the mirror, she thought she looked like Shrek, with her bruises looking so green and yellow. She looked even scarier than Becky had been with her green face mask.

"I'm feeling perkier," Clarissa grinned, "Tobi keeps insisting on kissing all my bruises."

"Yeah, and I bet he's been kissing other body parts too, you naughty bitch," Hayley laughed.

Mary began to blush.

"Now, don't get jealous," Clarissa told her. "It's about time I got some decent attention."

Becky nodded profusely. "Amen to that, sister!"

Mary poured the wine while the girls made themselves comfortable and at home.

Clarissa smiled at her mum, loving the fact that she was there spending time with her.

"Mum, I promise that will be the mildest comment of the evening. Tobi and I have an idea for my very own company, and I'll warn you now, you may be blushing all night."

Mary's eyes widened. "Maybe I should have put more foundation and powder on before I came over." She laughed. "Never mind, it's too late now. I'll just have to blush and keep you all warm with my burning cheeks."

"You're going to start your own company?" Hayley asked with a big grin.

Clarissa nodded excitedly. "That's our plan."

"Ooooh, spill the beans," Becky said, just as excited.

Clarissa's camera app pinged on her phone. "I think Ann's here, so I'll tell you all together." She grinned.

Mary let Ann in, and it was a wonderful reunion. They had always kept in touch, but they hadn't seen each other for a long while. They hugged on the doorstep like long-lost friends, telling each other how good the other looked. It was heart-warming to witness such love between old friends.

Becky's eyes welled at the sight.

"We'll be like that one day," she said as she looked at her best friends.

Clarissa and Hayley nodded.

"Come on in, Ann, before my mum squeezes the life out of you," Clarissa said jokingly.

Mary and Ann released each other, laughing at Clarissa's comment.

"I think it might be the other way round," Ann said as she took her jacket off and sat beside Clarissa.

"Ann, would you like some wine?" Mary asked, showing her the bottle.

Ann nodded. "When have you ever known me to turn down a glass?" She smirked.

"Mmm, never!" Mary told her with a grin.

Ann turned to Clarissa with sympathy written all over her lovely face. "Clarissa, I was so sorry to hear what happened to you and the boys. You see that kind of thing on the news and movies, but when it happens to people you know and love.; it's completely different."

Hayley, Becky, and Mary all nodded in agreement.

"The scary thing is that the bastard was getting away with it for years," Hayley said, shaking her head.

"I'd like to know how he got the gun?" Becky said in disgust.

Mary shook her head. "I asked Daniel the same thing, and he said that he probably knew some low life on the streets or online, willing to sell him one. And let's be honest; it's only decent people who follow the law. The criminals don't give a hoot."

"Anyway, let's talk about something positive," Ann said, giving Clarissa a warm smile. "I'm so happy to see that you're okay and on the mend. Thank you for inviting me tonight. I'm always up for a girl's night. I haven't had one in ages."

Clarissa grinned. "Well, I actually have an ulterior motive."

Ann raised a perfectly shaped eyebrow. "Now I'm intrigued."

"She's spilling the beans," Becky said, grinning at Hayley.

"Tobi suggested that I should start my own business, so I never have to work for another creep like my old boss, and to be honest, I love the idea of being my own boss."

"I can understand that," Ann told her, nodding. "I started my business because I was sick and tired of working for bad bosses and companies who didn't care about their staff. Working for male bosses was even worse when your mum and I were young. They thought they could do whatever they wanted, and we didn't have human resource departments with any clout back in our day."

Hayley tutted. "There are still many male bosses like that and HR departments who don't do what they're supposed to. Janka Industries, Clarissa's old company, is a perfect example."

"So, who's Tobi?" Ann asked.

Immediately, Mary, Hayley, and Becky started to grin.

Clarissa smiled at the grinning faces before her. "Tobi is my new boyfriend and the guy I told off when I was in your shop."

Ann laughed. "Wow, he was quite the handsome stud, if I remember rightly."

"That's an understatement," Becky added.

"Does he not already have a girlfriend? If I remember correctly, he was buying some very sexy women's knickers when he was at my shop."

Clarissa laughed. "This goes no further, ladies!" She told them firmly. "The knickers were actually for himself, and I have to say he makes them look good."

"No shit!" Hayley exclaimed in surprise, her eyes as big as saucers.

Becky burst into laughter. "Holy shit. Now that I would love to see."

Mary started blushing again. "Well, after what you told us about that Harold man, nothing would surprise me."

"Interesting," Ann said with a smirk. "Is Tobi a submissive?"

Clarissa was shocked. It was the last thing she expected to be asked, especially by Ann, but considering Tobi's business idea and what she wanted to discuss, she didn't see the point in holding back or lying.

"He is," she replied, making Ann smile.

"What the hell, Clarissa? You didn't think to tell us that sooner?" Hayley exclaimed, grinning from ear to ear.

Becky sat up straight, pointing at Hayley. "Yes, what she said."

Clarissa waved her hands down her injured body. "Look at me, ladies. I haven't had a chance to tell you."

Hayley and Becky gave her sympathetic looks.

"Okay, you're forgiven, but now you have to tell us everything before explaining you and Tobi's business idea," Becky stated.

"Like how and when Tobias became Tobi," Hayley added.

Mary took everything in, smiling at Clarissa's banter with her best friends while blushing profusely.

"Tobi ended up staying the day my ex-boss vandalized my car, and that night I discovered that only does he like wearing women's knickers, but he also loved the idea of being dominated. So, I did," Clarissa explained, blushing slightly. "Tobi is now only Tobias when he's been naughty, and I send him to my room to be punished, then rewarded."

"Holy hell, you kinky little minx," Hayley told her.

Becky and Mary looked at Clarissa with eyebrows raised in surprise.

"I'm going to blush every time I look at Tobi now," Mary said, her cheeks turning bright red.

"I didn't know you were into domination," Ann said as if it were an everyday conversation.

"I wasn't, but my new job is working on a phone sex chat line, and because of my husky voice, most of my callers are submissive or fetish fans. I had to get real good at it real quick," Clarissa explained. "According to Tobi, my new dominant vibe is what blew him away in your shop."

Ann laughed. "I can understand why. If I wasn't so dominant myself, I might have knelt before you when you told him off."

The girls cracked up, and even Mary started laughing.

"Anyway," Clarissa continued. "I want to start my own business called Darcy's Domination Desires, and I want to have my own domination and fetish chat lines, as well as selling toys, tools, and lingerie. That's where you come in, Ann."

Ann looked impressed. "Go on. I'm intrigued."

"Hayley and Becky helped me research domination and fetish clothing, and lingerie for my job, and we noticed a lack of plus sizes and things for busty ladies like Hayley and me. Then, when I researched wholesale products, I found the same thing," Clarissa explained. "Now, I know there's nothing you can't make. So, would you be interested in making custom products that I can sell on my business website for the domination and fetish market?"

Clarissa looked at Ann with hope in her eyes while mentally crossing her fingers.

Ann smiled, which Clarissa hoped was a good sign.

"I never thought of creating clothing for the Dom and fetish scene because it's so accessible, and I didn't even consider the plus and busty sizes," Ann told her. "I do make more profit on the bridal custom orders and special orders. So, I'm in, as long as you can give me plenty of time to make the items."

If Clarissa were not still recovering, she would have jumped for joy; instead, she made do with clapping.

"Yay, oh my god, Ann. I am so happy right now!" Clarissa declared. "If I email you some products I like with some drawings and notes on design ideas, do you think you could have a look to see if you could make them?"

Ann nodded and smiled. "I'll do one better. I'll make them in your size so you can put pictures on your website. Then I'll already have the patterns by making the examples, and you can take orders sooner rather than later."

Clarissa was thrilled, and even though it hurt because of her stitches, she grinned.

"I'll be happy to model, too," Hayley grinned. "I would love to try on something that would actually fit and could contain these puppies," she said, lifting her big boobs.

Becky rolled her eyes and giggled. "For god's sake, woman, put them down before you poke someone's eye out."

Hayley released her large boobs, feigning a sulky face. "I have a question, Ann. How did you know to ask if Tobi was a submissive?"

"Well, as Clarissa has been so honest, I'll confess," she said light-heartedly. "I've been part of the domination scene for nearly all my adult life."

"No shit?" Hayley said as everyone's mouths dropped open in shock.

Mary couldn't believe what she was hearing. "We have been friends for over twenty-five years; how did I not know that?" she squeaked.

Ann looked a little ashamed. "I'm sorry, Mary, but the only person who knew locally was my Albert; God rest his soul, and that's because he got me into the scene."

"Albert was into domination too?" Mary asked, wholly flabbergasted, her cheeks freshly glowing.

Clarissa, Hayley, and Becky kept their mouths tightly shut, not knowing what to say to Ann's confession. All three had known the older lady since they were teenagers. Now it was as if they were seeing her for the first time with fresh eyes, and their minds were blown.

"But Albert was so quiet and reserved!" Mary exclaimed.

"Albert was my submissive for the whole time we were together," Ann confessed. "You wouldn't believe the kinky shit he was into. If only every married couple could be as happy as we were." She sighed.

"I had no idea," Mary said. "I'm glad you had each other. Albert was a lovely man. Daniel and I still miss him."

Clarissa could tell how much Ann missed her submissive husband. Her loss was evident even though he had passed many years earlier.

"Anyway, I might be able to help your new business in other ways, too," Ann told Clarissa, putting a smile back on her face. "My current submissive and I often socialize in the domination and fetish scene. Not only can I possibly get you some callers for your domination lines, but I could wear some of your designs and be a walking advertisement when we go to events."

Ann's response to her proposal was far better than she could have hoped for, and Clarissa was stunned and thrilled simultaneously.

"You'd be willing to do all that for me?" Clarissa asked.

Ann took Clarissa's hand and patted it affectionately. "Clarissa, when I look at you, you remind me of myself at your age. I know we aren't blood-related, but your mum is one of my best friends, more like a sister really, and I love you like a niece."

"Thank you, Ann. I feel the same way," Clarissa told her truthfully.

"Well, now that's all sorted, let's have a look at the lingerie and clothing designs you like the look of, you kinky bitch!" Hayley declared.

Chapter 18

Clarissa's girl's night turned out to be a huge success. Not only was she offered help from Ann, but all the ladies helped her decide which lingerie designs looked the best. They also looked at the top sellers on the best online stores. Even Clarissa's mum, Mary, was a massive help, and her blushing lessened as the evening went on.

As Mary went to the kitchen to grab another bottle of wine, Hayley and Becky searched for more designs they liked. Ann leaned towards Clarissa, obviously wanting to tell her something out of Mary's earshot.

"If you want me to come over another time to tell you which toys and clothing are the most popular, just let me know. You've got my mobile number, so you can call or message me anytime."

Clarissa grinned. "Thank you, Ann. Tobi's just ordered a selection for market research, but I think he just wants to try them out." She laughed. "He wants to give everything his seal of approval."

Ann laughed. "My Albert was the same. We got together and married young, so he always wanted to try new things. Mind you, there's a lot more choice and availability nowadays. When we were young, we had to physically search or make our own toys. It's quite amazing what you can do with some household items."

Clarissa gave Ann a knowing look. "My callers and I are discovering that as well."

Mary walked back in with two more bottles of opened wine.

"Since none of us are driving home, I thought I might as well open two," she told them with a grin.

Clarissa was sure her mum was already tiddly, and she was definitely enjoying herself.

"I'll pour, Mary," Becky said as she watched Mary wobble a little on her way to the coffee table.

Mary handed over the two wine bottles and plonked herself down ungracefully. "Ann, how did you find out that Albert was into domination?" she asked, making Becky spill the wine she was pouring.

"Just after we married, I got sent home after a chemical leak at work. I caught Albert in our lounge with clothes pegs attached to his nipples and balls," Ann laughed. "The lounge curtains were closed, thank god."

Hayley snorted and choked on her wine simultaneously, spraying wine everywhere. She coughed and sputtered as Becky patted her back while laughing. Mary missed her mouth completely, spilling her wine down her floral blue blouse.

"Versatile little buggers, aren't they?" Clarissa laughed as Hayley and her mum tried to clean themselves up with paper towels. "They should advertise them saying, not just for laundry or sub's approved."

"What on earth did you say or do when you walked in and saw him like that, and what did he do?" Mary asked as she mopped her boobs and chin.

"To say that Albert was shocked is an understatement," Ann chuckled, "I was gobsmacked, seeing my new husband standing in our lounge with a massive hard-on and pegs sticking out from under his cock and from his nipples. All I could think of was, thank god I didn't catch him with another woman."

"I can understand that more than most," Clarissa agreed.

Ann gave Clarissa a knowing look. *'Yep, my mother has told her everything,'* Clarissa realized.

"Although I was beyond shocked to see Albert like that, seeing him so turned on had a positive effect on me," Ann admitted. "When I asked him what he was doing, he told me he found the painful discomfort pleasurable. From then on, we experimented together. Our sex life was amazing."

Mary was back to blushing profusely. "You found dominating arousing?"

Ann grinned at her best friend. "I sure did. There's something very arousing and empowering about dominating a man, especially if he's normally a powerful personality. My current submissive is a well-known brain surgeon, although you wouldn't believe it when he's wearing his leather bodysuit and is in his cage."

It was Mary's turn to nearly choke on her wine. "You put him in a cage?"

"Yes, but at his request," Ann told her as if it were an everyday thing to say.

"Fuck me sideways. Who would have thought my recommending a chat line job would lead to all this," Hayley declared, waving her arm around dramatically.

Clarissa grinned. "If you hadn't suggested it, I wouldn't have met Tobi."

"I don't care what Tobi's into. He's a lovely young man who makes you happy, and he worships my grandsons," Mary told Clarissa warmly. "And your dad thinks he's terrific too."

Becky raised her wine glass. "I'll drink to that!"

All of them raised their glasses.

"Here's to Tobi," Clarissa said.

"Here's to you both," Hayley said, grinning at her best friend.

They clinked glasses, celebrating Clarissa and Tobi, and Clarissa felt grateful for having so many amazing women in her life.

"Now we've finished being soppy and looking at the tame stuff —when are we going to check out all the toys?" Hayley asked, raising her eyebrows.

Much to Mary's embarrassment, Hayley and Becky checked out all the domination and fetish toys and tools that Clarissa had saved the links to on her laptop. Mary's expression was even funnier every time Ann gave a yay or nay because she had tried them. Ann's input was invaluable for Clarissa, and she made lots of notes.

Hayley and Becky had Clarissa, Ann, and Mary in fits of laughter with their comments as they browsed all the domination and fetish toys.

"Bloody hell, look at the size of that strap-on," Hayley blurted, reading aloud the description. "The supreme strap-on with adjustable straps, ten inches, and realistic for your pleasure. Ten inches isn't realistic." She laughed. "Personally, I prefer girth over length. If a todger's too long, it's just a waste."

Becky looked at the website with eyes like saucers. "It's no bloody wonder; so many men are paranoid about the size of their todger's. Some of these vibrators and dildos are just weird-looking and outrageous sizes."

"I wonder if they model them from real penises," Mary said curiously.

Hayley giggled. "Could you imagine putting that on your resume? Ten-inch vibrator, strap-on, and dildo model."

"That is probably something many men would like to brag about," Mary said with a serious face.

Between them, they managed to add many other items to

Clarissa's product list, and her excitement grew. She was starting to believe that she could make her business happen, with the help of the fabulous women in her life, of course.

—x—

When Tobi and Clarissa's dad finally arrived home from the local pub, Tobi was pretty much carrying Daniel. And both men were cheerily singing rugby songs.

"Oh, bloody hell Tobi, have you broken my dad?" Clarissa jokingly asked as they stumbled through the front door.

Tobi looked a little sheepish. "I'm afraid your dad bumped into a couple of old friends down the pub. They started to reminisce, and before I knew what was happening, they started toasting all their friends who had passed with shots of Scottish single malt whisky."

"It'll take him a week to recover," Mary told them, shaking her head. "The last time he got this drunk, he kept telling me I must be exhausted because I'd been running through his mind all day. Then he chased me around our house like a frisky teenager."

"Oh my god, Dad, you are so funny," Clarissa told him.

"It's true," Daniel slurred, "your mum is still a stunner. I'm a lucky bugger."

Clarissa couldn't argue with that. Her mum did look younger than her years, and she always dressed modern but classy.

"She sure is," Tobi agreed while trying to keep Daniel upright. He grinned at Mary. "I think I'd better drive you both home before he falls asleep where he lands."

It was an all-out battle for Tobi and Mary to get Daniel in Tobi's car. Especially as Clarissa's dad was in such a party mood, shouting, "Where are you, Steve? Where you at, Simon? We need another toast!"

Not long after Tobi left, Ann got up to go when her submissive boyfriend beeped his horn from outside.

"That will be my ride home. Thank you for a great evening, Clarissa. I have a feeling this girl's night will be the first of many, and I'm excited to work with you too. I'll speak to you soon. Ladies," she said, smiling at Hayley and Becky.

"Thanks for everything, Ann. I think we're going to do well between us. I'll send you over those designs and images as soon as possible," Clarissa told her gratefully.

—x—

By the time Tobi got back from dropping off Clarissa's parents, Hayley and Becky had cleaned up and left in their taxi. Clarissa was feeling worn out, but it had been a fantastic evening. Tobi carried her upstairs and helped her to bed.

"Did you have a good night with the girls, Ann, and your mum?" he asked as he kissed her softly.

"I did," she grinned, "it was a bit of an eye-opener."

Tobi raised a brow. "Really, in what way?"

"It turns out that Ann is a bit of a dark horse. She's a dominant, and she's on her second submissive. The first was her husband of over thirty years; my mum didn't know anything about it."

"Wow, I bet that was a shock for your mum." Tobi laughed.

Clarissa nodded. "That's an understatement; my mum was gob smacked. Anyway, Ann has agreed to make the custom wear, and she's offered to wear some samples at domination events to gain sales. She also wants me to give her some business cards as soon as possible."

"That's brilliant. See, everything's falling into place," he said, kissing her again.

Clarissa kissed him back, deepening the kiss.

"Thank you for believing in me."

Tobi sucked her bottom lips, making her giggle. "You are the strongest woman I know. Some people would be shutting out the world if they'd been through what you have, but you keep striving forward. I'm so in awe of you, gorgeous. Now, where are those bruises?" he asked, making her giggle again.

—x—

Tuesday morning was full of surprises for Clarissa. Tobi and her boys brought her breakfast in bed with the weirdest shaped pancakes she had ever seen.

"We made the pancakes all by ourselves," Luke had told her proudly.

Considering what the pancakes looked like, she believed him instantly. Clarissa praised them profusely for their efforts, and Luke and Matthew went to school with Tobi, full of pride and happiness.

When Tobi returned from the school run, Clarissa was still pampering herself.

"You have a large bouquet of flowers downstairs from someone," he told her while helping her to the stairs. "I found them on the doorstep when I got home."

Clarissa didn't have a clue who had sent the flowers. Tobi, her boys, her best friends, and her parents had already given or sent flowers while she was in the hospital. She was intrigued.

Tobi helped her down the stairs slowly, which was painful but getting more manageable. When they entered the lounge, Clarissa saw the beautiful flower arrangement set in a light-green watering can on her coffee table. Tobi helped her to the couch next to the bouquet. Once sitting down, she took the small white card from between the flowers as Tobi went into the kitchen.

"To our dearest Clarissa, wishing you a speedy recovery. Let us know if we can do anything to help. Love The Lawrence's."

Clarissa was touched. Unlike her ex-asshole, her ex-in-laws had always been there for her and the boys. She decided to shoot Sharon a message to thank her.

Hi Sharon, thank you very much for the flowers, they are beautiful. I'm improving daily, and the kids are great x.

As Tobi brought in fresh mugs of tea, Clarissa's phone pinged with a reply from Sharon.

We're glad to hear it. We were worried about you all. Nigel would have come to see you and the boys, but he got bitten by his new girlfriend's German Shepard, Karma, and he had to have twelve stitches on his butt cheek.

Clarissa exploded into laughter upon reading the message. Tobi looked at her, puzzled. He waited patiently as laughter tears streamed down her face as she squealed, "It hurts," while holding her sides.

"What on earth has made you laugh so hard?" Tobi asked, bemused.

It took a few more minutes for Clarissa's laughter to subside enough for her to speak. She wiped her face with her hands and took a long, slow, deep breath.

"I've always hoped and prayed that Karma would bite my ex, Nigel, on the ass for mistreating the boys and me. And guess what, she has!" Clarissa shrieked, bursting into more fits of laughter and throwing her phone to Tobi.

As Tobi read the last message from Sharon, his eyes widened, and he began to laugh.

"Bloody hell, we should buy that dog a bone!"

"I'm going to forward that one to the girls," she told him, trying to catch her breath, "it will make their week."

—x—

Two days later, Clarissa said goodbye to Sergeant Jameson after her visit. It had been a long two hours going over her statement, trying to remember information, and writing it all down. Unfortunately, she still couldn't remember much about the shooting and crash. Luckily, because Clarissa's police protection had been there, they were able to fill in the blanks.

As Sergeant Jameson drove away and Tobi closed the front door, Clarissa closed her eyes, trying to psych herself up to have her stitches removed, and have her first physiotherapy session. She wasn't looking forward to either. Although Clarissa knew she would look and feel better without all the stitches on her face, neck, and chest, she dreaded it. Tobi, of course, had offered to take her and kiss her better when they returned home.

When Clarissa's name was called in the doctor's waiting room, she hobbled towards the treatment rooms on her crutches with Tobi by her side. Her stomach churned, and her pulse quickened.

"It'll be over quickly, gorgeous," Tobi told her quietly, sensing her nervousness.

Clarissa gave him a weak smile, feeling like a wimp. A male nurse with a friendly smile met them in the surgery corridor.

"Clarissa Darcy?" he asked brightly.

"That's me," Clarissa replied, trying to sound brighter and braver than she felt.

The nurse gave her a knowing smile.

"Please follow me. We're in room four."

—x—

After Clarissa's trip to the clinic, Tobi took her to lunch at her favorite small cafe in town. She sipped her tea as Tobi put in their food order, relieved that her nurse and physio appointments were over. As the nurse had cut each stitch and pulled them out one by one, she had kept her eyes closed, not wanting to watch what was happening. It had been a longer process than she had hoped, but with Tobi holding her hand and talking to her the whole time, it hadn't been as bad as she thought. Her face, neck, and chest felt much better, even though her skin tingled like crazy.

Clarissa's physiotherapy session had been much harder than expected, even with Tobi's encouragement. Forced to do exercises that hurt her healing body, she had left the session despising Julie, the physiotherapist who had tortured her. Clarissa pulled out the sheets of exercises that Julie had given her. *'Now I've got to torture myself every day,'* she thought as she went over each exercise in her mind.

As Tobi made his way back to their table, she slid the sheets back into her bag.

"Those exercises will get easier the more you do them," he said, giving her a reassuring smile. "I broke my left leg skiing a few years back, and my physio had me back on my feet in no time."

"I'm determined to get back to normal as quickly as possible, but I'm not looking forward to causing myself more pain. Even if it is going to help me." She laughed.

The way that Tobi smiled at her had her heart fluttering in her chest.

"You are such a badass. You'll be running rings around me again in no time."

Clarissa loved Tobi's unwavering encouragement. It was something she wasn't used to but cherished.

"I wish I'd met you before Nigel," she told him.

"Ah, but then we wouldn't have Luke and Matthew, and they're my little guys," Tobi said with a grin.

Clarissa felt she couldn't have loved Tobi more at that moment. His affection and bond with Luke and Matthew was something she had always wanted her boys to have from a male role model. They never had that bond with their dad, even when they were babies. And he definitely wasn't a role model.

"Anyway, I've cleared my schedule for today, so I thought we could get your website started and your company logo created when we get home," Tobi suggested.

Butterflies instantly started to flutter in Clarissa's stomach.

"You can do that in one day?"

"Gorgeous, I've created so many websites for clients, I could make you one with my eyes closed," he said, grinning. "However, I'm going to do yours differently. Instead of creating your site with my servers, I'm going to create yours through a third party, so if anything should happen between us, your business and website are under your control. Plus, you'll be able to edit and change your site anytime you want to," Tobi explained.

"You'd do that for me?" Clarissa asked, still not used to being put first.

Tobi leaned forward and brushed her soft cheek with his hand. "I'd do anything for you—haven't you realized that yet?"

—x—

After finishing the most romantic lunch Clarissa had ever had, they collected the boys from school and made their way home. Luke and Matthew were super excited to tell Tobi all about their day, and Luke proudly read aloud the school project he had finished about

World War One as they drove.

When they got home, Clarissa helped her boys with their homework as Tobi made dinner, and as she watched her boys writing in their workbooks, it suddenly dawned on her that they had become a family. Clarissa couldn't imagine life without Tobi, and her boys adored him. *'It's too soon? Should I slow things down?'* She wondered. Clarissa glanced at Tobi as he peeled carrots at the sink. The radio was playing softly in the kitchen, and she smiled as Tobi mouthed the lyrics, not wanting to disturb or distract Luke and Matthew from their homework. Clarissa realized that she didn't care that everything was moving so fast, and didn't want Tobi to leave when her parents left his house.

With Luke and Matthew tucked up in bed asleep, Clarissa and Tobi got to work, Tobi worked on Clarissa's website, and Clarissa worked on the chat line. Tobi had set himself up at Clarissa's modest desk while she worked from the couch with her laptop and phone on a tray on her lap.

Tobi didn't bat an eye as Clarissa took call after call. That was until she received a fetish call from a loud man called Dave, and she was stumped as to what to say.

"Hi, this is Mistress Adele. Who's this?" she asked in her sultry tone.

"Dave. My name is Dave," he said, sounding hesitant.

"Do you know you've called the fetish line, Dave?" she asked, knowing how many callers accidentally came through to the wrong line.

"Yeah, I do. I think I need some medical treatment, Mistress Adele," he said, his voice elevating in pitch.

That was something Clarissa hadn't heard before, and she wasn't sure where to take the conversation. Tobi turned to look at

Clarissa with a confused look that matched her own. She shrugged and smirked at him.

"Well, that's what I'm here for, Dave," she told him, trying to sound confident. "What medical treatment do you need?"

"I need a colonoscopy, but you aren't one of those nurses who wear those bloody awful scrubs, are you? I can't stand them!"

Clarissa knew what he meant as the male nurse who had removed her stitches had been wearing dark-green scrubs. She assumed Dave was into the more traditional nurses' uniform that she had seen when she was young.

"I'm wearing my light blue, knee-length nursing dress with a thick white belt," she told him while opening her search engine to look up what a colonoscopy was.

"What shoes are you wearing, Nurse Adele?" Dave asked, his voice wavering with excitement.

"I'm a charge nurse," Clarissa told him with an air of authority, "So I'm wearing low black heels."

Clarissa quickly scanned the search results on her laptop screen, clicking on the first one that looked medically official. When she read what the website said, she was stunned. Clarissa didn't know if Dave was turned on by having something pushed up his butt or if nurses turned him on. Either way, she had to wing it and hope for the best.

"Are you going to give me an anal exam first?" Dave asked, his breathing picking up speed.

"I am Dave. Now, I need you to remove your clothes, put on the gown, and lay on the bed on your left side, please."

Tobi was fascinated, with Clarissa's website temporarily forgotten; he watched and listened to her, seriously impressed.

They could hear rustling and humphs from Dave, and Clarissa

assumed he was stripping.

"Okay, Nurse Adele, I'm ready," Dave said excitedly as his breathing became heavier.

"Glad to hear that, Dave. I'm just slipping on my latex gloves, and now I'm going to squeeze some warm gel onto my fingers, so the process is comfortable for you," she said sexily but firmly. "Are you ready?"

By the noises Dave was beginning to make, it was obvious what he was doing on his end of the phone, and Tobi started to grin. Clarissa was seriously impressed that Tobi was so cool, calm, and collected about the whole thing.

"I'm ready, Nurse," Dave said, his breath fast and shaky.

"Good. I'm sliding my fingers gently between your buttocks, and I can feel how tight your anus...."

Suddenly Dave moaned loudly, and the line went dead, surprising both Clarissa and Tobi.

"Damn, he lost control quickly," Tobi said, laughing.

Clarissa giggled and shook her head, amused.

"Not all men have your level of control and stamina, Tobias," she said, giving him her stern look.

Tobi smirked. "You keep giving me that; I've been a bad man look, and I'll have to take you upstairs, Mistress Clarissa, and let you punish me!"

Having her wicked way with Tobi was more than tempting, she had to admit. However, after being off work for so long, she knew she had much catching up to do.

"I would like nothing more than to punish you, you naughty bad man, but I have a lot of hours to catch up on and bills to pay," she said while making a sad face.

Tobi gave her an understanding smile. "I know; we've got

plenty of time for us," he said, giving her a wink.

Chapter 19

By the time Clarissa got to the end of her shift, her throat was starting to feel like she had swallowed a cactus from feigning so many moans and orgasms. Tobi sat back in her desk chair, pulling his shoulders back and raising his arms to stretch his back. Clarissa took his action as her cue to log off.

"How are you doing?" she asked, feeling excited and curious about what he had created.

"It's nearly done, and I've bought your domain name, Darcy's Domination Desires, in your name. So, you're good for the next three years." Tobi grinned, looking very proud of himself.

"You didn't have to do that!"

His grin widened. "I know, but it's your get-well-soon present. Now, I just have to teach you how to edit and upload everything you want."

"You are very naughty, Tobias," she said, putting down her laptop. "Let's see it."

Clarissa was so excited. It was her first step to becoming a business owner, and she didn't know if Tobi was genuinely aware of how much it meant to her.

Tobi unplugged his top-of-the-range laptop and sat beside her, positioning the screen so they could both see. Clarissa stared in awe at her brand-new website home page. Her Darcy's Domination Desires website was classy and sultry, with a color scheme of jet-black, dark red, and gold. Tobi had even created various other pages for her, including an about page, a chat lines page, multiple product pages, and even a forum for members to chat. Clarissa was blown away.

"This is better than I could have hoped for; I love it," she said quietly, leaning into him. She kissed him, hoping he could feel her love and gratitude. "Now, if you help me upstairs, I think I want to show you how much I love it. And I believe you need to be spanked for being so naughty, Tobias."

No more words were needed as far as Tobi was concerned. With laptops discarded, Tobi gently scooped her up in his arms, not wanting to waste another second, taking her upstairs to the bedroom.

—x—

The next week passed in a blur for Clarissa. She had never been so busy with trips to physiotherapy, working on the chat line, and creating her new company. She had no idea about all the tax and legal information she had to learn until Tobi told her.

Luckily Clarissa's parents had offered to take over the school runs for Luke and Matthew, which gave her and Tobi extra time to work. Tobi had even bought another desk so they could work side by side.

Mary was still blushing whenever she saw Tobi, but not as often. Her dad, Daniel, was thrilled about Clarissa's new business venture, even though it was out of the norm. She was beginning to get the distinct impression that her dad always knew that Ann's husband, Albert, was her submissive. According to her mum, he didn't seem that surprised by the news. And it did explain why her dad was taking her new trade so well.

Clarissa sent all her design ideas to Ann, and her feedback was brilliant. Clarissa couldn't wait to see the lingerie and clothing samples. She got the impression that Ann was just excited. Tobi was impressed at how quickly she got the hang of uploading and editing her new website, and with her company logo created, she was ready to order her business cards and fliers.

However, there was one thing that was playing on Clarissa's mind. Should she tell her current boss, Michelle, what she had planned?

Clarissa hated deceit, and she didn't want Michelle to think that she was trying to steal business from Castle Communications, especially as they had been so supportive since her accident. The problem was, she didn't have enough money to quit or lose her job on the chat line. So, she would have to put up with her position between the rock and the hard place until she did.

—x—

On Friday morning, packages began to arrive for Tobi, and he was like a kid on his birthday, shaking them and trying to guess what was inside. Clarissa was relieved that the packages came in black wrappings, so her boys wouldn't know that the items were. She made an entry in her notes to research black packaging for her business. Clarissa had never seen Tobi so excited for the weekend.

As Tobi had been so amazing looking after her and helping with the boys, she decided to try and make the weekend special. Her parents happily agreed to have Luke and Matthew for the weekend, which meant she and Tobi could have some proper adult time, and she couldn't wait, especially as she was managing to walk without her crutches.

Clarissa and Tobi were getting Matthew and Luke ready for school, and to be picked up by their grandparents when Clarissa's phone pinged. She picked up her phone and was surprised to see a message from Ann.

Good morning, Clarissa. I have some good news for you. I've made three samples so far, and I want to invite you and Tobi to a Domination and Fetish event tomorrow night. Call me when you're free.

Clarissa was surprised and thrilled that Ann had already managed to make three samples. She wished Ann had told her which ones she had made. Clarissa couldn't wait to see them. She was also surprised and excited about being invited to a Domination and fetish event, especially as it would be her and Tobi's first.

Tobi walked into the kitchen with Matthew and Luke, ready to go.

"Bye, Mum," Luke said, giving her a gentle hug.

Both of Clarissa's sons were still treating her like she was a fragile china doll, but she understood why. She hugged Luke back, giving him a loving smile.

"Bye, honey."

As soon as Luke released Clarissa, Matthew moved in for his morning hug. It was a new routine they had learned from Tobi, and she loved it.

"Love you, Mummy," Matthew said as he hugged her and looked up at her with a grin on his young face.

"I love you too, honey," she told him with a wink. "Now, you both have a great day and be good for Nana and Grandad, okay."

Luke and Matthew nodded before heading to the lounge to wait.

Tobi wrapped his thick, muscular arms around her waist.

"I've got their overnight bags ready for your mum and dad by the door. I think they're excited. Will it be their first time at a football match?"

Clarissa nodded.

"The only balls their dad was interested in playing with were his own. We might have a first this weekend, too, if you're interested, and I don't just mean your recent purchases." She teased, grabbing his tight bum.

Tobi raised an eyebrow and pulled her closer to his body. "Tell me more, gorgeous."

Clarissa was about to explain when her doorbell app sounded on her phone.

"Nana and Grandad are here, Dad," Matthew called from the lounge as he looked out the window.

Clarissa and Tobi locked eyes. Both surprised.

"Did Matthew just call me dad?" Tobi asked, his voice wavering with emotion.

Clarissa nodded, suddenly full of mixed emotions and not knowing what to say. "I can talk to him," she said quietly.

"You don't have to if you don't want to," Tobi told her, "I know everything has moved quickly, but I love you, and I love the boys, and I'd do anything for you. I want us to be a family, permanently, but only if you want that as well."

Clarissa couldn't believe what she was hearing. Clarissa knew she deserved a decent man like Tobi, and she loved him with all her heart, but she had spent years thinking she would never find real love or a good man. Clarissa knew from experience that if someone you loved put you down enough times, you started to believe their lies. Luckily Hayley and Becky were always there to keep her on track, and they were definitely rooting for her and Tobi.

"I want us to be a family, too," Clarissa told him, taking his face in her hands and kissing him, "I love you."

The doorbell rang, and Luke rushed to open it.

"Dad, we have to go," Matthew called, grabbing his school back-pack.

Tobi kissed Clarissa, giving her his biggest grin so far. "I'm coming."

When Clarissa and Tobi got to the front door, Clarissa's dad was already putting Luke and Matthew's school and overnight bags in his car, and her mum was smiling at Clarissa, looking emotional. It was evident that Mary had heard Matthew calling Tobi, dad, and she couldn't miss how happy Tobi was.

As Luke and Matthew hugged Tobi goodbye, Mary hugged her daughter.

"Tobi is every bit a dad to those boys. Have a good weekend, darling. You deserve it."

Clarissa squeezed her mum, kissing her on the cheek. "Thanks, Mum, and thank you for having Luke and Matthew this weekend. Any problems, just call me, okay."

Mary nodded, turning to hug Tobi while mouthing, keeper, to Clarissa. Clarissa rolled her eyes and chuckled. Once Matthew and Luke were in the car with their seat belts on, Mary and Daniel drove off down the road with Clarissa and Tobi waving them off.

They walked back into the house, and Tobi turned to Clarissa with a glint in his eye. "So, Clarissa Darcy, what have you got to tell me?" he said, wrapping his arms around her.

Clarissa pushed the front door closed.

"Ann messaged, and she's finished three of the samples and invited us to a Domination event tomorrow night. Do you fancy giving it a go? I know you were hoping to spend the weekend trying out your new toys, but maybe you can wear your new harness under your clothes and try it out," she said with a sexy smile.

Tobi's eyes lit up. "Well, Mistress Clarissa, I think we should find out from Ann which samples she's made, and maybe you could wear something hot too."

"Let's find out, shall we," she said, smacking him on his bum.

"Where's your phone?"

Clarissa nodded towards the kitchen, and before she knew it, Tobi released her, racing to find it. She chuckled as she followed with less speed, still sore from her physiotherapy session the day before.

As she entered her kitchen, Tobi eagerly passed her the phone. She laughed at his enthusiasm.

"Okay, I'm doing it," she smirked while finding Ann's number.

Her phone began to ring, and Clarissa set it to the loudspeaker so Tobi could hear.

"Hello, this is Ann."

"Hi Ann, it's Clarissa. I got your message, and I'm so excited."

Ann chuckled, "So you should be. Your designs I've made so far look incredible, and I'm getting super excited too."

Clarissa grinned at Tobi, feeling over the moon. Ann was a hard lady to impress, so her excitement felt even more validating.

"Which designs did you make?" Clarissa asked.

"Let me sit down for a second. I've been working on the fourth all morning. Ahh, that's better. Okay, I'm sending you the images now," Ann said as Clarissa's phone pinged.

Clarissa opened her messages and the new message from Ann. Her pulse began to race as she looked at the stunning photos of her designs. The first image was of the sexiest jumpsuit Clarissa had ever seen, and she was in awe. The black jumpsuit was a soft leather corset and trousers combined, but instead of the corset part being completely covered around the torso, it was made with leather straps in scarlet red. She looked at Tobi with a massive grin on her face.

"Oh my god, Ann, the jumpsuit looks amazing. Better than I could have imagined."

"Good," Ann said with a chuckle, "I made the outfit in your size."

The outfit was stunning, and Clarissa tried to imagine herself wearing it. Tobi slid behind her, wrapping his arms around her while peering over her shoulder to look closer at the image. It was clear that Tobi liked what he saw. Clarissa could feel his hardness pressing against her backside, and she grinned again.

"Tobi loves it too." She laughed, catching him nodding out of the corner of her eye. "So, if we come to the domination and fetish event, I can wear it?"

"You sure can," Ann told her cheerfully, "and I've made the second in my size, so we can blow their kinky socks off."

Clarissa immediately swiped to the next image. The image was of a stunningly hot, deep-red leather corset with black leather laces up the front and black leather trousers with red leather laces up the side of the legs. Clarissa could picture Ann wearing it instantly.

"Damn, Ann. You really will blow their kinky socks off with that get-up!" She exclaimed.

Ann laughed. "I made the next outfit in Hayley's size. I know she gets upset because she can't find things in her bust size. See what you think."

Swiping again, Clarissa looked at the third and last image, and she knew straight away that Hayley would love it. It was similar to the jumpsuit that Ann had made for Clarissa but without the trouser part. The corset was a deep purple which Clarissa knew was Hayley's favorite color, with black trimming, a pinstripe pattern, and black velvet hot pants. Clarissa knew that Hayley would fall in love with the outfit when she saw it.

"You are so talented, Ann. Hayley will love this," Clarissa told her.

"I hope so," Ann said, "Why don't you ask Hayley and Becky if they would like to come to the dom event with their husbands? They don't have to be submissive's or dominant's to attend. It's a formal event, just an excuse for us all to catch up. The fourth sample I'm finishing now should fit Becky perfectly."

Clarissa had to admit; she would feel braver going to a new kind of event if she had her best friends with her, and they were always up for new and fun adventures.

"That would be amazing, Ann. If you can send me the event details, I'll reach out to them this morning."

"You'll look even hotter than usual in that outfit," Tobi whispered in her ear, pressing himself against her.

Clarissa's skin tingled as Tobi's breath heated her skin. She pushed against him, moving her backside from side to side, teasing his solid erection.

"I'm sending you the invite now, which you can share with the girls. I'll send my boyfriend, Philip, over with the outfits so you have them ready. If you don't come to the event, at least you'll have the samples to photograph for your website. I hope you do come. It's going to be a fantastic night," Ann said, hopefully.

Tobi nuzzled Clarissa's neck. "Let's go and see what it's all about," he whispered.

"Tobi and I will definitely be there," Clarissa said with a giggle. "Tobi's already pointing the way, and we don't know where we're going yet."

Ann laughed heartily down the phone. "Fantastic. If you have any issues with the outfits, let me know. If all is well, message me if you want to meet up, and we can all go together."

"Thank you, Ann. I'll message you soon."

Clarissa opened the new message from Ann and the invitation image. The invite was more elegant than Clarissa expected. The invitation was titled Domfeti Carnivale, a domination and fetish black whip event, colored in various shades of purple, black, and greys. A man and woman tied together with plaited black leather rope adorned the invite, and according to the details, there was going to be a buffet meal, a fashion show, live music, and a rope artist. The event was being held at a county house in Sparsholt, Winchester, which wasn't far from where Clarissa lived. It sounded exciting, and she hoped Becky and Hayley would think so too. Clarissa pressed forward to send the invite to her best friends on their group message, typing an accompanying message.

Ann's invited us to this event tomorrow night, and she's made four of my designs for us to wear if you fancy an interesting evening.

Putting her phone down on the kitchen side, Clarissa turned in Tobi's arms, sliding her hand down to his bulging crotch and gripping him firmly. "You are extremely bad, Tobias. I think I need to punish you severely for your behavior. Get upstairs right now!" she demanded.

Tobi's eyes lit up, and he lowered his head in obedience. "Yes, Mistress Clarissa."

"Have our new toys unwrapped, cleaned, and ready," Clarissa called out as Tobi excitedly rushed away.

Clarissa could hear Tobi thumping up the stairs. "Yes, Mistress Clarissa."

She was about to follow Tobi when her phone pinged. Clarissa looked at her phone.

It was a new message from Hayley.
Hell yeah, I'm up for that, and so is Adam. We'll be at yours early to get ready. I can't wait! Send me a picture of the outfit, please.

With a grin, Clarissa sent Hayley the image of the outfit made especially for her, hoping that Hayley loved it as much as she did.

Clarissa's phone pinged again; this time, it was Becky.
OMG, I would love to go. It sounds brilliant. I'll see if Martin's up for it. I might have to bribe him with a blow job, lol.

With a smile, Clarissa quickly replied.
Awesome. Let me know, Becky. About the event, not the blow job, lol. Xx

Clarissa put her phone down and headed upstairs, feeling excited about her clothing samples, the Domfeti event, and having some kinky fun with Tobi. She couldn't believe how much her life had changed in such a short time.

—x—

When Clarissa opened her bedroom door, she was immediately surprised. Not only had Tobias unwrapped all of his purchases—but he was already wearing the body harness—and he made it look damn good. His muscles strained against the many leather straps, taking her breath away. It was evident that Tobias was seriously turned on; his solid erection was hard to miss. Clarissa's eyes widened at the sight.

The rest of Tobias's kinky toys were neatly laid at the bottom of their bed, ready to be used, but Clarissa noticed something was missing, the bondage cross. She walked into the room and approached Tobias, her body responding to his magnificent form. Clarissa ran her soft hands over Tobias's hard chest, muscular stomach, and leather straps. He raised his head to look at her with hot desire in his green eyes.

"You look amazing," Clarissa said, running her hands down his muscular stomach again. She gripped the strap along Tobias's waist with her left hand, pulling him closer. Her right hand smoothed over his skin and pubic hair until she reached his hard cock. Tobias gasped as she gripped him. The thinner straps around his genitals were already making him throb, but Clarissa's firm hand made Tobias want to fuck her instantly. His breath caught in his chest.

"Thank you, Mistress Clarissa."

Clarissa's admiration made him twitch in her grip, and the pressure for Tobias was a sweet pleasure.

"You seem to be missing something," Clarissa told him, her eyes darting to the bed and the array of domination and fetish toys. She gripped him a little firmer.

"It's over there, Mistress Clarissa," Tobias told her, pointing to the closed en-suite bathroom door.

Clarissa turned and smiled. Tobias had already attached the over-the-door bondage cross, which was ready and waiting to be used.

Clarissa leaned towards Tobias, softly kissing him while sliding her hand to his balls, giving him a squeeze.

"You are being efficient, Tobias. I think we should give it a try, don't you?"

Tobias trembled with nervous anticipation. "Yes, please, Mistress Clarissa."

Without letting go, Clarissa led him to the bondage cross. His eyes grew wide. Obediently he let her position him against it. He could feel the cold metal of the buckles against his bare back and buttocks, adding to his excitement.

The more turned on Tobias became, the more Clarissa loved it, her body reacting to his excitement and arousal. She could feel herself getting wetter and wetter.

Clarissa lifted his left arm into position, wrapping the black leather cuff around his wrist, and fixing the buckle to restrain it. She looked into Tobias's green eyes while securing his right wrist, his breath becoming louder as his excitement grew. Clarissa moved closer, brushing her large boobs against his strapped chest. She could feel her hard nipples pushing against her black lace bra.

As Tobias's throbbing cock pressed against her pencil skirt, she slowly undid the buttons on her top, wanting to reward him a little. Clarissa's warm breath washed over him as she leaned forward to let her top drop to the floor, and Tobias's eyes darted to her glorious, curvy body.

Placing her knee between Tobias's bare thighs, Clarissa moved closer still, his hard cock brushing against her skirt, making him gasp. With a firm push of her foot, she forced his left leg over, then his right, making him spread his muscular legs.

Clarissa smiled sexily. "Are you ready for this, Tobias?"

"Yes, Mistress Clarissa," he said breathlessly, his arousal palpable.

Using Tobias's thick muscular thighs for support, she slid her hands down his body until she knelt on the floor before him. She attached first leather cuff around his calf, then secured the other.

"Do you remember our safe words, Tobias?" she asked, using

his thighs again to stand up while brushing her body against his.

Tobias moaned, his body thrumming as Clarissa teased him. He wanted her more than he had ever wanted any woman. Her natural scent was driving him wild, and her touch had his whole body tensing with need.

"Yes, I remember them, Mistress Clarissa."

"Good," Clarissa said as she turned and made her way to their bed.

Reaching behind her back, Clarissa unzipped her pencil skirt, letting it fall to the floor. As Tobias watched, she stepped over the red material, reaching for the nipple clamps on the bed while giving him a tantalizing view of her black lace-covered ass. Tobias moaned loudly behind her, making her smile.

"Enjoying the view, Tobias?"

Tobias took a deep breath, letting it out slowly. He looked at her with hooded, lustful eyes. "More than you know, Mistress Clarissa."

Clarissa slowly walked towards him, teasing him with every step and movement of her curvy figure, the nipple clamps dangling from her fingers, glinting in the morning light from the bedroom window. As soon as she reached him, his breath quickened, his eyes darting from hers to the clamps, but there was no doubt or hesitation. Clarissa knew that he wanted more. Her hand went to his erect right nipple, and she pinched it with her fingertips.

"You look ready for a little pain and pleasure, Tobias. Are you ready?" she asked, swaying against his throbbing cock with her heated body.

Clarissa wished Tobias knew how turned on and wet she was. She longed to have him inside her.

"I'm ready, Mistress Clarissa." he moaned.

Without hesitation, Clarissa opened the first clamp and slowly attached it to Tobias's erect nipple. He gasped loudly and began to pant, his eyes closing instantly.

"Ahh, thank you, Mistress."

She smiled, enjoying his pleasurable reaction. "Are you ready for the next one, Tobias?"

"Yes, Mistress," he said, his breath quickening.

Clarissa attached the second nipple clamp, aware that Tobias hadn't called her by her full name.

Chapter 20

Tobias gasped and moaned as the clamp pinched his other nipple, the exquisite pain sending his senses into overdrive. His whole body felt more alive than it had ever been. As Clarissa brushed against him, he thought he might lose control. Taking slow, deep breaths, he tried to control himself, wanting to last so he could show Clarissa how much he desired her.

"You have been very bad, Tobias. You didn't address me correctly. You know what that means, don't you?" she asked, raising a brow.

"I do, Mistress Clarissa," he whispered, instantly yearning to feel her hand back on his cock.

Clarissa took a step back, giving herself some space.

"I'm going to spank you three times, Tobias," she told him, looking into his bright green eyes.

Tobias nodded and took a deep breath. She scanned his magnificent body—every inch solid and tense with desire and need—his hard cock protruding proudly.

"One...," she said as she raised her hand, spanking his cock firmly.

Tobias moaned loudly.

"Two...." She spanked him again, gazing at his face.

"Ahh." he moaned, louder this time, his eyes closed in painful ecstasy.

"Three..." she said, spanking him for the third and final time.

Tobias moaned again and began to pant as his cock throbbed. The feeling was so intense that he barely felt the nipple clamps anymore. That was until Clarissa flicked them. Tobias opened his eyes, the pleasure and pain driving him wild.

Clarissa moved closer, kissing and teasing him with her tongue.

"You've done really well, Tobias. I think you deserve a reward," she told him, her hand wrapping around his solid erection, his breath catching in his chest.

Clarissa could feel the wetness at his tip, and she used it to make him slippery. Her hand slowly slid along his shaft and around his ball. He moaned with need.

"Don't come until I give you permission," she whispered, her breath sending tingles through his body.

"I'm so close, Mistress Clarissa," he said breathlessly.

Clarissa wanted to reward him for being an obedient submissive and for everything he had done since coming into her life.

Releasing his hard, wet cock, Clarissa reached up to his chest, releasing the nipple clamps, knowing the sensation would heighten his arousal. Tobias groaned, the pleasure and torture making him feel light-headed, but before he could gauge what Clarissa would do next, her hands began to slide down his body.

Clarissa lowered herself until she knelt before him; his legs trembled as he panted. Taking his throbbing cock in her hand at the base, she slid her warm wet mouth over its length.

"Oh god!" Tobias cried out in ecstasy.

The feel of her wet and warm mouth immediately sent him toward his peak.

Clarissa gripped him firmly, sliding him in and out of her mouth, alternating between sucking and teasing his tip with her tongue.

"Please let me come," he asked desperately as his knees buckled, the wrist restraints pulling taut on his muscular arms.

Clarissa released him from her mouth. "You have my permission," she told him quietly, instantly sliding him back into her mouth.

As Clarissa slowed, then quickened her pace, Tobias moaned, his trembling body pulling against his leather restraints. Tobias reached his peak, his back arching, and Clarissa relished his pleasure and her effect on him.

Standing up, Clarissa looked at the spent man before her—the man she loved. She stroked his face, and as he looked at her, his eyes were full of love and awe.

Clarissa smiled as she unbuckled Tobias's wrist restraints, and he immediately wrapped his arms around her, pulling her against him. She could feel the dampness and heat of his skin against hers. He kissed her deeply, his tongue exploring her mouth. Clarissa melted in his arms, and even though she knew he was spent, she wanted him to take her.

"My turn to make you a quivering wreck," he told her, his voice still deep with need.

Clarissa moved out of the way when he released her, and he bent down, unfastening his other restraints. As soon as he was free, he scooped her up in his arms, carrying her to their bed.

"I'm going to show you how much I love and adore you."

Tobias was true to his word, taking his time to show Clarissa how much he loved her, and she relished every moment.

As they lay in bed recovering, the doorbell rang. Clarissa wondered why she hadn't heard her doorbell app pinging, only to realize she had left her phone downstairs. Acting as quickly as she could, Clarissa threw on her dressing gown and headed downstairs, wondering who it could be.

Clarissa opened the front door to find a handsome older man holding aloft clothes encased in black garment bags. Then it dawned on her who it was.

Clarissa smiled. "Philip?" she asked, impressed with Ann's taste in men.

The older man returned her smile, lighting up his handsome face. Philip certainly didn't look or come across like a submissive, but then again, neither did Tobi.

"It is. It's a pleasure to finally meet you. Ann speaks very highly of you, Hayley and Becky."

"Ann is an amazing and wonderful lady. I've known her most of my life," Clarissa told him warmly.

"That she is. Ann asked me to drop these off for you."

Philip held out the clothing samples, and she took them, realizing Philip was stronger than he looked. The samples were heavy, but Clarissa wasn't surprised, considering the amount of leather and materials it probably took to make them.

"Thank you for dropping them off, Philip. My boyfriend, Tobi, and I are looking forward to the event. If you and Ann want to come here first, we could have a couple of drinks beforehand, and you can meet everyone," Clarissa suggested.

Philip nodded. "That would be wonderful, Clarissa. I will let Ann know of your suggestion. I'd like to meet Tobi and your friends. Until tomorrow," he said, dipping his head respectfully.

Clarissa waved and closed her front door, excited to find out what the samples looked like in the flesh.

"Tobi, Philip just dropped off the samples!" she called upstairs before making her way into the kitchen.

Clarissa hung the garment bags on her kitchen door, then popped the kettle on, needing to hydrate after her very hot sex session with Tobi. As she placed two mugs on the kitchen counter, she felt strong arms wrap around her waist.

"You haven't looked at them yet?"

"I was waiting for you," she told him as his hands began to roam inside her dressing gown opening. "We don't have time for shenanigans now, you bad man. We have things to do today, and I need to get some hours in on the chat line."

Tobi tweaked her nipple playfully. "You've been working your socks off all week, and we don't have the boys, so why don't you have today off so we can work on your website and new app?"

Clarissa knew Tobi was right. She had been pushing herself hard.

"You're right. And the sooner we get the business up and running, the sooner I can be my own boss," she agreed.

"Damn right, boss lady. I'll finish the tea, so you can unwrap those beauties," Tobi told her with a grin, pointing at the garment bags.

Picking up the samples, Clarissa hooked them over her top kitchen cupboards, making them easier to open and view. She had never been this excited over clothes. Even her wedding dress hadn't got her this excited. In hindsight, she should have taken that as a sign that her marriage was doomed from the start and Nigel wasn't the one.

While Tobi made the mugs of tea, she unwrapped the first outfit, instantly recognizing it as the sample for Hayley.

"Damn, Hayley's going to look bloody hot in this get-up."

Tobi turned to look. "Adam isn't going to know what to do with himself when he sees Hayley wearing that. She'll be able to get him to do anything she wants." He laughed. "I see four samples; Ann must have finished Becky's."

"I'll be able to send Becky a picture of hers. Hopefully, it will sway Martin into coming to the event," she said as she started to unzip the next bag.

Clarissa grinned as she pulled the bag off and looked at Becky's outfit. It was stunning and just the kind of style that Becky liked, but a hell of a lot sexier. The fitted bodice was deep green covered in black lace with a gorgeous black lace skirt, which was knee length at the front but lengthened around to the back. The outfit was perfect for Becky's beautiful red hair. Grabbing her phone, Clarissa took a photo and sent it to Becky, noticing there was already a message from her best friend in their group chat. She opened the message and smiled.

It's a go. We'll get ready at your house too. Well, I will. Martin will get ready here.

Like what you see?

Clarissa messaged back, including the image of Becky's outfit, keeping her fingers crossed for a positive reaction.

Tobi handed her the mug of tea and sat at the table, admiring Ann's work and giving Clarissa a thumbs up. His phone pinged with a message.

"Looks like your car will be back next week, gorgeous."

Clarissa was thrilled. "That's awesome. I loved driving the Mercedes, but I've missed my little Mini. Any news on the Merc?"

Tobi looked at her sadly. "I'm afraid it's a write-off, but I can get you another one if you want to upgrade from your Mini?"

It was tempting, but Clarissa wanted to keep her trusted little car for a while longer. "No, I'm good for now,"

While waiting for Becky's reply, Clarissa opened the other garment bags. She was amazed at Ann's quality of work. When she sent Ann her designs with her notes and ideas, she never imagined that her designs would look so amazing.

"I need to get my business cards done so I have them ready to hand out for the event," she told Tobi. "Would you be able to take some photos of the girls and me tomorrow night at the event if the girls are up for it?"

Tobi grinned. "If I can control myself while you're wearing that," he said, pointing to her sexy outfit.

Clarissa laughed. "It's a good job the girls are coming here tomorrow. Otherwise, we might never leave the house."

Tobi nodded, knowing how true her words were.

"I think it would be great to get some shots at the venue, especially if it's posh. They would look great on the website."

As Clarissa sipped her tea, she couldn't stop admiring the samples. Having them in her house suddenly made her new business a reality instead of just an idea, even more so than her website.

Clarissa and Tobi spent the day getting organized. Between them, they finished creating the logo for Darcy's Domination Desires, going with three D's as the main image in a modern but classy font. Clarissa loved it. When they went to a printing shop to have the business cards made, the man who served them blushed profusely. Clarissa was sure she saw him jot down her business details.

In the afternoon, Tobi started working on Clarissa's business app, linking it to her website and matching the website theme and colors. Even though Tobi thought of it as Clarissa's business, she considered them partners. Every now and again, Clarissa would stare at her new business cards, trying to let it sink in that she was now a business owner and her own boss.

As Tobi showed Clarissa what he had done so far, her phone rang. Seeing that it was Hayley, she answered cheerfully.

"Domestic goddess to dominatrix diva speaking."

Hayley laughed. "Hello, dominatrix diva. I have some amazing news for you," she said excitedly.

"You've won the lottery?" Clarissa asked, hoping for a yes.

"I wish, but that's not the good news. I heard from Janka Industries' solicitors today, and they've made a settlement offer."

Clarissa's heart began to pound in her chest. "Let me put you on loudspeaker so Tobi can hear."

"Okay."

Tobi gave Clarissa a puzzled look as she pressed the loud-speaker on her phone.

"So, Janka has really offered a settlement?" Clarissa confirmed in surprise.

Tobi's eyes widened, matching her stunned expression.

"They have, and I think it's because one of the top women's magazines has done a big feature on sexual harassment and stalkers, using your recent trauma as their main example. Janka can't afford any more bad press."

"How much are they offering Clarissa?" Tobi asked.

"They're offering one hundred thousand, but I don't think that's enough," Hayley told them. "The highest settlement for sexual hara-ssment I know of in recent years was seventy-five thousand—but your case is far more serious—especially as their employee went on to shoot at you and your boys. You also sustained injuries and had to have spinal surgery. If they had listened to you when you originally complained, all that could have been avoided."

"So, you think I should decline their offer?" Clarissa asked.

"I do. Taking everything you've been through into account, including being forced to quit, loss of earnings, your injuries, Luke and Matthew's whiplash, and the trauma you, Luke, and Matthew went through and are still dealing with, I think they should offer you a lot more," Hayley explained. "I'm going to ask for five hundred thousand and see what they counteroffer. Hopefully, they'll get back to me quickly. They clearly want this over and done with."

"Thank you again for doing all of this for me, Hayley," Clarissa told her gratefully.

"That's what best friends are for, honey. We'll see you around six tomorrow. Love you."

"Love you too. Bye."

Clarissa put down her phone, feeling overwhelmed. One hundred thousand pounds was a lot more than she thought Hayley and her team would be able to get, but the thought of five hundred thousand completely blew her mind. She was suddenly grateful for all the bad press Janka had received since John Mason attacked her and her boys. John's name, picture, and Janka Industries had been in all the major newspapers because of what he did. Clarissa could understand why Janka would want to put it behind them and move on. She was sure the ordeal affected their share prices and bottom line.

"That's a lot of money, gorgeous," Tobi said, still looking as stunned as she felt. "You could pay off your house and have plenty left to set up your business, including buying your stock."

Clarissa hadn't thought about how such a large sum of money could change her and the boy's lives. She knew Tobi was right. Not only could she pay off her small, modest home, but she would definitely have enough for her new business. However, what would make the most difference for Clarissa, was being able to buy her boys shoes and clothes when they needed them, take them on proper little holidays, not stress over birthdays and Christmas, and be able to buy herself the things she needed. Clarissa also knew she would never have to ask her ex-asshole for anything ever again. Not that he ever obliged, of course.

"That kind of money would change everything for me, Matthew, and Luke," she said quietly.

The only downside was that if she did get a big payoff, it would mean that she would be back in the press again. Large pay-off's always seemed to get coverage. With a bit of luck, the media would have bigger stories to write about.

Clarissa didn't know who was more excited about the domination and fetish event, Hayley or Becky. Once Becky replied to confirm she and Martin were definitely going, Clarissa's phone blew up with messages in their group chat. Luckily, Tobi was busy finishing her business app, and there was nothing for Clarissa to do. Tobi had worked on it all evening the night before and had started again as soon as they got up. If he weren't enjoying himself so much, Clarissa would have felt guilty. *'My hot and sexy nerd,'* she thought as she admired his muscular form sitting at the desk, knowing he was wearing her silky knickers under his tight t-shirt and sweatpants.

Clarissa had spoken to Luke and Matthew, and they were having a great time with her parents. She knew it was selfish, but she hoped her parents would stay longer in the UK, if not permanently. She had missed them terribly. Unfortunately, Clarissa knew that her dad had no intention of retiring any time soon, and her mum loved to travel.

With her house clean, the laundry done, and Tobi busy, Clarissa decided to bite the bullet and call her boss, Michelle. If she received over one hundred thousand pounds from her claim against Janka Industries, she might as well get the ball rolling with her domination and fetish lines for her business.

Clarissa went into her kitchen so she wouldn't bother Tobi and put the kettle on while calling Michelle.

"Castle Communications, Michelle speaking. How can I help you?"

Clarissa smiled at Michelle's friendly greeting. "Hi Michelle, it's Clarissa. How are you doing?"

"Hi Clarissa, I'm good. I've just been looking at this week's numbers, and you're in the top three again, you gem."

"Really?" Clarissa laughed. "That's amazing."

"Clarissa, you were made for this job, seriously."

"I do love the job, and that's what I wanted to talk to you about," she confessed. "I've decided to start my own business to cater to people into domination and fetish, and I want to offer a chat line service. I wondered if that's something I can do through you and Castle Communications."

Clarissa suddenly felt nervous, not wanting to ruin the good relationship she had built with Michelle and the company.

"That's definitely something we can help you with, Clarissa."

Clarissa breathed a massive sigh of relief.

"We supply many companies with phone services, including chat lines. We can offer you line services from fifty pence a minute right up to two pounds a minute. The calls come through to us as normal, and our ladies take the calls. You would earn a percentage, and so would we. It would be a win-win situation for you, I think," Michelle told her excitedly. "You could still do shifts on the line if you wanted to, and then you would earn at both ends."

The news was better than Clarissa had hoped for. She couldn't wait to tell Tobi and the girls.

"That is amazing, Michelle. How long does it take to set up, and how much would it cost me?"

"We wouldn't charge you anything for setting it up, Clarissa. You already work for us, and I know you'll be successful."

Clarissa was touched by Michelle's continued faith in her ability and support.

"Thanks, Michelle. I really appreciate that."

"I wish we had more ladies like you!" Michelle chuckled. "It would make my job a lot easier. Anyway, I'll email you all the details and the chat line price guides. I can also send you images to use for your chat lines if you tell me what you'd like. Just let me know what you need. We can set you up within a couple of days."

"Thanks, Michelle. I'll let you know as quickly as possible. I'll speak to you soon."

"Okay, bye for now," Michelle said cheerily before hanging up.

The phone call had gone much better than Clarissa had expected. She was kicking herself for not speaking to Michelle sooner, especially as she could have had the domination and fetish phone lines up and running before the Domfeti event. Clarissa walked back into her lounge feeling excited.

"Guess what?" she asked Tobi as he stretched his back, knowingly showing off the muscles in his arms, back, and shoulders.

"What, gorgeous?" He grinned.

"Michelle said that not only would Castle Communications supply my chat line numbers, but they won't charge me for setting it up, and the calls would go through them," Clarissa told him excitedly. "Michelle will also send me whatever images I need for the website. She's going to email me all the information."

Tobi stood, walked towards her, and wrapped his arms around her. "That's fantastic news, gorgeous. Your new business is going to be up and running in no time. Just remember, you're offering a specialized service, so you need to charge relevant prices for your merchandise and the chat line services."

In less than an hour, Michelle emailed Clarissa with all the details, and as she perused the information, it seemed pretty straight forward. She could have as many chat lines as she wanted, call them by any name, and charge as much as she wanted. Grabbing her laptop, Clarissa researched other domination and fetish chat line websites to get an idea of what they charged and how they marketed their services. Before long, and after writing lots of notes, Clarissa knew precisely what she wanted. With time to spare before Hayley, Becky, and their husbands arrived, she emailed Michelle back with what she required.

Chapter 21

Hayley and Adam arrived first at Clarissa's house, which didn't surprise her, considering how many excited text messages she had received. By the time Becky and Martin arrived with Ann and Philip shortly after, Clarissa and Hayley were already on the red wine, and the men were enjoying a beer. Ann looked absolutely stunning in the outfit Clarissa had designed. The deep red leather corset enhanced Ann's bust, and the black leather trousers showed off her curves to perfection. Philip couldn't take his eyes off her.

As for the men, Clarissa had never seen Adam and Martin look so handsome and hot. She was surprised that Hayley and Becky had managed to keep their hands off their husbands long enough to come over.

Clarissa knew the feeling. She was struggling to keep her eyes off Tobi, dressed in a black suit and tie, especially as she knew what he was wearing underneath, her red lace knickers and the black leather body harness.

Philip looked like a hot doctor from a television show, and she could understand why Ann was such a happy lady.

Clarissa had to admit that Martin and Adam were getting on with Tobi as if they had known him his whole life. It was a massive difference compared to their relationship with her ex-asshole. Nigel had a knack for pissing people off within minutes, and he had got worse with age.

"Ann, tell us what these events are normally like," Becky asked, her eyes bright with excitement.

Ann smiled. "These big events are seasonal, so this is our summer get together. There are smaller domination and fetish events all year round, but not all of them are this classy. Philip and I have been to some events that were basically orgies, and neither of us are into that, especially at my age. I think people would pay me to put my clothes back on," she laughed.

The girls giggled at Ann's humor.

"I would disagree with that statement! You are a beautiful creature," Philip told her affectionately.

Ann smiled and caressed Philip's cheek. Their admiration and love for each other clearly evident.

"I hear you, sister. If I'd realized what an amazing figure I had when I was younger, I would have been lethal to mankind." Clarissa laughed.

"You still are lethal, gorgeous," Tobi told her, wiggling his eyebrows.

"This event is more akin to a summer ball. There will be entertainment, a buffet, dancing, and a chance to connect with other like-minded people. We are a tight-knit community, and we like to support each other. So, it's a great way of making business connections. Which is why I was so determined to have your clothing samples ready for tonight," Ann explained.

"We got my business cards made yesterday, so we can hand them out tonight to anyone who might be interested," Clarissa told them as she grabbed the stack from her desk and began to hand small amounts to everyone. "I'll have more in my evening bag if you need them."

"Look at you, Miss Boss Lady." Hayley grinned, looking impressed.

Clarissa grinned back proudly. "If it's okay with you all, Tobi will take photos of us at the venue, so we can use the images for our website and app."

"Ooooh, I've never been a model before. Do I have to strike a pose?" Becky asked as she began to throw her arms in all directions.

"Depends what the pose is, Madonna," Clarissa laughed. "Anyway, us girls had better start getting ready."

"Can I have a look at your website while you're getting ready?" Ann asked.

"Of course. I'd love to know what you think."

"I'll get it up for you," Tobi told her warmly.

"That's what she said," Hayley shouted as she made her way upstairs with Becky.

Clarissa could hear everyone laughing as she followed her best friends.

"You are terrible." She giggled as they reached her bedroom.

Clarissa had all three of their outfits ready and waiting, and when her best friends saw them hanging from her curtain rail, she could tell they were in awe like she was.

"Bloody hell, Clarissa, these are so much better than any on those websites. I'm so impressed that you designed them yourself," Hayley said, amazed.

Becky nodded. "I agree. They are stunning. You and Ann are so talented."

Clarissa passed the outfits to her friends and grabbed her own. She had never seen her friends get undressed so quickly.

"I spoke to Michelle today, and she's going to set up the chat line numbers for our business. I'm so excited. I still can't believe I'm doing it," she told her friends as she undressed.

Becky began to put on her new outfit, admiring its feel as she slid on the dark-green lace-covered corset. "How will you advertise for women to work on your chat line?" she asked. "I can't imagine you posting an advert that says, do you like talking to kinky dudes who love to get slippy with penguins? Then we have the job for you! Or, have you always wanted to hear a man scream after hammering his nipples? Then join our chat line team." She giggled.

Clarissa and Hayley were in fits of laughter, not only because of what Becky was saying but also because of the TV advert voice she was making. Clarissa held her sides tightly, still getting twinges when she laughed too hard.

"Actually, all the calls will still be going through Castle Communications, and I can still take calls through them and earn twice for the same call," Clarissa explained as her laughter subsided. She slid on the black and scarlet-red jumpsuit before her friends had chance to make her laugh again.

Becky looked at her, stunned. "Seriously, you'll get to earn double bubble?"

"Yep," Clarissa nodded. "And if I get the claim money from those scumbags at Janka Industries, I'll have the funds to pay Ann for all the clothing samples and stock."

"They made Clarissa an offer today for one hundred thousand pounds, but I've put in a counteroffer of five hundred thousand. We'll see what they come back with," Hayley said in her solicitor's voice.

Becky's mouth fell agape in shock. "Holy shit, that's a lot of money, Clarissa."

Clarissa nodded. The reality of Janka Industries' offer hadn't quite sunk in, and she didn't want to count her chickens before they hatched. However, even if she received their first offer, it was still enough to make a huge difference in her life.

"Even if I get their initial offer, I can use it to set up my business and pay a chunk off my mortgage."

"Just remember your best friends when you're loaded!" Becky declared while trying to slip into her black lace skirt while giving Clarissa a stern look.

"I want to take you both on my business journey if you're interested of course. If it all comes off, I'll need people I trust to help me build it," Clarissa told them honestly. She couldn't think of two people she would like to work with more.

"You'd seriously like us to be part of your business?" Hayley asked, surprised.

Clarissa nodded, smiling at the two women she loved like sisters. "Of course, I would. Not only are you both amazing at what you do, but can you imagine how much fun we'd have working together?"

Becky giggled as she zipped up her skirt. "Oh my God, we would have a blast. Does that mean we'd get to test out all the sex toys to see if they get our seal of approval?" she wriggled her eyebrows and winked at Clarissa.

Laughing again, Clarissa nodded.

"Hell yeah! You do know that vibrators are better than most men," Hayley declared.

Clarissa slipped her jumpsuit over her shoulders, navigating her boobs in the right direction, which was always tricky. "How do you work that out?"

Hayley grinned. "Oh, dominatrix diva, let me enlighten you. Firstly, they don't come before you do: they are raring to go whenever you are, vibrators don't leave a wet patch, they can go all night, and vibrators don't get headaches or say they're too tired. Lastly, when you get bored of it, you can just buy another one."

Becky and Clarissa could barely breathe; they were laughing so hard. Laughter tears streamed down Clarissa's face as Becky declared she might mummy-pee in her new skirt.

"You are seriously too much," Clarissa tried to say as she held her sides again.

When all three were dressed and ready, they stood in Clarissa's bedroom, staring at each other in awe.

"Bloody hell, you both look absolutely amazing!" Clarissa declared.

Becky grinned like a Cheshire Cat. "So do you! I have to say, I've never felt so hot and sexy," she said as she ran her hands down her body.

Becky bent over, running her fingers through her fiery red hair, then throwing her head back. To Clarissa, her best friend looked like a sexy Irish goddess. She had never seen her best friend look so confident.

"If I come and work with you, I'm wearing stuff like this every bloody day." She giggled, making Clarissa grin.

"Amen to that," Hayley added. "I feel so hot wearing this; I don't ever want to wear a suit to work again." She laughed.

"Let's go and see what the men think," Clarissa said, opening her bedroom door and leading the way.

When Clarissa reached the lounge, Ann was sitting next to Tobi at his desk while Martin and Adam were chatting with Philip in the kitchen.

Tobi glanced around as she entered, and instantly, his mouth dropped open, his eyes growing wide in surprise. "Holy shit! My god, you look incredible. Are you sure we have to go out tonight?" he asked.

Clarissa laughed at his lustful expression. Tobi looked at her like she was a lolly that needed licking.

"I gather you like what you see?"

"Gorgeous, you look so fricking sexy; you should be illegal and come with a heart health warning," Tobi told her as he rose from his chair, striding towards her and taking her in his arms.

Adam, Martin, and Philip walked into the lounge to see what was happening. Adam and Martin suddenly froze.

Martin nudged Adam in the ribs with his elbow. "Don't look now, mate, but two smoking hot domination Mistresses have just walked in the room, and if our wives catch us drooling, they'll be wearing our balls as earrings."

Adam gawked. "No shit, Sherlock. I think we'll be on body-guard duty tonight to fight off the submissive groupies who will be kneeling at their feet."

Clarissa looked at her best friends, who both looked over the moon at their husband's reactions.

Ann rose from the desk, clearly thrilled by what she saw. "You three will be blowing some kinky socks off tonight, that's for sure!"

"All four of you will," Philip added.

Clarissa smiled at Ann. "These outfits are amazing, Ann. I can't wait to have them up on our website."

"Your website is also amazing," Ann told her, looking seriously impressed. "I've got a car taking us to and from the venue, so let's have a drink to celebrate what we've accomplished so far, shall we?"

While waiting for the car to arrive, the friends celebrated Clarissa, Ann's, and Tobi's work, all three complementing each other's efforts. By the time their car arrived, they were all raring to go.

—x—

The drive to Lanstern House, where the Domfeti Carnivale was being held, was a stunning journey. Clarissa, Tobi, and friends cha-tted about anything and everything during the drive while sipping champagne, courtesy of Philip. Clarissa had never felt so spoiled. She felt like a kinkier version of Cinderella.

Now and again, she caught Tobi staring at her with a smile on his face. She grinned back, knowing that he couldn't wait to get her home again.

As they drove off the country roads, their driver took them down a long sweeping drive lined with ancient oak trees. It wasn't long before Lanstern house came into view with a torch-lit circular lawn in the middle of a massive, gravelled driveway. The solid brick country house was like something out of a period drama, with numerous large windows draped with ivy and flowering climbing plants. Lantern House certainly wasn't the kind of venue Clarissa expected a domination and fetish event to be held. She began to wonder how many other well-off surgeons and other top profess-ionals would be in attendance.

When they drove closer to the entrance, a long line of expensive cars was waiting to be valet parked. Clarissa could hear music coming from either inside or around the grounds. Clarissa and the others watched as people exited their vehicles. Some women were dressed in attire similar to what Clarissa, Hayley, Becky, and Ann were wearing, while others were dressed down in subdued clothing with collars, clearly submissive's. Most of the male guests were wearing black suits with either a submissive collar or a necktie. Clarissa wasn't surprised to see a few people being led inside on thin symbolic chains from either their wrist or neck collars. She also noticed that there were quite a few single people entering.

Butterflies appeared in Clarissa's stomach, and she wondered if Hayley and Becky felt as nervous. She looked at her best friends, who both grinned at her.

"Make sure you have your invitation ready on your phones, ladies and gentleman," Ann told them as their driver pulled up to the front of the queue. By the time their car stopped, they were ready with invites in hand and raring to go.

A sharply dressed man in a black tuxedo approached their car, opening the door and greeting them.

"Good evening, Ladies, Gentlemen. If you would like to proceed through the main foyer, please."

With a nod the man indicated the old, heavy-looking, ornate wooden doors of the entrance. The music Clarissa heard from the car was now louder and definitely sounded like it was outside. She could also hear lots of chatter and laughter.

Holding hands, Ann and Philip led the way inside, with the rest of their group following. Clarissa's eyes darted left and right, taking in the elaborate building and its stunning decor. Old paintings adorned the walls of what Clarissa assumed were Lords and Ladies of Lanstern House, adding to the elegant feel. The music grew louder, and Ann led them through the foyer and outside to the main garden. Clarissa's eyes widened, mirroring her friend's expressions of awe as their eyes feasted on the sight before them.

Circular tables adorned the large, flat grounds of the country house, covered with white linen and decorated with elaborate flower centerpieces. Large peacock feathers protruded from the arrangements giving a slightly regal feel to the event. A large wooden dance floor had been laid on the striped lawn, right in front of a stage where a live band was playing lively jazz music as people danced. The stage was framed by a deep purple canopy and matching curtains with black twisted ropes looped from the center of the stage and tied to the sides. Clarissa smiled as the female lead singer sang while people twirled before her.

Clarissa didn't know what she expected as her eyes gazed upon the tables filled with people of all ages, dressed in their best and having a great time. It was a true social event, with everyone chatting, catching up, and greeting old friends.

Another man in a more uniform suit approached them with multi-colored cocktails on a silver tray. "Good evening. Would you like drinks?" he asked, offering the tray.

Hayley grinned. "Don't mind if I do," she said, helping herself to a cocktail.

As soon as they all had their drinks and thanked the uniformed man, Ann and Philip led them to the tables. Clarissa's butterflies fluttered in overdrive as people turned to see who else was coming through the foyer doors, their eyes roaming over them and their attire. She could see people nudging their friends and acquaintances so they could look at the new guests and what they were wearing. Clarissa and Ann smiled at each other. The other guests were obviously impressed and liked what they saw. Clarissa's confidence grew.

Ann picked a table in the center of the festivities, and Clarissa wondered if she was being strategic, knowing that people could see them from all directions. A wink from Ann confirmed her suspicion. *'Clever lady.'*

No sooner had they all sat down at their table; a steady stream of people approached, greeting Ann and Philip like old friends. Clarissa began to get the impression that the domination and fetish scene was, indeed, tight knit. Ann, as always, was friendly and warm, introducing all her friends to everyone at the table.

When Ann introduced Clarissa as the owner and founder of Darcy's Domination Desires, which was coming soon, Clarissa could feel her cheeks burning. She wasn't used to being pointed out, but she loved the fact that Ann was promoting her new business.

Everyone that spoke to Ann and their group complimented Clarissa and Ann's clothing, asking where they could buy them. Hayley and Becky were brilliant, handing out Clarissa's business cards to anyone who inquired. It wasn't long before Clarissa had to share out more business cards from her evening bag.

The Domfeti Carnivale event had a friendly and buzzing feel to it. The music and atmosphere had everyone relaxed and in the mood for fun. Clarissa watched as Becky and Adam took to the dance floor. She hadn't seen them look so happy and in love for a while. Both were hardworking parents, and it made Clarissa's heart happy to see them enjoying themselves so much.

"Would you like to dance, gorgeous?" Tobi asked with a grin. "I'll be gentle with you, I promise."

Clarissa loved to dance, but she didn't know whether her healing body would be able to keep up. "I'd love to, as long as you promise not to break me." She grinned back.

Tobi rose from his seat, holding his hand to her, and she let him lead her to the crowded dance floor. True to his word, Tobi gently led Clarissa around the dance floor, holding her closely, protectively. It was all new to Clarissa, as Nigel had always wanted to dance alone. Mainly so he could peacock to any watching women. Tobi, however, only had eyes for her. Clarissa swooned as Tobi effortlessly twirled her around to the hypnotic beat of the music.

"I can't imagine my life without you and the boys," he whispered as his warm breath washed over her neck.

"I can't imagine my life without you either."

Tobi suddenly stopped in the middle of the dance floor, looking straight into Clarissa's deep brown eyes. "Be mine forever?"

Clarissa's heart pounded in her chest as Tobi's emerald, green eyes mesmerized her. "Yes," she said breathlessly.

Sliding his hand into his trouser suit pocket, Tobi pulled out a small black and gold ring box. Clarissa's eyes widened in surprise. He smiled at her so sweetly, she thought she might melt in his arms, there and then. Tobi released her and lowered himself to one knee. She gasped. The whole crowded dance floor stopped, including Becky and Adam. Her best friend gave her a beaming smile. As the music teetered off and stopped—Clarissa looked back at Tobi—who had nothing but love and adoration in his eyes.

"Clarissa Isabelle Darcy, will you marry me and be mine forever?"

Tobi opened the ring box and laid on a cushion of black velvet sat a stunning Art Deco floral diamond ring. Clarissa's breath caught in her chest. She had never seen such a beautiful ring in her life, let alone been offered one, but as she looked into Tobi's loving eyes, she wouldn't have cared if it was a ring pop from a sweet shop. He wanted to be with her forever, and that was all that mattered.

The dance floor and the garden fell into silence. All eyes were on Tobi and Clarissa, but they were oblivious.

"Yes, forever."

Everyone cheered and applauded as they heard Clarissa's reply. Glasses clinked while some of the watching guests wiped tearful eyes.

Tobi rose from the dance floor, his beaming smile lighting up his handsome face. He plucked the engagement ring from the black and gold box and took Clarissa's left hand in his. As Tobi looked into her eyes, he slid the Art Deco ring onto her index finger. Clarissa felt like she was floating on clouds as he took her in his arms and kissed her deeply.

"Three cheers for the happy couple!" The beautiful lead singer exclaimed from the stage. "Hip, Hip..."

"Hooray!"

Clarissa and Tobi smiled while still touching their lips as everyone cheered their engagement. Tobi released her, twirling her before pulling her back against his firm body. "Let's get some champagne to celebrate." He grinned.

Chapter 22

As Clarissa and Tobi reached their table, all of their friends clapped, with Becky and Hayley whoop-whooping with huge grins. Adam, Martin, and Philip took turns shaking Tobi's hand, congratulating him, while Hayley, Becky, and Ann took Clarissa in a group hug.

"We are so happy for you," Hayley told her tearfully. "If anyone deserves a fantastic man who adores her and makes her truly happy, it's you, honey."

"I second that," Becky said, gently squeezing Clarissa. "Now, let's see that beautiful ring, you lucky bitch."

Clarissa could feel tears springing to her eyes as she felt the emotion in her best friend's words.

"Did you buggers know about this?" Clarissa asked, feigning a stern look.

"Yep."

"Sure did," Hayley confessed. "Your mum and Dad are thrilled for you, and so are Luke and Matthew."

Clarissa was blown away. "They all knew as well?"

Hayley grinned. "Not only did they all know, but Tobi asked your parents and your boy's permission for your hand last week."

Two of the waiting staff approached with a wheeled tray of champagne and crystal glasses. "Congratulations to you both," the older of the two men said with a smile. "Compliments of Lanstern House."

"Thank you so much," Clarissa said as the girls released her.

Tobi shook both men by the hand. "Thank you, we appreciate it."

As the waiting staff poured glasses of champagne for everyone, they took their seats. Tobi held Clarissa's hand, his thumb stroking her hand and diamond engagement ring. The moment all glasses were filled and distributed, Ann stood with her glass in hand.

"Congratulations, Clarissa and Tobi. Here's to a wonderful couple who are meant for each other."

They clinked glasses as the music resumed, and everyone returned to drinking, chatting, and dancing. Before long, a stream of staff poured out from the main doors with platters of delicious-looking food, heading to long tables on either side of the entrance stone steps that Clarissa hadn't noticed.

The music stopped, and the lead singer took to the microphone. "Ladies and gentlemen, may I introduce, Fire and Ice," she announced as the black ropes were released from the sides of the stage.

The singer and band walked off the stage as numerous staff walked on, quickly removing all the instruments. Dramatic music began to play, and as soon as all the instruments and staff were gone, two women dressed in skin-tight bodysuits elegantly tumbled onto the stage. Their bodies leapt gracefully into the air to gasps and applause from the audience. One artist wore colors of red and orange flames, while the other wore blues, white, and silver. Before their eyes, the artists leapt in the air, grasping the black ropes while in motion.

Everyone at Clarissa's table was in awe of the two young women as they spellbound them by gracefully dancing in the air, using the ropes. With each dramatic movement, either flames or bursts of snowflakes erupted from the back of the stage, creating more gasps and applause. Clarissa had never seen anything like it.

The moment the rope artists finished, everyone stood to appl-aud and cheer their performance. The women dismounted the ropes, gracefully bowing to their appreciative audience. As they leapt and tumbled from the stage, a smartly dressed compere walked on.

"Ladies and gentlemen, the buffet is now open."

The buffet was a sumptuous feast. Large white China platters sprawled across the long white linen-covered tables, with an array of sliced meats and cheeses, crackers, savory dishes, salads, and fruit, arranged in elaborate designs. Clarissa and her group took turns in their pairs going to the buffet so as to make the queue manageable while gentle music played in the background. As Clarissa and Tobi chatted at their table, partygoers approached to congratulate them on their engagement.

Before long, everyone had a mini feast on their plate and were back at their table.

"Thank you so much for inviting us, Ann. This is amazing, in more ways than one," Clarissa told her, giving Tobi a wink.

Ann grinned. "I'm thrilled you were able to make it tonight. It's been a fantastic night so far. I've had more inquiries about what we're wearing than I can count. I think we will be extremely busy once you're open for business."

"Really? That's fantastic. I suppose we'll have to get a move on then." Clarissa laughed.

"Here's to Darcy's Domination Desires!" Hayley declared, hold-ing up her champagne glass. "And to kinky buggers everywhere."

Everyone laughed and clinked glasses.

"I also had a few inquiries as to whether you dominate pro-fessionally, Clarissa," Ann said with a mischievous smile.

For a moment, Clarissa thought she had misheard. "You had

what now?"

"I'm serious," Ann told her, smiling. "A few of our single friends asked me if you dominate professionally. They're all in high-power careers and don't have time for relationships. So, they are seeking someone special to dominate them, as and when they need it."

Clarissa was gobsmacked. She looked at Tobi in surprise. He grinned at her. "But I'm with Tobi. I've just got engaged."

"They aren't looking for a sexual relationship." Ann laughed. "I keep forgetting you are so new to the scene. In a professional relationship, the submissive doesn't get to touch the dominant, and the submissive pays handsomely for the privilege of being dominated."

"I didn't know that was a thing," Clarissa told her honestly.

"Hell, I'd give it a go if I thought I could do it." Becky giggled. "I'd be too afraid I'd hurt the poor bugger, especially after hearing Clarissa on the phone with Mr. Senson, man."

Ann laughed. "How do you think I survived financially after Albert died?"

Clarissa hadn't even thought about that. "I had no idea, Ann."

"I had numerous high-profile clients who I used to see evenings and weekends after I lost Albert and his earnings. My clients were the only thing that kept me going, emotionally and financially. It's how Philip and I met, and when we fell in love, I withdrew from doing it professionally. My clients were never allowed to touch me, and none ever tried."

"Well, I think that's given all of us food for thought," Hayley said with a giggle as the music lowered and the compere took to the stage again.

"Ladies and gentlemen, if you would like to take your seats, our fashion show will begin courtesy of Red Cherri, Kinky Klothes, and Pink Bubble."

The music changed to soft rock, and Clarissa noticed that the black ropes had disappeared, replaced with black and silver drapes. The music grew louder, and a woman walked on stage wearing a very skimpy and kinky outfit of black latex. Diamond shape cut-outs revealed most of her amazing body as she confidently strutted across the stage. She twirled elegantly mid-stage, then strutted off as another model walked on. The audience cheered and clapped as model after model, male and female, walked on stage. Clarissa, Tobi, and their friends were impressed with the fashion show, but Clarissa didn't like the clothes as much as she liked her own designs. She wondered if she was just biased, but the show did give her ideas for designs she would like Ann to make.

Clarissa turned to Tobi as the fashion show came to a close, and the applause died down. "We haven't taken the photos of our outfits yet,"

Tobi comically slapped his forehead. "I completely forgot about that."

"We want our pictures taken too. We've never felt this hot and sexy," Becky said, waving her hand between her and Hayley.

"Let's go and do them now before we all look too inebriated," Clarissa suggested with a grin.

Ann rose from her chair. "I know the perfect place. Follow me."

—x—

Ann led them out of the large garden and away from the festivities to a private garden down the side of the country house.

"Are we allowed in this area?" Becky asked.

Ann smirked. "I started this annual event, and I know Edward, the owner, personally." She winked at Clarissa.

Clarissa wondered if Edward had been one of her kinky clients.

The private garden was stunning. Rows of white wooden chairs decorated with pink, white, and lilac flowers ran alongside a gravel path. At the other end of the garden, sand-colored stone steps led to a very old and ornate pavilion that sat in the center. Matching flowers adorned the pavilion's white stone pillars, and fairy lights sparkled everywhere.

"I think there's enough light here," Ann said as she walked down the gravel aisle.

"This is stunning," Clarissa said in awe.

"I wish we'd got married somewhere like this," Becky told Martin, nudging him in the ribs.

Martin huffed from the impact of his wife's elbow. "We could have done, babe, but a certain someone wanted a destination wedding because it was all the rage at the time." He raised his eyebrows.

"Yeah, okay. I'll let you off. We did have a fantastic wedding. Maybe we should renew our vows here?" She suggested.

Martin shook his head, laughing. "And pay for it with what, Monopoly money? We've got kids and a mortgage. We can barely manage a camping holiday in Devon."

Becky laughed. "I know, and I love our life." She kissed him on his cheek while squeezing his bum.

"Aye, aye. Later lady."

They all laughed at Becky and Martin's banter.

Clarissa couldn't stop admiring the beautiful private garden. The attention to detail was amazing.

"We didn't bring a camera," Becky said, her face dropping in disappointment.

Clarissa wrapped her arm around her best friend. "We don't

need a camera, honey. Have you not seen my nerdy fiancé's top-of-the-range smartphone?"

Realization struck. "Ooooh, I get you." Becky grinned.

"I think I want to photograph my fiancé first," Tobi declared, pulling out his phone from his inside suit jacket pocket. He pulled a glass cleaning cloth from his trouser pocket, wiping his phone's camera lens while giving Clarissa a wink.

She gave him a cheeky smirk. "Where do you want me?"

"Now that is a loaded question, gorgeous."

Clarissa comically rolled her eyes while sweeping her arms out. "I mean here, you bad man."

"I want you up against that stone pillar," he told her with a smirk of his own.

Clarissa shook her head. "Are we still talking about the photos?"

"Yes and no," he laughed, winking at her again.

"You two need to get married already," Becky declared as she sat down on one of the decorated white wooden chairs.

As everyone laughed, Clarissa walked up the stone steps to the pavilion. She turned and rested her back against its smooth surface while raising her leg, so her foot was against it too. She could feel the delicate flowering vine against her bare arms and neck, and smell the flowers perfume wafting in the cool evening air.

Clarissa suddenly felt self-conscious, knowing that her friends were watching, but these photos were going to be important. She knew she would have to lead by example, so her friends were comfortable having their photos taken as well. She took a deep breath, *'Sod it.'* Clarissa looked at Tobi. He was ready with his phone in hand, looking at her like she was the only one there.

As Clarissa looked at her new fiancé, her thoughts returned to their recent tryst and what she had done to him. The mental images of his hot body restrained against her bathroom door made her whole body flush, and her gaze smouldered. She had to be honest, she couldn't wait to do it again. Clarissa changed position, turning around and holding the pillar while wrapping her right leg around it.

Tobi snapped photo after photo, and the more he watched her move, the more turned on he got. He steadied his breathing, trying to gain some level of control.

"What about laying across the top step between the pillars and then sitting on the top step," Ann suggested.

"You look so hot right now, honey. If I were a lesbian and single, I would definitely hit you up," Hayley declared with a giggle.

Becky giggled the loudest. "I second that statement."

Martin and Adam glanced at each other with huge grins on their faces.

"We'd be happy to watch and supervise," Adam blurted, instantly regretting it as Hayley slapped him playfully at the back of his head.

Adam feigned indignation. "What? You started it, beautiful."

Clarissa giggled at her friends and nodded to Ann, knowing it was a good idea.

As soon as she was in position, lying on the top step, Tobi snapped more photos. The cold stone cooled her heated skin but not her thoughts.

"Damn, lady, you're going to melt Tobi's phone." Hayley laughed.

Clarissa rolled her eyes and giggled as she moved positions, sitting on the top step. "I think this will be enough."

"Just a few more," Tobi told her as she placed her elbow on her knee, resting her head in her hand and giving him a sexy glare.

"You wait till I get you home," Tobi smirked.

Clarissa raised an eyebrow.

"Promises, promises," she said, rising and walking down the steps towards him. When she reached him, she wrapped her arm around his waist. "Can I see?"

"Nope, you'll have to wait till later. Next!"

Becky jumped up from her seat. "Me! I want to go next." She plonked herself in the middle of the sandy-colored stone steps, ruffling her fiery-red hair. Becky looked like a fiery redheaded vixen, and she knew it. Martin's mouth fell open.

The group watched as Becky moved around the pavilion, striking various poses, each one as sultry as the last. Tobi snapped away happily, asking her to move slightly this way and that, trying to get the best shots with the fading light. Ann went next, and as she posed, Clarissa felt in awe of her confidence and poise. When Ann posed on a stone bench at the back of the pavilion, Clarissa thought that Philip might drop to his knees in worship. The adoration and love he felt for Ann was palpable.

As soon as Ann finished, Hayley stepped up, adjusting her clothing and mindset. She took a long deep breath. Clarissa had never seen her so nervous.

"Are you sure you're okay with this?" Clarissa asked, not wanting her to feel uncomfortable. Hayley had never liked having her photo taken in all the years they had been friends, even though she was usually the most confident.

"I've got this," she said, smiling at Clarissa's concern. "But I think I'd like to sit on the chairs instead."

Clarissa nodded as Hayley sat down in a center chair. The

numerous pink, white, and lilac flower decorations framed her slim, busty frame. Tobi walked towards her, positioning himself in front of the white wooden chairs, and he began snapping. Every few minutes, as she changed position, Clarissa could see her relax while her confidence grew. Adam looked on in awe of his wife.

"Okay, I think we've got enough. I just hope I did a good job," Tobi said as he slid his phone away inside his suit jacket.

"That's what photo editing is for," Becky told him.

"You aren't going to let us look, Tobi?" Martin asked as they started to group around him.

Tobi grinned. "Nope, you're going to have to wait until I check them."

"Well, let's get back to the party. I want to dance some more," Clarissa said, grabbing Tobi's hand and leading him towards the sound of Respect by Aretha Franklin. *'Very apt.'*

Clarissa was thoroughly enjoying herself, dancing, drinking, and chatting with her friends while making new ones. Every time she sat down to rest, another person would come and introduce themselves, asking her about her clothing line and what other services she would be offering. She was starting to get the impression that the word was spreading.

After saying goodbye to another new acquaintance, Clarissa turned to Ann, who had just sat next to her. "Thank you so much for telling everyone about our new business venture. We seem to be getting lots of interest."

Ann smiled. "I've already had people asking if they can place orders. So, I think we're both going to be very busy."

Abruptly feeling anxious, Clarissa wrung her hands in her lap. Planning a new business was one thing, but actually doing it and selling to clients was another. Ann picked up on Clarissa's nervous body language.

"You don't need to worry. You've got a talent for designing clothes and a head for business. We're all behind you on this, Clarissa."

Clarissa knew they were only words, but they were just what she needed to hear.

"Thanks, Ann. Do you think we'll be able to drag the others off the dance floor?" she asked as her eyes glanced back to Tobi, who was dancing with an older lady while mouthing help to Clarissa. She grinned, knowing that the older woman was thoroughly enjoying her dance with a young hunk of a man. At one point, Clarissa was sure the older lady had grabbed his ass. *'No wonder he's asking for help.'*

Ann looked at her watch. "I think this might be the last song. So, we might get them home if we are lucky." she laughed.

As the music died, Hayley and Becky returned to their table with their exhausted husbands in tow.

"That was good timing. Our car should be here soon to pick us up," Ann told them as her phone pinged with a message. She grinned at Hayley and Becky's worn-out men.

The relief on Adam and Martin's faces was comical. Considering they were both active and fit men, Clarissa was surprised that her friends were able to destroy them on the dance floor. She thought maybe Hayley and Becky would not get shenanigans when they got home after all.

When Tobi finally escaped the clutches of the older lady, he sprint-walked back to their table with an extremely flushed face, looking embarrassed. He plonked himself down next to Clarissa.

"You wouldn't believe what that lady said she wanted to do to me," he squeaked, instantly making everyone laugh.

Ann laughed heartily. "That's Mistress Gloria. I've lost count of how many submissive's she's worn out. Apparently, she likes her submissive's the same way as she likes her dogs—on all fours and wearing a choke chain."

"She looks like a sweet little old lady," Clarissa said between giggles.

"There's nothing sweet about what she was saying to me, gorgeous. Trust me," Tobi told her as his cheeks reddened again.

Philip popped out of nowhere, appearing behind Ann and slipping his arms around her slim shoulders.

"Are we ready to go? I believe our car is here."

Tobi glanced to the table near the stage—and on seeing the older lady he had just danced with grinning at him while thrusting her hips—he jumped from his seat. "Yep, I'm ready to go. Let's get out of here."

They were still laughing as they reached the waiting Limo and driver.

—x—

The ride home from Lanstern House was nearly as enjoyable as the event. Clarissa didn't think she had ever enjoyed herself so much, and she couldn't wait to do it again. Adam and Martin wilted in the back seats, and the moment Hayley and Becky got in the car, their heels were off, resting their weary feet on their husband's laps. Clarissa's best friends were still buzzing, chatting about people they had met and how impressed they were with the rope artists.

"So, will you tell us what Mistress Gloria said to you?" Clarissa asked Tobi, who instantly reddened at the mere mention of her name.

"She said she wanted to call me Snuckles, put me in a furry bodysuit, fuck me from behind with a strap-on while pulling on my choke chain."

The look of pure fear on Tobi's face had Clarissa and everyone in fits. Clarissa could barely breathe, especially as she knew what Mistress Gloria looked like and had a clear mental image of the scene. "No wonder you feel traumatized."

Tobi shook his head as if it would shake the thoughts from his mind.

Tears streamed down Hayley's face as she tried to catch her breath. "Bloody hell, that's kinky. The kinkiest thing we've ever done was try those edible body paints you can buy. It was a bloody nightmare."

Adam slapped his face. "Worst experience ever!"

"Well, now you have to tell us what happened. You can't just leave us wondering," Clarissa said, knowing she wasn't the only one intrigued.

"When we got married, someone gave us a pamper hamper as a wedding gift, so we decided to open it after a couple of bottles of red wine. Most of it was for a bath, but it also contained some edible body paints. So, feeling adventurous, we decided to give it a go," Hayley said while Adam shook his head at the memory. "It was fun and a turn-on at first, painting each other's bodies, and before long, we got frisky. Unfortunately, as it dried, it turned into super glue, and within minutes, we were stuck together like multi colored Siamese twins."

Becky began laughing while everyone else waited for Hayley to admit she was joking.

"You are kidding, right?" Clarissa asked, beginning to giggle.

"Nope. We had to literally pull ourselves apart. And the worst thing was—we were doing it doggy style. Adam's pubes ended up being stuck to my ass cheeks."

"The pain!" Adam declared, shaking his head. "I don't know how or why you ladies wax."

The whole car erupted in laughter. Even their driver snorted and laughed from the front of the car, making everyone laugh harder. The mental image of Hayley with curly pubes on her butt cheeks, while covered in body paint, was something Clarissa would never forget.

"I can't believe you never told us about this," Becky tried to say as she held her aching cheeks.

"Scarred for life," Adam said quietly, still shaking his head.

"I'm guessing you'll never try the back, sack, and crack waxing for men after that incident?" Tobi asked Adam with a grin.

Adam glared.

Ann and Philip dropped everyone off, and as Clarissa and Tobi excited the limo, Clarissa popped her head back inside the car.

"Thank you for a fantastic night and for everything," she told them.

"It was our pleasure. We'll pop by tomorrow to collect our car," Ann said with a smile.

Chapter 23

Clarissa woke on Sunday morning with a thick head, feeling as sick as a pig with an aching body, and not just from dancing. Tobi hadn't been able to keep his hands off her after getting home the night before, and he had pretty much adored every inch of her, with and without her domination outfit on.

As she turned in bed, the urge to vomit took over. She raced to the bathroom as quickly as possible, hoping she would make it. After sorting herself out, she realized that Tobi was already up, and she made her way downstairs to find him working on his computer. She sidled up next to her new fiancé.

"Morning, Snuckles," Clarissa greeted Tobi with a grin.

Tobi pursed his lips and shook his head. "I'm not going to live that down anytime soon, am I?"

Clarissa laughed. "Nope, it's just too good. What are you up to?"

Tobi wrapped his arm around her, gently pulling her onto his lap. "I've been editing the photos we took last night. Do you want to have a look?"

"Hell yes,"

Clarissa bit her bottom lip excitedly.

Clicking on his computer screen, Tobi opened the album he had created, making it full screen, and clicked the slideshow.

As the first image appeared, Clarissa's eyes widened. "I can't believe that's me!"

It was the image of Clarissa leaning against the stone pillar of the pavilion and the photo was stunning. She had never thought of herself as sexy, but she had to admit, she looked hot. The flowering vines on the pillar complimented her complexion and the clothes she wore.

"Wow, Tobi."

He grinned, "Wait till you see the rest."

Clarissa watched in awe as the images changed before her eyes. Ann had been right; the private garden had been the perfect place to do the photoshoot. Every single photo was stunning. Hayley, Becky, and Ann looked like models, and she knew they would be thrilled with the photos just as much as she was.

"Tobi, you have outdone yourself. The photos are amazing."

"All I did was adjust some of the lighting. You, ladies, didn't need anything changing."

"The girls are going to be gobsmacked when they see these," Clarissa said, hugging Tobi around his neck and kissing his face. "I'll get dressed and send them a message. Maybe we can invite them over for lunch so they can be together when we show them. The boys won't be home until late afternoon."

Tobi smiled at her excitement. "Good idea. I'll make breakfast while you get ready."

—x—

By the time Ann, Becky, and Hayley were dropped off, Clarissa and Tobi had prepared a light buffet lunch, and Tobi had his laptop connected to the television. Clarissa felt nervous, hoping and praying that her friends would be happy with what they were about to see. Becky and Hayley couldn't stop talking about how much fun they and their husbands had at the Domfeti Carnivale event.

"I swear my feet are still aching from all the dancing, but it was so worth it," Becky told them with a big grin.

Hayley nudged Becky playfully on her side. "Never mind your bloody feet. I want to see the photos, so grab your food, woman."

They sat in the lounge with full plates, and Clarissa nodded to Tobi. "Ready when you are hot stuff."

Tobi clicked play on his laptop, and the slideshow on the TV began.

"Bloody hell, Clarissa. You look like a model," Hayley exclaimed, making Clarissa grin.

"That's what I thought when I saw the photos of you ladies."

The next image appeared, and Ann nearly dropped her plate. "That can't be me!"

"It's you. You hot, sexy thing," Clarissa told her, grinning at her reaction.

Becky appeared next, and she was just as shocked. "Holy shit! If I didn't recognize my hair, I'd swear it was someone else. I want those framed and on the wall in my house. So, when I'm an old lady with saggy tits and no teeth, I can tell my grandkids that I was a sexy bitch in my younger day, and they'll have to believe me."

Hayley choked on her hummus, spraying bits all over herself. "Damn woman," she laughed, "You're going to kill me one of these days! You can't say things like that to your future grandchildren."

Becky grinned. "I'm going to be just like my grandma. The last time we had a family get-together, my dad got cheeky with her, and in front of everyone, my grandma said, remember where you came from, son, my vagina. It was funny as hell. She's my hero!"

Hayley began choking and spluttering again while Ann laughed and patted her on the back. Clarissa and Tobias also burst into laughter, nearly spilling their plates of food on the floor.

They were laughing so hard that they missed the rest of the slideshow, forcing Tobi to start it again. By the time they watched it through again, and this time till the end, Ann, Becky, and Hayley were all in awe.

"So, ladies, are you okay with us putting the photos on the website and later on the app when it's finished?" Clarissa asked.

Clarissa grinned when all three of her friends nodded.

"Can we get copies of our photos?" Becky asked, "I really do want to get them printed off. And I want copies for my parents; they will freak when they see them."

"Of course," Clarissa told her, feeling thrilled and relieved that her friends were so happy with them.

Tobi and Clarissa uploaded the photos to the website as soon as Ann, Becky, and Hayley left. Clarissa was beyond happy with how they looked on their new site. As they sat next to each other at Tobi's desk, she leaned into him.

"This is really happening, isn't it?"

"It sure is gorgeous. Why don't you let me pay for some stock and give Ann some money to make more samples?"

Clarissa knew Tobi only wanted to help, but there were still things he didn't know. She decided that if they were to get married in the near future, she would have to be honest with him.

"I can't bring myself to let you pay for my stock."

"Why not? I have the money. I don't understand."

"Nigel talked me into not working after I had Matthew, but the moment he had to start paying for everything—he would hold it over me—making me feel like a leach. He'd even behave like a bastard when he had to buy clothes for the boys. It's why I went back to work after eight months. I just couldn't bear him being an asshole all the time."

Tobi nodded, finally understanding where she was coming from. His body tensed, and he could feel his anger building, not because of Clarissa but her ex.

"I get it, and I don't blame you for feeling that way. I'm not a violent man—but the more I find out things about Nigel and the way he treated you—the more I want to knock his head off his shoulders. The only things stopping me from hunting the bastard down are that he's Luke and Matthew's dad, and if he hadn't been such a bastard, I wouldn't have met you."

Tobi turned in his seat, taking Clarissa's face in his hands, and he kissed her deeply. Pouring all the love he felt for her in that one moment. "I would never, ever treat you like that."

"I know, but I would still feel the same way. I wouldn't be able to stop myself. It's going to take time."

Clarissa's parents were excited when they arrived with Luke and Matthew. Both boys hugged Clarissa and Tobi, giving them congratulatory cards bought by their grandparents.

"Let's see your ring then," Mary said with a huge smile.

Clarissa held out her hand, beaming at her parent's reaction.

"Oh my god, darling. It is gorgeous. Massive congratulations to you both," Mary said as she started to tear up.

"Don't cry, Nana. You're supposed to be happy," Matthew told her while hugging Tobi's leg.

Tobi ruffled his hair. "Those are happy tears, little guy."

Matthew grinned, rushing forward to give Mary a big hug.

"Let's put the kettle on," Clarissa suggested.

Clarissa made her way to the kitchen with everyone in tow, and as she boiled the kettle, Luke and Matthew told them all about their weekend while showing them photos on Mary's phone. Clarissa made the tea and sat down with her family while thinking how lucky she was, especially as she watched Tobi chatting to her parents while having Luke and Matthew on both knees as they tried to show him yet more pictures.

"Can we watch TV," Luke asked once he and Matthew had calmed down.

Clarissa nodded, knowing that her boys were wilting fast. "Of course. Do you want some dinner?"

Both boys shook their heads.

"No, thank you, Mummy. Nana already gave us dinner."

"So, how was your weekend?" Mary asked soon as Luke and Matthew were out of earshot.

Clarissa beamed at her mum. "It was the best weekend ever. We managed to do a load of work on the website. Tobi is doing great with the app, and the Domfeti Carnivale event was spectacular, wasn't it, Snuckles?" she said as she grinned at Tobi.

Tobi rolled his eyes comically while Mary raised an eyebrow. "You really don't want to know, Mary."

Clarissa giggled.

"Would you like to see our website for Darcy's?"

"Of course," Daniel told her, helping to rescue his soon-to-be son-in-law.

Clarissa grabbed her laptop, and when she opened it on the kitchen table, she saw a new email. Ignoring it, for the time being, she clicked on her website bookmark and turned her laptop around for her parents to see. Daniel clicked on the various pages, and both of her parents nodded and smiled as he browsed the site.

"Blooming heck. The photos of you ladies are amazing." Mary grinned.

Daniel nodded, impressed with what he saw. "This looks really good. When are you hoping to have it all up and running?"

"Soon, hopefully. It looks like Janka Industries want to pay me off to end their bad media nightmare. They've offered one hundred thousand. Hayley's counter-offered, so we'll have to see what they offer next, but hopefully, it won't take long. And we can use the money to launch Darcy's and pay off some of my mortgage," Clarissa explained.

Mary smiled at her daughter. "I'm so happy something positive will come out of what happened, darling. We know you're going to do well."

Clarissa rose from the table, hugging her parents for their constant and unwavering support.

Mary hugged her daughter tightly. "Are you going to do a launch party? I went to Ann's when she opened her shop, and it was very successful."

The thought hadn't even occurred to Clarissa, but she loved the idea, especially with Ann having so many contacts in the domination and fetish scene.

"I didn't even think of that, but I think it would be a fantastic idea."

Clarissa could tell that her parents were genuinely excited for her.

—x—

Two weeks had passed since the Domfeti Carnivale event and Janka Industries' offer. Clarissa and Tobi had been constantly on the go, working on Darcy's Domination Desires website and app, looking after Luke and Matthew, and doing their jobs. Clarissa felt like her head was spinning with so much going on, but she loved every minute of it, especially now she had a goal to aim for, and her beloved little red mini was back.

—x—

Clarissa had the day and evening to herself as Tobi was picking up his parents from the airport. She hadn't met them yet as they had been visiting family in Italy. Clarissa was nervous, especially as they were apparently protective over him since his cheater girlfriend. Clarissa could understand it. She would feel the same way if someone hurt her boys like that.

While Tobi was out, Clarissa was multi-tasking, updating her website, and taking calls while Luke and Matthew were at school. Her body ached from another physiotherapy session, but her body was getting back to normal. Michelle had sent all the chat line numbers she requested, so now she was uploading all the images for her new chat line services and writing the descriptions. Clarissa felt proud of herself. She had always been decent at writing but never knew she had a flair for selling erotic services.

Clarissa's phone pinged with a message from Ann.

Call me when you get a chance.

With so many hours worked already, Clarissa was ready for a break. Quickly, before another chat line call could come through, she logged herself off and dialled Ann's number on her mobile while heading to the kitchen. The moment it began to ring, she put it on the loudspeaker as she made herself a fresh cup of tea.

"Hi, this is Ann speaking."

"Hi Ann, it's Clarissa. Is everything okay?"

"Everything is great. I've made a few more samples, and they are gorgeous. I'm going to message you with some photos."

Clarissa instantly went into panic and guilt mode. "But I haven't given you any money yet."

"Don't worry about that. Call it my investment in you and your business. I know we're both going to do well out of this. Anyway, that's not why I wanted to talk to you. One of the high-roller dominant's that inquired about you at the event has called me again. He's desperate for you to dominate him, and I promised to talk to you about it."

Clarissa nearly dropped her kettle just as she was about to fill it. "Bloody hell, I didn't think they were that serious."

Ann chuckled. "It might be worth considering, Clarissa. As I said at the event, it's not a sexual thing, and you would earn more in one session than two weeks' wages or more. Plus, he would pay for your fuel, travel, and other expenses."

"Do you know what he's into?" Clarissa asked. Her mind was working overtime, going over what a side job like that could mean, especially if it paid so well.

"Alastair is a top cooperation banker and negotiator who finds it hard being in charge all the time. His stress release is being de-meaned. You would have to tell him how pathetic he is and what a small cock he has."

Clarissa was gobsmacked. She'd had many callers wanting the same thing, but she never understood why some wanted her to demean them. *Could she do it in person? Hell, yes!*

"I'll have to talk it over with Tobi. I don't want to make him uncomfortable, especially now we're engaged," Clarissa told her. "Can I call you when I've discussed it with him?"

"Sure, just let me know when you can."

—x—

Tobi's parents, Lucy and Leon, were not what Clarissa expected. When they walked through the door with Tobi into Clarissa's house, they hugged and congratulated her on their engagement, gushing about how excited they were. And within an hour, they were chatting and drinking red wine in the kitchen, with Luke and Matthew showing them their favorite toys. Clarissa smiled as she watched Lucy hugging Matthew, who had instantly taken a shine to her.

"I was starting to think we would never be grandparents," Leon laughed, patting Tobi on the back.

Tobi grinned like a cat who got the cream, winking at Clarissa.

Clarissa felt like she was glowing. Never in a million years did she expect Tobi's parents to be so thrilled about her and her boys, let alone accept them instantly like family. She began to wonder how Tobi had prepared them for their introduction.

"Tobi told us you're soon to be a business owner, Clarissa," Lucy said with a warm smile that lit up her face.

Suddenly, Clarissa felt awkward, not knowing how much Tobi had told them. "Yes, we're excited about it. Everything seems to be going well, and we hope to launch it soon. Tobi's been an amazing help and extremely supportive."

"I truly admire any woman who is driven to make her mark in the world. Especially women who don't rely on men."

The respect was clear in Lucy's tone, and at that moment, Clarissa liked Tobi's mum even more. She smiled at Lucy, knowing they were going to be firm friends.

—x—

As Tobi and Clarissa laid in bed panting and recovering from another sexual adventure with their new domination sex toys, Clarissa turned and put her arm around her hunky nerd.

"Today went much better than I thought it would."

"I think my parents love you more than me," Tobi laughed. "If only they knew what a wicked woman you are and what you do to me on a regular basis. I might have to tell my mum."

Clarissa slapped his bare muscular chest. "How much did you

tell them about our new business and what I do for a job? Your parents asked about the website, and I didn't know what to tell them."

He grinned. "I told them everything. My parents are very open-minded. I told them you were a single parent with two amazing kids and that you worked on a chat line to support yourself and the boys. They didn't bat an eye. My parents started with nothing, and they've worked hard for everything they have. I know my mum would have worked any job to provide for us."

"I'm so happy they like me."

"They don't just like you, gorgeous. They already love you and the boys." Tobi pulled her closer and kissed her already swollen lips.

"I had a chat today with Ann. She's already created more samples, and they are stunning. I can't wait to get them on the website."

Tobi smiled at her excitement. "You're going to have to add clothes designer to your list of many talents."

"She also said that one of the high-rollers reached out to her about my domination talents." She waited for changes in Tobi's body language, a habit she gained from years of her ex-asshole's behavior.

Tobi stroked her arm affectionately. "What's he looking for?"

Clarissa smiled, relieved that he was still relaxed. "He wants me to demean him, to help with his stress levels. Nothing sexual. And he's willing to pay more than I can earn in two weeks on the chat line apparently. It would free up a lot more time for me to work on the business."

Turning closer toward her, Tobi kissed her nose. "I'll support you no matter what you want to do. I only ask that I come with you for your safety. I'll be your bodyguard."

The love Clarissa felt for Tobi was overwhelming. Never in a million years had she dreamed of having a man like him in her life. He wasn't perfect by any means. He still farted in his sleep, left the toilet seat up, never changed a loo roll, and wiggled his tackle at her when horny, but she wouldn't change him even if she could.

"I'll let Ann know. Now go to sleep, you bad man; you've worn me out."

—x—

After a hectic weekend of hanging out with both sets of parents, Tobi and Clarissa were ready for some alone time. Luke and Matthew had enjoyed every minute of getting spoiled and receiving so much attention, and neither wanted to go to school that morning.

Clarissa reached out to Ann over the weekend and now had Alistair's information. Of course, Tobi had insisted on researching him, and once again, Clarissa was grateful for search engines. Ann had been right, Alistair wasn't married, and he seemed to be a workaholic with hardly any social life. She could understand why he needed to let off some steam. With Tobi happy that Alistair appeared to be a decent guy, Clarissa reached out by text, not wanting to disturb him if he was working.

It was while Clarissa and Tobi were eating lunch that her phone rang. It was Alistair, and the call was friendlier than expected. With her phone on the loudspeaker so Tobi could hear, Alistair asked how she was and told her how impressed he was with her already growing reputation for clothing design. Clarissa could tell by how he spoke that he was used to being in charge, but considering what he was looking for, she made sure she spoke with a firm but friendly voice.

"I hope you don't mind, but Ann told me you dominate via phone. I was hoping that you might be willing to dominate me in person, purely professionally, of course. It would only be once or twice a month, and I would pay you handsomely for your services. Two thousand per session, plus expenses. And from how highly Ann has spoken about you, I know I can trust you to keep things confidential."

As Alistair spoke, Tobi nodded his head and mouthed, *'Seems a decent man.'*

Clarissa thought so too, and not having to work on the chat line while waiting for her claim to finalize would definitely alleviate her stress levels and give her some free time. Also, two thousand a session was a lot more than she expected.

"I think it would be a good idea to do one session and see how it goes. I might not be what you're looking for, but at least you'll know by the end of the session."

"I think that would be a splendid idea."

"Great, let me know when you would like to book your session and anything specific I need to know, including your address details, and we can go from there," Clarissa told him.

"Excellent. I have a free day on Wednesday if you are available. Let me know as soon as you can, and thank you, Mistress."

The line went dead, and none of it seemed real to Clarissa. She looked at her grinning finance` with a stunned look. "I know I've said it before, but can you believe how much my life has changed already this year? It's crazy! Things are moving so fast."

Tobi grinned. "Nothing ventured, nothing gained, gorgeous."

"If Alistair is free on Wednesday, I'd like to try and do it sooner rather than later. At least I'll know if I want to do it or not."

"I'll make sure I'm free to take you."

After Clarissa messaged Alistair to say she was available for Wednesday, he messaged her with his address and what he wanted.

She was pleased that he didn't give her a long list. The only things Alistair requested was that she wear a tight top, pencil skirt, high heels, and seamed stockings. Luckily, she had all those things.

—x—

With Luke and Matthew spending Wednesday night with Clarissa's parents and Clarissa ready to go, they set off to Alistair's address. Ann messaged Clarissa a good luck message on the way, but it only made Clarissa more nervous. Tobi had been fantastic about the whole thing, seeing it only as a paid job. However, he had made it clear that if Alistair pushed his luck and got frisky with her, he wouldn't be responsible for his actions.

Alistair lived out in the country, which didn't surprise them. Clarissa would, too, if she had the money. Clarissa's stomach started to churn with nerves as they pulled into Sleepers Hill, wondering if she could really do this. Dominating over the phone was completely different from doing it in real life.

Clarissa's mouth dropped open when they found Alistair's home. Set back amongst mature trees sat a massive house, which was obviously designed and built by a modern architect. Beautiful wooden and brick-built structures blended seamlessly to give you the impression of class and elegance. She admired Alistair's house but wondered why a single man would want such a large home, especially as it had at least five bedrooms or more. She took a deep breath as Tobi pulled up in front of Alistair's three-car garage, which was just as posh as his home.

"If you don't want to do this, I can turn the car around, and we can leave right now," Tobi told her.

"I've got this, and we are here now. As you said, nothing ventured, nothing gained."

Chapter 24

Taking another calming breath, Clarissa exited Tobi's car, grabbing her handbag and straightening her pencil skirt. With Tobi behind her, she strode confidently to the front door of Alistair's stunning home and rang the doorbell. Alistair instantly opened the door, and Clarissa wondered if he was by the door waiting for her. He smiled the moment he saw her. He looked young for an older man, reminding her of an older Chris Evans, and Clarissa could tell he worked out.

"Welcome to my home," Alistair said, opening the heavy wooden door to let them in.

"Thank you." Clarissa walked into a large, well-lit foyer, turning to face him. "It's nice to meet you finally." She shook his hand. "I'd like you to meet my fiancé, Tobi."

Tobi stepped forward and held out his hand, which Alistair shook while smiling. "Thank you both for coming and thank you for giving this a try, Clarissa," he said with a warm, friendly smile. "Let me get you both a drink before we start. Tea, coffee, wine, or beer?"

"I'll take a coffee, please," Tobi told him as they followed Alistair to his sizable, modern kitchen.

"Coffee for me, too, please. You have a beautiful home, Alistair," Clarissa told him as her eyes admired his minimalist decor and large spaces.

Alistair smiled broadly. "I was hoping to raise a family here;

unfortunately, that hasn't happened yet. That's what happens when you're a workaholic like me."

While Alistair made the coffee, they talked. Clarissa got the impression that Alistair was a genuinely nice man, although he seemed quite lonely. He was easy to talk to and more down-to-earth than she thought he would be, considering his high-powered job. And although Alistair was good company, she wanted to get their session over and done with before her nervousness got out of control and had her running back to Tobi's car.

"Right, shall we get started?" she asked, hoping to move things along.

"Yes, of course, Mistress Clarissa," Alistair grinned, clearly excited. "Tobi, are you alright to wait here? We will only be in my study next door." He pointed to the room. "Please help yourself to coffee or anything in the fridge."

"Yes, I'm good, and thanks." Tobi nodded.

Clarissa could tell by the tightness in Tobi's jaw that he was also getting anxious.

"If you'd like to get yourself ready, Alistair, I'll be there in a moment," Clarissa told him firmly.

Alistair gave a nod to Tobi before looking at Clarissa. She gave him a firm glare, and his eyes widened. "Yes, Mistress." He walked away quickly, heading for his study.

Clarissa heard the door close behind him.

Clarissa wrapped her arms around Tobi's neck. She could feel his body heat through her tight blouse. "I won't be long."

She kissed him, then headed to the study. She knew if she didn't go in now, she never would.

Taking another deep breath, Clarissa opened the study door and walked in, closing it behind her. Alistair was sitting on his desk chair with his head down, wearing only black PVC shorts and a studded leather collar. On his desk behind him lay numerous domination and fetish toys that were obviously his favorites, including a riding crop, mask, and various clamps. She could see his anticipation and excitement all over his face. Clarissa had to admit he had been hiding a toned and muscular body under his shirt and casual trousers. She was surprised that he hadn't been snapped up a long time ago, especially as he was such a nice guy.

Clarissa reminded herself of what Alistair wanted, to be demeaned. She confidently walked toward him.

"There are certain rules to follow if you want to be my submissive, Alistair," she told him with a firm but sultry tone. "Firstly, you will address me as Mistress Clarissa while we are in this room, or you will be punished. Do you understand, you pathetic little man?"

Alastair looked up, his eyes wide with excitement. "Yes, Mistress Clarissa."

She stopped a couple of feet before him, lifting her head as if he were beneath her. "Get on your knees, you worthless piece of shit."

Clarissa watched as he immediately rose from his seat, getting to his knees obediently. His already swollen cock was barely contained beneath his black PVC shorts. She reached for the riding crop and a set of nipple clamps from the top of his desk.

"You will not come unless I give you permission," she told him, his eyes darting to the clamps and crop.

"I understand, Mistress Clarissa." His breath quickened.

"You will obey me at all times, and your safe words are orange for enough and red to stop. Is that clear, you sad little worm?"

She flicked the tip of the riding crop against his left nipple, making him gasp. His nipple instantly hardened.

"Ahh yes, Mistress Clarissa."

Clarissa knew she had to be careful. Their provisional relationship was only just beginning, and it could go one of two ways if she said or did the wrong thing.

She had to discover what he needed and wanted.

"What do you think you are worthy of doing for me?" she asked, flicking his other nipple with the crop.

"I can clean your beautiful shoes, Mistress Clarissa." He looked at her with hope in his eyes.

'Now we're getting somewhere.' She thought smugly.

Pulling his desk chair towards her, she sat down before him, allowing her pencil skirt to ride up her thighs slightly, just enough to tease. Alistair's eyes widened at her seamed stockings and sharp, black, stiletto heels. Raising her right leg, she placed her foot on his bare muscular thigh while giving him a stern look. She leaned forward with the nipple clamps in hand, her heel pushing against his tanned skin.

"Before you clean my shoes, I think I need to give you some incentive to do a good job. Are you ready for a little pleasurable pain?"

"Yes, Mistress Clarissa," his voice quivered as his body trembled.

Clarissa leaned forward, her heel pressing harder into his muscular thigh. She felt his muscles tense, and she couldn't miss his throbbing cock restrained inside his tight shorts. However, even though she was enjoying her power over him, he wasn't turning her on like Tobi. It was different, purely professional.

Alistair's eyes widened as she leaned forward, attaching the first clamp. He moaned loudly. Clarissa hoped that Tobi wouldn't lose his trust in her while hearing his moans.

"I'm impressed, my little pet."

She attached the second clamp, making him moan louder this time. Alistair closed his eyes as he tried to control himself. "You're doing well so far. I think you deserve a small reward for your good behavior, Alistair. You may stroke yourself through your shorts for five seconds, as I count. Am I clear?"

His hooded eyes opened. Clarissa could see just how turned on he was.

"Yes, Mistress Clarissa. Thank you."

She nodded for him to start. Alistair raised his head, his eyes locking with hers, and she began to count as he started to stroke himself with a trembling hand. Clarissa held his gaze, refusing to look away.

"One...two...three."

His breath quickened.

"Four...five...and stop."

She flicked his hand with the riding crop.

"Mmm, thank you, Mistress Clarissa."

"Now, clean my shoe," She demanded, rubbing the riding crop against her shoe and his thigh. She leaned back in the chair.

With a look of adoration and reverence, Alistair lifted her foot in his hands as if he held a prized treasure. He lowered his face, licking the side of her shoe with relish. *'Thank god I cleaned them before I left.'* Using the riding crop, Clarissa flicked his solid erection through his shorts and pointed to another area on her shoe. He licked again, moaning as he tasted the black leather.

As Clarissa watched, he licked and cleaned her shoe from the tip to the back. She flicked the crop against his barely restrained cock again, then his nipple clamp.

"Have you forgotten something, or are you too busy thinking

about your tiny little cock?" She flicked his erection with the riding crop more firmly, pointing at her heel.

"Mmm, thank you, Mistress Clarissa," he said as his tongue ran up the length of her six-inch stiletto.

The session was great, considering it was her first time with no safe words being used. Alistair was clearly turned on and enjoying himself immensely. Clarissa allowed him to clean her other shoe, and once he was finished, she permitted him to stroke himself for another five seconds. Using the other toys on his desk, Clarissa teased him, demeaned him, and rewarded him for good behavior. She also made him stand by his study window—telling him that strangers were watching what she was doing to him—humiliating him while adding to his excitement.

As their time together was coming to a close, Clarissa knew she had to allow him to finish.

"You have pleased me today, Alistair," she told him as she released his left nipple clamp.

He moaned loudly, his knees nearly buckling as the blood rushed to his very swollen and erect nipple. She smiled as she released the right clamp, and he fell to his knees.

"Ahhh, thank you, thank you, Mistress Clarissa." He gasped.

Clarissa took a step forward, placing the sole of her left foot against his throbbing and restrained cock. "I give you permission to finish," she said as she turned and strode from the room. As she walked away, she felt amazing and powerful.

Tobi was nursing a fresh coffee when Clarissa walked back into the kitchen, and she could tell he was anxious. The look of relief on his face, when he saw her, was evident. His eyes looked her over from head to foot as if checking she was all there. She wrapped her arms around his neck and kissed him, feeling his body instantly relax against her.

"How did it go?"

Clarissa ran her fingers through his thick, dark hair, something she knew he liked. "I think it went well, but I don't know if Alistair feels the same. I guess we'll find out in a few minutes. Are you okay?"

"I'm okay." He smiled. "I'll make you a fresh coffee."

Just over ten minutes later, as Clarissa and Tobi sat at the breakfast bar drinking their coffee, Alistair appeared fully dressed with a large smile on his face.

"Clarissa, I swear you are better than any therapist," Alistair said as he pulled out an envelope from his back trouser pocket. "Thank you so much for today's session. If you're willing, I would like to make regular appointments."

Clarissa accepted the envelope, not bothering to count it. She honestly didn't think he was the sort of man who wouldn't pay his bill in full.

"Thank you, Alistair. I'm happy that you received what you needed, and I'd be happy to see you regularly. Just let me know your requirements before each session and when you would like to book me."

Alistair approached Tobi, holding out his hand. Tobi shook it, giving the older man a friendly, warm smile.

"Thank you for bringing Clarissa and being her chaperone. I'm grateful for you both taking the time to come here today."

Tobi nodded, sliding himself off the breakfast bar stool. "You're very welcome."

"We'd better get going and leave you to enjoy the rest of your day. I'll see you soon, Alistair," Clarissa said as she slid off her seat.

Alistair grinned, looking a lot happier and more relaxed than when they first arrived. "Sounds good. I will see you out," he told them, leading them to his front door.

Clarissa waved as they pulled out of Alistair's driveway. "Well, I think he's a happy client."

She grinned while opening the envelope, which looked more than her, and Alistair had agreed.

She counted the money inside and was stunned to find three thousand pounds. "This is more than Alistair said. That's a hell of a tip!"

Tobi pulled onto the main road to go home. "Just goes to show how good you are, gorgeous." He grinned.

"I'm sorry if you felt uncomfortable while I was in the study with him."

Tobi reached his hand to stroke hers. "I was okay, but ready to dash in if you needed me. Although, I should know better. You are more than capable of defending yourself, as the last idiot found out." He grinned.

Clarissa felt proud of herself on the drive home, especially now knowing she could earn more than working on the chat line. She couldn't wait to tell Hayley and Becky about it; they were going to be stunned that she did it.

—x—

Clarissa and Tobi had just got home and were opening a much-deserved bottle of wine when Ann called.

"So, how did it go?" she asked, not waiting for Clarissa to say hello.

Clarissa grinned. "I think it went really well. He didn't try anything and seemed very happy when we left. He also gave me more money than we agreed."

Ann chuckled. "I thought he was pleased. Alistair sent me a thank you message, and when I asked him how it went, he said, fantastic.

"He asked me for regular sessions, so I assumed I did well."

"Well, there you go, you domination queen. If you'd like me to pass your details to my other friends who were asking about you, let me know."

For a split second, Clarissa hesitated. She didn't know when her claim money would be coming, and the sooner she got her new business up and running, the better. However, did she want to be a professional dominatrix too? The money would allow her to do more personally and for the business.

"That would be great. We can buy more stock and create more samples then," Clarissa told her.

"Sounds good. I'll see you soon."

As Clarissa put down her phone, she looked at Tobi, relieved that he was smiling at her. "Are you okay with me possibly having more clients?"

"I'll support you no matter what you want to do, gorgeous, especially if you aren't working all those hours on the chat line, because I'll get to spend more time with you." He grinned.

—x—

Within a month, Clarissa had four new clients for in-person domination, and all of them were very different. Michael was a specialist engineer who traveled worldwide for his job but came home between trips. He liked food play while being handcuffed and put in his cage. Clarissa wouldn't have found it too bad if the food play involved human food. Unfortunately, Michael liked to be fed canned dog food. So, Clarissa charged him extra as the smell of the dog food made her feel like vomiting instantly. It was tough trying to be a sexy dominatrix while you were turning green. Luckily, a tiny dab of menthol balm on each nostril made the experience less unpleasant.

Clarissa's other client, Robert, was a secret cross-dressing surgeon whose wife, Freya, preferred to pay Clarissa rather than dominate and punish her husband herself. Clarissa got on so well with Freya, she now considered her a close friend. Her newest clients, Joseph and Charles, were strictly punishment clients, but professionally they were miles apart. Charles was a top solicitor for wealthy and famous clients, and Joseph was a London based politician. She could sort of understand why they wanted to be punished. Both of their professions had them feeling like morally bad men.

After earning so much money with her new clients, Clarissa was able to stop working on the chat line and begin promoting her own chat line numbers. Michelle had been brilliant and was more than happy with the uptake in calls. Ann had managed to make all the clothing samples, and after buying a new large shed, Clarissa's garage and new shed were full of stock. However, she was able to make deals with a few suppliers to have most items delivered directly to her customers using her packaging and logo.

Things were falling into place, and all that was left to do was organize the launch of Darcy's Domination Desires.

Clarissa, Tobi, and the boys were preparing food early Saturday morning. Clarissa and Tobi had invited Hayley, Becky, Ann, their husbands, kids, and both sets of parents for a barbecue with an ulterior motive. Clarissa wanted their help and suggestions on their new business launch. She knew that between them, they would come up with some good ideas. It was also a great excuse to celebrate their new engagement with family and friends.

With Luke and Matthew happily in charge of the salads and

Clarissa preparing the meat, Tobi organized the pop and juices for the kids and cocktails for the adults. Tobi had even bought a case of champagne and hidden the bottles in a cooler in the new shed. Clarissa pretended she didn't know, secretly cleaning and polishing the champagne glasses while Tobi was picking up the boys from school.

All four of them were busy with their jobs when Clarissa's doorbell camera app sounded on her phone. She knew it was still too early for anyone to be arriving. Washing and drying her hands, Clarissa opened her app, stunned to see her ex-asshole walking up her garden path. *'What the hell does he want now?'* Having her ex-husband turn up— on what was supposed to be a happy day— wasn't what Clarissa needed or wanted.

Clarissa didn't want Luke and Matthew upset, so she slipped her phone to Tobi. When he realized who it was on her doorbell camera app, he shook his head.

"Do you want me to go?" he asked quietly, fine worry lines appearing on his forehead.

She smiled, knowing he wanted to protect her. "No, it's okay. I'll go."

As Clarissa walked to her front door, she made sure all the doors were closed behind her. Her pulse quickened. She didn't want another confrontation with the man who didn't give two shits about her or Luke and Matthew. And after their last heated conversation, she wondered what lies he was going to come out with this time.

Although she wasn't looking forward to their exchange, Clarissa was determined not to let him ruin their day.

Clarissa opened the front door, mentally preparing herself. Nigel walked toward her with a smile on his face, but she knew that fake smile.

"I'm afraid today isn't a good day to pop over to see the boys," she told him politely, trying to be the better person, knowing full well that it wasn't his reason for turning up.

"I just wanted to see how you were doing after your accident," he lied.

He moved his body, trying to see around her, looking disappointed when he saw the closed lounge door.

"Our accident was weeks ago. You could have come to the hospital straight after the accident to check on your boys. Why are you here now, Nigel? And please tell me the truth this time. I can't deal with any more of your lies." Clarissa's anger was already building. She could feel her heart pumping in her chest. She slowed her breath, trying to keep control.

Nigel lowered his eyes, and he started to shift his feet uncomfortably. "I heard you got engaged."

'That's the reason he's here.'

"Yes, I did," she said proudly.

He looked at her with a hurt she had never seen before, which surprised her. She waited for him to speak, and an awkward silence stretched between them.

"Please tell me why you're here."

"I can't bear the thought of you being with someone else, Clarissa. Please take me back. I promise I've changed."

She couldn't believe her ears. "It wasn't long ago that you lied about possibly having cancer. You haven't changed, and you still don't even think to ask after Luke and Matthew, your own sons. Why the hell would I want you back, Nigel?"

"But we're a family!"

Clarissa could feel her blood boiling in her veins. "We have never been a family. You were even out whoring the days Luke and

Matthew were born, you bastard. You can't even remember how old they are. Tobi's been more of a dad to Luke and Matthew in less than three months than you have ever been."

Nigel's face abruptly changed from hurt to furious, color flushing to his face as his anger exploded. Within a split second, his hands were around her throat, choking her. She couldn't breathe—even a little—and panic coursed through her.

Clarissa was momentarily too shocked to defend herself. His hands tightened, and his face darkened with effort. By the time her hands went to her throat to try and prise Nigel's hands off, Tobi was racing towards them.

The rage Tobi felt was overwhelming as he witnessed Nigel lurching towards Clarissa, gripping her neck.

The moment Nigel saw Tobi barreling toward him, full of rage, he released Clarissa and backed off. She stumbled back, choking and trying to catch her breath. Tobi pulled his arm back, throwing a punch powered by his rage and love for Clarissa, hitting Nigel squarely in his face with a crunch.

Nigel flew backward from the force of Tobi's impact, blood exploding from a smashed nose. As soon as Nigel's body landed on the paved garden path—Tobi was on him—pinning him down with his body weight. Nigel was panic-stricken, holding his hands up in surrender as blood gushed from his face, running down his neck. Tobi held him down by his throat with one hand, his fingers gripping soft flesh. He raised a fist, ready to punch again.

"If you even look in Clarissa's direction again, I will kill you!" Tobi spat. "You will never come here again. Do you understand me?"

Nigel could barely breathe, let alone speak. Instead, he tried to nod his head.

Clarissa was still trying to control her breathing and not pass out when Luke and Matthew came running out of the lounge to see what all the commotion was. The moment they saw Tobi and Nigel on the floor, both of them panicked.

"Daddy!" Matthew cried out, instantly worried.

Clarissa tried to hold her boys back as Tobi snapped out of his rage, getting off the bloody and weakened man. He stood, eyes darting from Clarissa to the boys.

Matthew wriggled out of Clarissa's hold, running towards the two men as Nigel scrambled to his feet. By the look on Nigel's face, he expected Matthew to run to him. Instead, Matthew ran straight for Tobi.

"Are you okay, Daddy?" Matthew jumped into Tobi's arms, wrapping his small arms around Tobi's neck.

Tobi's heart felt like it was in turmoil. He didn't want to hurt the boy's father, but no one had the right to lay a hand on Clarissa, his future wife. "I'm okay, little guy. Let's make sure mummy's alright."

Tobi didn't bother to look back at Nigel. He knew the coward wouldn't attack him.

Clarissa watched as Nigel stood shaking on the garden path, holding his badly broken nose as blood ran down his designer shirt, dripping on his expensive jeans and shoes. He watched his sons ignore him, and instead of seeing sadness or hurt on her ex husband's face, she only saw contempt.

The moment she saw that look, her mind was made up, and as Tobi and Matthew walked into the house, followed by Luke, she slammed the door shut behind them. Tobi wrapped his free arm around her, his eyes narrowing with worry.

"Are you okay, gorgeous?"

Clarissa shook her head as tears sprang to her eyes. She sobbed as her whole body shook.

"He said he wanted us to be a family again. When I told him you were more of a father than he'd ever been, he completely lost it. He's never been violent before, nasty, yes, but not violent."

"Do you want to cancel the barbecue?"

"No, but I do want to report him and get an injunction to stop him from coming near us again," she told him, trying to get her words out coherently while feeling determined never to have Nigel darken their door again.

"I'll call the police. Why don't you put some ice on your throat? It's looking extremely red and sore," he suggested, kissing her softly on her flushed and clammy cheek. "Can you help mummy for me?" He asked Luke and Matthew.

Luke and Matthew, shaken up as they were, took Clarissa's shaking hands, leading her to the kitchen as Tobi reached into his pocket for his phone.

Chapter 25

The police left Clarissa's house half an hour before Hayley, Adam, and their kids arrived. Clarissa found a thin summer scarf to cover her bruised neck before their arrival. Feeling much calmer, she answered the door with a smile on her face. She hugged her friends while their kids, Alex and Cody, ran inside to find Luke and Matthew, who were playing video games upstairs.

"I have some amazing news!" Hayley declared.

"You've won the lottery?"

Hayley rolled her eyes. "Nope, you have to be in it to win it, and I never buy a ticket."

"You're pregnant?" Clarissa guessed again with a huge grin.

Hayley shook her head. "Seriously? That wouldn't be amazing news. My body is still getting over that last one. If my boobs got any bigger, I wouldn't be able to stand up straight anymore. And I don't want more wobbly bits than I've already got." She laughed.

"I love your wobbly bits," Adam told her, looking sullen.

Hayley playfully slapped his arm. "You're not supposed to acknowledge that I have wobbly bits, you plonker." She rolled her eyes at Clarissa. "Men, they never learn."

"Tobi's in the kitchen," Clarissa told Adam, trying to rescue him before he dug himself into a hole so big that he couldn't climb out.

Adam grinned and made a quick exit, heading to the safety of the kitchen.

Hayley slipped her arm through Clarissa's. "So, do you want to hear the good news or not?"

Clarissa grinned at her friend's excitement. "Mmm, yes!"

"I wanted to wait till I saw you in person to tell you. Janka Industries finally came back with their counter offer. They're willing to pay you four hundred thousand pounds as a full and final settlement."

Clarissa stopped in her tracks and stared at Hayley in utter disbelief, suddenly feeling light-headed. "Really?" She squeaked.

Hayley nodded. "Yes. Do you want to accept it?"

"Hell, yes! Oh my god, I can't believe it. That's so much more than I ever expected. Let's get some wine poured to celebrate," Clarissa declared, leading her best friend to the kitchen.

When Tobi's parents arrived, he was happy to introduce them to everyone. Of course, the moment they arrived, they asked where Luke and Matthew were, and after some much-needed hugs from their newly adopted grandchildren, Lucy and Leon began to relax.

"We feel like we already know you," Lucy told everyone with a smile. "Tobi's told us so much about you, and he speaks very highly of you all."

Leon wrapped his arm around his wife. "We're thrilled to be here," he said as he grinned at Tobi.

"Please don't believe everything you've heard. We are sane, honestly." Hayley joked.

Before long, Leon and Lucy were chatting away with Daniel and Mary like old friends, gushing about how fantastic Luke and Matthew were and speculating, not very quietly, about when the wedding might take place.

By the time everyone else arrived, it was already feeling like a party, especially as they had another thing to celebrate. And like with most parties, the men seemed to gravitate towards the barbeque, talking sport, while the women mingled in the kitchen with a good supply of wine.

Tobi, still feeling protective, walked into the kitchen for the umpteenth time, wrapping his arms around Clarissa and kissing her ear.

"Are you okay?"

She smiled and stroked his hand reassuringly. "I'm good."

"Shall I fire up the barbecue, gorgeous?"

Clarissa leaned her head back against him, kissing his cheek. "Yes, please."

Becky watched as Tobi walked back out to the back garden wearing his stocking and suspenders novelty apron, heading to where all the husbands were still drinking and talking about the latest football game travesty.

"Are you going to tell us why Tobi is being so clingy, or are you going to make us guess?" Becky asked, raising a brow.

Clarissa didn't want to tell them, but she knew her friend's minds would be working overtime all day and evening if she didn't. She wanted them to relax and enjoy the get-together.

"Nigel turned up today, wanting us to be a family again."

Becky couldn't believe it. "Seriously? What reality does that man live in?"

"He'd heard about Tobi and me getting engaged. Apparently, he doesn't want me to be with anyone else." Clarissa took a large gulp of her white wine as if it would take away the terrible taste she suddenly had in her mouth.

Becky scoffed as Hayley, Ann, Mary, and even Tobi's mum, Lucy, rolled their eyes.

"Wow, that's a red flag right there," Hayley told her. "It's also what stalkers and wife murderers say."

Clarissa nodded. "I know, right? If I can't have you, no one else will, springs to mind. It was stalker behavior. Anyway, he got nasty and attacked me," she told them as her hand instinctively went to her very bruised and sore throat.

"That son of a bitch!" Hayley's instant anger reflected all the other women's emotions. "When I get my bloody hands on that bastard, I'll...."

Clarissa held up her hands while smiling at her friend's protectiveness. "I wouldn't worry, honey. Tobi saw him attack me on the doorbell camera, and I think he smashed Nigel's nose. His face was gushing with blood."

"That's my boy," Lucy said proudly, making Clarissa smile.

"I don't think he'd try anything again, but we did report him to the police, and I've applied for a restraining order now. The police took photos of my neck where he tried to throttle me."

"That bastard," Mary seethed, "It's a good job Tobi sorted him out. Otherwise, your dad would be hunting him down tonight to give him a taste of his own medicine."

Clarissa knew her mum was right. Her dad was very protective, and he despised Nigel for good reason.

"I'm going to go for full custody of the boys. Today was the final straw. He doesn't care about the boys. He didn't even ask if they were okay after the accident." She shook her head as if she could shake away what had happened. "Anyway, Darcy's Domination Desires is ready to go, apart from the app, which is nearly done. Tobi and I have everything set up. Ann has made an amazing clothing sample selection, and my chat line numbers are up and running. So, I need ideas for the launch party." She grinned.

Following Clarissa's cue for positivity, they all began offering ideas on venues and themes, taking the conversation to the garden where all the men were hanging out. Clarissa was impressed with all their ideas, from a masquerade ball to a Vegas games night, especially Lucy's idea of a Cabaret theme party.

"What about holding the launch at Lanstern House?" Ann suggested. "I'm already long-term friends with the owner, as you know, and I'm sure I could get a good price if you want to have the launch there."

Clarissa loved the idea, especially as so many people in the domination scene were already familiar with the venue.

"I think Lanstern house might be a real possibility," Clarissa told Ann with a grin, "Especially as Hayley gave me good news today."

Tobi's ears pricked up. "What good news?"

"Janka Industries has made a final settlement offer of four hundred thousand pounds, and I'm going to accept it."

Tobi dropped his spatula and whirled around, rushing forward to hug Clarissa and spin her around as everyone cheered.

"Congratulations, gorgeous. You deserve it; you really do." He put her down and kissed her. "I'll be right back."

The moment Tobi rushed off, heading towards their new shed, she knew he was retrieving the champagne he had stashed away. Clarissa's dad took over the barbecue duty like a pro, turning the filet steaks and chicken kababs. Clarissa and Hayley grabbed the champagne glasses while all the kids raced downstairs, rushing outside to find out what the noise was about. Becky grabbed the fizzy pop, juice, and tumblers for the kids, knowing they would want to join in.

As everyone received filled glasses of champagne, fizzy pop, or juice, they toasted Clarissa and Tobi's engagement, their new business, and Clarissa's settlement.

"Here's to a new chapter and a fantastic fresh start!" Clarissa toasted with a big smile on her face.

Thank you for reading.

If you want to help and support your favorite indie authors,
here is what you can do.
Leave reviews everywhere possible.
Tell your friends and family about their books.
Like, follow, and share their social media posts and author
pages.

Your help and support mean everything to us.

About the author.

Beth Worsdell is an English science fiction, fantasy, and women's comedy fiction author. The first to publish sci-fi fantasy books in adult and YA editions. giving readers the choice between books, with naughty bits and language, or without.

Beth Writes about badass women, strong female characters who will do whatever it takes to protect their families, friends, and humanity.

Founder-Host of The Witty Writers Show live from her Facebook author page and YouTube channel. Beth interviews other authors, book bloggers, reviewers, and publishing professionals of all genres. Join in to ask questions and have fun with Beth and her guests. Available to watch live on YouTube and Facebook. You can also listen to The Witty Writers Show podcast, via Spotify, Anchor FM, Google podcasts, and more.

Beth Worsdell published novels in adult and YA editions to help and encourage adults and teens to keep reading together.

Beth Worsdell and her husband have been happily married for over 28 years, spending most of their married life in Portsmouth, England. When Beth and her husband had the opportunity to move to America in 2011, they jumped at the chance. Beth and her family now live in Southern California.

Don't forget to follow Beth on Facebook, YouTube, Twitter, TikTok, Instagram, YouTube, Goodreads, Bookbub, and All Author. Please show your support for Beth by inviting your friends to her social media pages, and sharing her books, pages, and posts.

Send Beth a Book selfie with one of her books, e-book or paperback, to be featured on her social media and here on her website.

Other works by Beth Worsdell.

The Earth's Angels Trilogy is available in adult and YA editions.

Earth's Angels.

A mother's love will save her family.

Her determination will save humanity.

Her power will save the universe.

Melanie had everything. Four wonderful children. A loving husband. A good life. Until Earth died. Mel remembers none of it. Not even the apocalypse. Five years later, Mel wakes up in an otherworldly room and learns that angelic beings are using her as part of their plan to save Earth.

Thrust into a world of ancient races and alien wars, Mel soon yearns to join the battle over Earth. But that means putting her husband and children in danger.

Mel, a wife, and mom, must discover her courage, power, and destiny if she hopes to rescue Earth from the evil alien invaders determined to destroy everything and everyone she loves.

The Marilians.

Her determination will save humanity.
Her power will save the universe.

Melanie is shocked to discover her unborn baby has wings and extraordinary powers. But that doesn't stop her from joining the fight against the blood-thirsty Marilians.

When they discover a Marilian scout hiding near the human's quarters, Mel realizes the invasion is imminent. This means all surviving humans must train and prepare for battle, including her husband and four children. But there's no choice if they hope to stop the alien invasion.

As the angels and human survivors train for the battle of a lifetime, Mel wonders about the child growing inside her, a child like no other in the universe. Amid their hectic preparations, friendships build between not only survivors but also humans and angels. Unconventional love forms between races while facing a tragic loss. However, there is no time to grieve.

Meanwhile, Earth's angels make their own plans when they summon both their elders and an ancient alien race of dragons to help defend Earth.

Angels, dragons, and humans fight for Earth and the survival of humankind in a war where aliens control fire, and their bite or scratch transforms any lifeform into one of them.

Destination Unknown.

Her power will save the universe.

Melanie, her family, and the other humans must flee Earth if they want to survive.

Devastated by the battle with the Marilians, they find comfort in the newborn child who will forever change the course of the human race. Yet not even the miracle child, Faith, is enough for them to overcome their anger at the Marilians for leaving them homeless and planetless. ·

The Marilians must be stopped. They are the scourge upon the universe.

Fleeing to the Earth's angels' world, they meet the rest of the ancient dragons and set up a base. Together they form a plan, that will end the Marilians' reign of terror, but saving the universe won't be easy!

Mel, her family, and close friends visit amazing new worlds, enlisting the help of other alien races, decimated by the Marilians. Finding them all too eager to join in the fight.

There is only one way they can hope to win. Taking the fight to the Marilians on their home world. Except the Marilians have been busy…

Discover new worlds, the power of family, and the cost of upsetting a badass mother.

This isn't a revenge battle, it's a universal intervention.

Made in the USA
Coppell, TX
05 July 2023

18807210R00210